About the Author

Kenneth (Ken) Ansell is an agriculturalist and farmer turned professional artist, who graduated from Durham University and completed his two years of National Service as a second lieutenant in a transport company before starting his working career in Agricultural Education in Cornwall, and, eventually, Devon. A keen horseman, he has experience in breeding and schooling young horses together with point-to-point racing and hunting. He has a small farm on the edge of Dartmoor where he lives with his wife and family. Now in his eighties, Ken rides regularly and still does his share in the stable yard.

Also by Kenneth Ansell

The Fox
Pendogget's Mare

The Horse Traders

Kenneth Ansell

Published by
Filament Publishing Ltd
16, Croydon Road, Beddington,Croydon,
Surrey, CR0 4PA, United Kingdom
+44 (0)20 8688 2598
www.filamentpublishing.com

ISBN 978-1-911425-52-6

Printed by IngramSpark

CHAPTER 1

It was late afternoon and already the fickle September sun was touching the distant line of hills on the horizon as Matt Winsford turned the ancient Volvo estate off the A303 and onto the M5 heading towards Exeter.

'Not long now, Bullet'. He glanced at the brown rough-coated terrier that was curled up on the passenger seat. 'Looks as though we'll be able to spend a bit of time together, just you and me. Reckon it will do us both good, eh, Bullet?' The only indication that the dog had heard a word was a slight movement of the tail at the sound of his name.

At the next service station, Matt pulled over for diesel and a coffee, glad of the opportunity to stretch his aching legs. After filling up, he returned to the car park and sat for a moment watching the people making their way to the restaurant, then got out, opened the passenger door and clipped the dog lead to Bullet's collar. 'Come on, mate, time for a pee,' he said, dragging the reluctant animal over to the grass verge. The dog obliged by cocking his leg against the first sapling they came to. 'There you are, you old bugger, I told you so,' Matt said as the dog jumped eagerly back into the car to resume its original posture in the warm dent of the seat. The front door windows were lowered a few inches before Matt walked slowly towards the service area, safe in the knowledge that should anyone put so much as a finger through the gap, Bullet would taste blood.

The cafe was busy and the coffee warm and tasteless. He eventually found a corner table, took out the Ordnance Survey map of Dartmoor and spread it out, much to the annoyance of the elderly couple sitting opposite who viewed the young man with obvious disdain and moved to the next table, muttering inaudibly. Matt merely grunted and continued studying the map, tracing with his finger the winding lane that should take him to Coombe Cottage. 'Get away for a spell, go and do your own thing,' the doctor had said. Well this was far enough away, Matt thought as he memorised the route. He shrugged. It was just like old times, only now he would be on his own. He folded the map and stood up with a slight groan, taking the weight off his left leg for a moment before limping slowly towards the door. The elderly couple heard him mutter, 'Bugger it,' between clenched teeth as he passed their table.

Back in the Volvo, he rummaged in the glove compartment, found his painkillers, swallowed two tablets and washed them down with a gulp from a small water bottle. He sat for several minutes with his eyes closed before starting the engine and moving off, thankful for the fact that the car had automatic transmission which meant his left foot had very little to do for the rest of the journey. By the time they turned off the main road, he was feeling much better and even humming to himself a familiar tune, the words to which were not repeatable in polite company.

Skirting the small town of Bovey Tracey, he turned off onto a B-road and stopped at the first convenient gateway. 'First job, Bullet: get the keys.' He pulled a crumpled piece of paper from his inside pocket and studied it carefully. 'Right, all we have to do is follow this road, take the first lane on the left and it's the first bungalow we come to.' There was no name or number but he had to look out for a white gate on the right. He eased the car back onto the road and began the climb up a steep hill.

At the top, there was a sharp turn and a narrow lane branched off to the left. Almost immediately, the white gate appeared and Matt had to break suddenly to turn into the gravel drive.

The property was obviously well kept and the paint new, Matt noticed as he pressed the door bell. At first there was no response, but at the third press the door was opened by a plump elderly man who grinned and held out his hand. 'You must be young Winsford,' he said as Matt shook hands. 'Come in, we were just about to have a cup of tea.'

Matt hesitated. 'Er … I've got my dog in the car, Colonel Spreyton.'

'Then bring it in, boy, bring it in, and by the way, it's Charles and we don't use the military handle, that's all in the past.'

Matt shook his head. 'Bullet isn't the sociable sort, particularly if you have another dog in the house so I think he's better left where he is, but I would love a cuppa, thank you.' He followed Charles into the kitchen where a tall grey-haired woman was busy making tea.

'Margaret, this is young Winsford. You remember, his father John used to show South Devon cattle when we did in the old days? The family had the cottage while we did the Devon County Show and the Royal Cornwall.'

Margaret Spreyton turned and smiled. 'I remember a young man who gave us all heart attacks when he got lost on the moor.'

'I wasn't lost,' Matt said with a grin. 'I just went further than planned and then the fog came down.'

'Don't know what you were doing up there on your own anyway,' Charles cut in. 'Your mother and sister were worried to death.'

'I don't really remember except that I had just had my A level results and I suppose I wanted to get away for a bit to sort out what I was going to do next. It seems a very long time ago now.'

'Must be more than ten years because we've been out of farming eight years,' Charles said as he led the way into the sitting room and indicated to a chair. Matt sat down and Margaret busied herself pouring the tea. 'Do you take sugar?'

'No, thank you.' Matt accepted his cup and watched his hosts settle into the other two armchairs. They didn't seem to have changed very much in the twelve years since they last met; her face was perhaps a little more lined but she was still a slim, handsome woman. He had put on a bit more weight, the hair had receded and, like the short-clipped moustache, was now grey, but otherwise they were just as he remembered them.

'So, how are your folks?' Charles asked.

'Oh, much the same. Mother is wrapped up in the Women's Institute and Dad likewise with the NFU but, of course, they're both winding down a bit now and I don't know how long it will be before they decide to sell up and retire completely.'

'You've not thought of taking on the farm?'

Matt grunted. 'It wasn't on my agenda before this latest saga and even less so now.' He paused, wondering how much they knew and was relieved when they didn't ask. 'My sister Fiona is married,' he said, quickly changing the subject. 'Lives near Hitchin with one husband, two kids, three horses and countless dogs.'

'And you?' Margaret asked.

He shook his head. 'Once bitten, twice shy and I'm not much of a catch now, not till I get myself sorted anyway.'

'Well you've come to the right place,' Charles said cheerily. 'Coombe Cottage will give you all the peace and quiet you could want and we're always here if you need anything.'

Matt drank his tea and stood up. 'Thank you very much for the tea, but I'd better get myself moving before it gets dark.' He paused and looked round the room. 'Bit of a change from Lidstone Manor.'

Charles grinned. 'It's called downsizing. It's what us old 'uns are supposed to do.'

'So what happened to the house and the farm then?'

'The farm was easy. The Harveys bought it almost as soon as it came on the market, but, of course, they didn't want the house: too big and it needed a lot doing to it. We put it up for sale, hoping that one of those celebrities or a footballer might be interested but no luck; too out of the way, I suppose. Then along came this chap from a company involved in rehabilitating young offenders, Gainsborough House, I think they call it. Anyway, they wanted to take it on a lease. Well, of course, we jumped at it, particularly as they agreed our terms without a murmur. They wanted Coombe Cottage as well but I told them it was already taken as I had already spoken to your father and had agreed to let you have it as a winter let until next Easter.'

'Did father tell you why I wanted the cottage?' Matt asked pensively.

Charles put a hand on his arm. 'Just that you'd had an accident and needed time to recuperate. He didn't tell me any more and I didn't ask.'

They walked out to where the Volvo was parked. Charles handed him the cottage keys. 'By the way, you'll see an old boy called Spud Wannacott. He looks after the place for me, you know, cuts the lawn and keeps the bit of garden tidy. Good sort, ex-sergeant major, looked after me in the Falklands. If you need anything doing, he's your man.'

Matt got into the car and lowered the window. 'Thanks again for the tea. By the way, is it alright if I use the back room of the cottage as a studio? It's got plenty of windows and looks out over the Coombe. I'll put something down on the floor so that it doesn't get splattered.'

Charles raised his eyebrows. 'Yes, that's fine. I didn't know you were an artist. How long have you been doing that?'

'Oh, on and off since I was at school, nothing serious but I find it very relaxing, and who knows, I might need an extra string to my bow in the future, the way things are going.' Matt started the engine, raised his right hand in appreciation and pulled out into the lane.

The gradient was steep for the next couple of miles as the narrow lane wound between high hedge banks until there was the rumble of a cattle grid and they were out onto the open moor. To the left was a sea of bracken, already turning brown in the autumn sun which was slowly disappearing behind a granite tor on the horizon. On his right, the ground fell steeply away to small green fields dotted with the outlines of cattle and sheep, and below that the road that led to Lidstone Manor ran parallel through a line of trees.

Matt slowed down so as not to miss the track that led down to the cottage. Suddenly he recognised the two granite gateposts, braked, turned right and pulled up sharply at the gate to Coombe Cottage. There was a yelp as Bullet slid to the floor and Matt lifted the dog up and fondled its ears. 'Come on, my old mate, we're home.' He got out of the car, opened the gate and drove through, remembering to stop and close it again. 'Don't want a garden full of sheep and ponies, Bullet,' he told the dog as they walked up to the front door.

The cottage was just as he remembered it: grey granite walls with a slate roof and a 'doll's house' front of four windows and a door in the middle. Inside, the walls and woodwork of the small entrance hall were painted white or cream to attract the maximum light. There was a modest sitting room, a fireplace with a granite lintel and two armchairs and a sofa. The kitchen was well equipped, and Matt was relieved to see that it now included a washing machine, which meant he would not have to make trips to a launderette once a week.

But it was the room at the back of the cottage which interested him most. It spanned the whole width of the property with large windows which looked out across the wooded valley to the little village of Lidstone a mile away. Halfway between the cottage and the village, nestling in the valley, were the imposing buildings of Lidstone Manor. From the vantage point of the cottage, Matt could only see the rear of the large rambling Georgian house with its numerous outbuildings. There were stables, he remembered, and a number of buildings that were once hunt kennels many years ago. Now he could see a rectangular area of sand had been added, which he instantly recognised as an exercise arena for horses, and there was a very large horsebox parked at the rear of the house with several people milling about.

He unlocked the door into the garden and went out to give Bullet a run round the lawn and stood listening. The only sounds he could hear were the occasional bleat of a sheep and the trickling song of a robin perched in a nearby elderberry bush; it was literally just what the doctor ordered. He walked round the cottage to the car and began to unload it, starting with half a dozen canvasses, an easel and a varnished wooden box that contained his paints; these he took through into the back room, which he now looked upon as his studio, and set them against the wall. Next, he took out two large cases, trundled the largest into the kitchen and carried the smaller one up to the larger of the two bedrooms and deposited it on the nearest of the twin beds. He then dragged out a large padded dog bed, picked up two stainless steel bowls and took them through into the kitchen. He arranged the dog bed in the corner nearest the cooker and immediately Bullet went to it, turned round three times and flopped down. 'Just make yourself at home,' Matt said as he returned to the car for a large cardboard box containing various items of food which he placed on the kitchen table. He stood for a while gazing out of the window, then he turned slowly, unzipped the case, foraged around inside and brought out a bottle of Bushmills whiskey. He poured himself a generous 'three fingers', walked through into the 'studio' and sat in a high backed chair to look out over the valley.

One by one, the lights were beginning to go on in the direction of the village. Rooks cawed in the oaks behind the manor and somewhere a female voice was repeatedly calling a name. Matt could not determine whether it was for a dog, a horse or perhaps a child; eventually it tailed off into silence as the shadows lengthened.

At Lidstone Manor, he could see more activity round the horsebox. The ramps had been lowered and horses were being led out one at a time; he counted four plus a pony. 'They must have had a long haul to be unloading at this hour,' Matt said out loud to himself. The lights went out behind the manor and the horsebox began to move. Matt could just make out three people, one a woman, who were standing together watching the vehicle as it disappeared down the drive. When they eventually went into the house, Matt's eyes closed as the Bushmills began to take effect. Suddenly he shook himself awake, drained the glass and stood up. He looked at his watch: half past nine. 'Come on, Bullet. Time for some grub,' he said as he walked back into the kitchen.

The cardboard box contained most of the items he might require over the next twenty-four hours. He found a can opener, selected two tins, one of baked beans, the other of dog food. The latter he opened to give a now wide awake and excited Bullet his supper. Then it was a case of finding the necessary pans and utensils from the kitchen drawers to complete a meal of beans on toast with a couple of rashers of bacon followed by a mug of black coffee.

After piling the dishes in the sink he contemplated watching television but instead opted for an early night. 'Come on, Bullet, time for a poop and a wee,' he called as he went out of the back door. Outside, he thought for a moment before taking out his mobile phone to check that he had a signal. Satisfied, he dialled a number. 'Hello, Mother … Yes I'm okay, got here about seven … Yes it's just as I remembered but they've modernised it: washing machine and flash telly, that sort of thing. Tell Dad that Colonel Spreyton asked after him and mentioned when we used to come down to show cattle … Sorry we're breaking up, signals are always dodgy up here on the moor so I'll say cheerio.' He clicked off the phone, called to the dog and went inside.

He went into the sitting room, changed his mind and turned on the television to some sort of quiz show. He flicked through the channels, found nothing that took his interest and switched it off. Another Bushmills and his aching leg eased so that he relaxed into the chair and dozed.

Suddenly Bullet began to growl and ran to the back door barking furiously. 'What the hell's up with you?' Matt called as he pulled himself up out of the chair and limped towards the irate dog. 'There's nothing out there, you daft old fool, look!' He opened the door and Bullet launched himself into the bushes at the bottom of the lawn, the growl still rumbling in his throat. It was too dark to see anything and, as the growl subsided, Matt called the dog back. 'There you are, I told you so. Come on in. Probably just an old fox on the prowl.' He closed the door and turned the key in the lock. 'Come on, time for some shut-eye.'

He left the dog in the kitchen and went upstairs for a shower, found his wash kit and was pleased to find that the water was hot and, although it was necessary to stand in the bath to complete the process, the result was very satisfying and he felt refreshed and ready for a good night's sleep … he hoped. Brushing his teeth, the reflection in the mirror showed a dark stubble: it would have to go in the morning and he would need a hair cut soon. He gingerly felt his skull behind his left ear; the lumps were still there but the scars no longer showed and he hoped fervently that the hair would not grow back white along the lines where the stitches had been.

In the bedroom, he pulled on a pair of pyjama shorts and sat on the bed to sort out the medication they had given him. The painkillers he placed carefully on the bedside table; there was an anti-inflammatory that he put in the top drawer along with the packet of sleeping pills, which he hoped he would not need. There was also a tube of analgesic cream which he held for a few moments while he studied his left leg. He had been told that it was a miracle it was still there and was only saved by the prompt action of the paramedics. Now it had more metal in it than a plumber's tool bag: going through airport security was going to be interesting, to say the least. He squeezed out some of the analgesic cream and began to rub it into the long surgical scar that ran from his foot to just above the knee, pleased to see that it was beginning to fade to a dull purple where the stitches had been. He flexed his foot and winced before carefully massaging the cream into the scarred area from ankle to toes while the memories flooded back, or at least some of them did; there was a blank area, a dark time. They had told him what had happened but he could recall none of it, only the pain and the feeling of guilt when he eventually gained consciousness in the hospital.

*

Sleep came easily, thanks to the Bushmills, but it didn't last, thanks to Bullet. The dog was barking furiously. Matt turned over with a groan and glanced at his watch: half past two. He swung his legs out of bed and yelled at the animal. 'Shut up, Bullet! What the bloody hell is up with you!' For a moment, the dog was quiet, then there was a distinct noise outside. Was it a hoarse scream, a cry for help or the harsh bark of a vixen? That must be it: an old vixen calling to a dog fox. Bullet was barking again. Matt went down to the back door and let the irate animal out. 'All right then, go and see for yourself,' he told him as the dog slipped through his legs and ran out across the lawn, still barking furiously. Matt peered after him but, as he expected, saw nothing other than the elderberry bush waving in the wind that rustled through the trees bordering the cottage. 'Come on, you old fool, there's nothing there,' he called as the bark subsided to a low growl and Bullet reappeared from the undergrowth. Matt shivered, caught the dog by its collar and dragged it inside. 'Now just settle down, for God's sake, and let's get some kip.' He took a final glance towards the bushes, closed the door and made his way upstairs with a curt, 'Now go and lie down, and let's not hear any more.'

Back under the duvet, Matt lay awake as memories of his childhood drifted through his mind. The sound of the fox barking took him back to starlight winter nights on the farm, Christmas Eve, helping feed the cattle in the barns – always the last job before supper – and the sound of a fox barking somewhere in Bolters Wood the other side of the valley. Strange, it's a bit early in the year to hear a vixen calling for a mate, but you never know with this climate change business. He turned over, closed his eyes and clung to those childhood images in the hope they would see him through the night.

CHAPTER 2

The first light of dawn showed through the thin bedroom curtains. Matt turned over and opened his eyes. There was no need to look at his watch, he knew it would be half past six – old habits die hard. He lay on his back, hands folded behind his head, gazing up at the ceiling. It had been the best night's sleep he had experienced for months: no flashbacks, no black holes or screaming panic and, above all, none of the terrifying grinding noise that always accompanied a splitting headache. Perhaps things were looking up, perhaps the doctor was right and getting away from it all would do the trick. He swung his legs out and sat on the edge of the bed to flex and massage his injured limb, then, as ordered by the physiotherapist, twenty sit-ups, twenty press-ups and finally a walk round the room on tip-toes, the latter being the most painful for his left foot. That done, he made his way to the bathroom to wash and shave.

A new pair of jeans, a red check shirt, and Matt felt more confident as he entered the kitchen to find Bullet whimpering and scratching by the back door. 'You'll have to wait,' he told the dog as he unpacked the new pair of specially made walking boots and sat down to carefully ease them on. He stood up and tentatively walked across to the door: they felt good and the special padding in the left boot supported his damaged foot so that his limp was barely noticeable.

'Right, dog.' He opened the door and Bullet squeezed through as soon as the gap was wide enough, just in time to chase a large rabbit across the lawn and into the brambles by the gate into the track. Matt grinned as he took a deep breath of morning air and watched the last wisps of mist rise to the tree tops: it was going to be a fine and sunny day. Suddenly he heard a female voice cry out something about a dog and Matt knew it could only be Bullet. He put two fingers in his mouth and gave a shrill whistle. The dog appeared over the hedge bank looking very pleased with itself. 'What the hell have you done now?'

Matt growled as he grabbed the dog's collar and dragged it towards the back door.

'Is that your dog?' The voice came from the direction of the track. Matt looked up to see a young woman on a chestnut horse emerge into the gateway. 'I said, is that your dog?' she repeated. 'If so, you should keep the damn thing under control. It just shot across in front of me like a … '

'Like a bullet?' Matt couldn't resist a grin.

'It's not funny. It spooked my horse and I nearly got dumped!'

Matt pushed Bullet through the door and turned to study the speaker. Mid-twenties, he reckoned, blue eyes flashing with annoyance, and wisps of blonde hair that straggled from beneath a black crash hat. Her face was distorted by a tight chinstrap, but even so, it looked interesting. As for the rest of her, the long waterproof riding coat she was wearing obscured her figure, but Matt could tell that it was slim.

'I said, it spooked my horse.' The blue eyes had narrowed to slits.

'I'm sorry, I didn't mean to be frivolous, it's just that Bullet is the dog's name and that's how he got it. I mean, he sort of shoots around like … '

'Well just keep the damn thing on a lead.' She swung the gelding round, nudged it with her heels and trotted on up the track, across the road and up onto the open moor. Matt watched as she disappeared into the morning mist, shrugged and went back into the house.

Breakfast was a Spartan affair: cereal, toast and black coffee. Bullet was banished to his bed where he curled up with his nose between his paws, still growling quietly. Matt left the washing-up and went into his studio. He set up his easel where it would catch most light but allowed him to still see down into the valley in the direction of Lidstone, the village and the hills beyond. It was scene he might try to paint, particularly in the early morning when the sun came up over the horizon. Blank canvasses were stacked against the back wall and the three that he had already started he placed near the easel, selecting one to put up and work on. It was a landscape with a multitude of shades of green; he was good at green, a colour that so many amateur painters got wrong. Trees were his specialty and he knew the configuration, branch and leaf structure of most of the common British species. He used photographs but for reference only, always insisting that if a photograph was good enough, it did not need to be copied. He had sold a few paintings at very modest prices and mainly to friends and relatives, but it gave him encouragement and kept him interested in something that he hoped might become more than a hobby.

Setting out his paints, oil, turpentine and brushes took a while longer but before he could set about painting, a bark from Bullet caused him to look up to see a battered green Land Rover pick-up draw into the front drive and park beside the Volvo. 'What now?' he thought as he went out of the back door to see a tall grey-haired man lifting down a lawn mower from the back of the pick-up. He turned as Matt approached and held out his hand.

'You'll be Mr. Winsford. Spud Wannacott. I expect Colonel Spreyton has told you about me.' Matt shook hands and nodded.

'That's right, he told me that you are his ex-sar'n major.' Spud raised one eyebrow and grinned.

'Well, if you don't mind, I'll get on with the job then. Oh, and don't mind old Jen there, she'll be no trouble,' he nodded towards the open passenger window where the head of a grey rough-coated lurcher looked out with sad, quiet eyes. 'She's getting on a bit and will be content to stay where she is.' He started the mower and move onto the lawn.

Matt watched as the lean figure guided the machine backwards and forwards across the grass. From what Charles Spreyton had said, Matt reckoned he must be at least seventy but looked and moved like a man ten years younger. As he watched, he became aware that there seemed to be some sort of a commotion down at Lidstone Manor. Several people were milling about near a yellow minibus and he could hear shouting.

It took a little time to fetch his binoculars from the Volvo but when he returned the scene was the same. Spud had also noticed and had stopped to take a look. 'What do you reckon is going on there?' Matt asked.

Spud gave a grunt. 'You might well ask but if you want an educated guess, I'd say they're taking in another bunch of young yobs that don't want to be there. I don't know whether you know, but they are supposed to take 'em in and sort 'em out. Can't say I like the idea of having that lot down there, and that goes for most of the folk round here.'

'Do they cause any trouble?' Matt was still watching with the binoculars.

'No, not really. You get the odd one that absconds but they soon fetch 'em back or they have to go back to court. I'm not sure how it works but I'm told the Government pay them a hell of a lot of money and, by the way, the chap who runs it and his wife must be making a packet. She runs the horse side of it – exports and imports horses from all over but mainly Eastern Europe, they reckon.'

'Seems to have calmed down a bit now,' Matt commented.

'Just two or three folks standing around looking up this way.' He lowered the binoculars. 'That bit of excitement is over for today.'

Matt started to make his way back to the house, then paused. 'What's the Lidstone Arms like these days? Any good for a meal?'

Spud shrugged. 'Depends what you're looking for. I'd say it's about average, none of your fancy stuff but good enough for the likes of me.'

Matt smiled. 'Then I'm sure it will be good enough for yours truly. I'll find out for myself at lunchtime.'

*

The Lidstone Arms was a long granite and slate building standing back off the main street. The car park was full so Matt had to park in the reserve area which was tucked away at the rear. Inside, it was just the same as he vaguely remembered from the brief visits with his parents when they last stayed at Coombe Cottage some twelve years ago. It was a place of stone flagged floors and oak beams with a long panelled bar and a small eating area at the far end, although most of the lunch customers seemed to be content to eat their meal sitting at the wooden benches in the bar room.

The man behind the bar was large and bearded with a very red face that beamed at every new customer that appeared in front of him. Matt knew he must be the landlord and ordered a pint of the locally brewed ale while he looked at the bar menu and settled for a jacket potato with a cheese and onion filling. He looked round the bar. 'Quite busy this morning,' he commented between sips.

The landlord grinned. 'It's about usual these days since they took over the manor for that rehabilitation business. Most of the folks that work there come here lunch time. Mind, there are one or two odd 'uns among them, foreign, but they keep themselves to themselves and are no trouble.' He paused. 'You staying round here or just passing through?'

'I've taken Coombe Cottage for the winter.'

The landlord nodded. 'I wondered if the old colonel had let it. I could see the lights were on last night and one of the Lidstone Manor blokes asked me if I knew what was going on. Between you and me, I think they were hoping to put one of their people in there but you must have pipped them to the post. By the way, I'm Tom Slater.'

'Matt Winsford.'

'Right, Mr. Winsford, your order is just coming up. Enjoy.'

The meal was served by a plump dark-haired girl who, Matt estimated, couldn't be much more than sixteen years old. Probably the landlord's daughter. After a few minutes, she returned to ask, in a high-pitched sing-song voice, if everything was alright. He assured her it was and, as he ate, he couldn't help wondering why staff were encouraged to talk like that. It was the same when women spoke over the tannoy in supermarkets and railway stations, that same up and down monotonous tone.

His thoughts were interrupted when a door banged and a large man in a smart tweed suit walked up to the bar and ordered a pint of larger and a vodka and tonic. The man turned to glance round the room and Matt registered the high-coloured cheeks, short bristling moustache and receding brown hair; ex-military, perhaps. He was joined by a slim blonde woman whose tanned and slightly lined face spoke of the outdoors. Matt judged the man to be somewhere in his mid-fifties, the woman perhaps a bit younger. The landlord was talking to them and Matt detected a slight nod in his direction. They were talking about him, but so what. He was new in the district, and in a small place like Lidstone, any newcomer was a source of interest.

By the time Matt had finished his meal, the couple had moved to a table near the door and he was conscious that they were watching him. He got up and walked over to the bar with his empty glass. The landlord smiled and lent towards him. 'Those are the people who run the Lidstone Manor outfit,' he whispered. 'He does the bad boys side of it and she manages the horse business. Spends a lot of time travelling all over Europe and beyond buying and selling horses, she does. Made quite an impression in the village with buyers coming and going. It's meant a few more jobs locally and it's done my trade no harm, and that's a fact.'

'So, all in all, a good thing.'

'As far as I'm concerned, yes.'

'What about the bad boys, as you call them. Do they cause any trouble? I mean, do they ever get out at night and make a nuisance of themselves, or worse?'

'Lord no, they shuts 'em in at night – lights out at nine o'clock. What makes you think they could be larking about after dark?'

Matt shrugged. 'Only that I thought there might have been someone in the garden last night, at least my old dog reckoned so, and then I thought I heard a yell, but that could have been a fox or something.'

The landlord shook his head. 'I don't think you've got anything to worry about Mr. Winsford. They keep a pretty tight rein on 'em. It's more likely some of the village lads mucking about after they've had a few jars.'

'You're probably right but I'll keep an eye out just the same, not that I've got anything worth pinching but I don't like being woken up in the middle of the night with my old dog going berserk,' Matt said with a grin as he paid for his meal.

*

As he drove back to the cottage, he realised he could have walked to the village down the track that led from Coombe Cottage past Lidstone Manor. It was probably not much more than a mile: half an hour's steady walk down to the village and a bit more going back up. It would do him good, he reckoned, and there was the added attraction of taking a peak over the hedge at what was going on at the manor.

As he approached the back door, he could hear Bullet barking furiously. At the same time, somebody or something brushed through the shrubbery and disappeared down the garden towards the bottom hedge. Matt followed and was just in time to see someone scramble over the bank and run along the hedge in the direction of the manor. He paused to watch the hooded figure climb over a gate and drop from sight into the track that led to the village.

'What the bloody hell was that all about?' Matt asked himself. 'Naughty boy or village yob?'

He shrugged, walked back to the cottage and let the irate dog out to vent its anger in the direction the intruder had gone.

'Come on, settle down, you old fool, it's all over'. He led the animal back and began to check the doors and windows to make sure there had been no break in, then he studied the soil in the flower beds and the stone flags of the path. There were distinct imprints made by a pair of trainers which seemed to indicate that whoever it was had walked round the building several times, presumably to look through windows and perhaps find an easy access.

Inside, Matt was relieved to find that nothing had been disturbed. He considered ringing the police but decided against it. After all, he thought, they had better things to do than go chasing hoodies that might only be curious, and anyway, no crime had been committed other than trespass and a depleted force would not be best pleased to be called out for that.

The cottage felt cold and it was a relief to discover that what looked like a wood burner set into the fire place was in fact electric. He turned it on and sat down in the armchair to ponder the events of the day. It had started well enough: the meeting with the young horsewoman was interesting, if a little disconcerting. The pub seemed to be a good enough place to eat and the landlord was a decent enough sort with the typical pub landlord's grasp of local goings-on and tittle-tattle. The establishment would make a decent headquarters for the next few months and would save cooking as well as providing a bit of genial company as the nights drew in.

The afternoon was crisp and sunny, too good to sit indoors at the easel, so Matt retrieved his thick tweed coat and thumb stick from the back of the Volvo, whistled for Bullet and started to walk down the track towards the manor. The first part was quite steep and he was glad of the support the long stick gave as he negotiated the numerous large stones that littered the way. About half a mile down, the track levelled off as it skirted the fields and paddocks of the manor. Horses trotted up to peer over the hedge bank, curious at the movement and snorting with alarm as Bullet pushed his nose through the undergrowth after the scent of a rabbit. Matt called him back and wished he had brought the lead to keep him at heel.

As he approached the stables, he could see the bobbing hat of a rider just the other side of the high bank. He wondered if it might be the girl he had encountered earlier that day and, curious, he eased himself up the bank to peer over. Sure enough, the young blonde girl was riding the same chestnut horse round the sand school, keeping close to the rails which ran close to where Matt stood. He could hear her talking to the animal as it responded to the commands coming from her heels and hands. She was good, Matt could recognise a good horsewoman: he had been brought up by one and had been brother to another. Then it happened; with a single yelp, Bullet put up a rabbit, which made for the sand school.

Matt watched with horror as the chestnut swerved away, put in a couple of bucks and deposited the girl onto the sand. It took only a few seconds for Matt to scramble over the bank, through the rails to where the girl lay. By the time he got to her, she was sitting up and muttering words through her gritted teeth. She looked up as Matt arrived breathless to lean on his stick, panting from his run across the sand.

The girl looked up. 'Oh my God, it's you again!' she said angrily. 'Why the hell can't you keep that damn dog of yours under control?'

'I'm so sorry,' Matt said as he went to help her up. 'I should have put Bullet on a lead.'

She shook her head, fended off his help and stood up brushing the sand from her jacket sleeves. 'Just go away and take your bloody dog with you.' He watched as she limped towards the chestnut standing in the far corner, the reins wrapped round its front legs. He heard her talking softly to the animal as she lifted each foot to disentangle them, checking for any damage, then she brushed the remaining sand from her backside, put her foot in the stirrup and swung into the saddle to sit perfectly still. The horse put its ears back, bounced twice then stood ridged while the girl patted its neck and talked quietly: the ears went forward, and seconds later it was walking steadily towards Matt who stood still as the rider approached and then stopped in front of him.

'You still here?' she demanded, the voice now showing annoyance rather than anger as she looked down at Matt.

He stepped forward and took hold of a rein. 'I just wanted to apologise again and perhaps make amends for what happened.' He paused. 'I wondered if I could take you out for a meal or something?'

'No, thanks.' The reply sounded abrupt and final.

Matt nodded and was about to turn away when he stopped, stepped back and looked intently at horse and rider. 'Does the horse belong to you?'

'Yes, why?'

'How would you like to have his portrait painted?'

'Are you an artist?'

'Sort of.'

'What does that mean?'

'I don't do it for a living.'

The girl nudged the chestnut closer. 'Horses are not easy to paint, you know. You've got to know the anatomy and how they move. I've seen some pretty awful attempts at it.'

Matt grinned. 'Well, I'm not exactly a Munnings or Lionel Edwards but I was brought up on the farm with horses so I guess a bit has rubbed off.'

The girl thought for a moment. The idea of a portrait of her beloved Harry hanging on the wall in her room was appealing. 'Okay,' she said, and smiled for the first time.

'Brilliant,' he held out his hand. 'Matt Winsford.'

She nodded and responded with a brief handshake. 'Kate Lethbridge. How do you want to set about it?'

'Well, I will want to get a good look at him, make a few sketches, then take some photographs. We can start whenever you like.'

'What about tomorrow? I get most afternoons off thanks to my six o'clock start in the mornings. Come to the stable yard. I'll have to let them know who you are and why you're there. They are not keen on any strangers, probably because there's a lot of valuable kit around that's worth pinching, I suppose.'

Matt nodded. 'See you tomorrow then.' He turned and started to walk back the way he had come.

She called after him. 'There's a gate onto the track in the next field, if you want to avoid scrambling back over the bank again.'

He raised his hand before climbing back through the rails and making his way up the field. He found Bullet halfway down a rabbit hole a couple of yards beyond the gate and grabbed hold of his tail to pull him out.

'Come on, you old bugger. You've got me into quite enough trouble for one day. Let;s get you home.' Although, on reflection, Matt thought, it perhaps was not such a bad day after all.

CHAPTER 3

'So what's this fellow like, the one that wants to paint Harry?' Mary Lethbridge was busy laying the table for supper, her ample frame blocking the doorway to the kitchen while her daughter sat reading the latest edition of the *Horse & Hound* magazine.

'I don't know, Mum, I've only met him once. No, twice, I suppose. He seems alright as far as I can tell.'

'No, I mean, what does he look like? How old is he? What does he do beside paint people's horses?'

Kate put down the magazine and groaned. 'Mum, are you trying to pair me off again?'

'Well, it's about time you had a proper boyfriend. You're coming up to twenty-five years old, young lady, too old to be still living in Hotel Mum and Dad. But anyway, it's interesting to have someone different about the place, and you should know by now, I like to know what's going on. So?'

'So he's nothing special: about six one or two, thirty-ish but I haven't had a chance to look at his teeth so can't be sure, slightly lame near hind, short dark brown mane, good condition, I would say.' Kate grinned.

Her mother sighed and shook her head. 'We're talking about a man, not a blasted horse, Kate.'

Her daughter shrugged. 'Horses I know, but blokes, count me out.'

'What about young Bob Slater you went out with in the Young Farmers' Club? I thought that was getting quite serious.'

'I thought so too until he dumped me for that Sally Brimblecombe, she of the big boobs, the only daughter of a man with three hundred acres. There was no way I could compete with that.'

Mary stepped back to survey the laid table. 'Your father is going to be late. He phoned to say there had been a difficult calving and he needs to call in at the surgery on the way home. He said to start without him so we might as well get cracking.' She went into the kitchen and returned with a steaming shepherds pie and a dish of mashed carrot and swede.

They were halfway through the meal when the door opened and the tall lean figure of Jim Lethbridge appeared in the doorway. 'Sorry I'm late, love,' he said as Mary got up to retrieve the remains of the pie and vegetables from the oven.

She put them down onto the table. 'A bit dried up, I'm afraid, but at least it's hot.'

He smiled, and sat with the knife and fork held vertically as he waited for the meal to be dished out. Kate cleared her plate and watched him demolish the food hungrily. She was very fond of her father and it had been a great sorrow for her and disappointment for him that she had not achieved good enough A levels to be accepted at veterinary college as her elder brother had. Tom had followed in his father's footsteps, was now a practicing vet in New Zealand, and married with two children. She waited until the last mouthful had been eaten and her father was sitting back with a look of keen anticipation as sounds of more preparation came from the kitchen.

'Busy day tomorrow, Dad?'

'When haven't I got a busy day?

'I thought you ought to know they have just got another load in. They are settled in so they will be wanting you to do the usual examinations and paperwork checks.'

'Oh hell, not another lot of foreign passports and stuff I can't possibly read without the help of that dreadful chap Ivan, or whatever his name is.'

'Ivanovitch, or Ivan the Terrible to the rest of us. You're lucky you only have to deal with him occasionally, I have to put up with him every day.'

'Well they'll have to wait. I've got a TB test tomorrow that will take most of the morning and I can't put that off, then there's surgery in the afternoon so I suppose I'll have to get Alison to do that for me. Anyway, she's better with the smaller animals than I am. Just hope we don't get any emergencies, we could really do with a third member in the practice now.' He looked across at Kate who got up suddenly and went into the kitchen where her mother was dishing out the freshly made apple crumble.

'So what's with this Ivan chap then?' Mary asked as she reached for the custard. 'I heard you on about him when you were talking to Dad. What's so terrible about him that you have to give him that name?'

'Oh, I don't know. He just gives me the creeps, and I'm not the only one, but he's well in with the boss so we have to toe the line or risk getting the boot.'

Mary shook her head. 'Seems odd to me why they have to employ some foreigner when there are plenty of experienced local men and women who could do his job, I'm sure.'

Kate shrugged. 'It's because of where he comes from. We buy a lot of horses from eastern Europe: Poland, Hungary, even as far as Ukraine, and he comes from that part of the world, knows the language, the different laws and the geography, so he's pretty indispensable when it comes to doing the necessary deals and keeping the right side of any international regulations.'

Her mother paused for a moment. 'It seems a hell of a long way to go just to buy a few horses. What's so special about the animals from that part of the world?'

'They seem to produce good quality horses, particularly the Poles, and they are cheap. On the other side, there is a growing demand for British thoroughbreds, particularly sport horses: eventers, show jumpers, that sort of thing. The market in places like Germany, the Netherlands and France is good at the moment and, of course, Greta has plenty of contacts in that part of the world.'

'Greta being Mrs. Burford, your boss?'

'I thought you knew that, Mum.'

'I didn't know she was called Greta. That sounds a bit foreign too.'

'She was born in Germany and met Mr. Burford when he was in the army over there. That's what she told us anyway and I've no reason to believe it's not true.'

'And you're on first name terms?'

'Of course we are, Mum. This is the twenty-first century, not the eighteen hundreds. Anyway, she's okay to work for, knows her stuff and is hard but fair. Could be worse and if it wasn't for Ivan the Terrible, it would be a really easy number. I sometimes think that even Greta is a bit scared of him, not to mention his two sidekicks. Nobody is quite sure what they do, apart from going with him on the very long trips, as relief drivers I suppose. They do help over at the manor from time to time, and I've seen them with Mr. Burford and some of the boys on the allotments in the old walled garden.'

'Are we going to get pudding or are you two going to carry on nattering?' It was Jim's voice from the dining room.

'Sorry. Blame your daughter.' Mary said as she put the plate of crumble in front of him. 'She was just giving me the low-down on the goings-on at the manor.'

Jim grunted and resisted the temptation to start his dessert before the others had sat down.

'For heaven's sake, get on with it, Jim, before you start salivating all over the plate!' Mary grinned and sat down next him, giving him a nudge.

They finished the meal in silence until Mary got up and started to clear away. 'Come on, you two, I cooked, so you wash up, that's the house rule.'

Her husband gave a muted groan, picked up his plate and walked slowly to the kitchen closely followed by Kate who had an equally glum expression on her face. 'Time we had a dishwasher,' she muttered as she turned on the hot tap.

'We've got one,' Mary called from the dining room. 'It's your father!'

Kate smiled and looked at her father. 'What time are you likely to get down to the stables tomorrow?'

'Depends how the morning goes and whether or not Alison can cope. She'll have to get William to pick up the kids from school and he won't be best pleased in the middle of getting a second cut of silage. Why do you ask?'

'It's just that I arranged to meet this chap who is going to paint Harry at three o'clock but if you are sorting out the new arrivals, then Greta will want me to be there in case any of them get a bit fractious. That means he will have to hang around until we're done, and they are not going to like that. They just don't like strangers in the yard, least of all an unknown man.'

'Well, they have a lot of valuable kit there, saddles and the like, so I reckon they have to be careful, but to get back to your question, I hope to get to you straight after lunch. You can tell them that. I don't suppose it will take much more than an hour.'

Kate nodded and resumed the task of washing the plates while her father did the drying. When they had finished, she dried her hands, reached for her wax jacket which hung on the kitchen door and, putting it on, called out, 'I'm just going to give Harry and Molly their evening feed then I'm off to the manor. They want me to bed down the new arrivals for the night, sort out any rugs etc. we might need.'

She opened the door and went out into the yard. The Lethbridges' property had once been a farm house. Constructed of stone and cob, it nestled in a steep hillside, much of which still belonged to the Lethbridges. The remaining farm buildings consisted of a yard with a row of three loose boxes, one of which was used as a feed store while the other two housed Harry, the chestnut gelding, and Molly, a black cob mare. There was a tack room, a hay barn and an open shed which acted as a garage for Jim's battered Range Rover and Kate's little Fiat Uno.

Both horses whickered as Kate pushed open the yard gate and walked towards the feed store. She measured out a full scoop of crushed oats for the gelding and a handful for the mare. Both had a generous helping of chaff with a mineral supplement.

When both had been fed, she adjusted Harry's night rug, gave him a pat on the neck and walked across the yard to the shed-come-garage. The Fiat started reluctantly and Kate made a mental note to get the battery charged as she backed out of the shed and drove through the open gate onto the lane. A quick stop to shut it and she was off down the hill towards the main road to Lidstone.

The lane was very narrow and it was getting dark. She switched on the headlights and kept a watchful eye for the first hint of lights coming towards her. There were few passing places and it was wise to find one well before the oncoming vehicle reached you. It was always a relief to reach the junction with the main road. She turned left towards the village and was startled by a white minibus which came round the corner at well above the speed limit and continued down towards Bovey Tracey. 'Someone in a hell of a hurry,' she said out loud as she cut her speed through Lidstone village.

It was less than half a mile from there to Lidstone Manor and she was soon driving up the short drive towards the main gates which were always locked after eight o'clock. Five yards before the gates, she pulled over to the right, wound down the window and reached out of the car to a post where a faint green light illuminated a series of numbered buttons. She punched in the code number and waited as the large ornate iron gates slowly opened. Once through, it was a short distance to the front of the house where a gravel drive led off to the left towards the stable buildings. She pulled up in the parking area beside the green long wheelbase Land Rover used by the manor as an all-terrain people carrier.

The gate into the yard was unlocked and the lights were on at the block of six loose boxes that housed the new arrivals. Greta was already in the first one, her red puffa jacket clearly visible as she examined a big grey horse.

'Ah, there you are,' she called as Kate approached. 'Come look at this one. Don't you think he is superb? And I think we may already have a buyer.' She pulled off the night rug to show the whole animal while Kate nodded her approval.

'Looks a good sort,' was her only comment.

'A good sort!' The exasperation in Greta's voice was very evident. 'What do you think, Ivan? Don't you think he is superb?'

Kate turned to see the man in question standing behind her. He walked past her with a cursory nod to stand beside the horse, then stepped back to get a fuller view.

'Yes, he is very good. I think we may make money on this run.' He glanced at Greta and gave a wry smile. 'But I have other things to do so I will let you get on.' With that, he brushed past Kate, a little closer than was necessary, the young woman thought.

There were another four animals to be looked at, and of those, only one, a French Warmblood, was not pulling at the hay net which hung at the far end of the box.

Greta told Kate to stay for half an hour and keep an eye on the animal. Colic was always suspected after a long journey and Kate knew she had to watch for signs of discomfort or sweating. She switched off the lights in the other boxes and decided to check the liveries in the main stable block. As she walked across the yard, she noticed that the gate into the paddock and sand school were open and there was somebody standing the other side, apparently looking up towards the distant lights of Coombe Cottage.

It was almost dark now but she immediately recognised the back view of Ivan.

'What on earth are you doing out here at this time of night?' Her voice caused him to turn abruptly and she noticed he was holding what looked like a pair of large binoculars.

'Who is that?' he demanded angrily.

'It's me, Kate, and I asked what you were doing.'

'If you must know,' he paused before holding up the binoculars, 'I test these.'

'What, in the dark?'

'Yes, they are night vision. Just got them so I try them out. Good for finding bad boys if they go off in the night.'

'Good for poaching the odd deer more like,' Kate muttered as she resumed the inspection of the livery horses. There were seven to be looked at, four that were hunters and three competition animals. When she was satisfied all was well, she returned to the new arrivals and was relieved to see the French mare was quietly munching her hay. Turning off the light, she called to Ivan to lock up and made her way back to the car park.

*

At Coombe Cottage, Matt was busy converting the sun lounge into a workable studio. He had paused to watch the comings and goings down at the manor: the departure of the white mini bus, the lights going on in the stable yard, the arrival of a small red car and, finally, lights out. The activities at the manor roused his curiosity, little knowing that the feeling was reciprocated down in the stable yard.

CHAPTER 4

It had not been a good night. Matt turned over in bed to gaze, bleary-eyed, at the emerging light of a cold dawn, which seeped into the room through the half-closed curtains. He looked at his watch: six-thirty, so at last he could get up and the night was over. He pushed away the duvet, swung his legs out to sit on the edge of the bed, elbows on knees and head cushioned between his hands, staring at the carpet without seeing it, his mind still wrestling with the images and sounds that had once again deprived him of sleep: the black impenetrable fog, the screech of grinding metal and, above all, that face looking up at him with open sightless eyes. Images and sounds that recurred over and over again to haunt his nights. He groaned as he slowly eased his body to an upright position, got to his feet and limped towards the bathroom.

Freshly showered, he began to feel normality return to his exhausted body. He dressed slowly, taking care not to put pressure on his injured foot as he pulled on his jeans and socks. With the check shirt over his shoulder, he made his way downstairs determined to do his morning exercises in the comparative warmth of the kitchen.

When he arrived downstairs, Bullet was whining by the back door, so with a sigh of resignation, Matt pulled on his wellingtons and opened it as the dog squirmed past his legs and ran out onto the small lawn to cock its leg by the nearest tree. Matt followed Bullet onto the grass and looked down the coombe.

A thick white mist shrouded the whole of the valley bottom where the tower of Lidstone Church stood out like a square rock in a sea of cloud. Above him, the sky was clear and the autumn sun was just clearing the wooded horizon to the east. It was the sort of September morning that if you painted it, nobody would believe you, Matt mused.

He called Bullet and wished he had put his shirt on as the morning chill struck his bare shoulders.

'Come on, Bullet. You've had enough time, let's get inside,' He turned back towards the cottage when he heard his name called.

'Morning, Mr. Winsford!' Spud Wannacott was leaning out of his Land Rover cab by the gate onto the lane.

'I'm glad I've caught you. Saves me making a special journey. Just to say I'll be popping over later. The colonel wants those bushes trimmed at the bottom of the garden before they grow too tall and block the view across the valley. Apparently that's one of the selling points for a holiday let, a good view.'

Matt became aware that the speaker was looking at him intently as though making a detailed appraisal of his physique. It made him feel uncomfortable. He shivered and vigorously rubbed his left shoulder. 'Okay, help yourself when you like.' He paused and grinned sheepishly. 'I just had to get the old dog out fast before he peed on the carpet. Should have put my shirt on.'

The last remark caused Spud to laugh out loud. 'Just remember that September up here is a sight colder than what, I suspect, you have been used to.' He raised his hand in a gesture of farewell, there was a grind of gears and the vehicle disappeared up the lane towards the moor.

Back inside the cottage, Matt did about half his morning workout before the nausea returned and forced him to slump into a chair while he coped with the pain in his ankle and foot. It was half an hour before he got up to take his medication, fervently wishing he could take a stiff tot of the whiskey instead. The temptation passed and he finished dressing, gave Bullet his breakfast and set about getting his own, which was going to consist of a single glass of milk as anything solid he didn't think would stay down very long. He sipped the milk slowly and, when it was finished, he went into the newly fashioned studio to sit in a comfortable chair to contemplate the strategy for the afternoon's work.

*

He woke up two hours later, stiff but feeling much better. The nausea had gone and the pain was bearable. He went back into the kitchen and put on his walking boots and jacket: both he and the dog needed to get some fresh air. Calling for Bullet, he reached for his stick and went out of the door.

The mist had lifted and the day was bright and crisp so he decided to turn right out of the gate, then along a rough track that led up to the open moor. The bracken on either side was tinged with brown. Soon, Matt knew, it would go completely that colour and eventually shrivel to a crumpled carpet that would cover vast areas of the moor.

Higher up, the gorse was in bloom and he recalled the old saying 'when gorse is in bloom kissing is in fashion' – of course, it bloomed all year round. He watched Bullet scurrying about in the undergrowth and tried to remember the last time he had walked up that track. It was more than ten years ago: eighteen years old and trying to come to terms with A level results that were not as good as he had hoped, certainly not good enough to do engineering at a top university. Agriculture wasn't on his list, much to his father's disappointment, and neither was biology, his mother's suggestion. On that day, twelve years ago, he had wandered up the track, out onto the open moor, where the sense of space and distance clinched a thought that had been running through his mind for several days: he wanted to travel, he wanted a job that took him to places like this, wild with unending horizons. Then the fog had come down and it had taken him two hours to find his way back.

To Matt, it seemed such a long time ago and so much had happened since then. He came to the end of the track and struck out towards a distant tor that he remembered was called Hound Tor, a place of legend and tragedy, so the guide books said, but today in bright sunshine, the huge granite boulders held no aura of mystery. Instead, he felt an urge to climb them as he had done all those years ago, except now there was an added challenge. He glanced down at his left leg. It was beginning to ache where the damaged tendons stretched at the ankle – his Achilles' heel – as one of the doctors had jokingly commented. Well it was no joke now, he would have to turn back.

It was then that he noticed the line of half a dozen cars parked along the narrow road that ran near the foot of Hound Tor, one of which he was sure was Spud Wannacott's vehicle. Then he heard a sound that took him back to his early years on the family farm – the sound of hounds in full cry. Of course, it was September, the time to begin to train the young hounds, and early morning was the best time to do it. In the days of his youth, it was called cub hunting but since the ban on fox hunting, the name had been dropped. Now they would be hunting a laid trail, or at least that would be the intention. He realised that was where Spud was going when he called in at the cottage.

Matt called Bullet to heel and grabbed his collar as the sound got nearer. There was no point in running the risk of a small dog suddenly popping up in front of a pack of hounds in full cry. Two red-coated horsemen appeared followed by a small group of riders dressed in either tweed coats or waterproof jackets of various colours. Matt watched them disappear into a wooded valley below the tor as the various onlookers scrambled to get into their vehicles and drive off at speed in as near the same direction as the moorland roads would allow. He wondered if the young woman, Kate, was among the riders on Harry. He hoped not, only because a sweaty horse was not the best subject for a portrait photo. It depended how long they went on. If they blew for home before lunch, it would probably be okay. The thought of lunch reminded him that he would need to drive into Bovey to replenish the larder with basic essentials. He turned and began the walk back.

The trip to the little moorland town was uneventful. Most of the summer visitors had returned home, and as he walked up the single main street, it seemed that the population consisted mainly of well-to-do pensioners. There were fewer shops than he remembered twelve years ago and more estate agents and charity shops, but that was a sign of the times and something he had noticed even in his home county of Hertfordshire and that was relatively near London. There were enough good food stores to satisfy his needs and it was reassuring to see a thriving post office and two banks with the necessary cash machines,

Back at the cottage, lunch was a frugal affair: a ham sandwich and a glass of milk. The night trauma had left Matt with little appetite and he was glad of the opportunity to spend time sorting out his canvasses and paints ready for the work to come. As always, the contemplation of a new commission caused a feeling of excitement and anticipation tinged with concern that he would get it right. He checked his digital camera, picked up his sketch pad and prepared to walk down to meet his client.

Leaving a whingeing Bullet shut in the kitchen, Matt decided to walk down to the stables without his stick; confident that he could stay on his feet providing he avoided the stony track. He took the first gate into the fields above the manor. Several horses wearing rugs were grazing in the paddocks behind post and rail fencing and he paused to watch them remembering how, when a small boy, his mother had made him help look after his pony, something his sister did much more willingly. He walked on doing his best to disguise the inevitable limp as he made his way to the field gate that led into the stable yard. As he pushed it open, he saw her standing on the far side with the woman he had seen in the pub and a short dark-haired man, while a tall middle-aged man was examining a horse that was being led out of one of the loose boxes. When the gate clicked shut, she turned and smiled at him, putting up a hand that said, 'I'll be with you in a minute'. Matt nodded and watched as the animal was trotted across the yard and back. Finally, it was returned to the box and the group moved on to the neighbouring animal, except Kate who detached herself and began to walk towards him.

It was the first time Matt had seen her without a riding hat and it was a pleasant surprise to see that her hair was long and blonde and fell to her shoulders. It framed a very pleasing, if not actually beautiful, face. She was wearing a dark blue puffa jacket and jeans which were tucked into a pair of black half chaps. The smile was genuine and Matt took comfort from the indication that he was no longer considered a pariah.

'Nice to see you Mr. er … '

'Matt.'

'Oh, yes, sorry, Matt. I'm dreadful at remembering names.'

'Well, I remember yours. Kate. Short for … ?'

'Kathryn with a k and a y. Sorry to keep you waiting but we are running a bit behind. Dad is taking longer than usual with this lot so I am going to have to ask you to amuse yourself for about twenty minutes or so until we are finished.'

It was Matt's turn to smile. 'That's okay. I'll just mosey around and perhaps take a few photographs for future reference.'

Kate frowned. 'I don't think that would be very wise here. They're not very keen on strangers taking pictures, probably something to do with next door and the inmates at the manor, so best to just wander around the yard and look at the equine inmates here.' She turned to walk back to where the other three were examining a second animal.

Matt watched her go and his mind went back to another incident five years earlier when another good-looking young woman had walked away from him, but that time it had been for good. He stood for several minutes just looking around when he noticed the large horsebox, obviously being washed down and cleaned out, just the other side of the gate that led to the large gravel car park. He walked over to see a man with a long mop and brush swilling down the outside of the vehicle while a second man was lowering the rear and side ramps, presumably to do a similar job inside.

Suddenly Matt became aware of somebody behind him. He looked over his shoulder to see the dark-haired man who had been with the group examining the horses standing a few yards away staring at him. The man, wearing a black zip-up jacket and grey corduroy trousers, came up to stand beside him.

'You interested in horseboxes?' he asked.

Matt shrugged. 'I suppose I'm just fascinated by large vehicles.' He walked forwards to glance up at the front of the lorry. 'Ah, yes, a Scania and she's a six-wheeler. Bet she takes a bit of handling. How many horses can you get in there?' He nodded towards the ramps where the two men had stopped work and were idly watching.

'Why you want to know?' The tone was abrupt and Matt detected a foreign accent which he could not place.

'Just idle curiosity. I'm waiting for Kate over there. I'm going to paint her horse. I'm Matt Winsford, staying up there.' He indicated towards Coombe Cottage.

'Oh, yes, the painter, ah!'

Kate must have told him, Matt thought, but was not sure whether the final expletive indicated interest or disbelief. He also had the distinct impression that his presence there was not welcome. 'I'm sorry, I didn't mean to interrupt your work, it's just that I used to be in the transport business so things like this', he nodded towards the lorry, 'naturally interest me.' He glanced towards the two men who immediately resumed their tasks while his interrogator, who looked to be their boss, gave him a cursory nod and walked back towards the loose boxes.

For the next quarter of an hour, Matt wandered casually round the yard looking at the animals stabled in the main block of loose boxes and eventually ended up next to a high stone wall that separated the stables from the walled garden of Lidstone Manor. There was a small door made of weathered oak panels, its rusty hinges indicating that it had not been opened for a very long time while the stout padlock clearly said to keep out. He could hear voices the other side; there was some shouting while a loud voice seemed to be giving orders; The sounds were muffled through the thick wood but Matt had no doubt that he was eavesdropping on Lidstone Manor's young inmates, the bad boys the pub landlord had hinted at. He wondered what they had done to be sent there, probably not much more than some of the young men he had known during the past ten years. To him, it seemed a thin line between those youngsters who were considered criminals and those who were just a pain in the arse and needed a kick up the backside to put them straight.

His thoughts were interrupted by a tap on the shoulder and he turned to find Kate standing behind him.

'Sorry to keep you waiting but Dad was a bit slower than usual this afternoon and he's not the sort you can push.'

'Dad being?' Matt asked.

'Oh, sorry. He's the vet.'

'The tall gentleman?'

'Yes, that's right.' She looked puzzled for a moment. 'Oh my god, you didn't think Ivan the Terrible was my father, surely?'

Matt shrugged, then said with a grin, 'I guess I just hoped not. I thought he didn't quite fit the age group but you can never tell with foreigners, some have their kids very young. Where does he hail from?'

'He says he was born in Poland but I wouldn't bet on that being the truth.' She shook her head. 'Did you really think I could be related to that self-opinionated bastard?'

'I gather you don't get on.'

'It's just that I don't like the way he treats the staff here, or the horses if it comes to that. He says he's a retired jockey and I suppose that bit might be true. Anyway, Greta thinks he's the bee's knees so we have to put up with him.'

'Greta being the other female in your little group?'

'Greta is the boss of this side of the business.' Kate indicated the stabling. 'Her husband runs the other show.' She nodded towards the manor.

They were walking towards the gate where the horsebox had been parked for its clean up. The vehicle had been moved to a parking place adjacent to the house and Matt could not resist the temptation to take out his camera and take a few quick snaps as they walked past.

'Don't see many of those,' he said by way of explanation.

'You'd better put that away,' Kate said as she guided him towards her car.

'Where are we going?' Matt asked as he squeezed himself into the passenger seat. 'I though you kept the horse here.'

'Lord no. I couldn't afford the livery cost, although they do let me use the sand school. It's a small perk but very useful. No, I keep him at home and home isn't very easy to find so I thought it better to meet you here.'

During the drive, Matt made a note of the route just in case he needed to visit his subject anytime in the future. The gate onto the lane was open and they drove in to park in front of the barn.

'He's over there.' Kate nodded towards the loose boxes. 'I've kept them in specially. Normally I rug them up and turn them out during the day but I didn't want the job of scraping the mud off before you came.'

They walked over to where the two horses stood with their heads over the stable doors. Matt looked them over while Kate went to the tack room for a head collar.

'This one's nice,' he said, patting the neck of the black mare. Kate was putting the head collar on the chestnut.

'Old Molly, yes, she's a dear, pure bred Dales cob. Getting on a bit now but put a pack of hounds in front of her and you would have a job to hold the old girl. She belongs to my mother but Mum hasn't ridden her for a couple of years now so I have to trot her out now and again just to keep her going. Mum wouldn't part with her for the world so I suppose Molly is with us until she drops. Molly, I mean, not Mum.' She grinned and led Harry out into the yard. 'Where do you want him?'

Matt took out his small sketch pad. 'Just let him relax for a few minutes while I get down a few details. There's just the white star on his forehead and that white off-hind pastern.' He walked round the animal, making a few quick sketches. 'I'm relieved you haven't clipped him out, that would have made the job much more difficult.'

Eventually, he stuffed the pad back into his pocket and took out the camera. 'Okay, this is the important bit.' He began to take a series of photographs at various angles from the front and side of the horse. 'Now all we need is something to make him cock his ears forward.'

At that moment, the opening of the kitchen door achieved the desired effect and with a grateful 'Yes!' Matt took several shots before turning to see the plump grey-haired woman dressed in grey slacks and a flowered top standing in the doorway.

For several seconds, no one spoke until Kate finally said, 'Matt, this is my mother.'

Mary Lethbridge smiled and walked into the yard to offer her hand as Matt put away his camera. 'I'm pleased to meet you, Matt,' she said and he had the distinct feeling that, for the second time that day, he was being critically appraised; this time, he was glad he had his shirt on as he shook her hand.

Mary looked at her daughter. 'I hope I haven't interrupted you but I thought you might be ready for a cup of tea.' Kate gave an exasperated glance heavenward, shook her head and informed her that they had just finished but they needed a few more minutes. 'Right then, I'll go and put the kettle on.' She turned to Matt. 'You would like a cup of tea, wouldn't you?' It sounded more like a command than a request.

He nodded. 'Thank you, that would be very nice.'

'She's just being nosey, you know that, don't you?' Kate said irritably.

'I'm sure she is just doing what any mother would do,' Matt said as they led the horse back to the stables, 'and to tell you the truth, I wouldn't mind a cuppa right now. It's been one of those days.'

Kate led the way through the kitchen door where Matt took off his coat and boots to follow her in his socks. 'Boots off please, Kate.' The command came from the living room where Mary was setting out the cups and saucers together with three small plates.

'You're getting cake,' Kate whispered as they entered the room. 'Doesn't happen very often in this house. You are honoured.'

The sitting room was spacious but with small windows that cut the amount of light coming in. There were three oak beams running across the ceiling and a large fireplace with a granite lintel set in the far wall. A wood burner, flanked by piles of logs, gave a comforting glow.

They sat down opposite each other at a small, low table, she on the sofa and he in one of the armchairs while Mary poured the tea. She looked towards Matt. 'How do you like it?'

'Oh, just as it comes, no sugar.'

The large fruit cake was carved into three generous portions before Mary sat down to sip her tea. No one spoke until she lowered the cup onto her saucer and stirred it slowly. 'So, you are the new tenant of Coombe Cottage?'

'Yes. That's right.'

There was a pause. 'Will you be staying long?'

'That depends on how things go but probably until the New Year, perhaps longer.' He was beginning to feel slightly uncomfortable.

'Oh, not very long then. Is it just a holiday?'

'Something like that I … '

'Mother!' Kate interrupted angrily. 'Mr. Winsford didn't come in here to be cross-examined.'

'Oh, that's alright' He turned to his questioner and in a quiet, hesitant voice, said, ' You see I … I had an accident. Mashed up my leg and various other bits of my poor old carcass so the powers that be decided I should get away for a bit. We used to come here on holiday when I was a kid so it seemed the obvious place.'

'Well I hope you soon get better. It's a bleak old place up there to be on your own without your family.'

Matt shook his head. 'I'm not sure my parents would be much help but in any case, they have a farm to run.'

Mary gave a faint smile of satisfaction. 'Would you like another cup of tea?'

It had taken Kate a great effort to restrain herself from yelling at her mother as she sat listening to her extracting personal information from someone who, to her, was a complete stranger. She knew what her mother was up to and to some extent, she had been successful: she had established that the man did not have a wife.

She turned to Matt as they walked across the yard later on. 'Don't mind Mum. She doesn't get to see many folk, particularly strangers, so she tends to run on a bit. You know, wants to find out as much as possible so she can gossip to the rest of the Ladies Luncheon Club. So next Wednesday, you will be the topic of conversation at one o'clock in the Lidstone Arms.'

Matt grinned. 'Sounds just like my mother, but thanks for the tip. I'll steer clear of that particular hostelry on future Wednesday lunchtimes.'

They got into the Fiat. 'I'll run you home,' Kate said as she drove out of the farm gate. 'Save you having to walk up the track to Coombe Cottage.'

'I'm perfectly happy to go back the way I came, thank you,' he said. Then he thought, I'm not a bloody cripple.

Strange man, Kate thought as she put the car into gear and drove off.

After Kate had dropped him off, Matt stood for a while and watched the car disappear round a bend in the lane before making his way up the track towards the cottage.

He heard it before he was halfway up the track: the sound of a car alarm. There was only one car at the end of the track, and it was his. He started to run and wished he had brought his stick as the pain shot through his injured leg. He saw the lights flashing as he turned the final bend in the track, and to his dismay, he could see the reason why: there was a star-shaped crack in the rear window where someone had obviously had a go at it with something heavy; a rock or possibly a hammer. He felt in his pocket for the keys and quickly turned the alarm off and it was then that he noticed that the back door was open. He could not remember whether he had locked it and since he could see no damage, he assumed he had not.

Inside, his immediate impression was that someone had just gone around chucking things on the floor: towels, cooking utensils, some smashed crockery. It looked as though whoever did this simply grabbed things at random as they walked round. It was the same in the studio room; canvasses were strewn over the floor, several had been slashed and the paints had been scattered over the top of them.

Matt stood in a state of shock. Why would anyone do this? He leant against the doorpost trying to take it all in, trying to work out the motive for such senseless vandalism. If whoever did this was looking for something to steal, they would have been disappointed, he thought, for there was nothing of any value worth pinching downstairs: but there was up in his bedroom. He went up the stairs two at a time to where he had left his laptop on the bed and to his astonishment, it was still there exactly where he had put it. Theft was either not the motive or the intruder had been disturbed before he or she had been able to search the whole house.

On inspection, it appeared that no other rooms had been entered and as Matt made a thorough search of the rest of the house, he suddenly realised there was something missing. Bullet.

He went back into the kitchen hoping that the dog had slipped out when the intruder had opened the back door. As he stepped over the debris on the floor, he suddenly noticed some tea towels piled in the corner where Bullet normally slept. Protruding beneath them, he saw something which made his stomach churn – a bloodstained paw.

'Oh, Christ no!' The words blurted out as he quickly reached forward and whipped away the coverings to reveal the motionless body. He gently lifted the dog to cradle it in his arms; there was no sign of life as he stroked the limp head. He slumped back into a chair as the tears welled up in his tightly clenched eyes.

CHAPTER 5

Jackson Williams opened his eyes as he heard the door latch click. 'Are you up yet, Jacko?' His mother's voice came from the living room as, walking backwards, she manoeuvred her ample frame and a pushchair from the corridor into the flat.

Jacko sat up, quickly pushed away the duvet and swung his legs out of bed. For a moment he panicked, glancing at the bedside clock, which told him it was eight-thirty: he would be late for school. Then the relief as his mind caught up with his body and he relaxed back onto the bed. 'Yes, Mum. What's the hurry? I'm sixteen now, I don't have to go to school no more, so I'll just have me breakfast and take it easy for a bit.'

'Never mind about taking it easy. You can get your arse out of bed and start looking for a job.' Peggy Williams picked up a fair-haired two-year-old from the pushchair and dumped him into a playpen at the far end of the room. 'And you're old enough to get your own bloody breakfast while I change Bobby's nappy.'

Her bedroom door banged, which set off a wail from the child causing Jacko to get up and stomp angrily to the bathroom. He looked at himself in the mirror and ran his hands through the mop of frizzy black hair which, he contemplated, he could now let grow as long as he liked, perhaps even an Afro with dreadlocks and there would be no one in the shape of a bloody school teacher to tell him otherwise.

His ablutions completed, Jacko got dressed in jeans and a bright yellow T-shirt that had the words I'M THE ONE printed on it. A pair of red socks and blue trainers completed the job and he felt confident enough to face the world as a proper man and no longer a school kid. He set about a meagre breakfast of cereal and coffee accompanied by Radio 1 turned up as loud as he could.

There was a yell from the living room. 'Turn down that damned racket, Jacko! I'm trying to get Bobby off and there's no way he's going to get to sleep with that noise.' The sound diminished slightly as Peggy entered her eldest son's bedroom. She began to straighten the pillows then stopped abruptly as she detected a scent that was all too familiar. 'Have you been smoking that stuff again, Jacko?' she demanded angrily. There was either no reply or it was drowned by the latest music hit. She picked up the duvet from where it lay half on the floor, threw it petulantly onto the bed and left the room praying fervently that the boy was not turning out to be like his father. She went into the kitchen. 'Did you hear what I said? Have you been smoking weed again? And don't say no 'cos I can smell it in your room.'

Jacko finished his coffee, banged the mug down on the table and stood up to face his mother. 'I told you, I don't do it no more and what you could smell wasn't anything I had smoked.'

'So that means you've got some hidden away in there?'

'It means I *had* some. It's all gone now, I got rid of it.'

'You mean you sold it. Now look, young man, I don't want any repeat of what I had to go through with your father, so unless you give me your word you're clean, it'll be another visit from your social worker, so there.'

'I told you, I don't do it no more, Mum, and why bring the bloke you call my father into this when he's been long gone and no one knows where? Probably inside or buggered off back to Jamaica or wherever.'

'That's enough, Jacko, and don't swear like that, I don't like it.'

'So it's alright for you to swear, but not me, is that it? Mum, I'm sixteen now, I'm not a child anymore.'

'Let's get this straight, young man! As far as everyone else is concerned, you are *still* a child and will be until you are eighteen so don't start getting any big ideas.'

The boy merely gave a grunt in response as he reached for his grey hooded fleece which hung on the back of the door and started to put it on. He turned to see his mother go back into his bedroom and start opening the drawers in his battered bedside cabinet. 'What are you doing, Mum? Leave my things alone,' he yelled as he followed her.

'I want to know what you are up to, young man! It's not like you to be up much before midday when there's no school.' Peggy turned to look at her son. 'So what's got you going at this hour? Where are you off to and who with? That's what I want to know, Jacko. I don't want you getting into no trouble, I've got enough problems as it is without you making it worse.' She slammed the last drawer shut. The noise woke the child in the next room: the sound of its crying caused Peggy to dissolve into tears. Jacko began to leave, then stopped in the doorway and turned towards his mother.

'It's alright, Mum,' he said quietly. 'I'm just meeting Scag Thompson and some mates down the park.' His mother brushed aside a wisp of blonde hair from her face, dried her eyes on her sleeve and moved closer to face him. He was already taller than her by several inches and the fact made her feel even more uneasy.

'Who is this Scag bloke and how did he get that label? Don't tell me, I don't wanna know but what I do know is I don't want you mixed up with no drugs. You hear what I'm saying?' Her voice rose to a crescendo as she hurried over to the playpen to pick up the screaming child. 'And don't forget dinner's at one o'clock. Don't be late 'cos Andy wants a word with you.'

'What does *he* want?' Jacko did not get on with his mother's latest partner, Bobby's father,

'He wants to talk to you about an apprenticeship at the factory.'

'Tell him to get stuffed.' Jacko murmured under his breath as he opened the door and went out.

Out in the corridor, Jacko pulled the hood up and set off down the stairs. The two-bedroomed flat was on the fourth floor of the six-story block. There was a lift but it was often out of order and also stank of a mixture of tobacco smoke and urine so that most of the female occupants preferred to bump their pushchairs up and down the stairs rather than endure the few minutes incarcerated in the stinking hole.

Out in the street, he headed towards Kilburn station. He had a job to do before joining the gang at Gladstone Park. He glanced at his watch; plenty of time before Scag would arrive at the meeting place by St. Gabriel's Church so he took the opportunity to slip into a familiar Pakistani run grocery store. He emerged a few minutes later with a bottle of high alcohol cider and a packet of twenty Malboro, which he stuffed into the pockets of his fleece. It was not the first time he had done this and the elderly man behind the counter had never questioned his age.

At the church, he sat on the low wall that separated the building from the road to wait for his friend's arrival. Passers-by took no notice of the seated figure fumbling in his jeans pocket for his lighter. They were used to seeing groups of youngsters perched on the wall, waiting for a bus or just killing time. Jacko lit the cigarette and leant forward, elbows on knees, supporting his head with one hand ,and stared blankly at the tarmac while he flicked ash onto the pavement. He thought about the things his mother had talked about, conscious of the fact that he had lied to her. He had smoked a joint and he *did* have some weed stashed away, not in his room but in the bathroom, securely wrapped in plastic and hidden behind a loose wooden panel that surrounded the bath.

'Hi man, what's with you?' The sound of Scag's voice brought Jacko back to the present as he looked up to see the pale pock-marked face looking down at him. Scag Thompson was a year older than Jacko but was shorter and more heavily built. He was wearing a similar grey hooded fleece with jeans that were a size too big tucked into the tops of a pair of heavy workman's boots.

He sat down next to Jacko with a groan. 'I walked most of the way from Willesden and me bloody feet are killing me. The guy what sold 'em to me said the steel toecaps were just the thing for kicking someone's arse in a tight spot. What he didn't say was that they're bleedin' murder to walk in.'

Jacko sat up, took out the bottle of cider, unscrewed the top and took a swig before handing it to Scag. 'What was that you were saying about boots?'

Scag shook his head and, putting the bottle to his mouth, gulped steadily for several seconds before giving a long drawn-out sigh and wiping his mouth with the back of his hand. 'We might as well finish this off between us,' Scag said as he rubbed the top with his sleeve and handed the bottle back. 'We're in good time and I don't reckon our friend Bart will be doing much if things are too quiet.'

Jacko nodded and offered the packet of cigarettes.

Scag shook his head. 'No thanks, mate. I'd prefer a joint if it's all the same to you.' He fumbled in his pocket and brought out the small tin box which contained the cigarette papers and a small amount of cannabis. He held a paper between his fingers, sprinkled a thin line of the drug along its length and expertly rolled a thin cigarette.

They sat for several minutes without saying a word until Jacko broke the silence. 'Had another row with Mum this morning.'

'Well that's nothin' new.'

'She don't like the idea of me hanging about with someone that's got a handle like Scag. She always thinks the worst of me.' He paused before turning to look at his companion. 'How did you get that nickname, Scag? You ever screw the white stuff?'

'Heroin? Nah, you know me better than that. No way I could get the dosh for that sort of caper.' He chuckled. 'It was all a bloody daft mistake. I was doin' one of me regular postin' jobs – you know, delivering to a regular – when the guy can't wait to get his hands on the stuff, grabs the packet and, before you know it, half of it was down the front of me, at least fifty quid's worth. He yells blue murder, belts me one in the eye and rings up Bart to tell him I've buggered up the delivery, lost half of it and he should sack me and get someone else to do the job. When I got back with a real shiner, they all thought it was a great joke. O'corse I didn't get me back-hander, nor anything for the next couple of jobs but at least Bart kept me on and it was him what dubbed me Scag.'

Jacko grinned, stood up and stuffed the empty cider bottle behind the wall. 'Better get going, I suppose,' he said, giving Scag a nudge. 'Don't want you to get into no more trouble for being late.' Scag nodded, got to his feet and tightened the drawstring of his hood to give the maximum obscurity to his features. Jacko followed suit as they made their way to the station.

The number of people at the station was about average at that time in the morning. The rush hour was over and the crowd had thinned to a steady flow of people in and out of the main entrance which was on the corner of two thoroughfares. At the right-hand side, shaded by the overhead railway bridge, stood a tall pale-faced man in a long grey overcoat, a blue woollen hat pulled well down over his ears, and a brown scarf that hung loosely round his neck. He held a battered leather suitcase in his right hand and looked as though he was waiting for a bus or a taxi

As the two youngsters approached, he nodded in recognition and walked towards them, his eyes glancing anxiously at anyone else that came into his proximity. 'Right, boys, you know what you have to do,' he said in a hoarse whisper. 'Scag, you take the Christchurch side, and you, young Jacko, look out on the corner by the burger stall and don't forget, if you see any signs of the filth, don't panic, just walk towards me a few steps where I can see you, give me a nod, then bugger off as fast as them legs'll carry you.' He reached down into his overcoat pocket and drew out a wad of twenty pound notes, gave one to each of the lads and followed it with a small, cannabis-filled plastic bag. 'Just a bit extra to keep yer spirits up,' he said with a grin.

Jacko took up his position and watched Bart as he resumed his place by the station entrance. It was not the first time the boy had done the lookout job but he was still curious to see the sort of customers that brushed casually past the tall figure: the few seconds it took to complete the transaction obscured by the brown scarf. An elderly stout man in a blue pinstriped suit, a middle-aged woman in a mock fur coat and numerous young men all came through the doors of the station at various times with their money ready in their hands; they all made the transaction and left with a look of pleasure and contentment. These were the top-grade customers: the heroin addicts, the main money-spinners for the likes of Bart.

Intent on watching the proceedings at the station, Jacko failed to notice a dark blue Ford Focus that was parked on a double yellow line fifty yards up the side street he was supposed to be watching, nor did it register when two men got out and began walking leisurely towards him. One wore grey trousers and a black leather zip-up jacket, the other wore jeans and a thick, blue woollen jersey. By the time it did register, it was too late: he felt a firm grip on his arm, and at the same time, a voice close to his ear told him he was nicked. At the same moment, two uniformed policemen burst through the station entrance, grabbed Bart by both arms, and quickly handcuffed him. The man holding Jacko nodded to his partner who immediately began emptying the boy's pockets. While this was happening, one of the uniformed officers was talking into his mobile phone to call up the necessary transport. There was no sign of Scag.

The two plain-clothes policemen bundled Jacko into the back of the Ford. One of them sat next to him while the other drove at a moderate speed to the police station.

*

The middle-aged sergeant behind the desk raised his eyebrows as the young coloured boy was brought in. 'So, what's this one been up to?' he asked the taller of the two officers.

'We've done a bust on that lot trading drugs,' he told him. 'Mostly heroin, up in Kilburn. Only the tip of the iceberg, of course. We got one of the bigger fish that was doing the dealing and this little blighter was the tiny sprat on lookout. Been watching 'em for a couple of months now.'

The sergeant nodded and began entering Jacko's name, age, address and telephone number into the computer together with the details of his arrest. The contents of his pockets were placed on the desk; thirty-five pounds and sixty pence, cigarettes, lighter and the small plastic bag. The sergeant shook his head. 'If I'm not mistaken, that is not the sort of stuff a young lad like you should be in possession of.' He sniffed the packet. 'Cannabis, that's a Class B, young man, which puts you in deep trouble.' He looked over Jacko's head at the tall policeman who gave a nod and the slightest suspicion of a wink before he led the boy to an empty cell.

On his way out, he paused at the front desk where the sergeant had just finished a telephone call. 'I've left the door open,' he told him. 'He's only a bloody kid, hardly out of school.'

The sergeant grunted. 'The only way is to frighten the shit out of 'em, that's my opinion. Teach 'em a lesson they won't forget.'

The tall policeman shook his head. 'Things have moved on since your day, Tom. What he wants right now is his mum and then someone to put him on the right track.'

*

It was late afternoon before Jacko was allowed to return home accompanied by his mother and Sonia Caley, his social worker. They walked in silence to the car park where Sonia had left her VW Polo. Not until they had all squeezed into the car did anyone speak: it was Peggy, wiping her eyes, who broke the silence.

42

'What the fu … What the hell do you think you are playing at, boy?' Her fierce rebuff moderated by Sonia's presence. The social worker pretended not to hear and kept her eyes fixed on the road ahead. This was 'old hat' to her: she spent most of her time listening to distraught parents coming to terms with the misdemeanours of their offsprings. She herself had suffered the discrimination experienced by many black children and had watched her younger brother struggle with alcohol and drugs while her parents battled to change his life, fortunately with the degree of success that saw him eventually in a steady job. It was partly that and the fact that, like her parents, she was a dedicated Christian, which had prompted her to opt for social services on completion of her university degree.

As they walked up the stairs to the flat, Jacko, for the first time, felt scared. He had heard of the places that young boys were sent to: borstals, boot camps, detention centres, even jail. They all sounded grim. The fact that Sonia Caley was black gave him some comfort: she would be on his side, coloureds had to stick together. He was a few steps behind when they reached the corridor and he could hear Sonia talking to his mother, something about an STC, whatever that was, and seeing a magistrate. They paused at the door of the flat while Peggy went next door to retrieve Bobby from an obliging neighbour. With the child in her arms, she unlocked the door and went in, indicating that Sonia should sit on the sofa with Jacko beside her while she was going to make a cup of tea. The boy slumped down without taking off his fleece.

He sat, staring blankly ahead, thinking of the words he had overheard as they came up the stairs.

Oh God, he thought. That means court and all that bloody stuff. They'll put me inside.

*

The waiting room reminded Jacko of the local health centre, except it was much smaller and the chairs were fewer and much harder. He sat between his mother and Sonia while people came and went through the glass panelled door on the other side of the room. The young woman at the reception desk had taken their particulars and told them there was a slight delay of about twenty minutes and asked them to sit in the waiting room until called. Jacko was not sure what was happening. He had been told he was not going to court but he would be seeing a magistrate. What that meant, he had no idea. Sonia had tried to explain that, because of his age, it had been decided that he should not be subjected to the full legal system: there would be a shortcut.

'Jackson Williams!' He jumped when his name was called and stood up, nervously looking round to ensure that Sonia and his mother were going to accompany him through the glass door. On entering, he was surprised to see that the office he entered was quite small, not the court room he had expected. There were half a dozen chairs facing a raised wooden desk behind which a large man in a blue pinstriped suit was taking out a sheaf of papers from a file. It was not the size of the gentleman that impressed Jacko, it was the grey moustache and sideburns, the tanned face and, above all, the dark blue turban.

'Mr. Milkha Singh', Sonia whispered. 'It could be worse'.

The magistrate beckoned Jacko to come and stand in front of him and, adjusting his rimless spectacles, leant forward to look intently at the young man. Jacko met his gaze and found himself looking into a pair of dark piercing eyes, but eyes that offered no threat. He resisted the temptation to look away and suddenly realised he was no longer afraid.

'I have discussed your case at length with my colleagues.' Milkha Singh spoke slowly with a clear articulate voice which Peggy would have called posh. 'It seems to us that you are at a tipping point, young man,' his eyes scanned the paper in front of him. 'It would appear that there have been two cases of shoplifting in the past year for which, fortunately for you, the victims decided not to prosecute. There may have been others that we don't know about but that's as it may be.' He paused as his eyes scanned the document in front of him. 'But now there is the more serious offence: the possession of a Class B drug, namely cannabis. However, in mitigation it is plain that this was for personal use and not for trafficking; even so it is an illegal substance and certainly should not have been found in the possession of such a young person. In addition, it is clear that you were aiding and abetting persons who were selling drugs.' He looked across to where the two women were sitting and, with a smile, asked them if they would please join Jackson in front of him.

Peggy and Sonia placed themselves on either side of Jacko. Sonia was calm and gave the impression that she knew what was coming while Peggy stared anxiously at the magistrate, unsure what his words meant as far as punishment was concerned and terrified that her son would follow his father and sink into a pit of crime from which there was no return.

'Mrs. Williams,' Milkha Singh's voice jarred Peggy out of her reverie. She swallowed hard and, with a slight nod, waited to hear what was to become of her son. 'You will by now realise,' he continued, 'that there has to be a price to pay for the conduct of your son, Jackson. I have taken into consideration the fact that he is only just sixteen years old and that his childhood has not been the easiest. Ms. Caley has persuaded me that he should be given the chance of a better life and I am therefore recommending that he goes to one of our training centres for a period of six months. We have a number of STCs dotted round the country. At the present time ,they are experimental: there are no brick walls and no barbed wire but should an inmate attempt to abscond, then a far worse fate would befall him.' He directed those final words at Jacko, then, turning to Peggy, he continued, 'Your son is not unintelligent, Mrs. Williams. He has C grade GCSEs in Media Studies and English, and not many young men that come before me can say that. It is one reason why we are taking the course I have suggested. The secure training centres are as much educational as remedial, and I am confident Jackson will benefit from the experience. I am informed that there is a place available at Gainsborough House, which is at Lidstone in Devon.'

Milkha Singh sat back in his chair, removed his glasses indicating that the interview was over. 'Thank you, ladies.' He smiled and turned to Peggy. 'Mrs. Williams, you will be informed of the travel arrangements and Ms. Caley will tell you all you want to know about visiting. Thank you again, good afternoon.'

CHAPTER 6

It seemed to Matt that he had been sitting in the dark for at least an hour when in fact it was less that half that. The bundle in his arms was still motionless and, in despair, he was about to place it back on the floor when he stopped: he was sure something inside the limp body was moving, or was it just his imagination? He placed Bullet gently in the chair, reached up and switched on the light. As he did so, he was certain he saw the dog's eyelids move. His heart missed a beat: Bullet was still alive.

Matt's immediate priority was now the welfare of his dog: informing the police or ringing Charles Spreyton would have to wait. He carried Bullet outside and placed him carefully on the passenger seat of the Volvo. A quick examination of the vehicle reassured him that there was no further damage and it started at the first turn of the key. Breathing a sigh of relief, Matt pulled out into the lane and drove slowly towards Lidstone, grateful for the fact that he knew exactly where he could find the nearest veterinary surgeon.

It was now pitch dark and not easy to see the turn into the narrow lane which would take him to the Lethbridges. He almost missed it and had to brake suddenly so that it was only the quick reaction of his left hand that prevented the dog being catapulted onto the floor. Determined not to make the same mistake at the entrance to the house, he crawled along at twenty miles an hour until he recognised the gate into the front yard. Luckily, it was open and he was able to drive straight up to the front door.

It was Kate who answered the bell. 'Good Lord, it's you,' she said as Matt stepped forward, Bullet cradled in his arms. She glanced down at dog. 'Oh dear, what's happened? Has he been run over? You'd better come in, I'll fetch Dad.' She turned and led Matt to the sitting room where Jim was watching a documentary about Africa. He looked up as they came in and immediately got to his feet when he saw Matt.

'Oh, hello,' he said brightly and, then stopped when he saw what was being presented to him. He studded the limp body for a second before leading Matt into the kitchen and indicated to lay the dog on the kitchen table. 'Was it a vehicle accident?' he asked as he began to examine Bullet.

Matt shook his head and told him what had happened. Kate and her mother had joined them at the table and both expressed genuine shock and disbelief that anything like that could happen in a quiet little place like Lidstone.

Jim Lethbridge paused in his examination and looked at Matt. 'Have you told the police?' There was anger in his voice. 'People who do things like this should be locked up.' Matt had to admit that he had not informed anyone yet and that his first thought had been to get Bullet to a vet. Jim nodded. 'Yes, of course, but you can phone up from here if you like. You'll have to use the landline as the signal here is very dodgy. The phone is in my little office,' he pointed to a recess which was partitioned off from the rest of the sitting room by a full length green velvet curtain.

Matt shook his head. 'Let's get the old dog sorted first, then we'll worry about the rest of it.'

Jim laid his stethoscope down on the table. 'Well the good news is that his pulse is normal and, as you can see, he is slowly regaining consciousness.' Bullet had begun to blink and move his head slightly. 'The bad news is that he has almost certainly fractured his ribs on the left side and there is the added problem of the blow on the head which rendered him unconscious. If you are agreeable, I would like to take him down to the surgery where we can get an X-ray just to check there is no internal damage. We can also give him something to help the pain and inflammation, then I think we should keep him under observation for a few days to ensure he doesn't get dehydrated and we can check for any follow-up infection. My partner Alison is very good with dogs, I'm sure she will get him going again. Would you like to come down to the surgery with me now Mr. … er … Winsford, isn't it? Mary did mention that you were an artist and were going to paint Harry.'

Matt did not want to follow that line so he merely said that was correct and that he would like to accompany him to the surgery.

He sat in the front passenger seat of the elderly Range Rover with Bullet on his lap, trying to fathom out why all this had happened. What had he done to provoke such a vicious attack and what sort of person could inflict such pain on a poor defenceless animal?

The vehicle bumped over a pothole causing Bullet to whimper. 'Sorry,' Jim said. 'We've had to get used to those, but at least it got a response from … What do you call him?'

'Bullet. He used to shoot across the yard like a streak of lightning whenever anybody came through the gate. We thought of calling him Lightning but decided that Bullet sounded more appropriate for a small, fast object.'

That prompted a chuckle from the vet. 'He's getting on a bit now. How long have you had him?'

'On and off for eleven years, since he was a puppy.'

'On and off? What does that mean?'

Matt paused to consider his answer. 'I had, have, the sort of job that means I have to spend time abroad and I can't always take him with me, so he's had to get used to spending time with my parents.'

'Well let's see what we can do for him,' Jim said as he pulled into his parking space outside the surgery.

To Matt's relief, the X-ray showed no damage to the internal organs but three ribs were broken and there was extensive bruising. The gash on the dog's head had not penetrated the skull which was intact.

'Better than I had feared,' was the vet's initial remark. 'He'll need to be watched carefully over the next few days to ensure there is no internal haemorrhaging, but apart from that I'm confident we can pull the old chap through this one.'

Bullet was placed in a small cage that was solid on three sides to isolate it from the neighbouring cages which contained a variety of recuperating animals. It was comfortable and warm, and Matt was content that his old friend was in the best hands.

'Come and see him whenever you like. If Alison or I are not about, we have an efficient veterinary nurse who will let you know how things are going.' Jim looked at his watch. 'We were just about to sit down to supper when you called. I don't know if you've eaten yet, but I'm sure there will be enough chicken casserole for an extra mouth if you would care to join us.'

Matt hesitated. 'Thank you but I couldn't possibly impose on your wife at such short notice.'

Jim smiled. 'If I know Mary, she has already laid an extra knife and fork on the table in anticipation, and after what you've been through, I am certain she would not let you go back to the cottage on an empty stomach. Mary doesn't take no for an answer.'

It was Matt's turn to smile. He was hungry but there was another reason why he would not mind sitting at the Lethbridges' table that evening.

As predicted, the invitation to supper was made soon after they arrived back while Mary was laying the table. She looked very pleased when he agreed to stay; Kate said nothing as she went back into the kitchen to fetch the extra cutlery while her father ushered Matt into the office to make the necessary phone calls.

The reaction from Charles Spreyton had been one of disbelief, adding that such a dreadful occurrence could not be tolerated and he would send Spud Wannacott over in the morning to clear things up. The local police asked for more details but, on learning there appeared to be nothing stolen, seemed to lose interest, saying they would have an officer visit the property sometime tomorrow. When he told Jim that he was disappointed by the police response, the vet shrugged and told him that the local constabulary was so stretched that things like vandalism, unruly behaviour, even farm thefts and the hunting ban, were all low on their list of priorities.

There was little conversation during the first course until Mary got up to clear the plates ready for the apple pie. 'Glad to see you still have a good appetite, young man, in spite of all the trauma,' she said with a grin.

'Yes, that was very nice. It's been a long time since I sat down to a proper family meal, and I really do appreciate it, Mrs. Lethbridge.'

'It's Mary, please!' she called back from the kitchen.

It was Kate who spoke as she handed Matt his dessert. 'How is your leg now?'

'Okay. Why do you ask?'

'Oh, just that you were limping when I dropped you off and you refused a lift home.'

'It was kind of you to offer but I have to use the leg as much as possible to build up the muscle so the doctor says, so I'm hoping to get up on the moor as much as I can. Apparently I need to flex the ankle to strengthen the tendons. Not sure how to achieve that other than walking on tip-toes and that's a bit too strenuous for my liking.'

'Can you ride, Matt?' It was Mary asking the question.

'I've done a bit. Why do you ask?'

'It's just that when I broke my ankle some years ago, they told me that since I could ride a horse, the best thing for me was the rising trot. When you bump the saddle with your toe in the stirrup, your ankle flexes – as simple as that.'

'I'm sure you're right when you come to think of it. The only problem is, I don't have a horse.'

'I do and she really needs the exercise. Isn't that so, Kate?'

'If you say so, Mum.' Kate replied in a voice that indicated she had very little enthusiasm for the project.

'Oh, come on, my girl! You can surely find the time to hack out a few times with him, just to make sure he's okay.' Mary looked at Matt, who nodded and said that he thought he could probably cope.

Mary looked very pleased, too pleased, Kate thought, as her eyes flickered up at the ceiling in a gesture that said, 'Oh no, you're at it again, Mother.'

The meal over, the two men retired to the sitting room where Jim put more logs on the fire, at the same time indicating to Matt that he should sit in one of the two armchairs that were placed either side of the stove. He eased himself into the other with a sigh of satisfaction.

'It's been a long day for me and not a very pleasant one for you, young man, so what do you say to a drop of whiskey to cheer us both up. I've got some single malt that should do the job.' He got up and went to the sideboard at the far end of the room and took out a bottle and two glasses.

'I'm not sure I should really.' Matt was torn between his need for a drink and the fact that he had to drive back to the cottage.

'Oh, one small tot won't do you any harm, and anyway, if you'd like to make an evening of it, you could stay the night. We've got a nice guest room – en-suite and all that. I'm sure Mary would be delighted.'

Matt shifted uneasily in his chair, he could feel – no, he knew – the night to come would not be a good one and the last thing he wanted was to spend it in a strange bed in the same house as these nice people. 'That's very kind of you but I'll have to go back. There's medication I have to take which I haven't got with me and I really can't impose on you any further.' Nevertheless he accepted the glass of whiskey and settled back into the armchair to enjoy the flickering warmth of the wood burner. It reminded him of home.

There was a long period of silence before Jim said that he quite understood and that sticking to a drugs regime was one of the most important things in recovery from any trauma.

'So,' he paused. 'Was it a car accident?'

Matt gave a faint nod but did not elaborate.

'I'm sorry, I didn't mean to pry but sometimes it helps to talk about these things.'

'That's okay. Yes, it did involve vehicles and … there was a fatality.' Matt's eyes gazed fixedly at the flames; then he added under his breath, 'Sometimes I wish it had been mine.'

The conversation was interrupted by Mary. 'Sorry to butt in but I was just wondering if you would like to stay the night, Matt? We've plenty of room.'

Jim shook his head. 'We've just been through that, love, and there are reasons why he has to get back tonight.' Matt was glad he did not give those reasons. He had no wish to go through another explanation.

Mary made herself comfortable on the sofa in front of the wood burner. 'I see you two have sampled the drinks cabinet so if you don't mind, Jim, I'll have a G & T. You can forget about the ice and lemon.' Her husband grinned and eased himself out of his chair to go and pour her gin and tonic. As he did, she turned to Matt. 'Kate sends her apologies but she has to be up at five tomorrow so is turning in early. She said she hopes everything will get sorted out and that Bullet makes a full recovery.' The fact that her daughter had said none of those things but had simply told her she was going to bed had caused Mary some consternation. As she sipped her drink, she asked Matt when he was likely to come and ride Molly.

'I'll have to get kitted out first. Hard hat, suitable footwear, some half chaps. It means a trip into town so I don't suppose it will be for a few days. In any case, I'd like to get all this business cleared up first, then I can decide what to do next.'

'Yes, of course, I quite understand.' She paused to take another sip. 'When you say "decide what to do next", does that mean you would consider moving?'

Matt shook his head. 'I don't scare that easily Mrs. … Mary.'

She gave an inaudible sigh of relief and took another sip of her gin and tonic before adding, 'I dare say Kate could find what you need at the manor, save you buying new stuff; they usually have spare hats and chaps available for the occasional holiday rider but the right footwear might be more difficult.'

'That's no problem, I can send home for my old jod. boots, supposing they can still find them.' Matt grinned at the thought of his mother rummaging through the pile of old gear at the back of their tack room in search of a pair of well-worn jodhpur boots that hadn't seen the light of day for at least ten years. He had to hope they still fitted as he did not relish trying new boots on his damaged left foot. The thought of riding again cheered him up and, for a time, the black cloud of depression he had experienced earlier in the evening began to fade; it would have faded even quicker if Kate had condescended to join them.

As the evening wore on, he was not sure he could keep up the polite conversation much longer, so turning down the offer of a second glass of whiskey, he got to his feet to thank his hosts for their hospitality and made his way to the door.

'If there's anything else we can do, just let us know,' Mary called as Matt got into the Volvo. 'And you can come and ride Molly whenever you like.'

He nodded and turned to Jim. 'I'll pop in to see the old dog tomorrow about ten if that's alright.'

The vet indicated that it was and told him to take care down the lane as there would probably be some traffic coming from the Lidstone Arms at that time of night.

With a parting wave, Matt turned out of the gate, but not before noticing that a light in one of the upstairs windows had suddenly been switched off.

*

The drive back to the cottage was uneventful, although he did have to pass the big Scania horsebox going in the opposite direction. 'Well, that lot are definitely night birds,' he muttered to himself as the lorry turned onto the main road and headed down towards Bovey Tracey.

Lidstone was relatively quiet as Matt drove through; just a few loiterers hanging round the front door of the pub and what seemed like a minor argument going on where the lane turned off to Lidstone Manor, causing him to slow down long enough to see a man with long fair hair and a scraggy beard being hassled by the two men he had seen swilling out the horsebox in the stable yard: all pretty routine stuff for a country pub after closing time, Matt considered as he pressed on up the hill towards the cottage.

There had been some rain earlier in the evening but now the sky had cleared and an almost full moon cast long shadows across the lawn and lit up the puddles on the drive as Matt pulled up outside Coombe Cottage. As he got out of the car, he felt suddenly very vulnerable: he was alone, a situation he was not accustomed to.

He stood for several minutes, reluctant to enter the cottage, then walked into the garden to look down the valley. A tawny owl called from somewhere in the woods below, another answered close to him, then all was quiet and Matt realised he was experiencing something very rare in modern Britain: a natural silence. No car noise, no human voices, even nature was asleep. He began to feel calmer as he steeled himself to enter the mayhem that was inside the cottage.

When he switched on the light, he noticed that whoever it was that had trashed the rooms had not touched the bottle of Bushmills whiskey that had been left on the table in the kitchen, so it was unlikely that the escapade was the result of some drunken spree, Matt concluded as he reached for a glass and poured a generous tot. He no longer cared whether or not the liquor inhibited the action of his medication, he needed the oblivion that alcohol could bring more than the effect of the painkillers and anti-inflammatory pills.

The glass drained, he instinctively looked towards the dog bed to call Bullet, stopping short as the fact that his friend was no longer there hit, a fact that led to another glass of Bushmills which he sipped as he walked through to survey the damage in the makeshift studio. The canvasses were strewn over the floor and since there were only half dozen of various sizes, it had been easy for the intruder to slash them all. The easel was also on the floor but appeared to be undamaged, while the tubes of paint had been thrown in all directions. Matt tried to comprehend the reason for this vandalism as he picked up the nearly finished painting of the Winsford's farmhouse, which he was going to give to his mother on her birthday: it had a large hole torn in the centre. 'Bastards,' he growled as he turned off the lights and made his way up to the bedroom. It was cold. He took off his shoes and lay on the bed fully dressed, head and shoulders propped up on the pillows, the glass in his hand.

*

He woke as the empty glass rolled off the bed and hit the floorboards with a thud. Checking to make sure it had not shattered, Matt eased himself off the mattress and began to undress. A quick glance at his watch told him that it was past midnight: he had been asleep for over an hour, a sleep of oblivion, a sleep uninterrupted by those images and sounds that made up the nightmare he dreaded.

He pulled on his pyjamas and crawled under the duvet, the warmth lulling him back to sleep, and then it began: the grinding noises, screams, the struggle to get away and, worst of all, those lifeless eyes looking up at him as the black cloud descended. He cried out and sat up feeling sick and with a drumming headache. He reached for the painkillers, retrieved the glass and went to the bathroom to retch into the toilet bowl, but nothing came. He filled the glass, took two of the pills and gulped down the water before returning to the bedroom and the warmth of the duvet. He lay on his back looking up at the dim outline of a single oak beam which seemed to divide the ceiling into two halves, the half nearest the window now brighter than the other. Perhaps it was like his own life: divided into before and after, but after was not the brighter and neither was it going to be the easiest.

CHAPTER 7

It was eight o'clock on a cold September morning. Jacko and Peggy stood on the pavement outside Kilburn station waiting for the vehicle that would transport the youth to the place called Lidstone Manor. As instructed, Peggy had provided a packed lunch which she had put into a tin box together with a small bottle of orange juice. She held a brand new canvass holdall contained the basic necessities for Jacko's time away: wash kit, underpants, a spare pare of trousers and T-shirt. She had been told that Lidstone would be providing everything he would require but she was taking no chances.

At twenty past eight, a yellow minibus came from the direction of Hammersmith and the M4. It pulled up in front of them and a man in a blue uniform jacket and peaked cap got out and came over. 'Mrs. Williams and Jackson Williams?' Peggy nodded as she handed the bag and tin to her son and gave him a gentle nudge forward. The man took hold of his arm in a gesture to guide him to the open door of the minibus. Jacko shook his arm free and, without looking back, clambered into the vehicle and took a seat at the back.

A second man, also in a blue jacket and peaked cap, sat in the driving seat. 'All okay, Fred?' he asked.

'Yep,' came the reply. 'Better push on, we're running late and we've got two more of 'em to rope in before we're done.'

Peggy was left standing at the kerb. She waved but there was no response from her son. She felt for her handkerchief as the tears rolled down her cheeks.

Instead of going back the way they had come, the driver turned the minibus northwards and Jacko recognised Wembley Stadium and then the slip road onto the M1. Mill Hill and Elstree passed in quick succession. He had heard of Elstree, something to do with films, but the other places on the route were completely lost to him until they crossed the M25 and the sign for St. Albans came up. He had been there once on a school trip to see the cathedral and Roman ruins.

This time, the rendezvous place was the main bus station where a bearded, gaunt-looking man of Asian extraction and his teenage son stood apart from the bus passengers while they waited for the expected yellow vehicle to arrive. As the youth clambered into the minibus, his agitated father demanded to know why they had to be picked up from such a public place.

'Two reasons,' Fred replied as he got back into his seat. 'First, it saves us searching the back streets of St. Albans looking for your house, and second, I'm sure you would not want your neighbours to be in on what's happening to your lad.'

The man replied in a language that Fred could not understand and turned away abruptly without acknowledging the brief hand wave from his son. The newcomer ignored Jacko and took a seat just behind the driver to stare blankly out of the window.

Back on the M1, the driver took them south to join the M25 link road and from there to the M4: the route to the south-west. For Jacko, the journey now became totally boring: just miles and miles of nothing, fields, a few trees and the occasional animal. He gazed with envy at the long, straight black hair of the boy in front of him, wishing his own frizzy locks could be transformed into something as smooth and sleek as that. He was always wishing he could look different, that he could be another person, not the Jacko Williams that looked back at him from the bathroom mirror every morning.

The next stop was a service station near Swindon. A young woman waved as they drew into the car park and walked towards them accompanied by a slim teenager with fair, close cropped hair and carrying a small battered leather case. He was wearing a crumpled grey suit that looked to be a size too small, white socks and black trainers. The minibus pulled up beside them and Fred got out with a clipboard in his hand.

'Morning, Miss Watson.' He smiled at her before turning his attention to the youth at her side. He studied his clipboard. 'So, who have we got this time? Let's see, this is Robson?'

'That's right.'

'Steven Robson, was in care, Wiltshire County Council?'

'Correct.'

'Thank you, Miss Watson, nice to see you again.'

The social worker nodded and walked back to her car while Fred asked if anybody wanted to go to the loo. Nobody did, so he told the newcomer to find a seat in the back and climbed in as Bill, the driver, engaged first gear and drove onto the motorway.

Robson hesitated for a moment before deciding to sit next to Jacko. 'Hi,' he said cheerily as he sat down and push his suitcase onto the vacant seat behind, then turning to look at Jacko, he said, 'Me name's Steve Robson, what's yours?' He spoke with a northern accent.

Jacko said nothing for several seconds, then shrugged and replied that his name was Jackson Williams.

'Are y' named after that pop star? You know, the singer, moon walkin' and that?'

'No.' Jacko was not sure why he had that name. It could have been his father's but his mother had never said.

Robson lowered his voice to a whisper. 'D'ya know the Paki in front?' Jacko shook his head as the person in question turned to tell them his name was Patel. When he turned back, Jacko and Robson looked at each other and said nothing.

The minibus pulled off the motorway onto the forecourt of a service station near Bristol and they were told to eat their lunch. Visits to the toilets were accompanied by either Bill or Fred: they were not going to be allowed anywhere on their own. That fact began to break down the barriers between them and soon they were telling each other how they came to be in their present situation. For Robson, it was 'nicking' from shops and in particular those selling electrical goods which could be sold easily. It was a similar story from Patel, who had a long history of shoplifting.

When it came to Jacko's record, his companions were very obviously impressed by the fact that drugs were involved. Robson simply said, 'Wow!' while Patel shook his head in disbelief. It was then Jacko realised that he was 'one up' in their eyes, so that by the time their journey ended in front of Lidstone Manor, he was feeling slightly superior: a feeling that would be knocked out of him in the months to come.

*

The three youngsters stood in front of a curved wooden desk behind which was seated a large, red-faced man in a brown tweed jacket. He stroked his short stubble moustache with one finger as he studied the sheet of paper in front of him before reading out their names in alphabetical order: Asiz Patel, Steven Robson, Jackson Williams.

'Welcome to Lidstone Manor, lads,' he said with a degree of sarcasm that was not lost on the trio. Patel shuffled nervously while the other two simply stared at the floor in front of them. 'My name is William Burford and I am the head of this establishment. You will call me Mr. Burford or Sir, is that clear?'

There were imperceptible nods from Patel and Robson while Jacko continued to study the polished floorboards.

'This is not a prison, there are no walls or barbed wire to keep you in, but,' he paused to ensure his words were going home, 'should any of you transgress, abscond or break the rules in any way, you will find yourself in a much harder place, I can assure you.' He stood up and walked from behind the desk to stand in front, one hand in a pocket of his red corduroys, the other pointing at the young men. He was considerably taller than any of them and his now relaxed attitude was misleading. As he scrutinised his new inmates, William Burford had no doubts about his own ability to steer these young people away from crime through the strict regime at Lidstone.

Jacko looked up, his eyes meeting those of the man in front of him: hard blue eyes that told him not to expect anything resembling sympathy or understanding. He watched as Burford paced up and down the big room, pausing every so often to gaze out of one of the tall windows as he elaborated on the routine at Lidstone: the fact that they would be up at six in the morning and lights out was at twenty two hundred hours, no cigarettes, phones confiscated and, of course, no booze and no 'highs, legal or otherwise.'

Jacko was not listening, he was already trying to fathom out how to get away from this place, reckoning it would not be too difficult to get out of the immediate premises but the surrounding countryside was a different matter. Jacko had never been outside London, had never experienced a world where there were no houses, no paved streets and, if there were any buses, they were very few and far between.

His thoughts were interrupted when Burford suddenly banged a fist on the desk and yelled, 'Are you listening, boy?' while looking directly at Jacko. 'And stand up straight when I speak to you.' He looked round. 'That goes for all of you.' Robson responded immediately while Patel did his best to hide a grin. Jacko simply closed his eyes and waited until Burford moved away to press a button on the desk. 'Mr. Pearson will take you to your quarters and fill you in regarding the routine here and the uniform you are required to wear.'

A moment later, the door opened and a short, thin man entered wearing a blue boiler suit and carrying a cardboard folder which, with a nod to his superior, he opened, took out a page and read out the names. At this point, Burford left the room.

As soon as he had gone, Pearson relaxed and propped himself on the edge of the desk. 'Right, lads, I'm Jack Pearson and I will be doing woodwork and a bit of bricklaying with you.' For the first time since arriving, the three youngsters saw someone smile. 'And if you follow me, I'll show you round.'

As they followed, Jacko reckoned their guide was probably in his forties and that his stiff upright posture was related to the fact that he was inches shorter than any of the young men following him and he had to try and make it up by never slouching. They were first shown to their sleeping quarters up a narrow staircase to the top floor.

'Three to a room,' Pearson was saying, 'and you will each be bunking with two existing inmates. They'll put you in the picture as to what goes on here.' He pushed a door open to show three beds, on one a bright red T-shirt and the same coloured zip-up fleece jacket were laid out, each had the word GAINSBOROUGH in large white lettering on the back. Pearson picked up the T-shirt. 'This, you will wear at all times and when it goes to wash, you will pick up another one from the laundry. The fleece you will wear outdoors.' There was another smile. 'We'll always know where you are and what you are doing.' He turned to Jacko. 'So try 'em on, Williams, 'cos these are yours and this will be your room. Any problems, we'll sort out later.'

While Pearson showed the others to their respective rooms, Jacko took stock of the situation. The room was not large and the three beds were lined up against one wall with cupboards between them. On the opposite wall, there were three wardrobes, one of which had its door open and was empty: he concluded that one was his. The single window was small and high up above the beds: it had vertical bars set in the frame. He sat on the bed and picked up the T-shirt and, holding it against himself, reckoned it would fit okay, likewise the fleece.

At that moment, Pearson's head appeared round the door. 'I said put it on, Williams, and when you are told to do something, you do it, understand?'

Jacko got to his feet and slowly began to strip off and put on the red T-shirt, taking his time to fold his own and place it in one of the empty drawers in the bedside cupboard next to the bed.

Pearson was in the room and Jacko could see that Patel and Robson were standing behind him wearing their red gear. 'Come on, lad! Look lively! If you dawdle about the place like that, you'll find yourself doing extra chores when the others are putting their feet up in the television room.' Pearson stretched himself up to his full five foot six inches and led them out along the corridor, past a bathroom and down another set of stairs at the far end.

There were three more bedrooms for inmates on the first floor but the four largest had been converted into en-suite bedrooms and a sitting room for the three live-in instructors, of which Pearson was one. The main classroom was situated on the ground floor in what had once been the drawing room. It was now empty and Pearson explained that afternoons were spent in the workshops or the gardens and that he was due to take a woodwork class in about ten minutes and would leave them in the hands of John Griggs, the P.E. instructor, who also doubled up as the vehicle maintenance teacher.

Griggs was over six foot, bald with a three-day stubble, and the physique you would expect of a physical instructor except that, now edging forty, he was very conscious of the growing bulge in his midriff. Dressed in a tight black vest and matching tracksuit bottoms he strode out in front of the three newcomers to show them the workshops in the outbuildings at the rear of the house.

Now for the first time, Jacko could see some of his fellow inmates. There were three young men in blue overalls busy building a brick wall at the far end of a large shed. Three more were demolishing a similar structure next to it under the watchful eye of Mr. Pearson. Griggs had said very little during the tour except to tell them their personal belongings would be held in the front office and they would be kitted out with all they needed as soon as he had finished with them.

'Just got time to show you the gardens,' he said, looking at his watch as he led them through an arched wooden door in the stone wall that separated the old walled kitchen garden from the rest of the premises.

He stood in the corner on the far side of the garden, a man in his mid-thirties, the slight breeze ruffling his shoulder-length blonde hair. Jacko stopped suddenly to look intently at the tall lean figure as the man turned to walk towards the newcomers. For a second, he was tempted to turn and run, that gaunt face with the thin beak-like nose was unmistakable in spite of the pitiful attempt at facial hair: Jacko knew him.

He also knew the things the man had done to him and many other boys at the comprehensive school, before 'Beaky' had suddenly disappeared halfway through the summer term amidst rumours of drug dealing and cannabis farming. That had been two years ago and Jacko fervently hoped that he would not recognise him. He dropped behind Patel and Robson and looked down at the gravel path.

Griggs introduced him as Mr. Able, which caused Jacko to smile. He had been wondering what Beaky Andrews called himself now. 'As you can see,' Griggs continued, 'he is responsible for growing the vegetables we eat and, at the same time, giving you a grounding in horticulture, which we hope will stand you in good stead in the years to come.' Able said nothing but simply nodded and moved away to supervise the six inmates variously digging potatoes, cutting cabbages and rescuing the last of the runner beans. Jacko was very glad they did not have to shake hands and was the first to turn away and head back the way they had come.

They were escorted back to the front office where a middle-aged woman with dyed blonde hair was seated at a desk. She smiled as they came in, nodding to Griggs as he turned and walked down a short flight of steps. 'If you follow Mr. Griggs,' she told them, 'he'll take you to the stores and sort you out. Your personal belongings will stay with us and you'll get all you need while you are at Lidstone from there.'

They retrieved their bags from behind the desk and followed to a door. Further steps took them down into the basement where Griggs led them into a room lined with deep shelves containing an assortment of clothing. He selected three pairs of grey trousers, grey socks and dark blue trainers together with vests and underpants and told them to put them on. Robson had to change his trousers for a shorter pair, but other than that everything fitted, more or less. They were told to put everything else except wash kits back into their bags which were then placed on a shelf alongside twelve others. Each was given a pair of grey PE shorts, a red vest and pyjamas which were all stuffed into a plastic bag with their wash kits.

Griggs looked at his watch. 'Right, lads, up to your rooms first, then I'll take you to the dining room where, if you're lucky, you'll get a cuppa and a biscuit and can meet your roommates. They will sort you out and tell you all you need to know, and a bit more, I've no doubt.'

Twelve young men, all with close cropped hair and wearing red T-shirts, were sitting at a single rectangular table in the middle of the dining room drinking tea or coffee obtained from two dispensers situated on the wall nearest the door. There were three plates of biscuits placed evenly along the table. Griggs called out a name and a tall black youth in his late teens stood up and walked over towards him.

'Clayton, this one will be bunking with you and Wiggins,' he put a hand on Jacko's shoulder. 'Jackson Williams. He's nearly your sort so I expect you to take him under your wing and get him sorted.'

Clayton nodded and turned to Jacko indicating the chair next to him. 'Want some tea, man?'

Jacko found the London accent reassuring. 'Yep ... please.'

'Okay, I'll get it for yer, but it'll be the first and last time, understand?'

Patel was allocated to a dark-haired young man who walked with a slight limp, the result of a stumble on the morning's run. Robson was next and was heard to call out 'Haway the lads!' when he learned that his partner also came from Newcastle.

Jacko became aware that Clayton was looking at him intently as the plastic cup was put down in front of him: he was being scrutinised, appraised and categorised and it made him feel uncomfortable. The older youth sat down beside him. 'So, what do we call yer?'

Jacko was beginning to get angry. 'I'm Jackson Williams,' he said, turning to look at his interrogator.

'Yeh, I know that but I ain't going to put that handle on yer.'

'I'm Jacko.'

'That's more like it. I'm Richard 'enry Clayton but you can call us Clayton,' he grinned and beckoned to a stocky, ginger-haired boy further down the table. 'Wiggy, this is Jacko, our new bunkmate.'

Wiggins came over to stand between them. 'Well, well,' he said, looking down at Jacko, 'All I can do is offer you a hearty welcome to this wonderful establishment.' He waved an arm in the general direction of the door and the rooms beyond.

Clayton laughed. 'Don't mind him, Jacko. He went to one of them posh schools, which only goes to show it takes all sorts.' Wiggins raised two fingers and went back to his chair.

A bell rang and everybody stood up as Burford entered the room. He was carrying a clipboard from which he read out the names of the three newcomers and told them to raise their hands in turn so that everyone would know who was who. 'You three,' he continued, 'hair cuts nine hundred hours, report to Mrs. Gazely, front office. For all of you, morning run as usual, six-thirty hours, and this time you will all wear reflective armbands. I don't want anybody getting knocked over or lost as the mornings get darker. Any problems, see Mr. Griggs. Our speaker this evening is Mr. Gibson from Dartmoor National Park and his subject is to do with caring for the environment. You will pay attention, there will be no nodding off, and Clayton, you will get up and thank him at the end. I shall be watching. That's all.' He turned and left the room: there was an audible sigh of relief as the door closed.

'He thinks he's still in the bloody army,' Clayton said, turning to Jacko. 'Come on, we'd better get going.' He led the way towards the door. 'Are you coming, Wiggy?'

'No, I'm cleaning the bogs till supper.'

Clayton grinned. 'That'll teach yer not to call old Unable Able a poof behind 'is back.'

'Well he is,' Jacko said. 'I can tell you, if you ever find yourself alone in a room with him, keep your arse to the wall.'

'You know him?'

'Yeh, he was the caretaker at school, looked after the bits of garden and playing field. We called him Beaky. He left half way through the term and we reckoned he got done for growing cannabis. His real name's Andrews, at least that's the one he used with us.'

Clayton chuckled. 'Well, bugger me. He's as bad, if not worse, than us.'

'It's a small world. I just wonder what he's doing at a place like this?'

'Don't ask me, man, but come to think of it, he's not like the others, is he? I mean, they're all ex-army blokes and he's, well, a bloody fairy.'

The talk about Dartmoor was not as boring as Jacko had expected. Nevertheless he was glad when Clayton stood up and thanked the speaker: he was hungry and looking forward to the evening meal.

Jacko ate the sausage and mash without looking up, too intent on clearing his plate to join in the general conversation going on round him. They were talking about a boy they thought was Polish: he had landed a punch on Able and had been hauled off by a couple of toughs from the stables next door. Wiggy said he had seen a BMW draw up outside and Burford talking to a man. No one had seen or heard anything of the Polish boy since. Wiggy wondered if there was a connection.

'Naar,' Clayton growled. 'Y'er always imagining things, Wiggy, like the time you thought you saw them birds getting into our minibus in the middle of the night and anyway, what the hell were you doing wandering about the place after dark? Not looking for a way out, were you, man?' Clayton gave him a playful dig in the ribs.

'If you must know, man, I couldn't sleep. Got up to go to the bogs for a pee, looked out of the window and saw four birds being bundled in the bus by the heavy mob from next door.'

'Probably four pros who had finished their jobs for you know who and were going home.' Clayton stood up. 'I'm ready for pudding.' He took his dirty plate to the kitchen where two boys were busy washing up and picked up a bowl of rice pudding: a queue formed behind him.

After supper, there were a couple of hours when they could relax, watch television, read one of the three newspapers delivered daily or, as in the case of Wiggy, read a book. After a short while, Jacko decided to turn in early. He found his way up to the bedroom, changed into his new pyjamas and got into bed. It was the end of his first day at Lidstone, the experiences crowded into his exhausted brain: confused and fearful, he drifted into sleep.

CHAPTER 8

'I still don't understand, Kate, why you went off to bed without saying a word the other evening. I was quite embarrassed, you could have at least said good night.' Mary Lethbridge handed a freshly washed plate to her daughter who, washing-up cloth in hand, began to rub it more vigorously than was necessary. It was almost a week since the episode with Matt Winsford's dog and Kate reckoned that her mother had mentioned it at least three times since then.

'I wasn't feeling very well.' It was a lie, but there was no point in trying to explain to her mother that she was not interested in the man, not least because she sensed he was a very disturbed individual. There were things he did not want them to know and having overheard the conversation between him and her father, she was convinced that something disastrous, probably unlawful, had happened concerning the supposed accident that he was so reluctant to talk about. It all led her to the conclusion that what had occurred was the reason why he had chosen to hide himself away in a remote cottage on the edge of Dartmoor.

That idea spawned another: one that was much darker. She leant towards her mother and, in a conspiratorial whisper, said, 'What if all that roughing up of his cottage was done by a rival gang, somebody that wanted to scare him, you know, get revenge for something he's done.?'

'Don't be so daft, Kate! I'm sure he's not that sort.'

'Well, old Ivan at the stables thinks he's a bit suspicious. I overheard him tell Greta that they would have to keep an eye on him.'

'If I were you, my girl, I would get all that nonsense out of your head and concentrate on … '

'On getting a bloke?' Kate interrupted cynically.

'On getting on with your life, Kate. Horses are all very well, but there will come a time when being bucked off a fractious four-year-old won't be just part of a day's work as it is at the moment. In a few years' time, you'll find you don't mend as easily as you do now, and anyway your father and I are always scared you'll end up in hospital with something serious.'

'Mum, broken bones are part of the job, ask any jump jockey. In any case, we break horses differently now, we use the Monty Robert's softly softly technique. I haven't been bucked off for yonks riding a youngster.'

'What about the incident with your artist friend when you came off Harry.'

'First of all, he is not my friend and whether he is an artist or not remains to be seen. Secondly, if it hadn't been for that damn dog, it wouldn't have happened.'

'Friend or not, he's been in to see that damn dog every day this week. Anyone who would do that can't be all that bad. I think you should go and see how he's getting on, then at least you will know how the painting is going and if it's any good.'

Kate put the final plate away. 'I'm going to be too busy this week; there are three Dartmoor ponies to go this week so that means an early start at the crack of dawn tomorrow, then there are four hunters to clip out and the horses they brought in last week have got to be shown off to prospective buyers. The days are getting shorter and I won't have a minute to myself.'

'You are just making excuses. You don't have to go in daylight so why don't you give him a ring and go up one evening? Dad has got his number.'

'Okay. I suppose I'll have to and, since you told him he could ride Molly, I expect you'll be wanting me to ride out with him just to make sure he's competent. After all, we don't want him deposited somewhere out on the moor, do we?' The note of cynicism had crept back.

Mary dried her hands and turned abruptly to walk through to the living room where her husband was reading the report of the incident at Coombe Cottage in the local weekly paper. Apparently the police had come to the conclusion that some mindless yob, probably drunk, was to blame. 'Took them about five minutes solve that, I expect,' Jim said as he leant forward to put another log on the fire.

Mary made herself comfortable on the sofa and watched the log burst into flames. 'Kate thinks it's much more sinister,' she told him. 'She seems to think that he's some sort of criminal hiding away from the police.'

'That's silly, he would never have reported it to the police if that were the case.'

'Just what I told her, but you know Kate. Once she gets an idea into her head, it takes some shifting.'

'What takes some shifting?' Kate was standing in the doorway.

Her father looked up smiling. 'A ton of rubbish.'

'I've no idea what you are talking about.' Her puzzlement was genuine. 'I just looked in to tell Mum that I'll go and see Mr. Winsford tomorrow and arrange to take him out on Molly at the weekend.'

*

Matt clicked off his mobile and went through into his studio to consider the next phase of Harry's portrait: he would need to get some colour into the outline sketch if she was coming to see him that evening. The week had been a busy one starting with the clean up of the cottage with the help of Spud who set about the task with energy that belied his years. He had recommended a garage in the town specialising in Volvo cars who had replaced the rear window of his vehicle the following day, while daily trips to check on Bullet and the drive to Newton Abbot to buy fresh canvasses and replenish paint stocks had left him little time to produce something to show to the young woman who was, at that time, his one and only customer.

He sat down at the easel and began to mix the Raw Sienna, Light Red and Zinc White paints that would form the basic chestnut colour of the horse. As he worked, the trauma of the previous days gradually subsided and he was back to a time when painting was the one form of relaxation that gave him a sense of peace and quiet, the essential contrast to the stress and responsibility of his day job. As he worked on the image of the horse, his thoughts drifted to its rider, the young woman introduced to him by his dog: pleasant face, good figure, very nice family; he could do worse. Now, he realised, he was fantasising; why on earth would a young girl like that want anything to do with the likes of him? He stopped painting and shut his eyes tight while the thoughts of his own predicament crossed his mind, then he took the largest brush he had, dipped it in the paint and wrote the word KILLER across the top of the canvass. He sat and looked at it for several seconds before taking a cloth and attempting to rub it out: he would have to paint over it before the girl arrived.

It was six o'clock, just beginning to get dark, when the knock on the door interrupted Matt's efforts to create a plausible image on the canvass.

'I hope I'm not too early,' Kate said as he led her into the kitchen.

'No, not at all but I have to tell you that I haven't got very far with your painting, what with the events of last week and trying to get things back to normal. I'm afraid I just ran out of time.' He was beginning to feel nervous, apprehensive, and as they walked through to the studio, he wondered if his offer to paint this young woman's horse had been misguided.

She stood in front of the easel and studied the painting for several seconds without making any comment, then she turned to him and, with a faint smile, said that it was a good likeness and she liked the red sunset sky.

With some relief, Matt led her back to the kitchen and suggested a cup of tea or coffee; he was disappointed when she declined, making the excuse that she had to get back to feed Harry and Molly.

'I really came to see you about riding Molly. My mother seems keen to see the mare get a bit more exercise and it would appear that you might get some benefit out of it.' Matt thought that she was sounding very clinical as she continued. 'So mother suggested that we should ride out together a couple of times just to get you acclimatised to the old mare and then you can go out whenever you like, if that's okay with you.'

Matt got the impression that she was not overenthusiastic about the project as he replied, 'Thanks, that's very good of you, I'll look forward to it.'

'Okay then, what about next Sunday morning about ten o'clock?'

Matt nodded. 'I've sent home for a hat and some boots, so let's hope the come in time.'

She turned abruptly and with a brief, 'See you then,' opened the door and went out. Matt watched as she walked back to her car, disappointed that she had been in such a hurry to leave.

As she drove out of the cottage gateway and onto the lane, Kate realised that she was still uncertain about the true identity of the man she had been talking to. On the face of it, he seemed quite genuine, he could certainly paint horses and was a nice enough guy, but there was something about him that puzzled her. He was not like the young men she was used to; she knew that he did not spend his evenings drinking in the pub. He drank alone; she had noticed the half-empty whiskey bottle on the kitchen table. There was the question why he had chosen to spend his time isolated in a remote cottage, alone and without any obvious friends locally. She sighed and wondered why so many of the men she got to know had a 'but' attached.

*

The parcel arrived the day after Kate's visit. It contained an old black crash helmet – the sort jockeys wore under their silk caps – and a new pair of black full-length riding boots which had zips up the back. A note from his mother stated: 'I found the head gear at the back of our tack room – hope it fits. The boots were suggested by our local saddler in Wheathampstead. They are your size (I hope) and the zip-up backs should make it easier for you to get them on your bad leg. Glad to hear you are riding again, let us know how you get on. Dad sends his love. Love Mum. P.S. You mentioned you were painting a girl's horse when you phoned. Is it that horse you are riding? Send us an email and what about a photo or two?'

'Good old, Mum,' Matt said as he tried on the helmet which was a little too big but could be easily padded out with some plastic foam and a bit of Sellotape. The boots were fine, a bit stiff and must have cost the earth. He knew his mother would not accept money from him so he made a resolution to buy her an expensive present when he eventually got home. In the meantime, he would have to explain that there was no Wi-Fi in the cottage and he wasn't that good at texting so it would have to be a letter. He had not told them about the events of the previous week and had no intention of doing so. That could wait.

The other good thing to happen that day was the fact that he had been told by Jim Lethbridge that Bullet was ready to come home. His daily visits had seen a marked improvement in the old dog's condition so that the news did not come as a surprise. Nevertheless he felt suddenly elated as he laid the soft dog mattress in the back of the Volvo ready for the journey to the surgery.

The young veterinary nurse took him through to the now familiar room containing the animal cages. The sound of his master's voice brought Bullet up on his hind legs, his front paws against the wire, his stump of a tail wagging furiously. The nurse opened the cage to allow the dog out.

'As you can see,' she said, 'he's nearly walking sound but will need a bit of TLC for a week or two before he's completely right. I've got some medication for him in the office if you would pick it up on the way out.' Matt expressed his thanks as he carefully picked Bullet up and followed her to the office where she stuffed the paper bag containing the pills into his pocket. 'Instructions are on the packets,' she told him as he gently placed the old dog in the back of the car.

*

Sunday morning dawned bright and cold. There had been a slight frost in the night and the sky was clear blue except over the moor where a mist still lingered over the highest tors. Matt dug his heel into the lawn as he let Bullet out before breakfast: the ground still had some 'give' in it so he knew it would be okay to ride at ten o'clock. As he watched the dog sniff its way through the long grass on the edge of the lawn, he began to feel apprehensive about the forthcoming ride. It had been ten years since he had last ridden a horse and he did not know how the injured leg would react. He consoled himself that it was like riding a bike – once you've done it, you never forget.

Kate was waiting in the yard when Matt pulled up in the drive. He had managed to get the left boot on his injured foot without too much difficulty and the zips at the back of the boots made it easier to tuck his jeans in. He buttoned up his jacket and, with the helmet under his arm, walked over to greet her.

'Hope I don't look too much of a freak compared to you,' he said eyeing her smart fawn breeches and shiny black riding boots.

She gave him that faint smile again and told him that she had only just got back from showing one of the imported horses to a prospective customer. 'Got to give the right impression,' she told him as they walked towards the tack room which was a converted loose box adjacent to the two that housed the horses.

There were two saddles set high in racks with bridles hanging from hooks beneath. Kate indicated which one was Molly's and watched as Matt reached up to take it down, lodge it on his arm and dust it off with his sleeve.

'Sorry, hasn't been used for a bit,' she commented as she handed him the bridle. 'I've brushed both horses so you can tack up. I'll give you a hand if you like.'

Matt shook his head and smiled. 'Thanks, but I think I can manage.' He placed the saddle on top of Molly's door, slipped the bolt and went in with the bridle in his hand. Kate noted that he was talking to the mare and that he expertly slipped the bit into her mouth and pulled the bridle over her ears: this was not a new experience for him. Kate did not know whether to be relieved or disappointed. Part of her had hoped that he would be a complete novice and she could tell her mother that the idea of him riding her mare on his own was not on. She went to saddle Harry, still trying to fathom out where this guy fitted into the normal scheme of things.

Matt put the saddle on Molly, tightened the girth and led her out. Kate saw him adjust the length of the stirrup leathers then pause and look round.

'I'm afraid I'll need a mounting block,' he said pointing down at his left foot. 'I'm not sure that will stand the strain from the ground'.

Kate pointed to a neat pile of six concrete blocks at the end of the stable block and watched as he stepped up on them and, with an audible groan, swung himself into the saddle. He slipped his right foot into the other stirrup, neck-reined the mare away from the blocks and waited for Kate to mount Harry.

As they walked their horses out of the gate, she again watched him as he sat comfortably in the saddle, gently assessing the mare's mouth by the slightest movement of the reins. 'You said you had done a bit of riding,' she said with a rare smile. 'I reckon you've done more than a bit, Mr. Win … '

'Matt. Please,' Matt interrupted. He shrugged. 'I have to admit that I'm not that "horsey" but I come from a family that is. Both my parents and elder sister hunted most Saturdays so from an early age, I either had to learn to ride and go with them or spend the day with my aunt who lived in the village. I chose the former and eventually loved every moment. I had come to the conclusion, rightly or wrongly, that hunting was for men while the pony club was for girls. I thought it would all change when the ban came in but I was never interested in what went on at the front, just the riding, so as far as I could see, it was still the same.'

Kate was interested, it was not the sort of background she had expected, and for some reason, she wanted to know more. 'When did you give it up then?'

There was a pause before he replied. 'Couldn't fit any of it in with my job.'

'You didn't go to uni then?'

'No.'

'Nor me.' At least we have some things in common, Kate thought.

Matt changed the subject before the conversation could go any further. 'It's an interesting place, Lidstone,' he said as they trotted through the village. 'I still don't know anything about the goings-on at the manor. I gather it's some sort of remand home – you know, like a borstal.'

Kate shook her head. 'As far as I know, it's neither of those. Greta tells me it's something new, a cross between confinement and rehabilitation. Apparently, if any of the lads show real interest in a practical subject like woodwork or mechanics, they let them out to a local carpenter or garage for work experience; in fact, and you won't believe this, we've got one coming to work at the stables, a kid called Wiggins, who says he is interested in horses. Ex-public school, they told us. Apparently has a horsey mother and the boy went off the rails when his parents divorced, but if he wants to spend his days shovelling horse poo, so be it.'

They turned onto the track that led past Coombe Cottage. Matt began to feel a sharp pain in his ankle and slowed to a walk. 'Sorry, the old joints playing up a bit. I'll just have to give it time to settle down for a minute or two and then we'll trot on again.' Kate nodded and reined in Harry to lead the way over the rough, stony ground.

As they passed the cottage, Matt could hear Bullet barking furiously. At least, he thought, the old dog had not lost his sense of hearing. It cheered him up and helped alleviate the pain which had spread to the whole of his lower leg. He gritted his teeth; he had seen men endure worse than what he was having to go through.

Kate interrupted his thoughts as she pulled up to let him come alongside. 'You're still going to stay on there after all that has happened? I mean, it does look suspiciously as though someone has got it in for you. If you wanted to move out, I'm sure Dad could find somewhere else for you not too far away. He gets around and knows a lot of people with holiday lets.'

Matt shook his head. 'I'll be damned if I'll let whoever it was scare me if that was their intention. No, I'm bloody staying and if they try it on again and I catch them at it, they'll be sorry.'

Kate led the way onto the lane and turned left onto the bridleway that led to the moor and asked if he wanted to try a canter. Matt nodded, shortened the reins and nudged the mare with his heels. She responded immediately and he began to feel the old thrill of a horse under him; he was sixteen again – no pain, no guilt, just the pleasure of controlling a powerful animal at speed through a wild landscape.

Then the pain kicked in again and he reluctantly eased the mare down to a walk. He turned to Kate who had just pulled up Harry a few yards behind him. 'I think that might be enough for a first try,' he said reluctantly. 'Next time I'll remember to bring my painkillers with me.'

'Next time I think you'll be okay to go on your own,' Kate said as she turned Harry and led the way back. 'It'll give you the choice of how far you go and how long you stay out, and if you ever think you are lost, just drop the reins on the old mare's neck and she'll take you home. She knows this part of the moor like the back of her hoof, if you know what I mean,' she added with a grin.

Matt nodded. 'Thanks, I'll remember that, and it's good of you to let me ride Molly.'

'Don't thank me, thank my mother, she's the one who suggested it.'

Matt got the impression that his companion did not entirely approve of the decision. 'I don't want to be a bother to anyone,' he said easing his injured foot out of the stirrup for a moment. 'The last thing I want is a lot of fuss just because I've had a bit of a knock, and to tell you the truth, I wouldn't want to go on if you don't approve.'

Kate pulled up her horse and turning to look at him, saw the anxiety in his face and for the first time, she smiled. 'I'm sorry if you got that impression. It's just that my mother and I don't always see eye to eye, as you may have gathered, but I do sympathise with the problems you have with your injuries – the accident and all that – so please don't think I have anything against the idea.'

'You can keep your sympathy,' Matt muttered to himself. 'Save it for someone who deserves it.'

'We'll go another way back,' Kate suggested. 'Give you a chance to find your way around.'

They skirted the village and she led him through a heavily wooded area, a mixture of conifers and hard woods stretching up on both sides with wide but overgrown rides.

'This all still belongs to Colonel Spreyton,' Kate told him. 'The old boy is still keen on his shooting. Do you shoot?'

'Done a bit.'

Kate grinned. 'Where have I heard that phrase before?'

Leading down a steep hill to where the land flattened out, she stopped at a wooden five-barred gate that led onto a rough track at the edge of the woodland. The gate had a notice nailed to it: PRIVATE PROPERTY – TRESPASSERS WILL BE PROSECUTED. Kate leant over to pull the sprung lever that opened it. 'It's okay, we've got permission to ride through here any time, except a shooting day.' She indicated a track which branched off to the right. 'Old Spud Wannacott has his mobile home tucked away in there. He is supposed to be a sort of gamekeeper-come-forester but I suspect he spends most of his time knocking off the odd roe deer or brace of pheasants for his own use. The colonel knows what goes on but turns a blind eye: they are two of a kind.'

'What makes you say that?'

'Well, if you want my opinion, I reckon they are a couple of likeable old rogues with an eye to making a few quid wherever they can.'

At that moment, they met Spud coming up the track with a shotgun under his arm and his lurcher by his side. The feet of a freshly killed rabbit protruded from his shooting bag. He nodded at the two riders. 'Mornin', you two,' he said with a grin. 'Nice day for a ride.'

'Just showing Mr. … Matt around,' Kate told him.

'That's good.' He turned to Matt. 'How's it going, young man?'

'Not too bad.' Matt eased his foot out of the stirrup again to stretch his leg.

'And how's that little ol' dog of yours? I heard that he was knocked about quite a bit.'

'Thanks for asking. He's getting on fine' Matt replied as he replaced his foot gingerly back into the stirrup.

Spud watched him and, as Kate sat patiently on a fidgeting Harry, asked if he had any news about the events at the cottage.

Matt shook his head. 'No, Mr. Wannacott, I haven't a clue.'

There was a long silence while the old man seemed to be pre-occupied, studying the toes of his boots, deep in thought. He looked up and smiled. 'In your situation, it's not a good thing for you to be stuck in that place on your own all the time, Mr. Winsford. How would you like to come and have a drink with me one evening? I don't get much company out here and I could see that you were partial to the odd noggin' when we cleaned your place up. I've got a drop of good 'Irish' and perhaps we can sort a few things out for you. You never know, it might do us both some good.'

My situation. Matt thought. What the hell does the old bugger know about my situation. 'That's very kind of you, Mr. Wannacott, but I'm quite happy the way things are.'

'Well, you know where I live now, so any time you're passing … ' Spud raised a hand in farewell and walked off towards the green-painted mobile home.

Kate turned Harry and started off down the track towards a narrow hunting gate which led out onto another lane. The fastening was rusted and stiff. 'I'll get off,' Kate said.

'No, no, let me do it,' Matt insisted.

She turned to him. 'Don't be silly, in your condition, if you get off we'll have a hell of a job to get you back on again, so stay where you are.'

'Oh, shit,' Matt muttered through gritted teeth.

'This road leads round the top side of Lidstone Manor,' Kate told him. 'A couple of miles and we'll be passing the gates, you'll know where you are then.'

At that moment, Harry's ears pricked and, head up, he looked towards a bend lower down the road. A bald-headed man in a black tracksuit came jogging round the bend followed by fifteen young men in bright red T-shirts in single file. Kate patted Harry's neck, spoke a few soothing words and looked back at Matt. 'It's their Sunday morning run. The rest of the week, they go at crack o' dawn but on Sundays they get a lie in and start at ten o'clock. All weathers, hail or shine, you can set your clock by it.'

Matt watched as the line of runners passed in front of them. It brought back distant memories as the man in front barked out an order and the young men slowed to a disciplined walk, or at least most of them did, for there were several at the rear who were finding stones to kick and bits of stick to prod the shoulders of the man in front.

'Reminds me of the CCF at school,' he told Kate. 'Wednesday afternoons on parade – drill, route marches, shooting practice, the lot.'

'Sounds awful to me.'

'It was that sort of school but I enjoyed it. Stood me in good stead out in the wide world, if you know what I mean.'

Kate did not know what he meant and answered with a shrug as she nudged Harry with her heels and started off down the hill in the direction from which the 'red line' had come. 'This will lead us round the top of the estate for about two miles and then we'll drop down past the manor and back into the village. Are you okay with that because we can turn round and go back the way we came if it sounds too much?'

'No, that's fine. I think things are beginning to settle down in the ol' leg, just a few twinges so I'm fine.' He wasn't but he was not going to tell her that. In fact, the pain had shifted further up his leg so that gripping the saddle with his knee had become difficult. He was glad that Molly was content to walk quietly behind the fractious horse in front so that he could ease the pressure by stretching his left leg out of the stirrup and letting it hang loosely down Molly's flank. He was glad his companion had not noticed the move, at least not yet.

For Matt, it seemed a very long two-mile hack as they passed through the village and turned into the lane leading to the Lethbridges' farmhouse.

Mary Lethbridge, in jeans and a pink waterproof jacket, was standing in the yard as they walked in. 'How did you get on?' she called.

Matt quickly put his foot back into the stirrup and forced a grin. 'Not too bad, just a bit of a twinge now and then, but I'm sure that'll sort itself out, it's just a case of giving it time.' Now he was beginning to wonder how he could best dismount without collapsing in a heap on the cobbles. He realised that getting off the conventional way by taking both feet out of the stirrup irons and swinging his right leg over the saddle would probably mean him landing predominately on his left, which, he was sure, would give way and land him on the ground. After a moment's thought, he nudged Molly towards her owner. 'I'm afraid I'll have to dismount like a cowboy,' he told her with a grin as, with his left foot still in the iron, he swung the right leg over the saddle and stepped down. It hurt, but he was upright.

Mary was patting Molly's neck. 'Well done. Did you enjoy the ride, that's the main thing?'

Matt nodded and told her that he had, while reflecting to himself that it had been a bit of a 'curate's egg' – good in parts. He led the mare back into the loose box and unsaddled her; he could hear Kate doing the same thing with Harry next door. She was the first to hang up her saddle and bridle while Matt waited a few moments to get the feeling back into his cramped foot before walking out to do the same.

'Next time', Kate said with a smile, 'you're on your own. Is that okay?'

'Suits me.' It didn't quite; he would have preferred her company.

'So, when would you like to ride again?' It was Mary speaking as she watched them 'rug up' their respective mounts ready for turning out.

There was a long pause while Matt weighed up in his mind the pros and the cons – the pleasure against the pain. He turned to face her. 'How about next Wednesday about the same time?' It would give him a few days to work off any stiffness and, likewise, the mare would have a few days' rest before going again.

'What about you, Kate?' Mary asked.

'I've told him he's on his own from here on. Isn't that right?'

Matt grinned. 'Yep, looks as though I've passed my riding test and can ditch the L plates.'

CHAPTER 9

It was Sunday. The morning run completed, they were grouped round the noticeboard in the front office where the activities for the following week were posted. As Jacko had feared, he was due for gardening under the instruction of the dubious 'Beaky' Andrews – aka 'Unable' Able. It was Jacko's third week and he had done bricklaying and woodwork followed by a week in the machine shed working on a variety of old cars and a motorbike. It was the one part of the curriculum that he had enjoyed most.

'I see you are going to be with your friend, Beaky.' It was Wiggins, who had pushed to the front to stand beside Jacko.

'You don't have to sound so bloody smug about it, Wiggy. I nearly shit myself when I saw who it was when I first arrived. Now I've got to face the bugger and I just hope he don't remember me.'

'Why? What do you think he'll do if he does recognise you?'

Jacko shrugged. 'Fuck knows. All I know is he's as queer as a nine pound note and quite capable of a spot of GBH if he's pushed.'

'So don't push him, that's my advice.'

'It's all right for you, Wiggy, it looks as though you're going to be farmed out to next door.'

'Yeah, spend my days shovelling horse shit. Just like old times with my dear mother, except I won't get a clout if I do anything wrong, and I've seen a nice bit of crumpet – that's what my old man would have called her – working in the stables, so who knows? Wahey!' He gave Jacko a hearty slap on the back and elbowed his way back through the group, leaving his roommate staring at the noticeboard feeling depressed and anxious.

As he turned to leave, the office door was pushed open and an anxious looking Griggs called out, 'Has anybody seen Bennet?' There was a sudden hush in the room followed by quiet murmurings until someone asked why he was looking for Barrel Bennet. 'Because he's bloody well not been seen since we got back from the run,' came the sharp reply. 'And you all know what that means? Agro from the boss, search parties and a lock up until he's found, so I'll ask you all again, has anyone seen him?' When there was no reply other than a few shaking heads, he backed out of the room and slammed the door, muttering, 'Oh, shit,' as he went.

Clayton was the first to speak. 'Last time I saw ol' Barrel, he was playing catch-up round that steep bend just before you get to the woods. Poor bugger looked like he might croak at any minute.'

'You reckon he's had a heart attack or something?' Wiggy asked.

'Well, with his weight, could be.'

'Could have done a runner,' Robson chipped in.

'Naah, not ol' Barrel. My guess is he's just flaked out somewhere, probably sitting under a tree waiting for the old green Land Rover to pick him up.'

'Still think he could have done a runner,' Robson repeated.

Clayton shook his head. 'Look, mate, to do a runner, you've got to have some cash, and that's something we don't have. How far do you think he'd get in our lovely red gear? He'd be spotted a mile off.'

'Perhaps he still had some of his old clothes and put them on under his T-shirt and just stripped off the red stuff and chucked it in a ditch.' It was Jacko who offered that idea.

An hour later, a dishevelled Bennet was delivered to the manor in the back of the Land Rover and marched to the principal's office to explain how he got left behind, and how he felt unwell and had to rest in the woods where he was eventually found. Burford decided he should have a medical check before being allowed back and added an additional two weeks to his period of detention. On his arrival at coffee break, he was immediately surrounded by a group of curious inmates all wanting to know how Barrel had managed to stay out for nearly two hours without being missed. Jacko was one of them.

*

Monday morning dawned overcast with a slight drizzle. During the early morning run, Jacko kept his usual place at the rear of the pack and managed to drop well behind several times, but each time Griggs had noticed, called him back into line, and finally made him run with the leaders. Griggs was not going to be caught out again and Jacko realised that dropping out was not going to be as easy now as it might have been before the Barrel Bennet incident.

That morning, the route took them up past Coombe Cottage and onto the open moor. As they laboured up the steep slope towards Hound Tor, they were suddenly enveloped into a thick mist. There was no way anyone could see the end of the line of runners from the front. It gave Jacko something to think about as they jogged round the huge boulders and dropped down a steep slope into dense woodland where Griggs marked time and counted them as they passed, before resuming his place at the head of the group: Jacko kept his position at the front.

Back at the manor, the mist had lifted but the skies were dull and there was a hint of rain in the air. As Jacko ate his scrambled egg and toast, he contemplated with trepidation the coming days under Beaky Andrews. Would he be recognised? How would Beaky react? He knew the man had a reputation for violence quite apart from his homosexual tendencies. So what was he doing here and what did the others, including staff, know about him? The bell rang to mark the end of breakfast as Jacko drained his cup and headed for the door.

There were five of them in the group that waited outside the locked garden door. Besides Jacko, there were Patel and Robson, a thin, spotty faced youth called Bates, and Barrel Bennet, who had been put back onto gardening in the hope that it would help get his weight down. Beaky was late and looked pale and angry when he arrived. Jacko guessed that a night on scag and the odd spliff was probably the cause of their gardening instructor's headache. He pushed past them and, without a word, unlocked the door and marched in. The group followed with Jacko at the rear.

The walled garden was big; Jacko estimated that it was at least as big as two football pitches surrounded by an eight foot stone wall. At the far end was a large Victorian glasshouse, its lower glass panels whitewashed so that it was impossible to see from the outside what was growing in there. Next to that was a large stone building with a chimney, and beyond that was a wooden shed with a corrugated iron roof. There was a wide arched gateway next to which stood a massive stack of horse dung. The whole area was divided up into equal sized plots, each planted with a specific crop that could be used in the manor's kitchen.

Beaky lined them up against the wall. 'Right, let's get some names.' His eyes flicked from one to the next as each youth called out his name. Jacko was last and was relieved when his name conjured up no obvious response in Beaky's face. The instructor led them over to the shed where a range of tools hung from racks along one wall while various cutting tools, such as saws, sickles and a range of pruning shears were carefully arranged on shelves on the adjoining wall. All of the tools were marked with a number which corresponded to the same number on the wall so that any missing implement could be identified at a quick glance. Beaky made a point of ensuring that the inmates knew that there was no possibility of anyone sneaking anything out of the garden for possible use elsewhere. Jacko was puzzled why anyone would want to pinch a fork or spade but then realised, of course, it was the cutting tools they were worried about; he knew about the screwed up guys who took pleasure in taking bits out of other people with anything sharp.

They were given overalls to put on while Beaky waited. 'Sizes nine, ten and eleven,' he called out, pointing to a line of wellington boots, arranged in order of size along the wall beneath the implements. 'Anyone who don't take them sizes, 'ard luck,' he told them as they began to take off their trainers and try on the boots.

Outside the sky had cleared and a cold wind gusted through the arched gateway making that part of the garden several degrees colder than the areas sheltered by the walls. The group lined up to hear what jobs they would each be doing that day. Beaky fumbled in the breast pocket of his overalls, took out a card and a stub of pencil, and proceeded to write names against the list of jobs that had to be done that day.

'Right. Bates, Robson and Bennet, pick a hoe each and come with me.' He glanced at Jacko and Patel. 'You two stay here. I'll be back for you later.' Robson and Bennet moved towards the rack of tools. Bates hesitated: he wasn't sure what a hoe looked like. Once equipped, they were led to a series of plots and set to work, Robson hoeing beetroot, Bennet turnips while their instructor did his best to show Bates how to use the implement in the swedes.

Patel turned to Jacko. 'What d'y think we're going to have to do?'

Jacko shrugged. 'Don't ask me, but I'll tell you this, when it comes to my part, you can bet it'll be some bloody awful job that nobody would want to do.' And it was.

'Now then you two.' The smile on Beaky's face was not a kind one. 'I've got something special for the likes of you,' he indicated towards the tool rack. 'Patel, pick yourself a digging fork and spade,' he paused, 'and you, my young Jackson, or should it be Jacko … Williams … fetch that nice dung fork.' There was menace in the tone of voice and Jacko's heart sank as they walked towards the muck heap. Beaky had recognised him. His cover was blown.

Beaky pointed to a barrow that stood inside the gateway next to the heap. 'All you have to do, Williams, is fill that with that,' he pointed to the pile of dung, 'I'm sure you'll make a first class shit shoveller, so all you have to do is wheel it over to your suntanned friend here who will have the job of digging it in.' He gave a satisfied grunt and walked back to the shed, brought out a plastic chair and sat with the local newspaper, studying the runners and riders at the forthcoming Newton Abbot races.

*

It had been a long day. Jacko's arms ached, his head buzzed and he stank of horse dung. He struggled out of his overalls and joined the rest of the group as they trudged wearily towards the door out of the garden. He was the last to reach it and was about to go through when he heard his name being called.

'Williams, come back here. I want a word.' Beaky Andrews was standing in the shed doorway beckoning with one finger. Jacko did not like the look on the man's face. He turned and slowly walked back. 'I want a word with you, young man. Come inside.' Beaky led the way back into the shed and closed the door. He caught hold of Jacko's arm and spun him round, the grip made the youth wince.

Jacko shook himself loose to face his assailant. 'What do you want with me, Mr. … er … Able?'

'Let's not beat about the bush, Jacko Williams,' Beaky growled. 'I know you … '

'And I know you,' Jacko butted in and immediately wished he had not as his arm was gripped even harder and the voice in his ear got louder.

'Now listen to me, my friend. I'm on a good number here and I don't want some bloody half-baked yob messing it up. Do you understand? So I suggest you keep your mouth shut and we'll get along fine, but if I find out you've grassed on me … Well, I know where you live and I wouldn't want your mum to come to no harm. You know I've got some very interesting friends that live round your part of the world and they would be only too pleased to do me the odd favour.'

Jacko stared blankly at the face in front of him and said nothing. He waited until the grip on his arm relaxed, then he turned, opened the shed door and walked away leaving the instructor standing in the doorway watching. Once out of the garden, Jacko slammed the old door shut, raised two fingers in the direction of the shed and trotted off to catch up with the rest of the group.

'What did ol' Beaky want you for?' Patel asked as they walked towards the back door of the manor.

'Nothin' much. Just to tell me that he knew who I was and to keep my trap shut about his past.'

'And will you?'

Jacko smiled. 'As long as it suits me and when it don't, I'll shop the bastard.'

'What if he turns bad on you?'

'He'll only hit me once, and then he's out and so am I.'

'What do ya mean?'

'Nothin'. Let's get a shower and some tea.'

*

The next four days passed without incident as far as Jacko was concerned. The weather varied from bright sunshine to cold drizzle as the group carried out their respective tasks. When the drizzle turned to rain, they went inside to the classroom to listen to a monologue from Beaky on horticulture supported by a series of video clips showing workers carrying out a variety of procedures. Jacko was not the only one to nod off during those sessions. By the end of the week, he found that his arms and back were less painful and he was not as tired when he finished work: he was getting fitter and that would be useful when the time came.

CHAPTER 10

The days were getting shorter and the light less reliable as the October mists descended from the moor. Matt was conscious of the fact that in a few days' time, the hour would go back and there would be even fewer hours when he could work in the studio in natural light. He rigged up a light over his easel; it was a fact of life that artists in the UK had to work that way. Gone were the days when painters went off to the South of France to enjoy the luxury of clear and relatively uninterrupted light.

Harry's portrait was nearly finished; Matt was pleased with the result and hoped that his client would feel the same. Kate had not seen the painting since the one time right at the beginning, and although Matt had invited her several times to come and look at it, so far she had not done so, giving pressure of work as an excuse. He began to wonder if he had made a mistake in offering to do the painting in the first place. True, he had made the offer partly in the hope of getting to know her, but also it had been a genuine bid to recompense the effects of Bullet's behaviour. He reluctantly came to the conclusion that she was avoiding him.

For Matt, working under artificial light always seemed more tiring than working in natural light. He took down the portrait and replaced it with a large landscape of the moor which he had started immediately after the studio had been trashed. 'A change is as good as a rest,' he told himself as he set to work on the completely different subject, but in less than a hour he began to feel the ache behind his eyes getting worse until he could take no more. 'Come on, Bullet. Time for a walk.' He switched off the light and went into the kitchen to change into his walking boots.

A glance through the window told him to put on a waterproof jacket, and as he reached for his cap and stick, he made a mental note to take a trip into Newton Abbot to buy a New Zealand-style long raincoat to wear when it rained hard and particularly when he was riding Molly.

The fine drizzle cleared and there was a brief moment of sunshine as man and dog walked steadily down the track towards Lidstone village. Matt had decided to take the route he and Kate had ridden on his first ride, except in the opposite direction.

As he turned into the narrow lane that led to Lidstone Manor, a white minibus suddenly appeared travelling at a speed which made him quickly grab hold of Bullet's collar and flatten himself against the hedge bank as it sped by. As far as he could see, there were no passengers, but the driver was leaning forward over the steering wheel, obviously intent on getting the maximum speed out of the vehicle. Matt doubted that the driver even noticed him.

Matt walked on to the manor gates where the road had been widened to allow vehicles to turn. There was also now a grass verge opposite so Matt was able to stand for a few minutes to allow Bullet to relieve himself and have a sniff around. It was while he was standing there that the manor gates slowly opened and, a few seconds later, the nose of the Scania horsebox came into view.

Matt became conscious that the driver was looking at him intently rather than concentrating on his driving. The result was the lorry had to stop suddenly and back up in order to negotiate the turn. He heard the rattle and bang of horses losing their balance and there was the muffled sound of someone calling out. As the driver passed him, Matt recognised the shaved head and tattooed arm of one of the men he had seen cleaning the lorry on his first visit to the stable yard. He looked at his watch: half past four. They were off on another late journey.

'Come on, Bullet. Let's get going.' Man and dog continued up the hill towards the forestry plantation as a mist came down making the remaining daylight even dimmer. Matt was looking for the hunting gate and the bridle path that led through the woodland to the top road.

Rooks cawed overhead as they circled and wheeled before descending into the branches of the oak and ash trees that lined the road. 'Roosting early,' Matt told Bullet as the old dog trotted up, panting from the exertion of the hill. 'It's a sign that winter is coming on.' He looked down at his canine companion and grinned. It was as though the animal were a real person and the thought served to remind him that he was living a solitary life, devoid of human company; he ate alone at the pub, there was rarely anyone to speak to when he collected Molly, and when he rode on Wednesdays and Sundays, it was always just him and the horse: Kate had never volunteered to go with him.

Somewhere in the distance, a chainsaw buzzed: a reminder that the forest was a workplace and it was probable that before long the narrow roads would be congested with huge eight-wheelers loaded with the harvest of larch and spruce. But for now, the road was deserted and only one 4x4 had passed him going in the direction of Lidstone.

At the brow of the hill, there was a right-hand bend where the woodland thickened, and as Matt turned the corner, he saw the gate he was looking for. As he went through, he called Bullet. 'Come on you, old bugger. I bet there are some smells in here that will get you going.' As though he understood every word, the dog immediately disappeared into the undergrowth of brambles and long grass that bordered the track. It was not long before frantic barking told Matt that he had been right: there were interesting smells and this one was taking the hunter further and further away from him. He tried calling the dog, to no avail. His whistles had no effect, so there was only one thing to do: he would have to try and follow. He found a gap in the scrub, scrambled over a dry ditch, and began to run between the trees in the direction of the sound. 'Damn, I bet it's either a fox or roe deer,' he muttered to himself between breaths.

The going was not good. There were old tree stumps to be avoided, plenty of ruts where tractors had hauled logs in the distant past, and innumerable piles of dead branches that littered the forest floor. Matt's foot was beginning to hurt badly, forcing him to slow down to a brisk walk using his stick to take the weight off his left side. At one of the rides cut through the woodland, he paused to listen: the dog was still 'giving tongue' and he was getting closer to the sound of the chainsaw. He hoped the sound might scare Bullet into giving up the chase. But there was no sign of that at the moment, so there was no alternative but to go on. Now the ground was sloping away down a steep bank. He found himself sliding through the mat of dead leaves and soil, finally ending up on his backside in a wide overgrown ditch at the bottom.

When he tried to stand up, there was a sharp pain in his ankle, but this time it was the right one. 'Damn,' he muttered to himself, as he used his stick to lever himself upright and began to clamber painfully out of the ditch. Once on firm ground, he began to yell again for the dog to return to him. Suddenly, the barking stopped and so did the sound of the chainsaw. He called again but the forest was silent except for the sound of the wind in the treetops. He tried a step forward and managed to limp slowly towards a fallen tree trunk; he sat down on it with a grateful sigh and began to take stock of his situation. He had no idea where he was, Bullet was God knows where, he was more or less immobile and, on top of that, he was exhausted. Matt propped his stick against the trunk and slumped forward, elbows on knees, to contemplate his next move. It was no good attempting to get help using his mobile; for one thing, there probably wasn't a signal, and for another, he had no idea who he could call. Minutes went by and he tried one more yell for the dog and listened for any sound that might indicate that Bullet was coming back.

'Oh, it's you.' The voice came from behind and Matt turned to see Spud Wannacott standing a few yards away. At the same time, Bullet bounced up onto the log, tail wagging, to lick his master's face. Spud was wearing an orange-coloured safety helmet with ear protectors. 'Good thing I'd finished the job I was doing otherwise you could have been yelling there for the next couple of hours.' He grinned. 'So what's the problem? Apart from the antics of your four-legged friend, who I found halfway down an old fox earth near where I was working? It was lucky that when I pulled him out, he led me straight to you.'

Matt stood up and, leaning heavily on his stick, explained what had happened.

'Can you walk?'

'Not very well. It was bad enough with just my damaged foot but now the other one has gone as well. It's bloody painful every step.' He grinned. 'If they ever tell you a horse that's lame in both front legs trots sound, you can tell them from me that it's a load of cobblers.'

'In that case, I had better help you to the nearest ride then go and fetch the Land Rover. Is that okay?'

'Yes, thanks.'

'Okay, put your right arm over my shoulder and we'll get you going,' Spud told him as Matt took the first tentative steps.

Ten painful minutes later, they reached the edge of a broad ride and Spud found a large tree stump for Matt to sit on. 'I'm afraid I'll be quite a while. I've got to collect my gear then get home for the Land Rover so make yourself comfortable,' he grinned, 'and I'll be as quick as I can.'

Matt nodded and stretched his legs out to ease the pain. 'Come on, you old bugger,' he said to the dog as he grabbed its collar and lifted the mud-spattered animal onto his lap.

Time seemed to stand still as they waited; the air was getting colder and the throbbing in Matt's foot was getting worse. He untied the bootlaces and took the boot off. It helped ease the pain but he quickly realised that there would be some difficulty in getting it back on again if the swelling increased any further. He looked at his watch: Spud had been gone for just over half an hour, but it seemed much longer.

At last, the distant sound of a vehicle came from somewhere to his right, the drone of the engine punctuated by a variety of bangs and rattles as the old Land Rover negotiated the ruts and bumps caused by timber hauling in the past. Finally it came to a halt where Matt was sitting, and a grinning Spud leant across and opened the passenger door window.

'Hang on a minute, I'll turn this ol' girl round before you get in. Save you getting knocked about across these ruts.'

Matt watched Spud complete the manoeuvre before attempting to stand. Eventually, boot in hand, he began to hop towards the vehicle using his stick as a third leg. Spud reached out to take the boot, which he tossed into the cab before once more offering his shoulder to help Matt round the vehicle and into the passenger seat. Bullet was pushed into the middle while Spud settled himself into the driver's seat. 'Sorry to be so long but I had to collect my saw and these old rides are a sod for an old crate like this,' he patted the ledge above the instrument panel.

'That's alright. It's good of you to take the trouble.' Matt stretched his leg and groaned. 'I hope to hell I don't have to get myself to the MO in the morning.'

The grin on Spud's face broadened. 'You'd be better seeing a GP.'

'Oh, yes.'

Nothing more was said until the Land Rover jerked to a halt a few yards from the green-painted mobile home. 'Here we are then,' Spud said as he climbed out of the driver's seat and walked round to help Matt.

They walked slowly towards the steps that led up to the door. Spud opened it and helped Matt inside, at the same time switching on the light. 'Right, I should take your coat off and settle yourself down there,' he indicated to a sofa along the far wall. 'I'll find us a drop of medicine that will do us both good.' The grin was still there as he went back through a doorway to, what Matt assumed, was the kitchen area.

A glance round showed that Spud led a comfortable and ordered life; the room was clean and tidy, and the sofa and easy chair were covered in a light fawn material that looked smart and did not show any excessive wear. Against the opposite wall, there was a small table and two dining chairs next to which stood a mahogany sideboard which displayed various items of crockery. There was a wood burning stove to provide heat. It seemed all very well ordered: exactly what you would expect from a man who had spent most of his life in a very well ordered profession.

Spud returned carrying a bottle and two glasses. 'I noticed, when I helped to clear up the cottage, that you were fond of a drop of Irish so I thought you might like to try this,' he held up the bottle. 'It's a Connemara blend, a bit expensive but it's a whiskey I got hooked on during the "troubles".' He poured two generous tots. 'It'll help deaden the foot pain for you and the backache for me.' The grin came back as he raised his glass. 'Cheers!'

Matt did the same and took a sip. 'Wow, that's good.' He drained half the glass before putting it down on a wooden stool that his host had placed at his side.

Spud nodded. 'Glad you like it.' He paused. 'Hang on, I'll get something for that foot.' He put his glass down and went outside. Matt could see him through the window entering a nearby wooden shed. There was the sound of an engine starting and Matt guessed it was probably a generator for the electricity. A few seconds later, Spud emerged carrying a small package. Matt heard him come through the door, and a moment later he was standing in front of him holding a bag of frozen peas. 'Take your sock off, put your leg up and stick this on your foot. It'll help get the swelling down. In the meantime, I'll have to go and let Jen out. I had to put her in her kennel at the back while I was using the saw. She's a quiet old girl so I don't think she'll trouble your dog.' He drained his glass, put it down on the table and went out.

This gave Matt time to think. He wondered how he could repay the kindness old Wannacott had shown and why the old man had indicated such an interest in him. His thoughts were disturbed by a sudden growl from Bullet as the rough-haired lurcher bounced into the room and immediately came to sniff him. Matt grabbed hold of his collar. 'Steady boy, she's not going to hurt you.' And he was right. After the preliminary encounter, Jen turned back to greet her master and curled up at his feet beside the armchair. Spud sat back and closed his eyes, elbows on the chair arms and hands clasped in front of him, deep in thought.

There was a long silence during which Matt finished his whiskey and turned over the packet of frozen peas to get the most out of the cooling effect. Still Spud was silent. Matt was beginning to feel uncomfortable in more ways than one. He cleared his throat. 'Thanks very much. I'm very grateful for what you've done, and I'm sorry to cause you so much bother.'

The old man opened his eyes and smiled. 'It's no bother. The fact is, I feel I have a sort of duty to look out for you.'

Matt looked up. 'Sorry, I'm not with you. What do you mean a duty?'

Spud sat up and looked at him intently. 'I'm an old soldier and you know what they say, "it takes one to know one". Isn't that so, Mr. Winsford? Or should I say, Captain Winsford?'

It was Matt's turn to sit up. 'My God, who told you that?'

The old man pulled a face, rolled his eyes and stretched his arms out in front of him. 'Oooh … No one told me,' he said in a low growling voice. 'I'm psychic,' and ended with a raucous belly laugh. 'No, I'm not bloody psychic, but I can put two and two together, and you gave me plenty of clues. As I said, it takes one to know one, and I'm right, or at least pretty close, aren't I?'

It was several seconds before Matt slowly nodded and said quietly, 'I guess someone must have told you, though I can't think who, even Colonel Spreyton didn't know, and I'm sure my father would not have told him. I had made it clear that I wanted them to forget the whole episode and let me get on with sorting myself out.'

Spud pulled himself up out of the chair. 'Time for another,' he said as he picked up the empty glasses, put them on the table and began to pour two more generous measures of the whiskey. 'So, would you like to tell me about the episode, just as one soldier to another?' he said as he handed Matt his glass.

'I would much prefer to forget about it, if you don't mind.'

Spud settled himself back into the armchair and raised his glass as though to study the contents before putting it to his mouth and drinking. This was followed by a satisfied 'Ahh!' as he put the glass down carefully on a small table beside the chair. There was a moment's silence before he said, 'I'm afraid you'll find there are some things you can never forget. I know, I've been there.' He leant forward. 'There were things I saw and did in the Falklands that still get to me, and that was over thirty years ago. Yes, I know about PTSD, Post-Traumatic Stress Disorder. It cost me my job and my marriage. How do you think I got down to the point of living in a place like this? We didn't get any help in those days, and if it wasn't for the colonel, I'd probably be kipping under a hedge every night. I wouldn't want to see a nice young chap like you going the same way and ending up thinking that this stuff,' he pointed to the whiskey bottle, 'is the only cure. I know that if only I could have had somebody to talk to, things might have been different.' He got up out of the chair. 'It's getting chilly in here. I'll get a few more logs in.'

While he was gone, Matt took the time to think about what the old man had said. What he had told him had struck a cord so that when Spud returned with an armful of logs, Matt decided was ready: he would tell him.

Spud placed the logs next to the stove before opening the glass door and feeding two onto the fading embers. He opened the flue and watched as the glow turned into flame. 'There, that's better.' He turned and pointed to Matt's glass. 'Have another?'

'No, thanks. I think I've had enough, need to keep a clear head.'

'Very wise.' The old man smiled. 'So?'

'How did you suss me out without anyone giving you that information?'

'It wasn't all that difficult really. Remember, I was a senior NCO and summing up young men was part of the job. Things you did, things you said, and your general appearance.'

'Such as?'

'Well, for a start, here was a young fit man, living on his own, who did not go around unshaven and scruffy. Old habits die hard, as they say, and soldiers have to look smart. You have a good all-over tan and you didn't get that laying on Paignton beach. Of course, you might have had a job in sunnier climes, but my guess was Afghanistan. Then there was the business of seeing an MO. Civilians don't have Medical Officers, they have GPs. That clinched it.'

'So how did you know my rank?'

'Oh, that was relatively easy. First off, no tattoos: they would be very much frowned upon in the officer's mess. Finally, when we first met, you said you had been told that I was an ex-sar'n major – that's officer speak, no private soldier or junior NCO would dare abbreviate the word sergeant, even in front of an old retired one. As for your actual rank, pure guess work. You're about thirty and there were three possible options. If you'd had a bad start, you might still be a lieutenant, but on the other hand, if you were exceptional, you might have made a major, but my guess was that you were about average, a captain. So there we are, I rest my case.'

Matt closed his eyes and remained silent for several minutes, then he took a deep breath, opened them and began to talk, his voice barely above a whisper.

'We were in Helmand, 2nd Logistics Transport Company, and had just delivered a consignment of ammo and stores in three Leyland MMLCs to a forward post manned by a company of Rifles … '

'I'm a bit out of date, what's an MMLC?'

'Sorry, it's medium mobility load carriers. Used a lot for medium loads in rough terrain. Anyway, we'd done the job and my lads and the vehicles were to remain there to bring back some infantrymen to HQ while my driver and I were due to return in the Snatch Land Rover.' There was a long pause before he continued. 'That worked well because I was keen to get back as quickly as possible. I was due for home leave and didn't want to miss the chopper that would take me out. It was just bad luck that we were delayed for an hour by a freak sandstorm, which meant we would have to go like hell to make it in time, and the road – if you could call it that – was not exactly the M1, more like a baked version of the track up to this place. We had strict orders not to leave the road, which had been cleared of IEDs by the sappers as it was possible that the odd improvised explosive device could have been planted nearby. We were doing well until we came up behind a Yank Oshkosh doing about fifteen miles an hour.'

'What the hell's an Oshkosh?'

'Sorry, it's an American tank transporter. Don't ask me how it gets its name, probably called after some Indian tribe, I shouldn't wonder. The road was too narrow. We couldn't get past, and it was then that I gave the order to pull off and overtake.' Matt shook his head and closed his eyes. He was asked if he would like another drink but declined. He sat motionless, his voice once again descending to a whisper. 'I remember we had just passed the Oshkosh and were pulling back onto the road. Oh, God! I remember the noise of the explosion but nothing else until I came round and began to feel the excruciating pain. I must have passed out again because I faintly heard an American voice say, "Gees, I guess this one's had it." I thought he was talking about me.'

Spud leant forward and gently put a hand on Matt's knee. 'But it wasn't you because you are here. So, your driver, was he the one he was talking about?'

Now Matt was cradling his head in his hands and, with something that sounded like a sob, whispered, 'That's the point, Spud. You see, it wasn't a *he,* it was a *she.* Corporal Alice McGovern, a gritty Scot, twenty-two years old with all her life in front of her and … Oh God, man, I can still see the blood and those pale blue sightless eyes staring up at me … she was dead … and I bloody killed her.' At that point, Captain Matthew Winsford broke down and wept like a child.

Spud said nothing and, with a faint nod, leant back in the chair, chin resting on his clasped hands, in an attitude of deep contemplation. There was muffled 'Sorry' from Matt as he took out his handkerchief to blow his nose and wipe his eyes. Eventually, the old man stirred and leant forward again. 'War is bloody terrible,' he said quietly, 'and I mean that literally. I know. I've seen it all.' He reached for his glass. 'I need another and I reckon you should have one too.' This time, Matt did not refuse and gladly took his filled glass and emptied it in one gulp causing him to screw up his eyes and shudder. 'Whoa, steady old chap, you'll burn a hole in your guts at that rate.' There was the ghost of a smile on the old man's face.

'I wouldn't care if it did.'

'Now you are talking rubbish,' Spud's voice was firmer. 'And don't think you are the only soldier to make a wrong decision resulting in some poor sod getting killed unnecessarily! It happens all the time when a situation gets tense and you have to react instantly. I know.' He took a sip from his glass then rotated it slowly between his thumb and forefinger, watching it intently. It was several minutes before he spoke. 'I suppose one of the things that people remember about the Falklands war was the famous seventy-five mile 'yomp' by the Marines from San Carlos to Port Stanley. The papers were full of photographs and articles describing the march, but what they didn't tell you was what happened at the end of it. We didn't just walk down into a undefended town. Despite what the British public were led to believe, the Argies put up some pretty stiff resistance, at least they did where I was.'

There was a long pause while the old man finished his drink. He got up and put another log on the fire before continuing. 'We were pinned down by a machine gun post situated about a hundred yards up the slope. Had to deal with it before the rest of the company caught up. I'd not long got my third stripe so was keen to get the job done – too keen, as it turned out. I just turned and tapped two of my lads on the shoulder and ordered them to go and "knock 'em out" with a couple of grenades. I watched as they got halfway before they were torn to pieces by a rake of machine-gun fire. Two young lads, about the same age as your driver, and I had sent them to their deaths, on a spur of the moment decision.' He closed his eyes and slumped back into the chair. 'Should have gone with them, used my experience to keep them out of trouble, but I didn't. Instead, I sent two young men to their deaths.' He repeated the phrase twice, before opening his eyes again and leaning forward. 'That was more than thirty years ago, Captain Winsford, and it still gives me nightmares, so don't think you're alone. I know what you are going through and I can assure you that there are plenty of poor sods out there who have come home from combat that are in the same boat.'

He relaxed back in the chair and watched as Matt slowly shifted his position to face him. It was obvious that the recently injured foot was still very painful and there was a low groan as he put it to the floor. 'You did not have to tell me all that, but I appreciate the fact that you did, Sar'n Major Winsford.' There was a faint smile on Matt's lips as he added, 'I reckon it's about time we got down to first names, so can it be Matt and Spud? Incidentally, can I ask how you got that name?'

Spud welcomed the informality and said so adding, 'I suppose it was my initials at school – Steven Peter David – S.P.D., then there was the fact that my father used to deliver the vegetables, including regular bags of potatoes, to the school kitchen, so I suppose it was almost inevitable. And while we are on the subject of food, I suggest you stay and have a bite with me, then you will have to stay the night.'

Matt gladly accepted the offer of a meal but said that he could not impose on his host any further and would make his way home, adding that it wasn't very far.

Spud gave a grunt. 'Don't be daft, man! You're in no state to walk anywhere and I'm in no state to drive after three stiff whiskies. We've got no choice, so make yourself comfortable while I sort out some grub.' He went out into the kitchen, pleased with the fact that his young guest appeared to be more relaxed and glad to have a bit of company, something that did not happen very often at Chez Wannacott.

Matt put his swollen foot back up onto the sofa, readjusted the frozen peas, which were beginning to thaw by now, and slumped back onto the cushions feeling mentally and physically exhausted. He had never spoken to anyone about the incident in such detail before, had never expected a sympathetic reaction nor the degree of understanding that he had experienced in the past hour. He knew the memories would never go away, but he now realised there was a chance that he could learn to live with them.

Bullet was now on the floor curled up under his feet and eyeing Jen with a look of restrained belligerence. Matt could hear Spud moving about in the kitchen area and soon there was the appetising smell of fried bacon seeping through the beaded curtain that separated the kitchen from the living area.

It was not long before Spud appeared carrying two plates of bacon and eggs, fried bread and sliced fried potatoes. 'Not for the faint-hearted nor the fat,' he commented as he placed them on the table, 'but I reckon it'll do us.' He took out knives and forks from a small drawer in the table and laid them beside the plates. 'Do you need a hand?' he asked Matt as the latter attempted to stand.

'No thanks, I'll be fine.' He limped across using the backs of the chairs for support and sat down in the chair opposite the one Spud was occupying.

They ate in silence, the 'fry-up' augmented by thick slices of white bread and butter. 'Real butter,' Spud was keen to point out. 'Not that margarine stuff that's supposed to be good for the old ticker and tastes of nothing.'

The meal was rounded off with two large mugs of strong coffee which they drank seated back in the comfort of the armchair and sofa respectively.

'Would y' like to watch some telly?' Spud asked pulling aside a curtain to reveal a small, slim TV fixed to the wall.

Matt expressed his surprise. 'Wow! Wouldn't have thought you could get any sort of signal tucked away in a place like this.'

Spud grinned. 'The aerial is stuck up on a thirty foot pole the other side of the track. Works okay most of the time but I can't get the BBC if it rains and blows too much. Mind, I don't watch a lot but it's useful for the news and the latest weather forecast.'

'If you don't mind, I think I'd rather sit back and take it easy for a while. Don't think I could cope with the soaps just at the moment.' Matt lifted his leg back onto the sofa and examined the ankle. 'I think it's feeling a bit better,' he said pulling up his sock and placing the foot gingerly on the floor.

'I'll get you some cold water to put that in.' The old man got up and went into the kitchen area, returning with a washing-up basin half-full.

Matt took off his sock and gently lowered the foot into the cold liquid with a gratified, 'Ah! That's better.' He began to splash water over the swollen area and, at the same time, massaged the leg and ankle. 'I see you've got running water then.' The comment came as Spud returned from the kitchen to top up the basin with a full jug.

'Yep. There's a natural spring halfway up the slope at the back and it was just a case of tapping it. The water is about as pure as you can get, but in any case, I rarely drink it without boiling for tea or coffee and if I do fancy a clear glass, well, I just purify it with a shot of the hard stuff,' he pointed to the empty whiskey bottle and grinned. 'And if you're wondering about the loo, the colonel put in a septic tank for me. We had to keep all that a bit quiet 'cos we're inside the National Park and the planners would wet their knickers if they knew I was living here permanently. It's supposed to be just for use in the shooting season you see.'

'So you've got all mod cons then, but must be a bit parky in a hard winter.'

The old man waved a hand in the direction of the forest. 'Fuel on me doorstep. Just a case of going out and getting it which, incidentally, is what I was doing when yon tyke arrived on the scene,' he nodded towards where Bullet lay snoring, curled up under his owner's legs. 'So, young Matt, would you like to tell me a bit about yourself, or do you think I'm being a bit too nosey?'

Matt thought for a moment as he watched the flames grow in the wood burner. 'No … ' he said slowly. 'I think you are, how shall I put it, being a bit too fatherly, and the fact is, I could never tell my real father the things I have told you. He would be sympathetic, I'm sure, but I don't think he could possibly understand the effect it had on me the same way you have.' There was a long pause before he continued. 'There's nothing much to tell really – brought up on a farm; happy childhood, I never wanted for anything; family into horses, hunting; my sister absolutely potty about the whole horsey business while I was much more interested in tractors and the machinery side – typical I suppose.' He bent down to massage the ankle again.

Spud got up. 'Hold on, I'll get you a towel. Get you dried off and a bit more comfortable.'

As he gently pulled on his sock, Matt told Spud how he had decided that the army was a possible career while he was on holiday with his family at Coombe Cottage. 'My A levels weren't quite good enough for university and in any case, I wanted a job where I could travel and see the world a bit. I had enjoyed being in the cadet force at school and so the army seemed to fit the bill.'

'And did it?'

'Very much so. It gave me a chance to do a lot of things I could never have experienced in any other organisation. For example, at one stage I was posted to the training battalion working with young recruits, lads and the occasional lass from all sorts of different backgrounds, religions and colours. I enjoyed that part: sorting out their problems – and there were a lot in some cases – and gradually welding them into disciplined soldiers and hopefully into future law-abiding citizens. I really felt I was doing something useful.' There was a long pause before he continued. 'Now I don't know what the hell is going to happen and there are times when I don't even care.'

'Was there any fall out? I mean, did you get hauled over the coals for disobeying orders?'

Matt shrugged. 'The only guys to see what happened were the American crew of the tank transporter, and they were too busy saving my miserable life to say anything to the medics about how the whole thing had happened. I was whizzed back home and spent the next month in hospital, and by the time I was able to talk to anyone more important, things were happening at the front. My CO was too pre-occupied with a new insurgent threat to ask questions. I was lucky.' He turned to look out of the window but could only see his own reflection in the glass. 'I tried to contact Alice's parents but it turned out that she was brought up in care in a series of foster homes so I couldn't even say I was sorry.'

The old man thought for a moment. 'You said you had passed the American vehicle and was coming back onto the road. So how do you know the bomb wasn't planted actually on the road, one the bomb disposal squad had missed, or perhaps had been planted after the clearance? If it was, then the Yanks would have hit it if you hadn't overtaken them, so it's possible that you may have saved the lives of some GIs. Have you ever considered that?'

Matt shook his head. 'No, not really. The whole bloody business is just a blank to me so I couldn't tell you exactly where we were when it happened.'

'So perhaps the reason nobody took any action against you is that you were on the road and the only people who knew you had disobeyed orders were the Americans who were only too glad you had because it had saved them.'

For a split second, there was a look of relief on Matt's face but it quickly clouded over. 'That doesn't alter the fact that Alice McGovern is dead.'

'No, but it does mean someone else is alive who might possibly be dead. It's worth thinking about.' Spud got up to draw the curtains. 'So where do you go from here? Back in the army or out into civvy street?'

The answer came with a shrug. 'I don't know. When I got back to Deepcut Barracks after the spell in hospital, they told me I could stay but it depended on how well the injuries responded to treatment. So far, so good, but they intimated that it might be a desk job, and I don't want that. I've got six months to consider the options, and in the meantime, I can enjoy the Devon countryside and indulge my hobby of painting.'

'I gathered that you were an artist when I cleaned up the cottage after the break in.'

'Well, I wouldn't really call myself that: an artist is someone who can create something interesting or beautiful out of nothing, who can take the ordinary and make it extra-ordinary. I just paint what I see and hope I get it right.'

The old man smiled. 'I'm told you got it right with young Kate Lethbridge's horse.'

'Who told you that?'

'She did. She said she thought you had an "eye for a horse", whatever that means, though I get the impression she doesn't have much of an eye for you, if you know what I mean.'

'I suppose she thinks I'm some sort of an oddball from upcountry hiding away in the depths of the countryside.' He paused to look intently at his host. 'I would be very grateful if you would keep what you know about me to yourself. I don't want the locals to know about … well, you know, all we've talked about. The last thing I want is folks making a fuss, and I certainly don't deserve their sympathy, so please let's keep it between ourselves.'

'If you say so, that's no problem. There's quite a lot I wouldn't want folks to know about me.' Spud grinned, So mum's the word, eh?'

'Thanks, I just want to keep things under wraps until I'm ready – then, well, we'll see.'

The old man looked at his watch. 'Coming up to ten,' he said. 'My bedtime. I don't know about you, but I'm ready to hit the hay.' He got up to shut down the wood burner. 'I'll take the dogs out before we turn in – don't think yours will do a bunk if it knows you're in here but stand in the doorway just in case.' Matt limped to the door as requested while Spud put on his coat and went down the steps followed by the two dogs.

The mist had gone and the sky was clear and starlit. As he looked up, Matt thought of nights spent under much clearer skies where the stars shone more brightly and temperatures dropped dramatically from the heat of the day; where horizons merged with distant mountains and roads stretched ahead to unknown destinations. He knew he would miss the life he had known over the past ten years if he had to change direction and settle into some mundane job in civvy street.

His thoughts were interrupted by the return of Spud with the dogs. 'No problems,' the old man told him. 'Both had a pee and your old dog is as keen as I am to get back into the warm. We're in for a frost tonight, or I'll eat my boots.'

Both men retraced their steps back to the fire where Spud put fresh logs on the embers. 'There, that should keep in all night if we're lucky. Come on, I'll show you your bunk.' He led the way through the kitchen area. 'Loo and shower in there,' he opened the first door, 'and you're in here.' The second door opened into a small room just big enough for a six foot single bed, a chair and small cupboard. There were hooks to hang any clothes and an ex-army sleeping bag was rolled up in the corner. 'Not exactly the Ritz, I'm afraid,' Spud commented. 'I guess it'll take you back to your basic training days,' he added, nodding towards the sleeping bag.

Matt muttered his thanks and then went in to sit on the bed and begin to undress down to his shirt and boxer shorts. This was followed by a brief trip to the tiny bathroom and, as he returned, he found Spud standing in the doorway with a glass of water in one hand and a small packet and tube in the other. 'Painkillers and anti-inflammatory ointment,' he announced as he handed them to Matt. 'When you get to my age, they are two of life's necessities, particularly when the old arthritis kicks in,' he added with a grin.

'Thanks, but I don't want to take … '

'Don't worry, I've got plenty in reserve, so just take what you need. Sleep well,' he called as he closed the door.

Matt swallowed two of the painkillers and sat down on the chair to massage the swollen ankle with the ointment. After a short while, the pain seemed to ease and he was ready to unroll the sleeping bag and get into it. Within minutes, he was asleep and, for the first time in many months, there were no dreams.

CHAPTER 12

Kate looked anxiously down at the road surface as she rode a young fractious four-year-old out of the manor gates. She had hoped to take it for its first day's trail hunting that morning, but the night frost meant the ground would have been treacherous at eight o'clock, the time of the meet. Now a warming sun had melted the frost to a glistening wet carpet on the grassland but there could still be thin pockets of ice on the uneven surface of the lane.

Satisfied that it was safe, she trotted off through the village and up towards the moor, disappointed to have missed introducing the young horse to its first gathering of mounted riders, foot followers and, most importantly, the hounds. The bay thoroughbred had been bought by a local solicitor in the summer and was at livery with the stables on the condition that it would be schooled for hunting by the autumn. Kate would have to try again on Saturday.

As they trotted up the hill towards the track onto the moor, Kate saw the familiar outline of Spud Wannacott's Land Rover coming towards her. He slowed down and pulled into a field gateway to give her plenty of room to pass.

As horse and rider came up, he wound down his window and put his head out. 'Morning, Miss Kate.' He had called her that since she was a toddler. 'That's a decent looking sort,' he indicated towards the bay. 'Should give some lucky soul a good day with the hounds.'

Kate nodded as the horse 'marked time' with all four feet. 'Belongs to Peter Ridley,' she told him. 'You know, the chap who helps the hunt with any legal matters.'

Spud smiled knowingly. 'A very useful man to have around these days.'

Kate leant forward and peered into the cab. 'I see you have a passenger,' she said.

Matt turned towards her and merely smiled, reluctant to take the encounter any further. Kate slowly raised a gloved hand in acknowledgement and turned back to Spud, who recounted most of what had happened the previous day, but not all. Matt's true identity was a secret he was honoured to keep.

'You seem to be perpetually in the wars,' Kate called out as she leant forward again.'

Matt had to smile at the irony of the comment and simply nodded as he watched the rider nudge the horse forward. 'Must get on,' she told Spud, glancing at her watch. 'I've got one of the "naughty boys" coming at ten o'clock for some work experience – or whatever they call it. Should be quite an experience for both of us.' She walked the skittish bay past the vehicle and trotted on up the hill.

'That's a grand little maid. Sorry, can't help thinking of her like that, I suppose 'cos I've known her since she was a little 'un,' he looked at Matt,. 'It would be nice if you two could get together.'

'That'll be the day,' Matt grunted as he glanced back at the receding rider.

*

Kate turned the horse onto the moorland track and, relieved to find there was some 'give' in the ground, pushed him into a canter up the slope towards the rocks of Hound Tor. As she came to the top of the rise, she eased the gelding to a walk: there was the unmistakable sound of hounds 'speaking' in the wooded valley to her left. She concluded the master had decided to move the meet to the sheltered woodland where the frost had not penetrated. Either that or they were a lot braver than she was and had started off on very unpredictable slippery ground. Either way, she was in luck and the morning would not be completely wasted.

The 'field' were grouped together just inside a narrow gateway leading into the wood. There were a mere half a dozen or so riders, the majority dressed in the grey/green thorn-proof jackets favoured by the 'old guard'; the remainder wore waterproof jackets of varying colours. Kate zipped up her dark blue waterproof to hide the fact that she was not wearing a tie but otherwise she felt sufficiently tidy to attach herself to the rear of the group, keeping well back to avoid any close encounter with another horse.

The bay was behaving reasonably well. Head up and ears pricked, he stood alert and listening as the sound of the huntsman's horn echoed through the wood, then, as the riders moved away, he spun round once before settling down to follow at a steady, if somewhat erratic, jog. Kate was pleased the young horse showed no signs of fear or panic, just excitement and interest: he would make a good hunter.

She followed for another half an hour, glad that the pace was no faster than a brisk trot; there was always the danger that a young inexperienced horse would put in a quick buck if asked to gallop after a receding bunch of excited animals, human and equine. A glance at her watch and Kate realised she would have to leave the hunt and make for home. It had been a brief but useful encounter, and the fact that the young horse was reluctant to turn away from the sights and sounds of the hunt was another indication that he would eventually do the job required of him.

Back at the stables, the bay was fed, watered and rubbed down by his attentive rider before being rugged up and turned out into a small paddock to relax and cool off. As she walked back into the yard, Kate saw a man in grey overalls and wellingtons with a youth similarly dressed standing in the gateway that led to the manor. The man was tall and thin with straggly blonde hair down to his collar. He nudged the youth forward as Kate approached.

'This is Wiggins,' he told her, nodding towards the youngster. 'Booked in with you for work experience for the next three weeks.' The thin lips broke into a smile that made Kate feel uncomfortable as he continued. 'Back to the manor for 'is dinner at twelve, then two till four in the afternoon, right?'

Kate nodded slowly and told him that she understood and would make sure the boy made himself useful while he was with them. There was a grunt as the man turned abruptly and walked back towards the manor.

Kate turned her attention to the young man. He was stocky, ginger-haired and stood with his hands in his pockets looking round the stables with a huge grin on his face.

Kate walked up to him and offered her hand, which he shook politely. 'So, you are Wiggins,' she said. 'I'm Kate, what's your first name?'

The grin vanished. 'Just call me Wiggy, everybody else does.' He was reluctant to tell her, or anybody else for that matter, that his christened name was Bartholomew, Bart to his family. It had caused him enough embarrassment in his short lifetime, and would certainly have done so in his present situation.

'All right then, Wiggy.' Kate found it difficult not to smile. 'What do you know about horses and stables that made you put in for experience here?'

'Mother was into horses and taught me to ride when I was still at primary school.'

'Have you done much since then?' She was intrigued by the youth's refined accent and wanted to hear more.

'No, they pushed me off to boarding school when I was eight, then my father walked out and things went from bad to worse and here I am.' He shrugged.

Kate had no desire to probe any further into the boy's troubled past. 'Okay then, you know what mucking out is.'

'Too true.'

She presented him with a muck fork, brush and barrow, and watched while he set to work. 'Who was the chap who brought you over?' she asked.

There was a pause before the reply came. 'He calls himself Mr. Able but that's not his real name.'

'How do you know that?

'One of my roommates knew him before. His real name is Andrews. By all accounts a bit of a dodgy character. At least, that's what my roommate told me. Into drugs and he thinks he might be growing cannabis in the big glasshouse in the garden.'

Good Lord, Kate thought for a moment. 'Surely the other instructors would know about it, and I'm certain Mr. Burford would not allow anything like that? No, I'm afraid your friend must have got it wrong. My guess is this roommate of yours bears some sort of a grudge against the man for some reason and is letting his imagination run away with him.'

Wiggy shrugged. 'Dunno, could be. He did tell me that when he was at school in London, Andrews worked there as a groundsman and was done for growing weed in the attic of a house, so I suppose Jacko thinks he is doing the same thing here, perhaps they're all in it, wouldn't surprise me.' He pushed a forkful of straw into a corner and began to separate out the droppings.

'If your friend Jacko thinks that, why doesn't he tell someone in authority?'

'Scared.'

'What do you mean scared?'

Wiggy stopped working and leant on the fork to look at Kate. He shook his head. 'When you're in a place like that,' he nodded towards the house, 'you keep your head down, don't cause any trouble.'

Kate was wondering how such an obviously intelligent youngster could end up in a place like Lidstone Manor.

And there's one other thing you ought to know.'

'And what's that?'

'The man's a perv.'

'A perv?'

'A pervert. Queer, a homosexual.'

'There's nothing wrong with that,' she told him. 'It's not illegal.'

'It is when you try it on with small boys.' Wiggy spat into the straw before continuing to separate out the droppings. 'I'll need a dung shovel,' he commented as he swept up a pile.

Most of the horses were turned out in rugs during the day, except those needing special attention. It left fourteen loose boxes to be mucked out, hay nets to be filled and soaked, and the concentrates for each individual animal measured ready for their return at five o'clock. Kate was pleased with the way young Wiggins had settled into the work, and when the time came for him to depart, she had no hesitation in ticking the box satisfactory on the progress card he presented to her.

As Wiggy departed through the gate, Greta passed him riding a tall grey horse that was lathered in sweat. She dismounted and handed the reins to Kate. 'Bloody thing,' she said angrily. 'For two pins, I would put a bullet in it. Yah!' She spat onto the ground and stomped off towards the tack room where Ivan was standing holding a piece of paper which he immediately gave to her. As she read it, Kate heard her utter a word which sounded like a curse, but in a foreign language. Ivan shrugged with a look that said 'not my fault,' and followed her through the gate towards the manor.

Kate led the grey into its box and began to rub it down, speculating on what had happened on the ride and also what Ivan had said to upset her boss so much. She had noticed that things had been a bit edgy recently and wondered if the problems with immigrants at the Channel Tunnel were effecting the horse trade. But for now, it was back to rub 'em down, rug 'em up and turn 'em out: the grey would get an hour in the paddock to cool off before five o'clock when the rest of the horses would be brought in.

*

'And what sort of a day have you had, Kate?' Mary was busy laying the table when her daughter walked in.

'Interesting.'

'Interesting? What does that mean?'

'I'll tell you later,' Kate said as she pulled off her boots and went upstairs

Jim Lethbridge was late for supper as usual. 'Sorry, love, more TB testing. God, how I hate that job. If it wasn't for the fact that the contract is a money-spinner for us, I'd give it up tomorrow.'

Mary put a hand on his shoulder as he sat down at the table. 'So not a good result then?"

Jim slowly shook his head. 'I've just committed twenty-two of Bill Dawe's heifers to death. Reactors. It could well mean them selling up. Both him and Dorothy are getting on now, and I can't see them building up the herd again.'

'What about the boys?' Kate asked as she joined them at the table. 'I overheard what you were saying about the Dawes' cattle.'

'The oldest one isn't interested and the other has got a good job in Canada selling real estate so I can't see them taking it on.' Jim smoothed the napkin on his lap and looked expectantly towards Mary.

'Any minute now,' she said making her way to the kitchen. 'Just need to brown off the roast potatoes.'

Her husband gave a satisfied 'Ah!' at the mention of roast potatoes.

'That's a very nice farm the Dawes have got,' Mary said as she put a joint of roast lamb on the table.

'It might be nice, as you put it, but it's barely a couple of hundred acres – hardly big enough to make a living nowadays unless they diversify into tourism or a farm shop, something of that sort.'

'Can't see them doing that at their age,' Kate said. 'Pity, it's a very nice house and they've spent a lot doing it up.'

'Just right for a young couple starting up,' her mother commented as she offered the carving knife and fork to her husband.

Kate said nothing as she watched her father carve the joint while her mother laid out the dishes of vegetables. They ate in silence and it was not until they had finished the first course that Mary ventured to ask Kate to elaborate on her 'interesting' day.

'Bit weird really when I come to think of it.' Kate leant forward, elbows on the table, as she recounted the conversation with the young inmate. 'I don't know how much to believe, or how much he was making up.'

'You don't need to believe anything those young scruffs say,' Mary chipped in. 'Don't forget, they're here at Lidstone because of something wrong they've done, it's not a holiday camp.'

'Yes, but if only part of it is true, somebody ought to do something about it, and it struck me that this lad is different from most of the others. He's well spoken and educated; apparently his parents are quite well off so I can't see why he should lie.'

'What's for afters?' Jim asked, seemingly oblivious of the conversation between the two women.

'Haven't you been listening to what Kate's been saying, Jim? There seems to be something going on up at the manor. And it's apple crumble, if you must know.'

'Oh, so apple crumble is going on up at the manor? Whatever next.'

'You know perfectly well what I mean. What do you think we should do?'

Jim closed his eyes and said, with a sigh, 'Just forget about it. We've got enough problems of our own without getting involved with that lot. I expect someone up there will sort it out. After all, it is a penal institution – they're probably used to that sort of thing, you read about it all the time.'

'It's not the same, Jim. These are young boys and it's supposed to be more like a school than a prison.'

'Okay, but what do you expect me to do? Go up there and tell the principal – what's his name, Burford? – that one of his staff is a crook and the only evidence I have is that one of the inmates told me so? Don't be daft, Mary, I wouldn't have a leg to stand on, and neither would the police. So as I say, forget about it.'

There was a long silence while Mary served the crumble. Eventually, she said, 'I still think somebody should say something, drop a hint in the right quarters, if you know what I mean. You're pals with Tom Gresham, you could drop a word in his ear and he can decide whether to do anything or not.'

'Okay, okay, I'll have a word with Tom, though I don't know how much clout a detective inspector has these days, particularly bearing in mind the force is greatly overstretched. Still, I'll give it a try if you feel strongly about it.' His eyes travelled from Kate to Mary and back again: there was no doubt they were expecting him to do something but he still was not sure anything would be achieved.

Another period of silence as the dessert was consumed. As she was clearing away the dishes, Mary casually asked her daughter if the painting of Harry was finished and, if so, when was she going to collect it.

'I don't know, but that reminds me, I met Spud Wannacott in his Land Rover this morning and he had our artist friend as a passenger. Apparently, he's ricked his ankle chasing after that ruddy little dog of his, so Spud decided to put him up for the night in his mobile home. The old boy seems to have taken him under his wing, though I can't think why, I wouldn't have thought they had much in common. I mean, the art world is a far cry from soldiering, which is where Spud has been most of his life.'

'I understood that the painting was just a hobby and that he did something else for a living before having an accident and coming to convalesce at the cottage,' Mary said as she handed Kate a drying-up cloth as a hint and followed her into the kitchen where Jim was already filling the washing-up bowl.

He stopped what he was doing and turned to Kate. 'I sensed, when he came to see us about his dog, that he was a very troubled young man. He seems a nice enough chap and if you want my opinion, I think all of us should do what we can to help him get over whatever it is that's troubling him.'

Mary nodded in agreement. 'You're right, Jim. After all, he's more or less part of our little community here at Lidstone. I'm thinking one of us should pop up there and see if there is anything we can do for him, seeing that he is probably going to be unable to drive and could be stuck in that cottage for days. If Kate won't do it, I will.' She looked at her daughter who was making a clucking sound and flapping her elbows while gazing intently at the ceiling. Mary frowned. 'What's that supposed to mean?' she asked angrily.

Kate shook her head slowly. 'You're going broody again, Mum, and my guess is he's not the sort to want outsiders probing around his personal space, if you know what I mean.'

'No, I don't know what you mean. All I'm saying is that we should offer to help out with things like shopping and general chores. We could have him down for the odd meal. It's not as though he's a complete stranger, he does exercise my horse and he's painted yours, so … '

'Alright, alright, don't go on, Mother. I'll give him a ring tomorrow and tell him that mother hen wants to take him under her wing. Will that do?'

'That's enough sarcasm, young lady,' Mary told her, but as she walked back to the dining room, she was smiling.

CHAPTER 13

The following day, Matt telephoned Mary Lethbridge to explain what had happened and that he would be unable to ride Molly until his ankle had gone down so that he could get a boot on. She sounded very sympathetic, asked him how he was coping and suggested that one of them, probably Kate when she called for the painting, could bring him back for some supper. He thanked her and said that the painting was finished and could be collected at any time, but could she or Kate give him a ring before hand to ensure he was there as Spud Wannacott had volunteered to ferry him about until he was sound again.

True to his word, Spud arrived at ten o'clock to take him to Newton Abbot Hospital to get the foot checked where it was confirmed that it was merely a minor sprain and, with the right medication, should be back to normal in a week or so.

On the way home, Matt asked how long Spud had known Kate. The old man smiled. 'Well, if you want to know, as I said, I've known her and the family since she was a toddler. I can see her now, sitting on her little skewbald pony trotting behind her mother's cob on their way to her first meet; couldn't have been more than four or five years old, great grin on her face and her long blonde hair plaited into a pigtail underneath her black riding hat.'

Matt studied the handle of the aluminium walking stick the hospital had given him. 'What about boyfriends?' he asked without shifting his gaze.

Spud's grin went even wider. 'She's a good-looking maid so, as you'd expect, she's had quite a few, and they're just the ones I know about.' He paused while he negotiated a busy roundabout. 'So, that's Kate. What about you, dare I ask?'

With a slight groan, Matt moved his injured foot to a more comfortable position. 'Nothing at the moment, and in my present state, who the hell would want to be saddled with a bloody cripple like me?'

'I've seen men in a much worse state than you, young man, make a success of their lives. At least you've got all your limbs and you're not disfigured in any way. In fact, you look pretty chipper to me, so stop running yourself down and start being a bit more positive. Why don't you just ask the girl out?'

'Because I know she would say no.'

'How do you know till you've tried?'

'I know because I've been there. I know because I discovered the hard way that women find it difficult to cope with me as I am now.' There was a long pause before he continued in almost a whisper, 'I had a girlfriend. We'd been living together for over two years when it … when the incident happened. She'd put up with all the business of me being away a lot of the time but I guess she just couldn't cope with me the way I am now, so she walked out and, to be honest I don't blame her.'

No more was said until they arrived back at the cottage. As he helped Matt out of the Land Rover, Spud told him that he would come in and rustle up a bit of grub for them both. 'Thanks but I'm not at all hungry, just knackered, so I'll take some painkillers and get my head down for a couple of hours. Thanks again for your help, Spud. It's been great having someone to talk to who understands. You push off and get your own lunch. I'll be in touch.' He waved a hand as the old man climbed back into the vehicle and drove off.

*

It was four o'clock when he woke to the sound of his mobile ringing. It was Kate to say that she would call at around six to pick up the painting and she had orders to bring him back for supper. Was that alright? He replied that it was and was about to ask her to thank her mother for him but she rang off before he could finish the sentence. He gave a resigned shrug as he put the phone back into his pocket and called Bullet.

'Right, old chap, time for walkies.' He eased himself downstairs in his stockinged feet and decided that he would have to wear one boot and one bedroom slipper. The old dog was bouncing up and down like a two-year-old which delighted his master as he grabbed his stick, hobbled to the door and went out.

The air was chilly and a dense mist was coming down from the moor. This afternoon's walkies would consist of a limp down the garden path, across the lawn and back to the cottage. Not much but enough to give Bullet a chance for a pee and a sniff round.

Back inside, Matt decided to do some tidying up. He did not want to give his visitor the impression that his domestic life was one of untidy chaos, although to some extent it was. In the army, there had always been someone else to clear things up, make his quarters clean and tidy, but now the chores were his: bad enough when he was fit but now …

After half an hour, he switched on the fire and was forced to sit down in front of it and rest both feet. Thoughts turned to the impending visit from

Kate. He would need a shower, some fresh clothes and a shave, and then would come the moment to present her with the painting. It was always something he dreaded, showing the finished commission to the client. Would it be good enough? Was it right? He crossed his fingers as he stood up and made his way upstairs. He found a clean shirt and decided on his fawn moleskin trousers and the well-worn brown sweater that had been part of his wardrobe since his first year at Sandhurst; no tie, casual, he was sure that would be right. The only problem, he would have to wear a shoe on his left foot and a slipper on his right. He grimaced at the though of hobbling behind Kate into the Lethbridges' dining room.

It was a little after six when a knock on the back door to the kitchen announced Kate's arrival. As Matt opened it, he saw that she was still dressed in her working clothes: knee-high rubber boots with buckles at the top, jeans and a grey polo-necked sweater, her blonde hair tied back in a ponytail. He smiled as he remembered Spud's description of the little girl on the pony, but, unlike the child, this young woman was not smiling.

He stepped back to let her in. 'Hello, nice to see you,' he said as she started to remove her boots. He told her not to worry as the floor was tiled and there would be no carpets to clean. There was an awkward silence before he said, 'I see you've come straight from work. Can I get you a cup of tea or something?'

'No, thank you, I don't think we've that much time. Mother likes to get supper on the table at seven.' Matt was relieved to see a faint smile on her face as she spoke.

'In that case,' he said, 'I suppose we'd better get on and have a look at what I've done.' He tried to sound confident in spite of the butterflies that invariably came whenever he had to show the results of his work. He led her through into the studio where the painting was placed on the easel illuminated by the overhead light.

She stood looking at it for several agonising seconds before a slight nod and the almost whispered words. 'It's good.' She turned to him and, this time with a broad smile, said, 'It's very good. I think you've caught him exactly and I love the background.'

Matt's sigh of relief was audible. 'Glad you like it,' he said. 'Would you like to take it now?'

'Yes, please.' She looked at him and grinned. 'I know Mum is dying to see it. She's been nagging me for days to come and see you.'

'Good, in that case, I'll find something to put it in,' Matt said brightly as he took it from the easel and gave it to her. 'Safest in your hands at the moment,' he told her as he limped back to the kitchen.

A plastic carrier bag large enough to take the canvass was found under the sink. Kate put the painting in it and carried it out to the Fiat to place it carefully on the back seat. Matt followed, after switching off the fire and making sure that Bullet had sufficient food and water. Satisfied that the old dog would be comfortable until his return, he eased himself into the passenger seat and waited for Kate to start the engine.

It was almost dark when they pulled into the yard behind the house. Matt had declined the offer to be dropped off at the front door to prevent him having to walk the distance from the barn to the house. 'Need to get the foot going,' he told Kate as he limped by her side. He had abandoned the walking stick and was determined to walk as soundly as possible up to the back door. As Kate led the way in, Matt assured himself that he was not hobbling.

'Hello, come in.' It was Mary's voice. 'Nice to see you again,' and as Matt went through the door into the dining room, she whispered to Kate, 'Have you got the painting? Is it alright?' Kate nodded and said that she would show it to them after supper. 'I can't wait to see it,' her mother said excitedly.

Matt was ushered through to the sitting room where Jim was sitting by the wood burner reading the latest edition of the *Western Morning News*. He stood up and indicated the armchair opposite. 'How's it going?' he asked with a smile. 'I heard you'd been in the wars again.'

Matt thanked him for his concern but, as he sank into the chair, he secretly wished people would stop using that particular phrase. 'It's not too bad, really. Should be okay in a few days, the doctor says. With any luck, I should be sound and back in the saddle by the end of next week.'

'Glad to hear that.' It was Mary's voice from the dining room. 'Old Molly has been looking so much better since you've been riding her out, isn't that so, Kate?' Matt did not hear the reply to the question but did hear Kate tell her mother that she was going up to change out of her working gear.

'Nearly ready,' Mary called out.

'We'd better get to the table,' Jim whispered. 'She hates it if we're not there on the dot in case things get cold.'

There was an appetising smell coming from the direction of the kitchen and both men glanced in that direction with an air of anticipation as Mary stepped into the dining room and placed a steaming dish on the table. 'Venison casserole,' she said proudly. 'Spud brought me a haunch this morning. He said it's been hung for a week so should be nice and tender.'

At that moment, Kate entered wearing a flowered skirt well above the knee and a tight pink sweater that accentuated her well-proportioned figure. Her mother glanced at her, raised one eyebrow, but said nothing.

Supper in the Lethbridge household was normally a simple affair: hot first course (except in high summer when cold meat might be offered), followed by a simple dessert of fruit, with water or cordial to drink. Tonight Mary had excelled herself by offering additional cheese and biscuits and had opened a bottle of her homemade elderberry wine. 'Kikapoo joy juice', Jim called it partly, because of its unpredictable potency, but also because it was only drunk on special occasions. He looked at her inquiringly but said nothing as she handed him the bottle to pour.

Initial conversation inevitably centred round Matt's recent injury and he had to recount what had happened giving ample praise to Spud for his help and generosity.

'Your little dog okay then?' Jim asked.

'Fit as a fiddle, thanks to you,' Matt replied with a grin.

'Don't thank me, thank Alison and Steph, the nurse. They did all the work,' Jim told him as he set about the venison casserole with an appreciative 'hmm'. The rest followed suit and there was silence until plates were empty.

Mary stood up. 'Anyone for seconds?'

There was a general murmur of, 'Yes please', from the two men while Kate shook her head and said she had to watch her figure. Mary nodded in agreement and decided to forego the second helping she had set aside for herself.

'To get back to your dog,' Jim said, 'we never found out who did it, did we?'

Matt thought for a moment. 'I wonder if it could have been one of the inmates at the manor? I presume some of them are pretty rough and quite capable of doing something like that.'

Kate shook her head. 'No, I don't think so. For one thing, they are all locked in at night, and for another, I don't think they are the sort of youngsters to do that sort of thing. No, if you ask me, if it is someone from the manor, it's more likely to be one of the instructors.'

'Good Lord, what makes you think that?' Matt's surprise was genuine.

Kate took a deep breath and told him what Wiggy had said.

Matt was puzzled. If it was true that a drug dealer and paedophile was working at an institution for young offenders, why had it not been picked up when the man was appointed? He turned to Jim. 'Surely they must have safeguards to prevent someone like that coming into contact with vulnerable youngsters.'

'You would have thought so, unless of course they do know about him and he's in some sort of rehabilitation programme under strict supervision.'

'Doesn't sound very plausible to me,' Mary said as she brought in the dessert of stewed apples and custard. 'Which reminds me, Jim, did you manage to have a word with Tom Gresham about all this?'

'As a matter of fact, I happened to bump into him in the Dolphin at lunchtime. Apparently he was at a meeting there, something to do with the cuts in rural policing.'

'So what did he say?'

'I'm afraid he didn't seem very interested but said he would "pass it on", whatever that means.'

'Oh well, at least we've done something,' Mary said as she offered round the cheeseboard.

Jim poured the last of the elderberry wine into Matt's glass, suggesting they should have coffee in the sitting room, and while the two women were in the kitchen, he explained that Tom Gresham was the local police inspector who seemed to be more interested in the night time movements of the stable's big horsebox than the information Kate had given him. 'Apparently there have been a number of complaints about the large vehicle travelling the narrow lanes late at night. The only explanation I could give him was that their business was transporting horses to and from the continent and that it was probable that some of the long journeys would inevitably end at night, and for the same reason they would have to start a journey in the early hours of the morning. I got the impression that he thought there might be more to it than that but didn't have time to explain any more. I haven't mentioned it to Kate and I don't want her to get involved, but I thought I would tell you as your cottage overlooks the manor and you might spot something if there is anything out of the ordinary going on down there.'

'It would help if I knew what I was supposed to be looking for,' Matt told him, then added, 'You don't suppose it could have anything to do with what Kate told us, you know, about the drugs and stuff?'

Before Jim could offer an opinion, the women entered the room, Mary with the tray of coffee and Kate carrying the painting which she propped up on the mantelpiece for all to see. Mary was ecstatic and gave a loud 'Wow!' while her husband nodded in appreciation and, with a grin, said, 'Looks as though we might have a real equestrian artist with us. Well done, you've caught him exactly.'

Matt felt slightly embarrassed, but at the same time gratified by the compliments and said that he had done his best and was glad that they liked it. He was particularly satisfied that Kate was pleased and he could now regard his efforts as suitable reparation for the unfortunate events caused by Bullet in the sand school. He also hoped her attitude towards him might thaw a little.

Matt opted out of the discussion on what sort of frame and where it should be hung. Eventually it was decided that it should have an old-fashioned gilt frame and the best place for it would be over the sitting room mantelpiece. When asked for his opinion, Matt grinned and told them that he was chuffed that his work was going to take pride of place , 'Like a Stubbs in a stately home.' The remark caused general laughter and the friendly atmosphere helped Matt relax and enjoy the rest of the evening.

It was ten o'clock before anyone looked at their watch. Kate was the first one to do so and Matt took the hint. 'It's getting late,' he said, looking at her. 'I ought to be getting back, and I know you have an early start in the mornings.' She nodded and said she had to be at work by six o'clock as the Pony Club Hunter Trials were on tomorrow and there were three ponies at livery with them that would have to be ready to box up at eight o'clock.

Matt started to get out of his chair when Mary said, 'As I've said before, you can always stay here the night. We've plenty of room.'

'Thanks very much, but I have to get back. The old dog needs looking after, but in any case, I'm not sleeping too well with this,' he nodded towards his damaged ankle, 'and I wouldn't want to disturb you in the night if I have to get up and hobble to the bathroom.'

'The bedroom's en suite,' Mary said, hoping he would change his mind.

'Mother!' Kate said no more, but got up and went into the kitchen to get her coat.

Her father called out. 'Hold on, Kate! I'll run Matt home if you want to get to bed.'

She shook her head. 'That's all right, Dad. It's only a couple of miles and anyway, I feel a bit responsible. It is after all my painting that has been delivered and the least I can do is take Matt home.'

Matt smiled and felt strangely elated, then realised why: it was the first time, as far as he could remember, that she had used his first name without a prompt.

Jim stood up and waited until Matt, with the occasional grunt and grimace, got to his feet, then he and Mary walked through to the kitchen with him to bid farewell. Kate was already warming the engine of the Fiat as Matt crossed the yard, his limp barely discernible.

As they made their way back to the sitting room, Mary remarked that she was pleased that the young man seemed so much more at ease this time.

Her husband smiled. 'Well, I suppose he's just getting to know us. Just you and me, that is. I'm not so sure about our beloved daughter.'

Outside the mist had lifted, there were no clouds and, directly above them, the stars were clearly visible. As Matt looked up, he noticed that in the direction of Torbay and Exeter, they were blurred by the glare of urban life. He got into the car feeling glad that he was living in the countryside and pitied the unfortunate town dwellers who would have no idea what the sky looked like on a night such as this.

Kate backed out and turned the car towards the gate. A full moon sent shadows across the lane as she drove slowly towards the village. 'It's a bit eerie,' she said, 'full moon, shadows. Bit like a scene out of *Dracula.*'

Matt chuckled. 'Don't worry, I'm not going to take a bite out of your neck … not unless you want me to,' he immediately regretted the words as Kate, staring straight ahead, said, 'I don't think so.'

The rest of the journey continued in silence until they reached Coombe Cottage. Matt knew there was no point in asking her to come in for a coffee, so he simply thanked her very much for the lift and the enjoyable evening and wished her a safe journey home. On her part, she thanked him again for the painting and said they had all enjoyed his company. As he got out of the car, he considered asking her if he could repay the hospitality by taking her out for a meal but decided that a rejection was almost inevitable, and so simply closed the door and waved goodbye.

CHAPTER 14

It was a busy morning at the stables. The two ponies were groomed and, with manes plaited and legs bandaged, they were ready to be loaded into the two-horse trailer when the two young girls and their mothers arrived at eight o'clock. Ivan would drive them to the course then return with the Land Rover to resume his duties before collecting them again as soon as he received a call from one of their mobile phones.

One of the ponies had been difficult to load, and Kate breathed a sigh of relief as the trailer disappeared out of the gate towards the drive followed by the parents' vehicles.

At nine o'clock, she went into the tack room and brewed herself a mug of coffee. At half past, Ivan returned and was seen walking across the yard towards her in earnest conversation with Greta. Kate was not involved in the horse trading business and was not particularly interested in what was going on between Ivan and Greta until he raised his voice and almost shouted, 'But our clients the other side will not be pleased. You must do something.' At that point, they noticed Kate sitting at the back of the tack room and, as they walked away, she heard Greta say that she would look for an alternative.

Wiggy arrived at ten as usual and, without being told, began his daily task of mucking out. Kate got the impression that the boy was 'out of sorts' as he carried out the work without his usual chatter. She left him alone to get on with it until just before the lunch break when she went over and asked him if everything was alright.

'No, it bloody isn't,' he replied angrily.

'Why, what's wrong?'

'They're only going to stop me coming here, that's what.'

'That's the first I've heard,' Kate said irritably. 'Why would they want to do that?'

'Dunno, I just got hauled up in front of bloody Burford and got told I'd been shooting my mouth off and that this would be my last day here.' He stopped what he was doing and looked at Kate. 'Just when I thought I'd landed a nice cushy number. Shit! … Sorry.'

'But you've only been here a couple of days. I don't understand. I'll have a word with Mr. Burford and see what I can do.'

Wiggy shook his head. 'If I were you, I'd keep well out of it. Don't you worry about me, it's my mate, Jacko, you ought to be concerned about. He's going to have a really tough time if our friend Beaky gets to know that I've passed on what Jacko knows about him.'

'Beaky being the chap who brought you here the other day?'

'That's right, he's threatened … never mind. Let's just say things might get a bit uncomfortable back in there,' he nodded towards the manor.

'I'm sorry, I thought you were getting on so well here. It's a shame.'

'I'm sorry too. I've felt almost human here,' he gave a wane smile, 'even though I've spent most of the time shovelling shit.'

Kate patted him on the shoulder. 'I'll tell you what, when you come back this afternoon, you can have a ride on the roan cob in the corner box. He's quiet and it will give you a bit of a send-off. I'll find you some kit.'

'Great!' Wiggy's eyes lit up. 'Thanks,' he paused. 'I haven't ridden since I was about ten, but I suppose it's like riding a bike, you never forget.' He grinned, put his tools in the barrow and wheeled them back to the shed. Kate recalled where she had heard that phrase before.

As he went out, he passed Greta coming in the opposite direction, obviously in a hurry. She handed Kate a piece of paper with a name and address written on it. 'Three ponies coming from these people,' she said, pointing to the paper. 'They should be arriving tomorrow morning. I will give your father a ring to get them signed off fit and they will be going to Deauville the next day.'

Kate was rarely, if ever, told the destination of the animals sent abroad but she did know there was a racecourse at Deauville and wondered what three Dartmoor ponies would be doing there. She looked at the names and address, which meant nothing to her. 'I thought you said there were some thoroughbred broodmares in the pipeline to go?'

'Nien. The owners have told us that the delays caused by the migrants at the Channel Tunnel means too much delay for such expensive animals, so they have cancelled. It is a nuisance but,' she shrugged, 'we have to keep the ball rolling, as you say.' She started to walk away, stopped and turned back. 'Oh, yes, I forgot to tell you. The Wiggins boy will not be coming again.' She gave no further explanation and Kate did not ask but wondered if, by any chance, Greta had overheard the conversation between herself and Wiggy and had reported it back to her husband. In which case, why had they taken no action against the man Wiggy called Beaky? She decided to take Wiggy's advice and keep out of it.

*

'Come in.' William Burford was sitting at his desk in the main office when the man who called himself Kevin Able walked in. Two weeks had passed since the Wiggins incident had made it necessary to remove the youth from his work at the stables. It had been a worrying time. 'Take a seat, Kevin,' Burford frowned and indicated the chair opposite. For a moment, he seemed preoccupied with the notes he had scribbled on a piece of paper in front of him. When eventually he did speak, there was anger in his voice. 'I don't know what this is about, Kevin, but I had a phone call this morning from a certain Detective Sergeant Price from the local constabulary. He's on his way here and told me a few things had come up that he would like to discuss with me. Didn't say exactly what but hinted that they had some concerns and he would like to clear up the matter before it went any further,' he paused. 'I hope you haven't been up to your old tricks, Kevin. The last thing we need is the powers that be poking their noses into our affairs. I'm sure you are aware that Gainsborough House here at Lidstone is an experiment as far as the penal system is concerned. One false move and the whole thing could fall apart round our ears.'

'What's it to do with me?' Able shifted uneasily in his seat. 'I ain't done nothing wrong, least ways not 'ere.'

'So there's nothing in the glasshouse you wouldn't want the law to see?'

There was a long pause before he replied, 'Well, I suppose I might have got a few sprigs in there, just for me own use, o'course.'

'Get rid of them,' Burford said angrily looking at his watch. 'You've got until four o'clock, and don't forget the scent of cannabis lingers. Make sure you deal with that. We've got much more valuable business on hand without being done for growing weed. You understand?' There was a brief nod from Able as Burford continued. 'And one other thing, it seems that someone has dug up your murky past. Greta tells me that young Wiggins has been shooting his mouth off in the stable yard.

'Bloody Jackson Williams,' Able muttered angrily.

'Sorry?'

'Oh, nothin'.'

'I just hope that's not the reason for the visit this afternoon because if it is, despite of the fact that you are a vital part of our business, it will be curtains for you, I'm afraid.'

There was a smirk on Able's face. 'So what about my connections up in the smoke? Who's going to deal with them?'

Burford closed his eyes and leant back in his chair. 'I dare say we'll manage but it won't be easy.' He waved a hand to indicate the interview was over.

At five minutes past four, an unmarked black BMW drew up outside the front door of the manor and a young man wearing a grey suit with a pink shirt but no tie got out. Burford went out to meet him and was relieved to see the policeman was in plain clothes. They shook hands and he led him into the office. 'Please take a seat.' Price made himself comfortable and took a file out of his briefcase and carefully placed on the desk in front of him. Burford settled himself behind his desk. 'How can I help you?' he asked.

The sergeant hesitated. 'Well, sir, we are aware that you are not entirely responsible for what goes on at the stables, but nevertheless I thought I should bring the complaints to your notice before taking up the matter with your wife.'

The look on Burford's face was one of puzzlement tinged with relief; this was not going to be as bad as he had feared. 'Sorry, I'm not with you.'

Price opened the file and took out a sheaf of papers. 'I'm afraid we've had a number of complaints concerning the movement of your large horsebox along the narrow lanes hereabouts. Most relate to journeys late at night, mainly the noise and lights through the village in the small hours of the morning. I was hoping you could have a word with your wife and perhaps they could reorganise their schedule to give less offence to the locals.' He leant forward and placed the papers on the desk.

Burford suppressed a smile and did his best to look serious. 'I will most certainly do what I can, Officer, you can take my word for it.' They stood up and shook hands. 'If you like, we can go and have a word with Greta now,' Burford said as they walked back to the car.

Price shook his head; his experience of confronting disgruntled horsey women had not been particularly enjoyable in the past, and Greta Burford had a reputation for being difficult. 'I'm quite happy to leave it to you, Mr. Burford,' he said as he got into the driving seat. Burford noticed he had a smile on his face as he drove away.

Burford decided that his best course of action would be to have a quiet word with his wife before discussing the problem with Ivan. Greta was bent down feeling the tendons of the off hind leg of the big grey horse which she had tied up outside the loose box. Her husband waited until she had finished the examination before telling her what the policeman had said. She straightened up, looked at him and shook her head. 'God, that is all I needed. We have a contract cancelled, and now this. It is going to make things very difficult, you realise that?' She lowered her voice as Kate and Wiggy walked past with the roan cob. 'Our clients will not like it, and Ivan will, as they say, do his nut. You had better send that Able fellow to talk to our main source and see if we can arrange something.'

'Okay, but it will take a day or two to arrange, so in the meantime, we'll wind things down a bit and then see if we can sort something out.' He gave her arm a gentle pat, told her not to worry, and set off back to the manor.

*

Kate watched him go through the gate. She had overheard some of the conversation, but apart from the realisation that Greta was very upset, it had meant very little to her.

She turned to Wiggy who had divested himself of his overalls and was now sporting a slightly too large riding hat and a pair of slightly too small jodhpurs which Kate had rescued from the back of the tack room. 'Okay, young man we'll put you up in the sand school and see how you get on.'

The cob stood patiently while Wiggy put his foot in the stirrup and swung his leg over to sit confidently in the saddle. Kate knew the roan was bomb proof;it belonged to a well-off middle-aged widow called Melissa Thompson, who now lived in a smart sea-view flat in Torquay. She came to hack out, usually once a week, and was happy to have the old horse ridden by anyone in the stables, as long as it was confined to a quiet jog round the lanes; no hunting, as she was anti.

Kate let the cob walk round her on a lunging rein and, once satisfied that Wiggy could actually ride, she allowed him to trot round the school on his own, noting, with a grin, that although he seemed to be 'all arse and elbows', the boy was comfortably rising to the trot and was able to push the animal into a controlled canter without too much trouble.

After half an hour, Wiggy looked as though he was ready to call it a day so she indicated for him to walk into the centre and dismount. 'Not bad,' she told him. 'I'm sorry you've got to leave us, we could do with a bit more help around here.'

They walked back to the stable yard where Greta was standing looking not too pleased with what she saw. 'This is not a riding school, Kathryn,' she said. Kate knew she was in trouble when her boss used her full name. 'The boy was here to work, not enjoy himself,' Greta continued, 'so get that animal back in its box and the boy back to the manor.' She turned abruptly to greet Ivan who had delivered his charges back to the yard. One of the girls was proudly showing off the rosette she had won as she led her pony down the ramp and into its loose box.

Kate helped Wiggy unsaddle the cob. 'Don't worry about Greta,' she told him. 'She's upset about something.'

'I bet she is.'

'What do you mean?'

'You know what I told you the other day? I bet Beaky has been found out and her old man is in trouble.' He grinned. 'Wow! I must tell ol' Jacko.'

'I think it's more likely to do with contracts being cancelled, so don't start jumping to conclusions.'

Wiggy was still grinning as he carried the saddle and bridle back to the tack room and hung them up in their allotted places. He sat down on the rickety wooden chair in the corner and removed, with some relief, the ill-fitting hat and tight boots, pausing for a moment to consider his situation. He was sure the reason he had been banned from the stables was because he had opened his mouth and somehow what he had told Kate had gone further than he thought; he wondered how that would affect his future, particularly with regard to Beaky who must know that Jacko had passed on the information. It suddenly occurred to him that he had put his friend in possible danger – would Beaky take it out on poor old Jacko? Slowly, he pulled on his overalls and wellington boots and prepared to go just as the young girl with the rosette came in and pinned it to the felt-covered board to join the coloured array of rosettes already there. She smiled at him as she left. Wiggy studied the display for several seconds before selecting an oldish-looking blue rosette to stuff into his overall pocket. A souvenir, he told himself – old habits die hard.

As he was leaving, Kate met him at the gate, and smiling, pushed a ten pound note into the top pocket of his overalls. 'Just a small thank you,' she said. He pulled it out, looked at it and shook his head. 'We're not supposed to have money,' he told her, folding the note carefully and transferring it to his trouser pocket.

'Why not? I thought you would have a tuck shop or something.'

'I suppose they think it's too much of a temptation. You know, nicking and all that. With some of them in there, you wouldn't feel safe with a few quid in your pocket.'

'I can take it back if you like.'

He grinned. 'Don't worry, I can take care of myself, and you never know when a bit of cash might come in handy.' He turned and, with a wave, walked briskly towards the manor. He went in the rear entrance and almost bumped into Beaky who was just coming in from the garden.

The man stepped in front of him, turned, grabbed him by the arm, and said through gritted teeth, 'I'm watching you, Wiggins, and that mate of yours, Jackson Williams. You can tell 'im from me, if I get any more agro from the pair of you, he'll be the one I'll be gunning for. Have you got that?'

Wiggy grimaced with pain and, suppressing the urge to yell, simply stared back defiantly. Eventually Beaky let go of his arm and stomped off in the direction of the main office.

'Take a seat, Kevin.' Burford nodded towards the chair opposite as he sat down at his desk. He settled back twirling a pencil between the thumb and forefinger of his right hand, obviously enjoying the alarmed look on Beaky's face. It was several seconds before he spoke. 'Well, Kevin, which would you like first, the good news or the bad?'

'The good,' Beaky said without hesitation.

'Okay. It appears that our friend from the fuzz was predominantly interested in the night time movements of our transport. Changing schedules and pick-ups will be a damned nuisance but probably something we can sort out without too much trouble, although problems at the Calais end of the tunnel don't make the job any easier. It means you may have to go up to town and have a word with your friends in London before long. It hasn't come to that yet but be prepared.'

'And the bad news?

'It's possible that your reputation has leaked out a little further than we thought. Sources tell me that a question was asked at police HQ concerning the possibility of cannabis being grown here. Fortunately, the idea was dismissed as improbable and it was decided that no action would be taken, but it's a warning shot and I suggest you take greater care in the future not to raise any more suspicions. Is that clear?'

Beaky said nothing. He was thinking of ways to prevent things getting worse. Eventually he asked who or what was his source of information.

Burford smiled. 'I thought you knew that Mrs. Gaymer's daughter works in the office at police headquarters. Quite useful, you must agree.'

Beaky nodded but he was not smiling.

The door opened and Greta came in, followed by Ivan. 'Come in, please. Don't bother to knock.' Burford remarked sarcastically, then turning to Beaky, he said, 'I thought we ought to have a get-together and decide where we go from here.'

Beaky nodded and looked at Greta who, in turn, looked at Ivan who sat, arms folded, slightly behind them. No one was in any doubt where the answers would come from. The three of them waited patiently for the little man to speak. 'I think,' he said, 'I think we must complete those things we have started. If we do not, there are others, as you well know, who will try to take our business from us.' There was another long pause. 'I have worries that, maybe, we are being watched.'

Burford leant forward and looked intently at the speaker. 'You don't mean that artist chap at the top of the hill?'

'Ya,' Greta said. 'Ivan has often seen him looking down this way with binoculars. Isn't that so, Ivan?'

'Yes. He clears bushes away to see better, and my driver says that he watches at the gate sometimes.'

Burford shook his head. 'Come on, Ivan, don't you think you're getting just a little bit paranoid about this fellow. He's probably just a straightforward holidaymaker admiring the view, and as for watching the gate, well, anyone walking the lane might do that.'

'He has been there too long for holiday,' Ivan said.

'Was it your blokes who did his cottage over?' Beaky asked.

Ivan shrugged with an air of whatever. 'We needed to know how he would react.'

'Well, 'e obviously don't scare easily.'

'You see my point. Firstly, he stays. A holiday person would pack up and go home, I think. Secondly, if not an ordinary holidaymaker, what is he doing there, and more importantly, who is paying him?'

'Are you suggesting he works for one of the agencies?' Burford asked.

Ivan shook his head. 'I am not so sure about that. I am thinking more that one of our friends from the other side of the channel might like to take over our business and is looking for the right time to move in.'

'How on earth could they do that?' Burford was looking anxious.

'Simple. You know as well as I that one wrong move and the clients lose confidence, and when that happens, they go elsewhere.'

'So where does that leave us now?' It was Greta's turn to sound alarmed.

Ivan got up and began slowly pacing round the room, his thumbs in his belt and a look of intense concentration on his face. 'It is important,' he said, stopping to face the other three, 'that we keep the right side of local police, which means reorganising things at this end to make sure we do not disturb local population by too much noise in hours of darkness. To do this, I think you load your horses afternoon or late evening, in any case before dark, and then take the back road to Haldon Forest and pick up our consignment there. That road is not much used at night, but in any case no one is going to be too concerned to see a horsebox there as there are many stables on that stretch of road. Then we do reverse on the way back, delivering in the early hours and arriving home in daylight. You can do, Greta?'

'If you can sort it out with the clients, I see no problem.'

'Good, we all know the importance of your horses in this business and they are something our rivals do not have.'

'No, but it won't take 'em long to find some other way,' Beaky told them. 'I know only too well how them sniffer dogs work.'

Burford gave him a wry smile. 'We all know about your unfortunate experience, Kevin, but we are trading on a somewhat higher level than your erstwhile little business.'

Beaky shrugged and was about to say something when Ivan butted in. 'Which brings us to the case of artist man,' he said. 'I do not like being watched. I think we have to persuade him that he is wasting his time and should leave us to get on with our business,' he grinned, 'which is, of course, horse trading.'

CHAPTER 15

'Had another visit from that woman selling tack and rugs this morning.' Kate was standing next to her mother in the kitchen as she began preparations for the evening meal.

Mary looked surprised. 'Didn't think she would be back so soon; can't be more than a couple of weeks since she was here last time. She must think folks round here are made of money.'

'I reckon the company she works for, what's it called, Posh Tack? I reckon it's scraping the barrel, coming all the way down here from the other side of Dorchester to flog a few saddles and second-rate winter rugs to the likes of us. Mind you, they can't be doing that badly. The Lidstone Arms isn't cheap and I'm told she doesn't spare herself when it comes to the best on the menu.'

'Well, I've only seen her once when she came here that time looking for you and she certainly didn't look like a young woman who overindulged. In fact, I thought she was as thin as a rail.'

'I suppose at the beginning of the hunting season, she's hoping to make a few sales. Good luck to her, but I don't think Greta will be putting much business her way, although I'm pretty sure Ivan might try. He took quite a shine to her last time, and as far as I could see, she didn't do too much to discourage him.'

'Good Lord! Well, I suppose it takes all sorts, but Ivan? Yuk!' Mary made no secret of her opinion of that ghastly little foreign man.

*

Matt sat down at his usual corner table in the restaurant area of the Lidstone Arms. The regulars from the manor were grouped at the bar ordering drinks. There were four of them: the usual three he knew as Burford, his wife Greta and the man called Ivan, but tonight they were also joined by a thin man with long fair hair who looked as though he had been 'pulled through a hedge backwards' as Matt's father would have said. The man wore a grey T-shirt and a pair of faded jeans ,which sagged round his backside as he leant against the bar.

His working boots still had traces of mud on them as though he had been called to the meeting at short notice. In contrast, his three companions were dressed for an evening dining out. Greta was dressed in a fawn woollen jumper and tartan skirt, Burford in a brown tweed suit, complete with something that looked like a regimental tie, while the ex-jockey was resplendent in a dark green corduroy jacket and matching trousers, but no tie. They were obviously engrossed in an animated discussion which was punctuated by occasional glances towards Matt as glasses were filled before they eventually moved to a table at the far end of the room.

Matt sipped his pint of local Dartmoor ale as he waited for the waitress to bring his steak and chips. The room was beginning to fill with people, mainly couples, looking for good traditional food at reasonable prices, and the Lidstone Arms offered both. When his meal arrived, he was too busy helping himself to the chips and peas from their respective bowls to notice the arrival of a young woman at the bar opposite. When he eventually looked up, he was taken with her rear view as she perched on a stool facing the bar. Matt stopped eating and began to appraise the figure from the bottom up, literally; what he saw seductively filled the tight black skirt and, for a second or two, caused his concentration to dip before taking in the rest of the tall, slim torso which was crowned with a head of dark wavy hair that trailed well below the shoulders of the matching jacket. He waited impatiently for her to turn so that he could see the face, and when she did, he was not disappointed. Dark eyes with long eyelashes glanced in his direction and well-shaped lips gave him a brief smile before she picked up her glass of red wine and moved to a table in the window alcove midway between himself and the four from the manor. He guessed her age to be about the same as his own and wondered what a smart young woman like her was doing in rural Devon: obviously in business of some sort, but what? He was intrigued.

Ivan was also watching the woman between bouts of intense conversation with his companions until eventually food arrived and the blonde man got up and walked out. The remaining three relaxed and began to eat: Greta, a chicken salad with vegetables, no chips; her husband, beef curry; and Ivan, a goulash. Intent with their meal, no one noticed that the woman in the alcove had been pointing her iPad in their direction and at various other diners, including Matt. He was only made aware of the fact when he looked up and saw her take a snap of the bar; the landlord grinned and waved. She raised a hand back and Matt concluded that the woman had been here before and was possibly connected with the hotel trade or perhaps a company advertising hotels and restaurants. He did his best not to look at her but became aware that she was looking at him. He sipped his beer and concentrated on the menu as he contemplated a dessert.

It was not until he had demolished the bread and butter pudding that Matt ventured a glance towards the alcove. The woman had finished her meal and was sipping a black coffee; she gave him a smile, and to his pleasant surprise, got up and with coffee in one hand and iPad in the other, walked over to his table. Matt struggled to his feet and raised a questioning eyebrow, but before he could say anything, she apologised for interrupting his meal and asked if she could join him for a few minutes.

'By all means,' Matt almost blurted out, 'please take a seat.' He attempted to move round in order to assist with the chair but was too late; she was already seated before he got there. He resumed his seat and tried to look as though this sort of thing happened to him frequently. He waited for her to speak. She crossed her legs and leant forward, her elbows on the table.

'Mr. Winsford, isn't it?' she asked with a smile. 'I was hoping to meet you ever since I arrived three days ago.'

'Oh?' Matt couldn't think of anything else to say.

'Yes, I understand that you are an artist specialising in animal portraits. Is that right?'

Matt cleared his throat and swallowed hard. 'Yes, I suppose you could say that, but how did you know?'

'Oh, I have contacts with the stables at the manor and the girl there mentioned that you had painted her horse. I wondered if you could do a similar job for me, but a dog this time?'

'Yes, of course.' Matt hoped he did not sound too eager. 'What sort of dog is it?'

'It's my Border Terrier. She's getting on a bit and I thought I'd like to get it done before … well, you know.'

'I do indeed, I'm a bit in the same boat. My old dog's a Border cross but it hadn't crossed my mind to paint the old bug … sorry.'

She laughed and held out a hand. 'My name is Serena Brent.' They shook hands.

'Matt Winsford.'

'When would it be convenient for me to bring Dot to see you, Mr. Winsford?'

'Matt, please.' He smiled. 'That's an interesting name.'

She laughed. 'Short for Dotty. We had a lot of problems when she was a puppy. Fortunately, she's grown out of her silliness and has settled into ripe old age.'

'I wish mine had'. He told her about the episodes with Kate and Harry.

'Oh, yes, they told me about that when I was at the stables. In fact, that's how I heard about you.'

'You're into horses then?'

Yes, in a way. I represent a company selling saddlery and tack. In fact, most things to do with horses, including riding gear.'

'Oh.' Matt sounded surprised and she laughed.

'I try not to appear too horsey when I'm off duty.'

'Well, I must say, you have succeeded.' There was an uncomfortable pause before Matt cleared his throat and asked if she would like a drink.

'Thank you, but I have some work to do and need a clear head.' She tapped the iPad. 'But to get back to the painting, would you by any chance be available tomorrow? I'd like to get started as we're only here for a few days. Oh yes, I forgot to ask how much you charge?'

He wanted to say he would always be available and he would do the painting for nothing, but instead he told her that they could meet any time tomorrow morning and the fee started at a hundred pounds, but depended in the size of the canvas.

She nodded in agreement and suggested ten o'clock at the cottage.

'That will be fine. I'll make sure old Bullet is well out of the way otherwise there will be chaos.' He grinned. 'I never had him de-knackered, and the old devil is still full of testosterone when nature calls.'

'I'm sure we'll be okay.'

'I hope so.' He regretted the words as soon as they were out, but it was too late. She grinned and stood up. He did the same. She lifted up the iPad. 'Got to send some stuff off before tomorrow.'

'Yes, I noticed you were taking a few photographs. Thought they might be to do with your work.'

She frowned then told him they were to send home to her mother who always wanted to know what sort of place she was staying at. Matt was glad they were for her mother and not a husband or boyfriend. He stood watching as she walked past the manor house table and could not help noticing the way the man in the green corduroy suit eyed her. He suppressed the urge to go over and intervene, but instead he went to the bar and ordered another beer.

It was pitch dark with a cold drizzle outside when Matt left, and he was glad his coat was warm and waterproof. He reached into a pocket for his small torch and, carrying his thumb stick horizontally, he walked on down the tarmac, determined not to limp, at least not on level ground.

Where the stony track that led up to the cottage joined the road, he paused to lean on the stick and take the weight off each foot, lifting them alternately until any pain subsided and he felt ready for the slog up the hill. Behind him, he could hear the sound of car doors banging and voices raised as the pub's customers began to leave. Car headlights flashed past while he stood between the high hedges that bordered the track, and as he looked back, he wondered how such a smart-looking woman as Serena Brent came to be flogging horse tack in the wilds of Dartmoor. Perhaps he would find out tomorrow. He took a deep breath and began the walk up towards the cottage.

The drizzle turned to steady rain as he reached the gate into the manor paddocks; it marked the halfway stage between the road and the cottage and he took the opportunity to stop and lean over it to rest his aching limbs. Below him, the lights were going out one by one, and Lidstone Manor was obscured by the rain driving across the valley. He pulled up his coat collar and was about to resume his journey when he heard something that sounded like stones rattling a few yards behind him. He turned and shone the torch down the track in the direction of the sound, but the beam was not powerful enough to penetrate very far into the rain swept darkness. He considered the possibility of a fox or badger crossing from one side to the other; on several occasions, he had noticed well-used animal paths crossing the track. Reassuring himself that this was the likely cause, he stepped out of the gateway and was about to continue his journey when a sudden strong grip on his arm spun him round.

A voice growled, 'Right, let's 'ave yer wallet and mobile, Mr. Arty-farty, you get me?' At the same time, a punch landed in Matt's midriff causing him to double up with pain. The torch was wrenched from his hand and thrown over the hedge. The balaclava helmeted man grabbed Matt's coat by the lapels and drew his face closer. 'Let's 'ave yer phone and wallet, then you can just pack your bleedin' bags and bugger off!' He expected his victim to nod in agreement, but the nod he received smashed into his face. At the same time, a knee slammed into his groin, and as he doubled over, a blow behind the ear sent him sprawling in the mud. Matt had only used his unarmed combat training for real once before and that had been against a fit and wiry Afghan; this overweight opponent was a doddle. As the big man went down, Matt became aware of another figure, taller and leaner, stepping forward towards him. The figure hesitated for a moment, just long enough for a blow on the side of the covered face from a well-aimed thumb stick to deter any further action. The man screamed and sank back into the hedge as his companion on the ground scrambled to his feet. Matt ran for the gate and scrambled over, but did not run across the paddock; instead he turned immediately to his left, ran a few yards and rolled into the water-filled ditch that ran along the hedge. He heard one of the men call out a name which sounded like Ken, or was it Kev? He was telling the other to come on.

As he expected, the two men followed him over the gate but ran straight on, presumably to catch up with him and finish what they had intended to do. As Matt lay there, the near-freezing water seeping through his clothes, he tried to work out what was happening. Two men had tried to mug him. They seemed to know who he was and where he lived; this was not a random mugging, it had been planned. Then there was the reference to packing up and leaving, but why? And was there any connection with this and the trashing of the cottage? He waited two more minutes before crawling back to the gate and climbing over. The old strategy of feigned retreat and waiting ambush had worked, except, of course, there was no ambush.

The rain eased as Matt jogged purposefully up the track towards the cottage. He needed to get there before the muggers; there was always the chance that they would try again. Breathless, he paused at the cottage gate to make sure he was alone, then quickly ran to the back door, unlocked it and went in.

Bullet jumped up to greet him as he switched on the light. The cottage was exactly as he had left it and he gratefully reached for the bottle of Bushmills and poured himself a generous helping, which he drank neat in two gulps. He was shivering violently, partly from the cold and partly as a result of the trauma he had just gone through. He quickly went round the cottage to make sure all the doors and windows were secure, then told himself he was being paranoid and that there was no way that a pair of such incompetent crooks would trouble him again. Nevertheless, as he stripped off his wet clothes and stepped under the hot shower, he decided he would sleep downstairs on the sofa.

*

It was midnight by the time the two wet, dishevelled figures appeared at the rear entrance to the manor to punch in the entrance code and make their way along the corridor to the main office. Burford was sitting at his desk, his jacket draped over the back of his chair, his collar unbuttoned and the tie loose round his neck. He leant back and eyed the two men as they came in.

'Well? Did you get it?' he demanded. There was no reply. 'Well?'

It was several seconds before the big man shook his head.

Burford stood up and walked round the desk towards him. 'I take it that's a no,' he said angrily. 'So what went wrong? It couldn't have been that difficult! Bloody hell, there were two of you.' He turned to Beaky. 'Dear God, man, what have you done to your face?'

The next few minutes were spent recounting the night's events. Burford listened, disbelief showing on his face. 'All you were supposed to do was relieve the man of his wallet and phone, no bloody fisticuffs, just frighten the bugger into giving them to you.'

'He don't frighten,' the big man said. 'An' it was 'im what started it. I just give 'im a tap in the guts and 'e did that to me.' He pointed to his bruised and swollen nose.

Burford shook his head. 'What a bloody cock-up.' He turned to Beaky. 'So what have you got to say for yourself, Kevin?'

Beaky gingerly touched the now purple bruise on his face. 'We didn't reckon on 'im being that good, I suppose.'

'Alright, alright.' Burfords said in a tone of resignation. 'Now I'll have to think of another way to get the information we want.' He pointed to the man with the bloodied nose. 'You, out, and get that nose fixed in the morning.' The man muttered something inaudible and moved towards the door. Beaky made as if to follow. 'No, not you, Kevin. We need to talk.' Burford returned to sit at his desk. He picked up a pen to twirl between his thumb and forefinger and indicated Beaky to take the chair opposite. There was a moment's silence before Burford confessed that the idea of stealing the wallet and mobile was not his.

Beaky grunted. 'I bet I know whose idea it was,' he said. 'What did Ivan expect to gain from it?'

'Information. Apparently he, or one of his associates, has the know-how to hack into a mobile and find out who the man has been in contact with. It would have told us exactly who he is and who he is working for.'

'What if it's blocked by a password?'

'Well, at least that would tell us that he is probably under cover for somebody.' Burford threw the pen down onto the desk. 'To tell you the truth, I'm getting fed up with this whole bloody business, and if it wasn't for Greta, I'd pull out tomorrow.'

Beaky said nothing. He had long ago suspected that the ex-jockey knew something about his employer's wife but he had no idea what.

Burford leant forward on the desk. 'I don't want any more mistakes, Kevin, so just watch your step. You understand?'

CHAPTER 16

Matt woke before dawn with a splitting headache. He had worn a thick woolly sweater over his pyjama top but he still felt cold under the thin blanket he had brought down from the bedroom. He sat up and, with a groan, began to massage his right ankle. The swelling had gone down but it was still throbbing from the previous night's exertion. He hoped it was down enough to get his riding boot on; the prospect of riding Molly again was comforting. After the recent traumatic events, a quiet ride across the moor was exactly what he needed.

He got up, switched on the light, then walked over to turn on the fire and stand with his back towards it as he contemplated what to do. He had already decided that reporting to the police would be a waste of time: nothing had been stolen, he could not identify the attackers and in any case, what happened was just a blur in his mind; he found it difficult to remember exactly how it happened and what the attackers had said. He knew what would happen if he did report it, some overworked bobby would come up, take a few notes, and that would be the last he would hear of it.

He went into the kitchen where Bullet was already whining to go out. 'You'll have to wait, old boy' he told him as he filled the kettle for his morning coffee. The climb up the stairs was not as painful as he had anticipated and the fact cheered him up a little as he felt in the cupboard drawer for his painkillers. Two pills were washed down with a glass of tepid water that had stood on the bedside table for the last two days. He sat on the bed and waited until the drug kicked in before going into the bathroom.

His refection in the mirror showed a large bruise on his forehead and, as he shaved, he wondered how he would explain it to his visitor later that morning. The thought of that visitor boosted his moral as he went back into the bedroom to find suitable clothes to impress her, ending up with best moleskin trousers, check shirt and a smart red sweater his mother had sent the previous week. He would not be doing any painting, just photographs and a few sketches, so there was no fear of his smart get-up being splattered with paint. He looked at himself in the full-length mirror on the wardrobe door: passable, except for the purple swelling on his forehead; he tried combing his hair forward but it was too short to cover the wound.

Next, he tried on his flat cap and pulled it down at the front as far as he could. It looked ridiculous, and in any case, he couldn't wear the thing in the house, even though artists were supposed to be eccentric when it came to their dress code. In the end, he decided he would have to cobble together some sort of explanation for the wound; it was either that or tell the truth, for he was in no doubt his guest would notice it and almost certainly be curious.

He could hear Bullet still whining in the kitchen as he finished dressing and hurried down the stairs to open the back door. Outside the sky had cleared. It was just getting light, and as he walked the dog onto the lawn, he could see the lights in the stable yard below coming on one by one. Kate would be somewhere down there beginning her day's work. The thought gave Matt a strange feeling of contentment. She was doing a job she obviously loved and not many people could say that. Suddenly he heard the revving of an engine and the big horsebox backed into the yard and the ramp was let down; obviously they were going to load some horses. He could not make out how many animals were to be led in and was tempted to go back inside and fetch his binoculars, but before he could, the ramp was pushed back up and the vehicle began to move slowly out of the yard and down the drive.

Breakfast was a matter of cereal, toast and coffee, eaten as quickly as possible to give plenty of time to tidy the place up, particularly the makeshift studio which he had not thoroughly sorted out since it was trashed. He made sure the landscape of the moor and Hound Tor he had painted as a Christmas present to his mother was prominently displayed on the easel. He was pleased with it and hoped it would make a suitable impression on his client. He also had photographs of previous work on his laptop and they included the portrait of Harry. An hour after breakfast, he was confident that he was ready.

The white van arrived promptly at ten o'clock and drew up behind the Volvo in front of the cottage. As he opened the front door, Matt was surprised to see that the Serena Brent who got out was now very different from the Serena Brent he had met in the Lidstone Arms. She was dressed in a grey polo-necked sweater, red puffa waistcoat and tight navy blue breeches tucked into brown knee-high boots that had two buckles at the top. Her hair fell in a single plait down the front of her right shoulder, secured by a blue ribbon tied in a bow. She smiled as Matt walked out to greet her. 'It looks like the weather is going to be kind,' she said, looking up at the few scudding clouds in an otherwise blue sky.

'That's always a bonus when you have to take photographs,' he told her, and there was an awkward pause before Matt asked if she would like to come in for a coffee while they discussed what she would like him to do. 'Don't worry about the boots,' he said as she began to undo the buckles. 'We'll go straight into the kitchen. I'm used to clearing up in there.' He led her through and indicated a chair at the small breakfast table. She sat down and watched as he filled the kettle and switched it on.

'This is very nice,' she said, looking round. 'How long have you been here?'

Matt thought for a moment. 'Must be nearly two months now,' he said as he took two mugs out of the cupboard and placed them on the table. 'Do you take milk and sugar?'

'Just milk please, Matt.'

She had remembered his name. Matt was chuffed. He smiled broadly as he poured the water onto grounds of the instant coffee. 'So, what would you like me to do?' he asked as he sat down opposite her. 'Do you want a whole body or just a head?' He showed her examples on the laptop.

'Oh, I think the whole dog would be nice.'

'Any particular background?'

'No, I'll leave that to you.'

While they were drinking their coffee, Matt became acutely aware of the scent of perfume emanating from the other side of the table. It had been a long time since he last sat close enough to a woman to sense the intimate aroma of expensive toiletry. It took several seconds to bring his mind back to the painting.

'Okay, when you're ready, we'll get started. I've shut my old dog in the sitting room out of the way. You can probably hear him whining already.'

Serena Brent smiled and said she hoped Bullet would not get too distressed. She was looking at him intently and, to his dismay, he knew the reason why. 'You look as though you've been in the wars.' *That phrase again.* Matt was about to reply when she added, 'Don't tell me, you walked into a door.'

He grinned, glad to be let off the hook. 'Yes, something like that,' he told her. 'Shall we get on now?' He picked up his camera and a large sheet of plastic before leading her to the back door.

They went outside and Serena reached into the front of the van, lifting out the small brown dog, which she began stroking gently while Matt walked onto the lawn and laid out the plastic sheet on the grass. He then got down and lay on his stomach, which caused an involuntary groan as his bruised muscles pressed on the hard surface. He looked up and saw a questioning look on her face and was not sure whether it was because of the groan or the fact that he was flat on the ground. He grinned. 'You have to get down to their level otherwise the image is distorted, so if you can get Dot to stand still about six feet away, I'll do my best to get some shots.'

Serena did as she was asked, but preventing the little terrier from darting off into the bushes proved more difficult and so it became necessary to put her on a lead.

'Don't worry,' Matt told her. 'I can paint that out, and the collar too if you want.'

Matt took a dozen or so photographs and selected four he thought would be useful. 'I'll get them printed up and use them as references, but I like to make a few sketches as well which means I get a good look at the animal, particularly the eyes. Most important the eyes, just the same as in humans.'

They went inside and into the studio where Matt gave instruction to place Dot onto the small table while he worked in pencil and charcoal. When he was satisfied with the sketches, he showed them to Serena who nodded appreciatively and told him she was confident that he would do a good job. A few minutes spent choosing the size of canvass, and the initial procedure was over.

They stood beside the white van that displayed the words POSH TACK in blue over a red prancing horse on the side. Dot was placed carefully back onto the passenger seat while her owner thanked Matt for his trouble.

'I have to thank you,' he said. 'I have to confess, I don't get many customers out here. In fact, you are only the second since I arrived.'

Serena gave him a knowing smile. 'Yes, so I've been told, but from what I have seen of your work, I'm sure I won't be the last.'

Matt felt a glow of satisfaction and was reluctant to end the conversation. He turned his attention to the vehicle, standing back to studied the logo. 'Do you sell clothes as well? Because I could do with a decent pair of breeches and a better hat.'

'Yes, that would be no problem. If you could give me details of colour and sizes, I'll see what I've got with me and, if necessary, get them sent from headquarters. You see, I don't often get asked for men's clothes.'

'Okay, then. Breeches, fawn, thirty-two inch waist. Hat, black, of course, size seven and a half.'

'Good, I'll make a note and give you a ring.' She reached for her notepad and pen and wrote down his mobile number. 'Is that all?'

There was a pause before Matt almost blurted it out. 'No, actually. I wondered if I could take you out to dinner sometime?'

Her smile was reassuring. 'I think that would be very nice, thank you.'

Matt nearly said wow, but managed to restrain his enthusiasm and simply asked when it would be convenient for her.

'I've got to sort out some orders, including yours, with the office this evening, so would tomorrow be okay with you?'

'Brilliant. Is there anywhere particular you would like to go? I would like to get away from Lidstone but I'm not very clued up when it comes to places to eat round about here. Do you have anywhere you could recommend?'

Serena thought for a moment. 'There's a pub called The Queen Bess in a small village the other side of Newton, which has a reputation for good food. I have a customer not far from it and they swear by the quality of the meals. Would you like to try it? Don't think you will need to book as it's mid-week.'

'Sounds just the job. What time shall I pick you up?'

'Better aim to eat about seven, that way we'll be sure of a table, so would six-thirty be okay?'

He wanted to say that it would be more than okay, but restricted his reply to a simple 'yes.'

Matt watched the white van disappear round the bend in the road towards Lidstone before returning to the cottage to let Bullet out onto the lawn. The old dog, excited by the new provocative scents that clung to the damp grass, ran backwards and forwards from the back door to the spot where Matt had photographed Dot. Matt watched with amusement. 'I know just how you feel, old feller,' he told him. He looked at his watch; just time to jog old Molly out for an hour before lunch. He changed back into his old jeans and sweater and managed to get both boots on without too much pain.

A phone call made sure Mary Lethbridge would be expecting him; she told him how pleased she was that he was fit again and said she would get the horses in ready for him. He liked Mary; she reminded him of his own mother, always ready to lend a hand, particularly when it came to horses. Mary would take the trouble to get both animals into their boxes, knowing that if she left Harry out in the field on his own, he would charge around like a mad thing trying to get to his companion with the risk of some unforeseen injury. It was not unknown for horses in that situation to jump a fence.

True to her word, Mary had not only stabled the animals but was busy grooming her mare when Matt arrived. 'I think the old girl has missed her jaunts out with you,' she told him with a smile. 'I reckon she's put on a bit of weight in the last few weeks. You'll need to let out the girth a couple of holes,' she told him as he put the saddle on Molly's back.

Matt decided to take the route avoiding the village and go to the lane that led through the forestry. He would ride past Spud Wannacott's mobile home in the hope of seeing the old man. He wanted to let him know he was literally back in the saddle and to thank him once more for his help.

As Matt eased Molly through the narrow hunting gate and onto the track that led up to Spud's home, he saw him standing just inside the wood, the lurcher by his side, a bundle of nets over his shoulder and a brace of rabbits in his right hand. There was a small wooden box on the grass beside him. He raised his hand as Matt approached.

'Glad to see you're getting back to normal,' he called out.

Matt pulled Molly up and grinned. 'Don't know about normal, but things are definitely looking up.'

'Glad to hear it.' Spud picked up the box by its leather strap handle and walked towards the rider.

Matt was glad his hat covered the bruise on his forehead: it would have been a lot more difficult to explain away under the old man's scrutiny. He indicated towards the box. 'I see your ferret has been doing its job.'

Spud nodded. 'Mrs. Spreyton asked if I could get her couple of rabbits for one of her dos next weekend. She's treating the shoot members to one of her game pie suppers. I've already delivered the pheasants and venison so the rabbits will make a nice addition.'

'No myxomatosis about then?'

'Not this year. Myxy seems to come in cycles: bad a couple of years ago down to hardly any this year. I'll be out again tomorrow so if you fancy a bunny for supper, I'll drop one in tomorrow evening if you like?'

'Thanks, but I've got a date so will have to miss that treat.'

The old man raised an eyebrow. 'Anyone we know?'

Matt grinned. 'None of your business, my friend, but I will tell you it's not Kate Lethbridge.'

'Oh.' The old man sounded disappointed.

'Glad I've seen you anyway. Just dropped by to thank you once again for your help and advice, and ask if you would come and have a bite and a drink with me sometime. I'm not much of a cook but I dare say I can rustle up something reasonable. I've got a fresh bottle of Bushmills, and if you go a bit over the limit, you can kip in the spare room. How does that sound?'

It took several seconds before the ex-sergeant major replied: there was a note of hesitation in his voice. 'Don't want you to go to that much trouble,' he nearly said 'sir'. 'I'd be just as happy with a pie and a pint in the Lidstone Arms.'

Matt was surprised by the old man's reticence and for a moment was not sure what to say, then the realisation dawned. 'Come on, Spud, don't be daft. I'm not inviting you to the bloody officers' mess, just Mr. Matthew Winsford's temporary pad for a pint and a natter,' he leant forward and lowered his voice. 'Honestly, Spud, I would appreciate it if you would come. I owe you and it would give me a lot of pleasure to return the compliment.'

The old man smiled. 'If you put it that way, I suppose I can't very well refuse.'

'Brilliant. How about next Saturday?'

'Sorry, first shoot of the season. I'll be looking after the beaters for the colonel.'

'You say when then.'

Spud thought for a moment then suggested the following Thursday. He was going to have a day with the foxhounds and would appreciate not having to cook for himself that evening.

'Good, gives me a bit more time to work out what to put on your plate,' Matt replied with a grin. 'Sevenish be okay?'

The old man nodded. 'I'll look forward to it. Take care.' He added the latter comment as Matt nudged Molly into a canter up the track towards the far gate onto the lane. He had to dismount to open and shut the gate, then had to lead the mare a few yards along the lane to find a bank that he could use as a mounting block. Once back in the saddle, he was agreeably surprised that the effort had not caused the expected pain in his injured leg and ankles. Nevertheless he walked Molly for the next mile until they reached the gate beside a cattle grid that led onto the moor.

They trotted along a well-used bridle path that led down into a wooded coombe where a moorland stream cascaded over granite rocks between oak and ash trees already bare of leaves. He found a place where the stream bed flattened and a muddy track crossed onto the open moorland; sheep scattered as Molly snorted and broke into a steady canter up the track towards a clitter of boulders that marked the crest of the hill. Matt pulled the mare up and stopped to take in the view. From there, he could look down into the valley where the tower of Lidstone Church was just visible through the trees; the yellows and browns of autumn still clinging to the branches of the beech and sycamore trees that lined the road to the village. Under the lee of the boulders, the world around him was silent; the only sound he heard was the croak of a raven as it glided down towards a larch plantation on the edge of the moor. He realised it was a world he wanted to live in: a world free from the brutality of organised warfare where death could come in so many different ways. He had experienced all that in Afghanistan and was glad that the campaign had ended and his erstwhile comrades were coming home.

He turned Molly and the mare walked steadily down the hill to where a narrow moorland road wound through open country to another gate and cattle grid. From then on it was a gentle walk past the larch plantation then through an easily manageable gate onto a bridle path that led down to the Lethbridges' fields. Matt had ridden that way many times and found it a very convenient route to avoid coming back through the village.

He looked at his watch as he rode into the stable yard: it was a quarter to one, and as he dismounted, Kate's Fiat drove in and pulled up outside the back door of the house. She got out and walked over to him as he led Molly into her loose box.

'Have a good ride?' she asked, leaning over the loose box door.

'Yes, thanks,' he patted the mare's neck. 'I think we're both glad to get going again.'

'Good, I know Mum will be pleased.' She turned to walk away. 'See you,' she called out. Matt hoped so.

Bullet was waiting for him, bouncing up and down on the passenger seat. 'Next time, you can come with me, you old bugger,' he told him as he got in the driving seat and started the engine.

At that point, he saw Kate hurrying from the back door. 'Mum wants to know if you would like to come for supper tomorrow evening?'

He looked up and smiled. 'Thank her very much but tell her that unfortunately I have a dinner date that evening.'

'Oh?' It sounded like a question: if so, there would be no reply.

Matt simply told her to tell Mary that he would be delighted to come any other time. As he pulled out of the yard, a glance in the rear-view mirror showed Kate frowning as she walked back to the house.

CHAPTER 17

Kate watched the white van draw into the stable yard. It was the second time that week and she wondered what Greta had ordered, but it was Ivan who walked briskly over and began chatting to the sales woman who was busy unloading a number of horse rugs. The woman stopped what she was doing and stood facing the him, the difference in height very apparent: she was at least a foot taller than the ex-jockey. Kate heard her tell him that she had a date that evening and so could not dine with him at the Lidstone Arms. He turned abruptly and walked away, his face betraying his anger and frustration.

Kate cast her mind back to the previous day and Matt Winsford's reason for not coming for supper – was there a connection, or was she putting two and two together and making five? For some reason, she felt miffed.

Ivan went out of the yard to where the Scania horsebox was parked. Kate could see him examining the vehicle's tyres which prompted her to think that another long journey was in the offing. She had noticed that the excursions to the continent had become less frequent recently; they were still trading regularly within the UK and Ireland, but the foreign transactions had come down to less than twice in the last month. One thing that had improved as far as she was concerned was the fact that animals were no longer arriving or departing after dark, so there were fewer late nights and early mornings when she had to turn out to load or unload horses.

She wished Ivan and Greta would spend more time helping her with the daily stable work. There were six full-time liveries to cope with, not to mention watching over the seven DIY liveries to make sure the owners stuck to the stable's rules, which ranged from car parking, feeding routines and mucking out, to the use of the sand school and grazing paddocks. She wished they could have kept the boy, Wiggins, in the yard; the extra pair of hands had proved very welcome during the short while he was with them. With a shrug, she turned, picked up the barrow of muck she had been taking to the heap, and spent a thoughtful five minutes forking the soiled straw and droppings into a neat pile.

She loved her job in spite of the long hours and low pay, but she was beginning to wonder just how much the horse trading side of the business was contributing to the income of the stables as a whole. Her father had often commented that the quality of the animals bought and sold was not always up to the standard one would expect, bearing in mind the high cost of transporting them to and from the continent. Kate just hoped they would stay in business and keep the stables going.

Her next and last task centred round the three liveries that were going hunting the next day. Her priority was Peter Ridley's bay horse. She knew the lawyer was meticulous when it came to turn out and she was keen to ensure he would not be disappointed. All three animals had been brought in from the paddock and their rugs removed ready for a thorough grooming to remove any traces of mud. Peter's bay, in particular, had a tendency to roll as soon as he was turned out, and so a muddy face and ears were almost inevitable. Kate spent the next hour grooming and combing manes and tails before rugging up the animals prior to giving them their concentrate mixture and hay nets. It was dark by the time she finished at six o'clock: it would mean an early start tomorrow to get the three animals' manes plaited, a final grooming, then saddles and bridles polished, all by ten o'clock.

As she reached the yard gate, she heard Greta coming in the opposite direction from the old gamekeeper's lodge where she and her husband lived. The look on her face betraying controlled anger as she asked Kate if she could spare a minute as there were a few things that needed sorting out. Kate had no choice but to follow her back towards the converted loose box that served as the yard office. Greta switched on the light. 'I will bloody murder that Ivan one of these days,' she said, pulling out several magazines and newspapers from the drawer in the old table that served as a desk and handing them to Kate. They were cuttings from local newspapers together with the latest *Horse & Hound* magazine. 'We have to find at least three suitable horses to go the day after tomorrow,' she said angrily. 'Ivan says it is urgent but why he gives such short notice, I do not know.'

'Did he say what sort of animals he was looking for?'

'No, he just say at least three, preferably hunter types over sixteen hands.'

Kate was mystified. 'I suppose he's got suitable buyers at the other end?'

'I have no idea. He tells me not much these days. All I know is we have to find them, so I must ask you to go through the advertisements this evening and pick out any, fairly local, that you think are possible so that I can start phoning tomorrow. Best to look for more than one at the same address. We shall be very short of time and may have to get them delivered unseen.'

Kate did not know what to say except 'right' in a drawn-out tone of disbelief as she picked up the magazine and put the other advertisements between its pages. 'I'll see what I can find and let you know first thing tomorrow.'

For the first time, Greta smiled. 'Good girl. Sorry to leave it all to you but we have people coming to dinner tonight at the lodge.'

Kate thought she did not sound too happy about that and decided the best thing to do was to change the subject. 'I see you've bought some rugs from Posh Tack. Are they any good?'

'Have not had time to look at them yet. Why do you ask?'

'Might get one for myself.' Kate paused. 'What's she like?'

'The rep? Seems a nice enough girl. Needless to say, Ivan is very struck with her and tried to, how you say, get off with her. He did not get very far and she was curious to know where he came from as she could not place his accent.'

'And did you tell her?'

'Yes, of course, it is no secret that he comes from Poland. She said his English was very good and he must have been over here quite a long time. I told her I did not know. If you want to contact her, the phone number is pinned up on the board there.' She pointed to the small noticeboard on the wall above the table.

'Thanks, I was just interested, that's all.' Kate looked at her watch. 'Better go, you know what my mum's like when it comes to being late for meals.'

'I had heard,' Greta said with a grin. 'Your father has the same problem sometimes when he is working here. So, some horses by nine o'clock tomorrow please.'

Kate drove the Fiat slowly through the village as a cold mist swept down from the moor cutting visibility down to a few yards. Nevertheless she was able to see Matt Winsford's Volvo parked outside the Lidstone Arms and she thought she knew why it was there.

*

Matt waited in the bar where Tom Slater was busy polishing glasses and preparing for the evening's main influx of customers which would be in about an hour's time. Sounds of frantic activity could be heard coming from the kitchen every time the swing door was opened by one of the young waitresses coming through to ensure the tables were laid and reserved. The landlord explained that members of the local hunt were having their annual supper there and they were expecting about sixty diners that evening so service might be a bit slow. The thought that Serena would probably be glad not to be dining at Lidstone that evening gave Matt added confidence that she would enjoy his company somewhere else.

Matt explained that he was meeting Serena Brent and they would be dining elsewhere. Slater said, with a smile, that she was very attractive and he was a fortunate young man. 'There's more than one around here that would be very glad to be in your shoes,' he added looking towards the door. 'She's asked me to keep that blighter at bay more than once.'

Matt turned to see Ivan coming towards them. The ex-jockey walked to the bar and asked for the six Lidstone Arms special pasties he had ordered that morning.

'Another trip?' Slater asked as he handed them over.

Ivan merely nodded, then he looked up at Matt and, with what seemed to be a derisive smirk, pointed to his forehead before walking back towards the door.

'What was that about?' Slater asked.

Matt showed him the bruise. 'I think he wanted to tell me something.'

At six-thirty precisely, Serena came through the door that led from the upstairs accommodation. She was wearing the same black skirt and jacket but the blouse was now pink and her open toed shoes had heels that were considerably higher than those she had worn previously. Matt turned to greet her and noticed that the shoes made her almost as tall as he was. She smiled and began to put on the knee-length fawn coat she had carried on her arm. Matt stepped forward to help her.

'Thanks, Matt. It's getting a bit chilly out there. I see you are well equipped,' she pointed to the rather tatty waxed coat that he was picking up from a nearby chair. 'That'll keep out anything nature likes to throw at it.'

Matt muttered a self-conscious 'yes' and wished he had something smarter to wear. At least his tweed jacket was respectable enough together with the moleskins and, unlike most of his contemporaries, he was wearing a tie: nothing special, just plain blue and white stripes; he had always avoided the regimental and old-school tie versions.

As they walked towards the door, it suddenly burst open and four smartly-dressed men pushed through, almost colliding with the couple. Matt heard his name called and looked up to see Spud Wannacott grinning at him. For a brief moment, the boisterous conversation stopped as eyes turned towards Serena. Spud gave a 'thumbs up', then, with a grin and a nod, ushered his three companions towards the bar.

'I recognise that old boy,' Serena said as she watched the party order their drinks. 'He bought some boots from me the other day. He seems to know you.'

'He does the gardening at the cottage and it turns out we share a few things in common.'

'Like what?'

'Oh, just an interest in the countryside and country sports.' Matt felt slightly uncomfortable at the question and concluded that his date for the evening was a very inquisitive lady. He opened the passenger door of the Volvo revealing a clean white table cloth draped over the seat. He smiled apologetically. 'I'm afraid old Bullet leaves a lot of dog hairs around, hence the cover-up.'

Serena smiled as she eased herself into the seat, showing a gratifying amount of leg in the process. 'Don't worry, I'm used to it. Dot is just the same.'

The journey to the Queen Bess involved the negotiation of a series of narrow lanes which in places were barely wider than the car. 'Bit tricky if you meet someone coming the other way,' Matt commented. 'Passing places seem to be few and far between.'

Serena chuckled. 'You should try it in a Ford Transit. I can tell you it's one of the reasons I don't like making deliveries after dark.' Matt had difficulty visualising her delivering at any time, let alone after dark. He wondered how a good-looking young and obviously intelligent woman came to be doing that job anyway.

It seemed a very long time but was in fact less than half an hour by the time the lights of a small village loomed out of the darkness. Serena instructed him to slow down as they approached the whitewashed building a few hundred yards beyond the last of the village lights. The entrance to the car park was narrow but the parking area itself was spacious with just a handful of vehicles taking up the spaces.

'Not too many in tonight so we should be okay for a table,' Matt said as he parked the Volvo next to a mud-splattered pick-up.

The young man behind the bar greeted them with a broad smile. 'How can I help you, folks?' Matt asked for a table for two. 'No problem, sir, help yourself.' He indicated towards the dining room where vacant tables outnumbered those that were occupied. 'You can leave your coats over there, if you like,' he pointed to a row of coat hooks adjacent to the dining room door, 'and the toilets are through the green door at the far end.'

Matt thanked him and helped Serena with her coat, glad he had left his own tattered garment in the car. He chose a table for two in the corner and asked her if she would like a drink before they ate. She replied that she would just have a glass of wine with the meal. He nodded. 'Me too, except mine will be a pint of the local brew. That'll last the evening for me. Don't want to go over the top, if you know what I mean.' He realised he was beginning to sound nervous and hoped it didn't show.

Serena declined a starter and, when the young bearded waiter came, ordered the duck a l'orange with salad and new potatoes while Matt settled for the game pie, chips and vegetables. Serena asked for a glass of

Chardonnay while Matt opted for a pint of local ale, asking the waiter to recommend a brand. 'Would you like to come to the bar, sir? We have four to choose from.'

Matt nodded self-conscientiously, excused himself and went back to the bar. As he returned to the table with the pint glass of amber liquid, he could not help noticing that he was the only male, as far as he could see, who was wearing a tie. The thought crossed his mind that he should make an excuse to go to the loo and take it off.

'Jail Ale,' he told her with a grin as he sat down, and as though reading his thoughts, she said, 'Like the tie. Is it special?'

She's noticed.

'No, just something my sister sent me last Christmas. I suppose it seems a bit out of date these days but I was brought up to believe a man was not properly dressed without one.'

'Well whoever told you that was correct in my opinion.' She smiled and for some reason it made him feel like a small schoolboy who had just got something right. She took a sip of the wine.

'Is it chilled enough?' Matt asked.

She replied that it was very nice. There was an awkward period of silence before she asked, for a second time, how long Matt had been at the cottage. 'A bit over two months now.'

'It's in a very attractive position overlooking the valley. I bet it's in demand during the summer.'

'That's right. I used to stay there with the family when I was a boy. Dad knows Colonel Spreyton from the days when they used to show South Devon cattle.'

'So your parents farm here?'

'No, in Hertfordshire. Very different from this part of the world.'

The conversation was interrupted by the arrival of the food, much to Matt's relief – things were getting a bit close to home.

Nothing more was said until Matt had cleared his plate and, while he waited for Serena to finish eating, he ventured to ask how she came into that business of selling saddlery.

She answered without looking up. 'It's a family business.'

'Oh, I see, you mean it's your family business.

'My parents.' She finished the last mouthful, placed the knife and fork on the plate and sat back with a satisfied, 'That was very nice, thank you. Matt got the distinct impression that no more would be forthcoming on the subject of the family business.

He smiled. 'Don't thank me, thank the chef.'

For dessert, Serena chose the pavlova and Matt decided on the chocolate cheesecake.

'So how long are you planning to stay at Coombe Cottage?' Serena was concentrating on the plate in front of her as she spoke.

'Probably until Christmas. It depends on how things go.' He anticipated the next question. 'I'm recovering from a road accident and can't go back to work until my leg has completely healed.' He hoped that sounded plausible and would satisfy her curiosity: he was wrong.

'That sounds as though the people you work for are pretty good when it comes to looking after their staff.' She swallowed the last spoonful, put her elbows on the table with the wine glass in her hands, and looked at him intently. 'It must have been quite a nasty accident to put you out for so long. Are they a local firm?'

Matt was beginning to panic. Should he tell her the truth? How would she react? His dilemma was solved by a plump, blonde girl in a fawn trouser suit.

'Hello, Serena,' she called out as she entered the restaurant area. 'Fancy seeing you here.' She walked over to their table while her escort, a stocky young man with a weather beaten-face, chose a table.

Although Serena smiled, Matt got a distinct feeling that she was slightly annoyed as she introduced him. 'Matt, this is Mavis, the customer I mentioned. She has a riding school just down the road from here. Mavis, this is Matt Winsford.'

Matt stood up and offered his hand, which the girl took hold of with a firm grip. 'Nice to meet you, Matt.' She glanced at Serena then back to Matt with a knowing smile. 'I'll leave you to it then. See you next week, Serena?'

'Yes your order should be through by then, probably next Wednesday. I'll give you a ring.'

'Thanks. I better get back to Rod. You know him, he doesn't like being kept waiting.'

Serena nodded as Matt returned to his seat. 'Sorry about that. She's a lovely girl but likes to get her nose into everything.'

Lovely girl or not, Matt would have happily bought her a drink just for saving his bacon. He quickly changed the subject away from his supposed accident. 'Can I get you another drink?'

Serena declined and said she wanted to keep a clear head as she still had a few things to finish that evening before she could turn in, 'and I've got a long drive tomorrow,' she added.

Ah well, that puts the kibosh on any romantic follow-up, Matt thought as he took a sip of his beer. 'Do you often work late?' he asked.

'It's a matter of finding enough time in the day,' she replied, 'and I can use the Lidstone Arms Wi-Fi in the evening if I want to get on the net.'

'Sounds as though you have a very busy life. I hope there is enough time for some coffee.' Matt grinned and called over the waiter.

Serena leant across and put a hand on his wrist. 'I'm sorry, Matt. I know it sounds as though I'm making excuses, but things have been a bit hectic recently and I've got a lot on my plate.'

'Well I suppose Christmas is not that far off so you are bound to be busy.'

'Oh, yes, that's right.' She sounded pleased that he understood.

'Will you be here over the festive season?'

Matt shrugged. 'As I said, it depends.' He wondered why she was interested and hoped she might be about to invite him to join her for Christmas: but it didn't happen. Instead she said something about the pleasure of being at home with the family. It suddenly occurred to Matt that she might be probing, in the politest way, to find out if he was married or had a partner. She had never asked and, likewise, he had never told her. Perhaps now was the time.

'I don't have any close attachments to go to other than my parents.' He almost blurted it out. It sounded an odd way of putting it but at least it got the point over as he felt a gentle tap on his wrist. It was very much like his mother telling him he'd been a good boy.

The coffee arrived and the conversation turned to more mundane matters such as the welcomed fall in the price of diesel and the fact that many of Serena's customers felt her prices should fall accordingly. 'I suppose the fact is they can get stuff more cheaply on the internet, but as with most things, it's the quality that counts, particularly when it comes to horse tack.' Matt smiled in agreement as she slipped effortlessly into her sales pitch.

It was ten-thirty when Serena glanced at her watch. Matt took the hint and nodded to the waiter. Having settled the bill, he fetched Serena's coat and held it while she put it on. There was a murmur of appreciation as they walked through the lobby and out into the chilly air.

The drive back to Lidstone was uneventful as fortunately all of the sparse traffic was going the same way as they were. As they drew up outside the hotel, Matt knew there would be no point in suggesting a possible coffee at the cottage; he had already been made aware that was not on. He turned towards her to say goodnight and was agreeably surprised when she leant across and kissed him on the lips.

'That's for a lovely evening,' she told him. 'Perhaps we could do it again sometime.'

Matt nearly said, 'Yes, please,' but managed to modify the reply to, 'I'll look forward to it.' He got out, opened the passenger door and escorted her to a rear door that led to the upstairs rooms.

She turned and looked at him, and for a moment said nothing, then she gave his hand a squeeze and said, 'You're a one-off, Matthew Winsford, did you know that?' He didn't know what to say as she turned back and walked up the stairs.

*

Back at the cottage, Matt poured himself a whiskey, switched on the fire and slumped into the armchair with his feet out towards the warmth. Bullet came and put his head on his thigh, and as Matt gently stroked the dog's head, he contemplated the evening. There was no doubt he had enjoyed it and he was confident that she had also,but, and there was a but, there were times when he had felt uncomfortable, even inadequate. He gave a long sigh and had to admit to himself that he had become out of touch with civvy street: too many years spent abroad in predominately male company.

He drained his glass. 'Come on, old man. Time you went outside for a pee.' He carefully pushed the dog aside and stood up, the sudden pain in his left leg reminding him that he would need to take his medication before he turned in.

Outside, the sky had cleared and once more the stars caught his attention. He tried to remember the course on night navigation but could only identify the Plough and Orion before cloud drifted in from the moor and saved him agonising over any further constellations. Bullet sniffed around as usual but there were no rabbits to startle nor rats to chase. All was quiet down at the manor and the last lights had gone out with the exception of the bright permanent light at the entrance to the main house. As he watched, a white minibus drew up and a number of people got out and made their way into the building. Matt looked at his watch; it was close to midnight, probably late night revellers, he concluded. He called the dog and went back inside.

As he lay in bed, he found sleep illusive. Quite apart from his usual aches and pains, the evening in the company of an attractive woman made him realise how much his life had changed since the IED had exploded in Afghanistan and how much he needed to sort his life out. There would be big decisions to be made in the near future.

When eventually sleep came, it was fitful with confused dreams where the hot, dry winds that blew down from Afghanistan's mountains suddenly became the chilling wet drizzle of Dartmoor's bleak landscape. He woke in a cold sweat and reached for the painkillers that, with a glass of water, were always at hand on the bedside table. It always took about half an hour for the drug to take effect and, when it did, he usually fell into a dreamless sleep, but tonight was different: his romantic advances had been successful, they were both in his bedroom and were about to make love, but the person sitting on the other side of the bed was not Serena Brent. It was Kathryn Lethbridge.

CHAPTER 18

Jacko watched the arrivals as they walked through the main doors and into the hall of the manor. It was the third Sunday of the month; visiting time. Most of the parents came in the yellow Lidstone minibus, which picked them up at Exeter's St. David's railway station. A few had their own transport, notably Wiggy's mother in her black Range Rover, which she always parked in full view of the occupants and staff. Jacko was not anticipating anybody coming to see him; the train journey from London was too expensive for his mother to find the money out of her monthly benefits. Coming by coach was cheaper, but the journey time was much too long for his baby brother.

Visitors and inmates were reunited in the main classroom where they could sit opposite each other at separate tables. Three members of staff were always present and anything seen to be passed between the two parties was immediately scrutinised and, if necessary, confiscated. Any classified drugs or legal highs would put the intended recipient's release back at least six months. Tobacco and cigarettes were also banned, much to the annoyance of inmates and visitors alike.

From where he sat in the adjoining common room, Jacko could hear the chatter and noise of people coming and going, the scrape of chairs being moved, even some laughter mixed in with the general hubbub. He was not alone; Robson was also there watching the football on the large screen television in the corner. He, as far as he knew, had no parents or relatives, and the only likely visitor would be one of his many foster parents, and that was extremely unlikely.

The recorded game between Manchester United and Chelsea ended in a draw, and Robson clicked off the set and turned to Jacko. 'Well, at least bloody Man U didn't win this time.' Jacko shrugged; football was not his strong point.

'Ah, see ya diven have nobody come again,' the Geordie commented.

'My mum's got better things to do.' Jacko was not in the mood for conversation and decided to go up to his room, leaving Robson to click the television back on and surf the channels.

Jacko took off his trainers and lay on the bed staring at the plaster moulded ceiling. It was a rare opportunity to be alone, to have time to think without the continual banter of his roommates. He had found the discipline of Lidstone difficult at first, but had to admit to himself that, if it were not for the presence of Beaky Andrews, this place was not that bad; Beaky's threats made it much worse. He was worried not for his own safety, but for the hint of possible harm to his mother. He felt he should try and warn her but that would be impossible without somebody knowing as mobile phones were not allowed and he knew that the once a week phone calls on the landline were listened to by Mrs. Gazeley in the office; Burford had warned them of the fact on the day they had arrived. On top of that, he had a shrewd suspicion that any letters would be read as they had to be handed into the office for posting unsealed, but then, neither he nor the majority of his fellow inmates wrote letters. Their preferred means of communication would be texting but because of the 'no phones' rule, that was out. Beaky was bound to get to know he had grassed on him and that could mean more trouble in the future. He was due to work in the gardens again on Monday and the thought frightened him.

Jacko had no way of knowing that events had already moved on and the hints that Wiggy had dropped in the stable yard had filtered out to people who would make life much more difficult for the horse traders.

*

Burford paced round his office, hands behind his back and a worried look on his face. There was a knock on the door. 'Come in, Kevin.' Beaky gave his boss an enquiring look as he walked across to stand by the desk and wait for Burford to stop his pacing and resume his seat behind it. 'Sit down, Andrews.'

Beaky was immediately alarmed: it was the first time anyone had used his real name since he arrived at the manor.

Burford leant towards him, elbows on the desk and the now familiar pencil gyrating nervously between his fingers. 'It looks as though we are well and truly in the shit this time,' he said angrily. 'No, I'll rephrase that. It looks as though *you* are truly in the shit. Word has got out concerning your past and our contacts in the smoke don't like it. For one thing, it makes our business vulnerable, and for another, it could bring the law down on us like a ton of bricks. We've had a visit from a couple of our friends from your part of the world and they are very concerned,' he paused. 'I'm afraid, old chap, your days here are numbered so we've arranged for you to go, with as little fuss as possible, back to where you came from. I'm sure your friends up there will find you something useful to do. You'll be catching the eight-thirty train from Exeter tomorrow evening. Okay? In the meantime, it's important that you carry on as usual on Monday so as not to raise any suspicion, and whatever you do, keep your mouth shut. Is that understood?'

Beaky said nothing but simply glared at Burford for several seconds before finally telling him to go to hell. 'You knew everything about me before you asked me to come down 'ere and join you lot. So what's changed? You'll still need me contacts in the smoke.'

'What's changed is that somebody has put your track record out there,' Burford said, pointing the pencil towards the window.

Beaky Andrews slumped back in his chair. 'Bloody Williams,' he muttered through gritted teeth, 'I'll kill the little bastard.'

*

Monday morning dawned bright and frosty. The morning run was brisk and, for Jacko, interesting. It was the familiar route through the wooded valley and up the winding road towards the moor, the same route where Barrel Bennet had flaked out going round the steep bend, and had not been discovered for over three hours. It was an incident that stuck in his mind as they toiled up the slope, their breaths hanging in the air while Griggs yelled out instructions to keep together.

As they left the shelter of the trees, a chilly wind suddenly hit them and Jacko was glad that they were now allowed to wear blue tracksuit trousers instead of shorts, and although the red T-shirts gave little protection from the cold, nevertheless he felt a glow of anticipation as they crested the hill and began the run back down towards Lidstone village. He was beginning to form a possible plan of escape.

The work day began with a lecture from Beaky on the merits of well rotted manure in the soil. Jacko leant towards Wiggy and whispered, 'That's shit talking shit.' They both giggled.

'What's that, Williams?' Beaky was staring at Jacko as he walked towards him and, for a moment, the youth thought he was going to get thumped, but at the last moment Beaky stopped short and said, 'I don't want no more agro from you, Williams, so just watch it.'

Jacko sat staring straight ahead, carefully avoiding any eye contact, but the look on Beaky's face told him that he had not heard the last from the man: he would have to be more careful in the future.

The day's tasks included cutting the last of the cauliflowers, the usual weeding chores and finally digging in of the manure Beaky had been talking about. The whole process bored Jacko; he much preferred the time spent in the machinery shed messing about with old cars and bits of farm machinery.

After the midday break, the group reassembled as usual in the big shed and waited for their instructor. After a quarter of an hour, they began to amuse themselves with an improvised game of football, suggested by Jacko, using cauliflowers as balls. By the time half an hour had passed, they were getting bored with the game, mainly because the cauliflowers disintegrated too rapidly and there was a general feeling of guilt at the growing pile of inedible vegetables.

It was after half past two before Beaky eventually arrived and, when he did, it soon became obvious that he was in a bad mood, made much worse by the sight of the mangled organic footballs.

'What the bloody hell's been goin' on?' he yelled. 'Just 'cos I'm a few minutes late, this happens,' he pointed to the green heap. 'Whose idea was it?' Nobody spoke but eyes turned towards Jacko who immediately recognised the half-vacant stare that told him the man was high on drugs. Beaky walked up and grabbed him by the arm. 'Right you, in the shed,' his voice vibrated with anger. 'The rest of you, bugger off back inside. That's it for today. I'm fed up with the lot of you.' He dragged Jacko into the shed and slammed the door.

It was pitch dark as Jacko struggled to free himself from the hand that clawed into his arm. Suddenly a fist smashed into his face, causing him to yell out in pain; this was followed by a viscous blow to his stomach. He crumpled to the floor and lay still, waiting for a kick that never came. Instead his assailant yelled, 'Bastard!' and walked out, slamming the door behind him. Jacko curled up on the floor and groaned, the groan ending in a choking sob: he was crying for his mother.

The rest of the group drifted back to the manor and gathered by the main office, waiting for someone to tell them what to do. It was Burford who found them.

'What's all this about?' he demanded. 'What are you doing here when you should be out in the gardens?'

'Mr. Able's done a bunk,' someone called out from the back of the group.

'What do you mean done a bunk?'

Wiggy stepped forward. 'He told us to come back inside, sir, then he just walked off and left us.'

Burford thought for a moment before telling them to go up to their rooms and wait.

It was not until Wiggy was sitting on his bed that he realised his roommate had not been with them outside the office. He was on the point of going back down to tell someone when the bedroom door opened and Jacko stumbled in. Wiggy got up and helped him to his bed.

'My God, what the hell's happened to you?' he asked when he saw the bruise on Jacko's face.

'Beaky duffed me up,' Jacko wiped his eyes on the palms of his hands so that Wiggy would not notice that he had been crying.

'What are you going to do about it?'

'Nothin.' He stretched out on his bed and clasped his hands over his injured stomach. 'Least, nothin' you want to know about.'

'What do you mean nothing I want to know about?'

Jacko did not reply but lay still, gazing fixedly at the ceiling.

'Come on, man, you can tell old Wiggy. I'd love to see you get old Beaky in the shit, so tell us before the others finish their stints and come piling in.'

There was a long pause before Jacko sat up and turned towards his roommate. 'I've got to get home,' he said quietly.

'What! Don't be daft. You'll only get yourself into a load of trouble if you try to do a runner, and you'll get caught for certain. It's a long way to London and there's no way you're going to get on a train.'

'I could hitch.'

'Up the M5 and M4. Are you kidding?'

Jacko put his head in his hands. 'He threatened to do something to my mum. I've got to get home somehow.'

Wiggy sat down beside him on the bed. 'I reckon you're making a mountain out of a mole hill, as my ol' dad would have said. Blokes like Beaky are all talk and no do. I reckon if you told Burford what's happened, there' a good chance they'll chuck the sod out and that'll be the end of it.'

Jacko shook his head. 'No, you don't understand, it ain't him I'm worried about, it's his mates back home, they'll do what he tells 'em. All he has to do is promise some free weed, or, better still, something a bit harder, and they'll do anything.'

'You could tell the local fuzz and they could pass it up the line.'

'And how long d'ya think that'd take? Bloody weeks.'

'Okay, if you must make a break for it, why not just get to the nearest pay phone, make the call and get back here before anybody twigs you've gone? Just reverse the charges and that's that, simple.'

'Naah, once I got away from here, there's no way I'm coming back. I've got to get to my mum somehow, a phone call would only scare her.'

'You would be mad to try a bunk but … ' there was a long pause. 'I heard my mother say that it was ridiculous that you could get from Newton Abbot to London for less than a tenner on a coach when train fares cost ten times that.'

Jacko shrugged. 'I aint even got that.'

Wiggy stood up and felt in his trouser pocket to fetch out the crumpled ten pound note that Kate Lethbridge had given him. 'Here, take this. I've got no use for it in this rotten place so you might as well have it.' He pushed the note down the front of Jacko's T-shirt and winked. 'I still think you're bonkers, but I suppose it's worth a try.'

Jacko smoothed out the note, stared at it for a few seconds, then carefully folded it and put it in his own pocket. 'Thanks, mate. I'll pay yer back as soon as I get some dosh.'

The statement caused Wiggy to shake his head and smile. There was no way he would ever see that ten quid again; he knew it and, in all probability, Jacko knew it. He was about to say so when the door burst open and Clayton rushed in.

'Have you heard what's happened to that bugger Able, your friend, Beaky?' He was looking at Jacko who shook his head and said he hadn't a clue. 'Well I'll tell yer, me old mucker. He's been given his marchin' orders, straight up. He's off tonight, back to where he come from.'

Jacko suddenly looked scared. 'Who told you?'

'I heard ol' mother Gazeley telling Griggs, and you know the old bat listens to every phone call that comes out of Burford's office.'

'Doesn't surprise me after what happened today.' Wiggy relayed to Clayton the events of the afternoon.

'Christ, he's really blown it, man, and a bloody good riddance, if you ask me.'

Jacko lay back on the bed with his eyes closed, his thoughts turning to the possible danger to his mother and what might happen to her if Beaky carried out his threats. The man was dangerous, he knew that from his own experience, and the thought made him more determined to make a break for it and get home the best way he could. A bell rang out in the corridor but Jacko did not move. Clayton walked over and tapped his shoulder. 'Come on, man, teatime,' he looked down at Jacko. 'Bloody hell, where did y' get that shiner?' He was pointing at the coloured bruise developing under Jacko's left eye.

'I tripped over a shovel in the garden.'

'If you believe that, you can knit fog., Wiggy called out as he walked towards the door.

Jacko groaned and turned onto his side. 'I'm giving tea a miss, so just bugger off and leave me be.'

Clayton shrugged and followed Wiggy into the corridor. 'What's with him, man? He don't trip over no shovel so what's the real deal?'

'What do you think? Beaky knocked him up for letting people know what a miserable shit he is and he threatened to take it out on his family.'

'Jesus, poor little sod. No wonder he's gutted.'

'In more ways than one. Apparently Beaky did his best to punch his guts out.'

'Is he gonna tell Burford?'

'No, worse than that. He's thinking of doing a runner back home. Says he's got to warn his mother.'

'Ain't there no other way he can do that? Why don't he just ask to use the phone?'

'I don't think he wants anybody here to know about it. He's got the idea it would make things worse, particularly if Beaky got to know; and the news today that the guy is on his way back has caused poor old Jacko to panic. I tried to persuade him not to try it but you know what he's like, once he gets an idea into his head … '

'When is he planning to do it, do you reckon?'

Wiggy shrugged. 'Your guess is as good as mine, but it's going to be pretty soon, you can bet.'

Clayton shook his head. 'He'll need cash if he's going to get very far. Has he got any?'

'I gave him the tenner I got from the stables and, as far as I know, that's all he's got.'

'How far is that gonna get him? Nah, man, it's a no-no.'

'I know that, you know that, but he doesn't, or at least he doesn't want to know.'

'Any clue on when?'

'I reckon he'll go for it tomorrow. Don't know exactly when or how, but I've got an idea he might try and make it on the run tomorrow morning. You remember when Barrel Bennet went missing? Well Jacko was very taken with the fact that he was out for over two hours before anyone noticed, so that's my bet.'

'Do ya think we should help him then?'

'If he asks, possibly, but otherwise we should keep out of it.'

'You're right, man, no need to pile shit on ourselves if it ain't necessary.'

They entered the dining room where there was a hubbub of excited conversation centred round the impending demise of the gardening instructor. Wiggy and Clayton barely had time to get a cup of tea before there was a sudden hush and William Burford appeared in the doorway. He tapped on a table with his knuckles, cleared his throat and called out, 'Quiet please!' Everyone stopped what they were doing and turned towards the principal. 'You will no doubt have heard,' he continued, 'that Mr. Able will be leaving us shortly due to unforeseen circumstances.' Someone in the room laughed. The laugh quickly turned into a cough as Burford glared at the assembly before continuing. 'He has been called away to London for personal reasons and unfortunately will not be returning.' There was almost a cheer from the assembled inmates which was luckily drowned by the bell announcing the end of the tea break. Burford left the room abruptly, leaving his listeners to debate the possible causes of Beaky's abrupt departure.

The period between tea and supper was taken up by a young woman giving an illustrated talk on local National Trust houses. The audience was much more interested in her than the subject and were surprisingly well mannered considering the recent spate of exciting news. Pearson was in charge and questioned the absence of Jacko when he checked the roll and was told that he had a stomach problem and did not feel well enough to attend. Pearson had given a dubious grunt and said he would check later.

Patel had been instructed to give a vote of thanks to the speaker. He was nervous but surprisingly eloquent considering English was not his first language. After this formality, the group dispersed to their respective rooms prior to the evening meal.

When Wiggy and Clayton entered theirs, they saw Jacko was sitting on the edge of his bed, obviously feeling better than when they had left him earlier.

'How's it going, man?' Clayton asked. Jacko shook his head, stood up and walked briskly the length of the room and back before resuming his seat on the bed. Wiggy watched with some amusement and asked him what the hell that was all about.

Jacko gently massaged his stomach. 'Just want to make sure I can do the run tomorrow,' he told him.

Wiggy nodded. 'So that's it?' he said knowingly. 'You're going to do Barrel Bennet, aren't you?'

Jacko did not reply but went over to his wardrobe to check his old grey T-shirt was still there.

The evening meal was ham, egg and chips, Jacko's favourite which he ate with relish. 'Not much wrong with you, Jackson.' It was Pearson standing behind him who spoke.

Jacko stopped eating and looked up. 'No, sir. I'm okay now, just a bit of an accident in the garden.'

'Good, any more problems and you report in sick, you understand?'

'Yes, sir.' Jacko resumed eating, aware that Pearson's odd way of putting it meant he would have to see Mrs. Gazeley in the morning and tell her about his injuries. He was not going to do that.

The dessert was rice pudding, which he did not like but there was also a plate of wrapped chocolate bars on each table. When he thought no one was looking, he grabbed a handful and stuffed them into his trouser pockets, then instead of going into the television room with the rest of them, he made his way back to the bedroom to prepare for the next day.

CHAPTER 19

'What the hell do you think you were up to this afternoon?' Burford was standing over Beaky as the latter sat in the chair in front of the Burford's desk. 'It's one thing to get our little sideline in the shit but quite another to do the same for Gainsborough House. I've told you many times this is an experiment as far as the authorities are concerned and it won't take much to close it down for good. That would mean curtains for all of us – you, me, the stables, "Uncle Tom Cobley and all", and we would be lucky to get away without the fuzz round our necks.'

Beaky wriggled uncomfortably in his chair but made no response.

'Have you made contact with your people in London?'

The reaction to that question was a smug grin. Beaky liked the words *your people* – it gave him an inflated sense of his own importance. 'They're picking me up at Paddington.'

Burford nodded. 'Good. I want you to tell them that we've got everything under control here and, once things settle down, we can carry on where we left off. Is that clear?'

'So you are going to suspend operations for the time being?'

'That's right. As you know, there is one person in the vicinity we're not sure about and that visit from the police concerning the lorry was disconcerting, to say the least. So we think we should lay low for a bit and see what happens.'

'My people,' Beaky emphasised the words, 'my people ain't goin' to be very chuffed about that. We've got a lot in the pipeline to shift and we are short of time to do it.' Again, he emphasised the *we* and the grin remained as he waited for a response.

'I expect you to do your best to smooth things out, Kevin.' The tone was more mollified as Burford reached into a drawer of the desk and took out a sealed envelope which he slid over the desk top towards Beaky. 'Two hundred quid travelling expenses and your train ticket in there, Kevin. Have a good journey.' He stood up, walked over to the door and opened it with a gesture that told Beaky the interview was over and he should go.

Twenty minutes later, the yellow minibus drew up outside the front door. Beaky dragged his suitcase and backpack into the baggage space and took a seat immediately behind the driver, who was the man who had accompanied him on the ill-fated mugging. The man skewed round in his seat.

'So, you're off, Kev?' Beaky did not reply. He was in no mood for polite conversation with Jake Crump and he had no intention of explaining why he was leaving.

They travelled in silence until the lights of the A38 loomed in front when Jake suddenly said, 'I hear one of your boys had a bit of an accident in the garden.'

'Who told you that?' Beaky sounded alarmed.

'Pearson.'

'Did he say what happened?'

'No. The boy clammed up, wouldn't say.'

The sigh of relief from Beaky was just audible, causing Jake to raise an eyebrow.

By the time the minibus pulled up outside at Exeter's St. David's station, Beaky was relaxed, even glad, that his stint in Devon was coming to an end. He hated the countryside; the blank lifeless vista of fields and trees gave him the creeps and the wild emptiness of the moor terrified him. He would be glad to get back to the familiar bustle of the city where things were alive and the lights never went out, where there was money to be made if you knew the right people. He glanced at his watch: ten minutes to spare, just time for a quick coffee in the station buffet. He nodded to Jake, grabbed his case and backpack and made his way into the station. There were fewer than a dozen people in the buffet as he carried his coffee to a table near the window that looked out onto the platform.

It was then that he noticed a good-looking young man, clean-shaven, dressed in dark grey trousers and a black leather zip-up jacket, looking through the glass at him. The man smiled briefly and sat down on one of the benches outside. Beaky had a sudden urge to go out and sit next to him; good-looking men did not come his way very often, and this one definitely looked interesting. He sat contemplating a possible move as he sipped his coffee, but his thoughts were interrupted by the loud clanging of a bell and a voice announcing that the Padington train was on time and due in five minutes. Beaky got up and went out onto the platform. The young man was leaning against one of the pillars talking into his mobile phone. Probably saying goodbye to his girlfriend, Beaky thought grimly; it would be just his luck the guy was straight.

There were fewer than a dozen passengers in the second-class carriage. Beaky stowed his luggage and settled into a window seat to watch the lights of Exeter pass into the darkness of the countryside. He wished he had brought something to read; it would be a long journey to just sit and twiddle his thumbs. He looked round the carriage and was surprised and pleased to see that the good-looking young man was seated in the corner behind him on the other side of the gangway. He contemplated moving over to sit nearer but decided against it when the young man took out a book and began to read. In the end, there was nothing he could do other than settle back and doze.

He woke with a start as the lights of Taunton flashed through the window and the train jerked to a halt. The carriage began to fill with more passengers. As he watched them file in, he realised that the young man was no longer there; he felt disappointed and was about to resigned himself to a tedious and boring journey when he saw him returning with a plastic mug, presumably containing tea or coffee. Beaky rarely travelled by train and the possibility of a buffet had not occurred to him: it gave him the excuse to speak to the man.

He got up and went over. 'Excuse me,' he said, putting on his best smile and poshest voice, 'but can I ask where the buffet is?' The man indicated the direction and told him it was two carriages down. Beaky thanked him and set off. He would get his coffee and make an excuse to sit next to the young man, but when he returned, the corner seat was empty.

The remainder of the two and a half hour journey was spent thinking over his current predicament and what to do next. It had been just his rotten luck that the boy Williams had turned up at the manor. Before he had arrived, the job had gone smoothly enough. Now he had to face up to the fact that he had let the organisation down and there would be a price to pay. The thought troubled him enough to ensure he stayed awake for the remainder of the journey.

The distant glow of the metropolis brought his mind back to the present and what to do next. They said they would pick him up at Paddington and he had arranged to stay at his mother's flat in Tottenham. She was not particularly pleased about it but it would have to do until he got his own place. He was consoled by the knowledge that he had enough stashed away to get somewhere decent in London, or even perhaps abroad.

His reverie was interrupted as the train came to a halt and passengers began to retrieve their luggage and move along the carriage to the exit door. Beaky waited until most had made their way onto the platform before he followed suit. As he stepped down, he looked round hoping to see the young man again, but the crowd made it impossible and he shouldered his backpack and dragged his case out to where people were lined up waiting for taxis or, like himself, waiting to be picked up by friends or relatives. He moved along the curb to a position less crowded, where he could be clearly seen by the driver who was meeting him. A glance at his watch told him that the train was on time. That was a good thing: upsetting anyone in the organisation by keeping them waiting too long was not wise if he wanted to keep his position.

Cars came and went. Beaky looked back towards the station entrance and there he was: the good-looking young man not more than twenty yards away standing back from the crowd obviously waiting to be picked up. As he watched, a black Ford Focus drew up and a tall slim person in a dark grey suit got out and walked towards the man, greeting him with a wide grin and a tap on the shoulder. Beaky estimated that he was slightly older and wondered if the younger man was gay after all and this was a meeting of lovers.

His thoughts were interrupted by the arrival of a dark blue Mercedes which drew up in front of him. The window lowered and a voice said, 'Hi, Kev. Long time no see.'

Beaky smiled and nodded. 'I wondered if they would send you, Chalky, seein' as how you're one of the few wot know my fizog.'

Chalky grinned. 'Your face, once seen, never to be forgotten.' Beaky grunted, walked to the rear of the car, opened the boot and stowed his case and backpack, then got into the seat next to the driver. 'You got a place in town then, Kev?'

Beaky shook his head. 'Nah, staying at ma's place in Tottenham.' He passed over a piece of paper. 'That's the address.'

Chalky glanced at it and tucked it into the top pocket of his smart blue jacket. 'All in good time,' he said as he drew away and manoeuvred the big car through a maize of vehicles towards the A501.

Beaky relaxed, closed his eyes and was just beginning to ponder his next move when the car jerked to a halt at traffic lights and he had put a hand out to the dashboard to steady himself.

'Sorry, Kev,' Chalky apologised as Beaky sat up and stared at a sign for Regent's Park.

'Hold on, Chalky, where the hell are you taking us? I said Tottenham, not the bloody West End.'

'Calm down, Kev. I'll be taking you there in due course, but apparently you've got a little matter to sort out with the boss.'

'What would Sandor want to see me about? I ain't done nothin' wrong.' Beaky was beginning to feel uncomfortable and wondered how much information about his exit from the manor had reached the top of the organisation.

Chalky was grinning. 'Yer never know, Kev. They might be going to give you a raise.' Beaky was pretty certain that was not the case.

The journey took them past Hampstead Heath where the traffic thinned and Chalky was able to put his foot down and increase the speed. 'Won't be long now, mate,' he said as they travelled along a route which Beaky recognised was the Finchley Road, eventually slowing down to the thirty mile speed limit through an area where a terrace of smart Georgian houses faced the open greenery of the heath. The car slowed to a crawl, finally pulling up outside a house which had an imposing portico with steps flanked by intricate wrought iron railings. 'That's it,' Chalky said as he pulled on the handbrake. 'I'll wait here until you're finished.'

Beaky did not like the sound of that last phrase as he got out of the car, slowly walked up the steps to the front door and pressed the button on the door. A voice demanded to know who it was. 'Kevin Andrews', Beaky said, hoping he sounded more confident than he was. There was a click and a voice said, 'Come in, Andrews.' He pushed open the door and went inside.

Outside a light rain was blowing across from the open heathland opposite, reducing the visibility to a few yards. Chalky switched on the internal lights of the car and began reading *The Sporting Times*. Moments later, the rain came down harder rattling against the car windscreen; he stopped reading and looked up just in time to see a black Ford Focus car drive slowly past and park fifty yards further on where the street lamps were dimmest.

<h1 style="text-align:center">CHAPTER 20</h1>

The morning bell rang at seven-thirty but Jacko had been awake since five, his mind turning over one idea after another. The problem was, he had only a vague knowledge of the area. He knew Lidstone was high and on the edge of the moor, which meant he would be travelling downhill, but in which direction? He had noticed at least three narrow lanes, but which one should he take? Would there be any chance of using some of his meagre ten pounds to catch a bus? He had never seen one nor had he noticed any bus stops on the morning run. Finally he decided he would drop out of the run and, if possible, lie low until they gave up looking for him, then he would take pot luck down the first lane he came to.

He dozed fitfully until the bell jarred him back to consciousness and the reality of what was to come. He lay half asleep until Clayton tapped him on the shoulder. 'Come on, man, you've got ten minutes to get yourself sorted.' Jacko gave a groan as he eased himself out of bed and stood up. His stomach was still very painful and his head ached as he made his way to the bathroom.

By the time he got back, Wiggy and Clayton were already dressed and ready to go. They were passing him on their way out when Clayton stopped and turned to him. 'I hope you know what you're doing, Jacko. If you get caught – and you will be, you know that – it'll probably mean another six months in some place much worse than this. Look, I'm a couple of years older than you, man, an' I've seen these places, my brother did time in one, an' I can tell you, they're not where you wanna be. So think about it.'

'I've gotta do it, Clayton.' Jacko was not looking at him; instead, he gazed steadily ahead as he went over to his wardrobe and found his old grey T-shirt. He took off his red one and placed it on the bed, then he put the grey T-shirt on and the red one over the top.

Clayton was watching and smiled to himself. 'Why did I know he'd do it?' he muttered to himself.

Jacko hurriedly stuffed the chocolate bars into his tracksuit pockets then turned to fold back the duvet and tidy the bed: there was the clatter as coins fell onto the floor. He bent down, picked them up and began counting: eight pounds and fifty pence. 'Wow!' he told himself, 'nearly twenty quid!' He looked up to hear Clayton whisper 'Good luck!' as he turned to go down the corridor.

They were lined up in the hall by the main office when Jacko hurried to join them, taking his usual place at the end. As usual, Griggs told them to stand up straight as he moved slowly along the line, giving each inmate a green fluorescent tabard to wear. Jacko hoped he would not notice the bulges in his trouser pockets caused by the chocolate bars. He kept his hands to his sides to cover them as Griggs approached.

The instructor peered at Jacko's face. 'Do you shave yet, Williams?'

'No, sir.'

'Well you do from now on. I'll see you get some kit.'

Jacko gave a sigh of relief and replied, 'Yes, sir,' as he put the tabard over his head and tied the cords at his waist.

Outside it was still dark. Griggs had a torch which he used to check numbers and to warn any early morning traffic. 'Right now, keep close together till there's a bit more daylight, then no more than a couple of yards between each man. Is that clear?'

There was a bored, 'Yes, sir.' He said the same thing every morning.

'Okay,' he continued, 'this morning looks reasonable, just a bit of mist coming up from lower down, so we'll start by going up onto the moor where it's clear and we will avoid any traffic, then it'll be back down to our usual run through the woods, down the top lane and home. You will be aware that we are short of staff and I will be in sole charge so keep together. I don't want any stragglers.' The last statement gave Jacko some encouragement. Since the Barrel Bennet episode, they had often had two instructors out with them. He had something to thank Beaky for.

Griggs waved a heavily-tattooed arm and they followed him out of the front door onto the gravel drive. The trees on the ridge of Haldon Forest were silhouetted against the dawn light and Jacko shivered as they began the run down the drive to the twin wrought iron gates that led onto the lane. Here they 'marked time' while Griggs tapped in the code to open them. The gates were illuminated at night by a light high on a metal pole fixed to the stone gatepost on the right-hand side. Jacko knew there was also a CCTV camera situated underneath the light which monitored any activity twenty-four seven. The gates would remain unlocked to allow normal access until six o'clock in the evening when a member of staff would lock them. This was usually Kate Lethbridge on her way home.

Out of the gates, they turned right and jogged on through the village where lights were on and the first commuters were getting into their cars for journeys to Exeter or Torbay, or even further afield to Plymouth. Griggs slowed them down to a walk past the Lidstone Arms until they reached the track that led up towards Coombe Cottage, where they resumed jogging. All except Robson, who muttered a curse, kicked out at a large stone and stood for a second holding the foot up and keeping his balance by putting a hand on the granite post that stood at the start of the track.

Griggs' torch flashed down the line. 'What the hell are you doing, Robson? Come on, man, keep up.'

The youth did not reply but resumed his jogging with the feigned limp. It made Jacko realise that dropping out would not be easy.

As they reached the top of the hill, there was a glint of light through the hedge from the windows of Coombe Cottage. Griggs let them stop for a minute to get their breaths back. A dog barked in the cottage. A door opened and the noise came closer as the dog barked furiously on the other side of the hedge. A voice called out, 'Bullet!' The barking ceased as the line of runners emerged from the track and crossed the road onto the moor.

It was beginning to get light. The track was wide and steep, and the muddy ruts caused by horse riders made it difficult under foot as the runners struggled to keep up with Griggs.

Eventually they reached the top of the rise where he stopped and indicated they should gather round. He pointed up to an outcrop of large granite boulders half a mile away at the top of a steep incline. 'Right, lads, that's where we're going. It's not easy so we'll go at a steady pace. Watch out for any potholes and follow the sheep track to the top. Okay, let's go.'

Jacko toiled up the hill in his usual position at the rear of the line which meant he was the last one to reach the top. The path had been difficult; the narrow sheep track was stony with the occasional narrow ditch where water trickled down towards a flat boggy area close to where they had started the climb. Jacko was irritated by the chocolate bars as they moved around in his pockets and rubbed against his legs at every stride; not only that but the weight of them meant he was continually having to hoist up his trousers to prevent them slipping below his hips. When he eventually joined the others, he was exhausted, but the view was worth it.

Griggs was pointing at the distant lights just visible through the morning mist. 'Those are the light of Newton Abbot and Torbay,' he told them, 'and you see where the sun's just coming up, there's a darker horizontal line? That's the sea.' The group appeared to be impressed, few of them had ever seen the sea, let alone have a holiday in a place like Torquay. The exception was Wiggy, who had not only experienced holidays by the sea but had enjoyed them in exotic and sunnier climes.

Of the whole group, only Jacko was not studying the far horizon. His gaze was fixed on the narrow winding road much closer to where they were standing. It wound across the moor below them and he could see the occasional car, presumably taking people to where those lights were shining. Then he saw it: a small bus. So they did exist in the countryside. If he could find it again, this would be the place to get his bearings and perhaps get to the road and, who knows, catch a bus.

'About-turn!' Griggs gave the command and began to lead them back down to the track. 'Go steady! I don't want any busted ankles!' he called out as they followed him to the bottom of the hill. Here Griggs stopped, lined them up and, satisfied they were all accounted for, he set off again, this time downhill to a narrow wooded valley, at the bottom of which a small stream tumbled over rocks between stunted growths of oak and alder trees. They followed the stream downhill by keeping to the narrow path that ran alongside until they came to a hunting gate leading into a meadow where black cattle grazed. Jacko, like many of the others, began to panic as the animals bunched and ran towards them. Griggs held up a hand to slow them down to a walk. 'Don't worry,' he called out. 'They're just curious, bullocks don't cause a problem but, a bit of advice, don't mess with cows that have got calves. I wouldn't take you through a field of those.' Jacko was not sure he could tell the difference as he moved up closer to Robson and Patel.

The cattle had access to the stream to drink, which made the path very muddy in places, and Jacko began to feel the damp seeping into his trainers. He was also getting hot now: wearing two T-shirts was beginning to take its toll and the movement of the chocolate bars was starting to make his thighs sore. Once they were out of the field and onto a narrow lane, he slowed down hoping that Griggs would not notice – but he did.

'Williams, keep up!' he yelled, and ran on the spot allowing the rest to pass him until he was level with Jacko. 'What's the matter with you today, Williams? You're running like a bloody old woman!'

Jacko did not answer but gritted his teeth and made the effort to catch up with Robson. The fact that he felt his guts were on fire was not something he was going to share with the instructor. Griggs waited to see him resume his place at the end of the line before making a sprint to the front where Clayton, as the oldest inmate, had been instructed assume the lead.

Half a mile on, they turned left into a bridle path which took them down past a white, thatched farmhouse where two horses, spooked by the sight of the runners, cantered round their small paddock. Jacko could see their breath hanging in the air as they eventually stood, ears pricked, snorting at the line as it passed on the other side of the fence. Jacko vaguely remembered going that way once before: he made a mental note of the farm and where the bridle path came out onto the road. He was lucky because there was a signpost at the junction stating that it was a public right of way. He would look out for it if he got that far on his bid to find his way home.

The road was lined with stone banks on the top of which trimmed hedges of hawthorn and hazel made an impenetrable barrier that kept livestock in and provided shelter from the cold winds that blew down from the open moorland. It meant that Jacko had no idea exactly where they were in relation to the viewpoint on the moor he would want to reach when he needed to get his bearings and find a road that would take him to a town. As they ran, he glanced through gateways hoping to see a landmark that would tell him the direction they were heading, but a thick mist was gradually coming up from the valley below and blotting out the view. He knew they were taking a wide circle that would eventually bring them back to Lidstone but Griggs had chosen a different route and it was not until they reached a heavily wooded area that Jacko began to recognise where they were. He now knew that in a few minutes, they would start the climb up the long steep hill with the sharp bend near the top. That would be the place.

'Keep up close all of you!' Griggs' voice indicated his concern as the visibility deteriorated and, due to the steepness of the gradient, the line of runners was now stretched so that the tailenders were out of his sight. By the time they reached the bend in the road, they had all slowed down to a walk, including Griggs who was looking anxiously back to check numbers, but the mist was too thick. It was a situation he dreaded. It was a situation that Jacko had prayed for.

*

He stood and waited for what he estimated was five minutes: he did not possess a watch; his had mysteriously disappeared the first week at the manor. It had started to rain. The last of the tabards had long disappeared into the gloom and the only sound he could hear was the drip of moisture from the branches overhead onto the dead leaves of the forest floor. He quickly took off his tabard, rolled it up and threw it into the ditch by the roadside, then he turned and began to retrace his steps down the hill, trying to remember the route back to where the bridle path led up to the moor.

He walked carefully along the narrow grass verge, keeping as close to the edge of the wood as possible: there was the possibility of traffic. His fears were confirmed when a set of dulled headlights appeared a few yards in front of him. He quickly climbed through the rails of the forest's wooden fence and flung himself down onto the mass of dead leaves on the ground. The vehicle passed slowly up the hill, its rear lights barely visible. Jacko remained on his stomach until the sound of the car had gone, then he stood up and began to think about his next move. He was sure to be discovered if he remained on the road. It meant going cross-country which would involve going through fields full of the cows and bullocks that Griggs had told them about. He was not looking forward to that.

His next action was to quickly take off his two T-shirts and reverse them, putting the grey one on top of the red; now if anyone saw him, he would pass for an ordinary jogger on a routine exercise. He waited in the shelter of the trees until the pain in the muscles of his stomach and ribs subsided into a dull ache. The run had taken its toll and he realised that he was exhausted and now confused. Which direction should he go if he was to keep off the roads? How would he cope in a thick fog across fields full of cows or horses? He sat down with his back against the trunk of a large beech tree, took out one of the chocolate bars, and began to peel off the wrapping while he thought about what he had done. There was still time to undo it, he could abandon the whole thing, turn up late and say that he had felt unwell, got lost or just passed out. The chances are that no one would question it and he would be let off with a few hard words from Griggs or Burford. He ate the chocolate bar: it did little to allay the hunger and fatigue.

Jacko had no idea how long he had been sitting there when he woke from a fitful doze. He looked towards the road and saw that the mist had lifted and the day was now clear. A chilly breeze rustled through the branches causing him to shiver as he stood up. He realised he would have to keep moving to stay warm; this, combined with his final decision to continue his bid for home, prompted a quick move towards the road. He stopped short as a vehicle passed rapidly down the hill; it was the green Land Rover from the manor: they were out looking for him already. That thought made him hesitate before crossing the road into the woodland on the other side. Here Jacko noticed the branches of the trees were still green and to him they looked like giant Christmas trees planted in straight lines as far as the eye could see.

The spruce plantation was dense and offered better shelter from the wind and rain. As he stood trying to work out which way to go, there was the sound of a vehicle coming up the hill. He flattened himself on the ground and watched as the green Land Rover appeared coming from the opposite direction. Suddenly it stopped and he heard a door open as someone got out and a voice he recognised as Griggs' called out to the driver. 'You're right, it is the tabard. I must have missed it as we came down the hill.' He picked it up out of the ditch, threw it onto a back seat and spoke to the driver. 'Hang on a minute, I'll take a look inside the wood and see if the little bugger is still in there. I suppose there's an outside chance he's injured or something so we'd better check it out.' He dodged through the fence and searched the ground for any giveaway signs. 'Yep,' he called out, 'I can see where dead leaves have been disturbed. It looks as though someone's been scuffing around here, and I bet it's our friend Jacko Williams. I'll poke around a bit, see if I can make out which way he went. In the meantime, better get on your mobile and call up for some help.'

Jacko had heard enough. He slid on all fours down a steep incline that ended in a dry ditch; there he paused to listen. Griggs was still talking but the sound was getting fainter: he was searching in the opposite direction. Jacko got up, scrambled out of the ditch and ran as hard as he could through the trees down to where a narrow stream ran between banks of grass and sedge. He stopped to catch his breath and listen. He could hear nothing above the sound of water trickling over stones. It was then he realised how thirsty he was. It prompted him to kneel and slake his thirst by scooping up the liquid in his cupped hands.

Refreshed, he set off again at a steady walk. Now the gradient was uphill, he hoped he could find an open space that would give him the chance of seeing where he was and what direction to take, but the trees seemed to go on for ever. When eventually he reached a wide track that led to a gate, he estimated he had been walking for over an hour. A pale sun was just visible through a thin layer of cloud. Jacko knew that the sun rose in the east and they had seen it coming up over Torquay, so although the sun was getting high in the sky, nevertheless it was still morning so if he went towards it, that's where he would end up: civilisation.

As he approached the gate, there was a sudden loud whirring sound and a loud *cack-cack-cack*. I made him jump with fright. He looked to see where the noise had come from but could see nothing but trees. In a scared panic, he ran for the gate and scrambled over, falling on his right knee as he landed. Jacko had never experienced the alarm call of a terrified cock pheasant before. He got up and leant against the gatepost as the bird skimmed away on its low flight across the field in front.

The forest edge stretched away on his left roughly in the direction of the sun. He decided he would keep close to it until he reached its end, then he would try and work out where he was in relation to his goal: the rocks on the moor. The forest was much larger than he had anticipated; there were more field gates to get through or over, and his progress was slowed by the new pain in his knee so that the sun was high overhead by the time he came to a final gate onto a road. He climbed over it and gave a sigh of relief – the only animals he had encountered were a few very woolly sheep that had white faces with black noses. He thought they looked as though they had been eating soot. He had smiled for the first time in the past couple of days.

Now his quandary was which way to go along the road and how long should he risk travelling on a public highway. He concluded the east was probably to his right and he would stay on the road until the next gate on the right-hand side then he would venture cross-country again and hope to get to some higher ground where he could get his bearings.

The next gate, which was made of galvanised metal, was padlocked and had a strand of barbed wire coiled along the top. Jacko could see several horses in waterproof rugs grazing in the field. One of them caught sight of him and came trotting over to stand snorting as though to warn him to keep out. Jacko did not need to be warned. There was no way he was going in with that lot, even if he could have scaled the gate. He continued along the grass verge as the increasing wind blew the few remaining leaves from the hawthorns that topped the roadside hedge. He began to shiver again and broke into a trot to get warm, all the while looking for a chance to leave the road and continue cross-country, but the thick hedge seemed impenetrable and the only gate he came to was a broken wooden structure that fronted a stone ruin, which looked as though it had once been a barn.

Jacko stopped and looked over the gate. The roof of the building had gone but the stone walls were almost intact and would offer shelter from the wind – a good place to take a break. He climbed over what remained of the gate and entered the ruin through a wide doorway. Inside was strewn with rubble and the remains of the wooden rafters that once held up the roof. In one corner, he found a slab of stone propped up by two chunks of granite. It made a comfortable seat for him to rest his aching feet and, at the same time, keep out of sight of any passers-by.

He began to realise how hungry he was and reached into his pocket for a chocolate bar. 'Two down, four to go,' he said to himself, as he bit eagerly into the chocolate. When it was finished, he contemplated eating another but reluctantly decided that he would need the few that remained to tide him over until he could reach civilisation.

In the shelter of the thick walls, it was not warm but it was less cold and Jacko began to relax. So far, so good; he had avoided any further detection and he knew, from what Clayton had told him, they would stop searching after twenty-four hours and turn the problem over to Central Office and let them sort it out. It meant he only had to keep under the radar until tomorrow morning when the local search would be called off. He had lost track of time but guessed, from the rumblings coming from his stomach, that it was close to midday and he had not yet reached the viewpoint he was aiming for. It was time to get moving before it started to get dark

Back on the road, Jacko decided the best thing to do was to behave like a fitness freak on a daily workout. He set off at a brisk trot along the grass verge hoping to find a gate into a field before anyone spotted him, but he was out of luck: a group of horse riders appeared round the bend in front of him. He could hear the chatter of female voices as they came closer. He jogged towards them without looking up.

As they drew level, he glanced up to see the leading rider, a middle-aged woman in a green fluorescent jacket, looking down at him. 'Afternoon,' she called out with a smile. 'Good day for a run.' Jacko gave a brief nod and carried on towards a small wood where he could see a gate which would give him the chance to head in the direction he wanted to go.

In the woodlands, he paused to get his breath. 'Bugger,' he said out loud, and wondered how long it would be before a rider told someone and that someone told Burford. He started off again down a broad track that led to another gate into a field covered in knee-high plants that looked like tall cabbages. Jacko had never seen a field of kale before. He climbed over and dropped onto soft, bare soil, his trainers sinking up to the lace holes so that he could feel his feet getting wet as he walked round the field edge, keeping as close as possible to the barbed wire fence that surrounded the wood. Nevertheless the wet leaves saturated his trousers from the knee down. He was so concerned trying to keep dry that he failed to notice the thin strand of wire stretching across the field until he almost touched it. The wire was supported at intervals by plastic posts: there was a faint ticking sound. Jacko had learned enough about the countryside in the past weeks to know that it was an electric fence and it was live. It was level with the top of his thigh and he had to drop down on all fours to creep under without touching it.

Now his hands and knees were covered in mud. He carefully reached through the fence to pull up a plant and use the leaves to try and wipe it off. The field on this side of the fence was a sea of mud where cattle had grazed on the kale. Jacko rightly assumed that the fence would be moved every day to allow the animals fresh food. He looked around nervously for any sign of the animals and was relieved to see the field was empty.

It was a slow plod to the next gate which led onto a farm track. Jacko could see that the cattle had come that way and he followed their trail, hoping it would lead to somewhere he could get himself cleaned up, a water trough, even a barn with straw; as long there was nobody about, he could get away without being noticed. He was lucky; the track did lead to a barn full of hay bales. It was an old wooden building with a corrugated iron roof, enclosed on three sides and adjacent to a covered yard where he could see a number of brown and white cows feeding from a large circular metal hay rack. There appeared to be nobody around, and Jacko was relieved to see that there was no house in the vicinity. He walked over to the yard, reached through the bars, and rinsed his hands in the water trough, before going over to the barn to wipe them dry with some loose hay near the barn. As he was about to look for a way out, he suddenly heard the distant sound of a vehicle coming up the track. He looked round for somewhere to hide and saw a wooden ladder propped up against the bales; within seconds, he was on top of the stack, lying flat and watching the track.

Eventually, a quad bike appeared with two people on it; one, a boy of about six or seven, seated behind a man. Jacko assumed it was father and son. They turned into the gate of the field, stopped just inside, dismounted and walked towards the electric fence.

'Wait till I've turned it off,' the man called out.

The boy nodded and stood by the hedge while his father walked to the other side of the field. Jacko saw the man bend down, then wave to the boy who immediately began to move the posts and wire. The pair worked steadily until the fence was a couple of yards further into the crop. The man stood back to view what they had done and, obviously satisfied, gave the boy a 'thumbs up' as they walked back to the quad bike. Jacko hoped they would go back the way they came and was disappointed when the vehicle turned towards him. He shuffled to the back of the barn and lay still, hardly daring to breath.

'Reckon we'll need a couple more bales, Toby.' As Jacko heard the man begin to clime the ladder, he squeezed himself into the far corner. There were two thumps as the bales hit the ground.

'Watch out, Dad! That one nearly conked me,' the boy called out.

'Then don't stand so damned close. Come on, let's get this done. Mum will have tea ready by now, and you know what she's like if we're late.'

There was the sound of cattle moving and the clatter of a metal gate slamming shut, then the engine of the quad bike started up. There was a cry of 'Hold tight!' and the sound of the vehicle receding into the distance.

Jacko breathed a sigh of relief and eased himself into a more comfortable position on the bales. The encounter, together with the gnawing hunger in his stomach, made him realise how the time had flown: it was obviously past school time. Back at the manor, they would be streaming back into the dining room for tea and sandwiches; the thought made his mouth water and he felt in his pocket for a chocolate bar.

When he finished the snack, he screwed up the wrapping, tucked it between a couple of bales and sat with his back against a wooden beam to contemplate what to do next. The hay was comfortable and slightly warm, the result of a late second cut that was still maturing. Down below, he could hear grunts and occasional coughs as the cows fed or laid down to chew the cud. The light was fading and it was not long before Jacko stretched out his aching limbs and dozed into a troubled sleep.

*

It was the hoot of an owl that woke Jacko, and he realised it was pitch dark. He crawled to the edge of the stack and looked out to see a full moon and stars; the air felt cold and there was a tinge of frost in the air. He had no idea what the time was, except that the countryside was now silent apart from the faint sounds from the cattle below. There was no doubt in Jacko's mind that it was now the middle of the night and there would be no point in him trying to find his way in the dark. He crawled back into the relative warmth of the hay and was soon asleep once more.

*

He saw the lights before he heard the now-familiar sound of the quad bike. Jacko stayed still, listening. It was still dark but the sky was beginning to lighten on the horizon in front of him. He made a mental note of where the sun was rising; that was the direction he would have to take and it coincided with the track down which the cows were now being driven by a man Jacko assumed was the same one he had seen the evening before. He could just see the cattle entering the field at a steady trot, obviously anxious to get to their daily feed of fresh kale leaves.

The quad bike started up again and Jacko watched the red tail light disappear round the bend in the track. He waited several minutes to make sure it did not return before descending the ladder.

Outside the barn, the air felt cold. He shivered and wished he had a coat to put on. The gnawing hunger was still there and he was thirsty again. He looked round for a tap and found one at the side of the barn with a plastic hosepipe attached. He quickly removed the pipe and bent down to drink directly from the tap. The water splashed over his face and down the front of his T-shirt, but he continued until his thirst was quenched, ignoring the chill of the ice cold water that now saturated his clothing. He wiped his face with his hands and reached into his pocket to take out two chocolate bars, leaving the last one to have when he caught that bus he had seen travelling along the road below the rocks. The two bars had little impact on his hunger but the chocolate gave his energy a boost so that he felt able to set off again.

The chink of the coins in his now almost empty pockets reminded him to check the money was still intact – there was always the possibility some had spilled out when he was squirming about on the hay. He stopped and carefully felt for the ten pound note and was relieved to find it still folded in the same pocket as the remaining chocolate bar. He scooped out the coins in his left hand and carefully counted: the eight pound coins and a fifty pence piece were all there; he was still in with a chance.

Now it was a case of heading towards the sunrise, except there was no sun, just a brighter patch in an otherwise cloudy sky. The track was muddy and strewn with cowpats so Jacko found himself dodging from one side of the track to the other in order to avoid as much muck as possible. It was slow going and drained what little energy he had, so by the time he reach the lane at the end of the track, he was exhausted and was forced to find a patch of grass to sit down and rest. It gave him time to look around, to try and decide which way to go next. Something puzzled him – the road looked familiar. He stood up to get a better view and thought he recognised the gate into a small wood further down the road and, as he walked towards it, he realised with horror that he had been travelling in a wide circle.

He stopped to lean on the gate with his head in his hands, looking into the wood where he had walked the previous afternoon. Close to tears, he began to wonder if it had all been worthwhile. Should he give up now, let them find him and accept his punishment? What was the point of trying to get to his mother anyway? Nobody would help the likes of him, and she was probably quite happy that he was where he was. But the thought of Beaky's threats still worried him. Confused and tired, he shook his head despondently and turned back onto the road, not knowing which way to go and not caring. In the end, he decided to carry on past the wood in the hope it would take him somewhere he recognised. And it did.

PUBLIC RIGHT OF WAY – Jacko stood for several seconds looking at the sign pointing up the bridle path the runners had come down the previous day. At last, he knew where he was, and the knowledge revived his spirits as he turned onto the track and made his way up it towards the rear of the thatched farmhouse. The horses were no longer in the field and he could see a man moving about in the yard. He bent below the level of the hedge bank to make sure he would not be seen. Once passed, he did his best to jog up the hill towards the end of the bridle path, which he knew led onto the moor.

He felt the first drops of rain on his face as he emerged from the bridle path and crossed the lane onto the track he remembered was going to take him towards the rocks on the hill and his chance to get to where there were people and buses, the things that were familiar to him. Deep in thought, Jacko failed to notice the darkening sky until a sudden squall of heavy rain and sleet lashed into his body, causing him to stop and look round for shelter, but there was none. A stone wall on his right offered little protection, and he found it difficult to see any further than a few yards ahead. He decided to battle on, hoping to find the way off the track that led up to the rocks on the hill, but he found it difficult to look ahead as the force of the wind made him keep his head down. He began to shiver as the cold from his soaked clothes seeped into his body.

The deluge eased as suddenly as it had begun, and, at last, Jacko was able to look around and get some idea of where he was. He did not recognise anything. The rain still made it difficult to see more than a few hundred yards and now a thick mist was slowly tumbling down from the rocks of the high moorland and would soon obliterate everything. He considered turning back as his shivering became more severe, but he was not sure which direction was back. All he wanted now was to get somewhere dry. He quickened his pace in an effort to get warm. Huge boulders loomed out of the mist and, as a small flock of sheep scattered in front of him, he noticed that some of them had been sheltering under a low overhang of rock at the base of the boulders. It looked dry and, despite the liberal deposit of sheep dropping,s he decided to crawl under. He would wait until the weather cleared and he could stop shivering, then he could get to the rocks on the hill and then on the bus and then … He was numb and did not feel cold anymore, he did not feel anything. His eyes closed, he was out of breath and dizzy. He pushed himself further under the rock and lay still, waiting for everything to come right, for everything to …

CHAPTER 21

The day had not started well for Matt. It had been three days since his date with Serena. The portrait of Dot had not gone as well as he had hoped and he was seriously thinking of scrapping it and starting again. On top of that, severe cramp in his injured leg had kept him awake until the early hours so that it was past eight o'clock before he had made it downstairs for breakfast. His intention was to ride Molly early that morning as Spud had told him that the fox hounds were meeting at the Lidstone Arms at eleven o'clock and, as neither he nor Molly were geared up for hunting, he was anxious to keep out of their way as far as possible, particularly as he intended to take Bullet with him. The dog had been getting too full of himself lately and had gone berserk the previous morning for no particular reason. Matt felt a good run behind Molly would calm him down.

The early hours of the morning had been dry and chilly, but soon after he had arrived at the Lethbridges', it had started to rain so heavily, he had contemplated calling the whole thing off. He had waited in the tack room for the rain to ease off, but as it did, the inevitable mist descended from the moor. He could have ridden down the lane towards Lidstone but that would have meant the possibility of meeting the hunt at some stage. The only option was to wait for the mist to clear then take the bridle path up to the moor.

It had been nearly an hour before Matt had been able to see further than the field gate at the other end of the yard. The mist had eventually lifted to be replaced by a cold drizzle. Matt had become used to the sudden changes in the weather that occurred on the moor and had taken the precaution of bringing his long waterproof coat, so that at least he could keep his knees dry. He finished tacking up Molly, called to Bullet, climbed into the saddle, and walked the mare out of the yard towards the gate that led to the bridle path.

For Matt, riding Molly was the thing that gave him the most pleasure in his mundane existence at the cottage. His painting kept him occupied but was often frustrating, as he had experienced in the past few days. Pain and disturbed nights were consistent features of his daily life, but once on board the little black mare, all of that was pushed aside: he was a young boy again, riding his pony round the family farm, taking in the delights of the open countryside. It was pure therapy and he wished he could spend the rest of his life doing nothing else, but he knew it was all a daydream, and before long, he would have to make those critical decisions concerning his future.

On the moorland track, he nudged the mare into a trot as Bullet scurried off ahead to investigate any patch of dead bracken in the hope of putting up a rabbit. Matt was pleased to see the old dog was back to his old self and was happy that he was enjoying himself, as long as he did not range too far; visibility was poor and the small brown animal was difficult to see, even in good light. He was therefore concerned when he heard the dog's frantic barking some distance ahead.

Matt turned off the track and headed towards the sound, urging Molly into a canter up the rocky incline towards a pile of boulders that loomed on the skyline. As he got closer, he pulled the mare back to a walk and peered ahead: there was no sign of Bullet and the sound was now a muffled growl. 'What's the old bugger up to now?' Matt asked himself, as he pulled up and dismounted to lead Molly up towards the rocks.

As he got closer, he could see the dog running backwards and forwards in a cavity beneath a large boulder at the base of the pile. Slipping the reins over Molly's head, Matt led the mare up to the boulder and, holding the reins at arm's length, peered into the dark recess and saw what he thought was a bundle of rags. Calling the dog off, he was about to turn away when he heard a groan and the sound of teeth chattering.

'My God, Bullet, what have you found?' Matt looped the reins on his arm and, talking soothingly to the mare, got down on his hands and knees and crawled under the overhang.

What he saw startled him: a pair of dark eyes staring blankly from a dark, young face, contorted with cold.

Matt's immediate reaction was to get whoever it was out as quickly as possible; easy enough if he had been on his own, but he had Molly pulling back on the reins: a sudden quick move might spook her, and the last thing he wanted was to see his mount disappearing into the mist. He slowly eased himself back out and stood up to look round for somewhere not too far away where he could tether the mare. A patch of gorse about twenty yards below the boulders looked a likely solution. He led Molly down and tied the reins to a thick stem, relieved to see her immediately start to nibble at the prickly leaves: they would do her no harm and would keep her occupied while he went back up to get the young person out. He reached in his pocket and took out his mobile phone but, as usual up on the moor, there was no signal: he would have to do what was necessary without help.

Matt eased himself back into the cavity on his stomach, took hold of both of the person's arms and pulled gently until the whole body was out in the open. Now he could see that it was a young coloured boy scantily clad in trousers and a T-shirt. Matt felt for a pulse: it was slow and weak, but it was there. He had seen hypothermia during a six weeks' posting to Northern Canada designed to train his drivers in the skills of negotiating ice and snow. All personnel had been trained to recognise and treat the condition, and he knew he had to get warmth into the body as soon as possible. He unzipped his long waterproof coat, put his hands under the youth's armpits, and pulled him up to a standing position pressed close to his own body, then he wrapped the coat round the two of them and waited.

The body warmth at first triggered violent shivering, then the boy opened his eyes and tried to speak, but no words came through the chattering teeth. Matt was feeling the strain of supporting the weight of the boy's body. 'Do you think you can stand, lad?' There was a faint nod and a shuffle of feet. 'Good, okay, now, I'm going to sit you down on that rock there,' he nodded towards a stone ledge that jutted out from one of the boulders. 'You sit there while I take off this coat, then I'll help you to put it on. Okay?' Again, there was a faint nod as, with Matt's help, the boy staggered towards the ledge.

The coat having been exchanged, Matt contemplated what to do next. He checked his phone: there was no signal. He knew he had to get the boy warm as soon as possible. His first thought was to get him to Coombe Cottage, but there was the problem of what to do with Molly when he got there: he had nowhere to put her. He would have to take him to the Lethbridges' where he was certain to get the care he needed.

The next question was, how? The boy could hardly walk and it would be extremely difficult supporting him and leading Molly. The thought of the mare caused him to look in her direction. She was still peacefully nibbling the gorse: there was only one answer. He walked down, untied the reins and led the mare up to where the boy was sitting. 'Do you think you could sit on this horse?' he asked him.

This time, the head movement was negative.

Matt brought Molly closer. 'If you can stand on that ledge, I'll bring the old lady up and you can easily put your foot in the stirrup and get on her.'

There was still obvious reluctance. Matt took off his riding hat, placed it on the boy's head, and fastened it under his chin. It was a couple of sizes too big but it would give some protection in the event of any accident. 'Come on, lad, you've seen cowboys do it often enough on the telly. Just put your foot there,' he pointed to the stirrup, 'swing your other leg over, and you're there. Hang on, I'll give you a hand.' This time, there was a faint, 'Okay,' as Matt moved to help him onto the ledge.

Molly stood patiently as Matt settled the boy in the saddle, making sure the long coat was properly zipped up and covering the boy's knees. Taking a hank of the mare's long mane, he put it in the boy's hands, telling him to keep a tight hold of it, then he called Bullet and gently led the mare forward down the slope, grateful that she seemed quite happy with her new and unbalanced burden.

The rain had finally stopped by the time they reached the track below the boulders, but Matt's polo-necked sweater was already soaked and he could feel the cold water trickling down the back of his neck; it was his turn to shiver. There had been several occasions when Jacko had slumped forward causing Matt to stop and push him back into a more upright position. Once they were down on more level ground, progress became much easier. Matt reckoned at the rate they were going, it would take approximately another half an hour to get back to the Lethbridges' house, and he was grateful when they reached the smooth surface of the road: riding boots were not designed for walking on rough ground. Only one vehicle passed them and it was going too fast to notice the odd-looking rider and the dejected person leading the horse and a small dog running behind.

By the time they reached the bridle path, Matt noticed that the boy was looking more comfortable; perhaps the warmth from the mare's body was having an effect or the subtle movement of his own body was generating some heat. Whatever it was, Matt could hear him muttering something. The words were indistinct and slurred, but it was an indication that he was beginning to recover.

As they entered the stable yard, Harry whickered a greeting. Molly responded and the sound seemed to waken her rider so that he suddenly sat up and looked around before slowly collapsing, causing Matt to quickly turn to catch hold of his coat before he hit the ground, one foot still in a stirrup.

Matt was now in a quandary: he could not leave the boy in the middle of the yard while he put Molly in her box. Likewise, he could not leave the mare while he took the boy into the house.

His dilemma was solved by the arrival of Kate's little red Fiat. She pulled up just inside the yard and got out to walk over to where Matt was trying to keep Jacko upright.

'What on earth is going on?' she demanded, the alarm in her voice matched by the look of concern on her face.

'Oh, Kate, thank heavens you're here! Could you give me a hand? I've got to get this lad to somewhere warm … I'll explain later, but if you could just take care of Molly while I get him indoors, it would be a great help. Is your mother in?'

Kate shook her head. 'She went to the meet this morning. I expect she's following in the car, she usually does when they meet at the Lidstone Arms.'

'Oh, yes. Is the back door open?' Matt asked as Kate took hold of Molly's reins.

'I expect so. Mother rarely locks the back door unless she's likely to be away for the whole day.' Kate was staring down at the semi-prostrate figure. 'What's happened to him?'

'Just let me get him inside and I'll tell you all I know.'

Kate shrugged and, as she led the mare towards the stable, Matt called out to her, 'You can take your time. I'm going to have to strip the lad of his wet gear. Oh, and stick Bullet in the Volvo for me, please.' He lifted Jacko and carried him to the back door. It opened easily and Matt was relieved to feel the warmth coming from the Aga stove in the kitchen. He switched on the oven, opened the oven door, and sat Jacko on a chair as close to it as possible.

The heat had the desired effect and a bewildered Jacko began to look around. 'W … where am I?' he stuttered. Matt unzipped the coat and began to pull it off Jacko's shoulders. There was immediate resistance. 'What're ya doin'?'

'It's all right, lad.' Matt's tone was consoling as he managed to remove the coat and begin to strip off the remaining clothes. 'We've got to get these wet things off you and get you dry. You'll feel better then.'

Jacko pushed him away. 'I c … c … can do it.' He was still shivering as he bent down to untie his shoelaces before taking off his trousers and underpants, then he pulled off his T-shirts and immediately sat on them.

Matt assumed he had done this because the wooden chair was too hard for his backside, but he needed to dry the wet garments. 'Give me your shirt and vest, lad. We need to get them dried.'

Reluctantly, Jacko handed over the T-shirts as the back door opened slightly and Kate's head appeared in the gap. 'Have you finished yet?' she called out.

Matt grabbed a kitchen towel and threw it to Jacko, who quickly covered his groin. 'Yes, okay, you can come in now.'

Kate stood for a few seconds, looking at the hunched figure in the chair. 'How is he now?' she asked, walking over to stand by Matt, who was busy taking Jacko's pulse again.

He looked up at her. 'He's getting there,' he paused and looked around. 'Have you got a blanket or something I can put round him until we get his clothes dry?'

Kate though for a moment. 'There's a new horse blanket I got from your friend Serena Brent the other day.'

Matt detected a note of disdain when she mentioned the woman's name. 'That'll do fine,' he told her.

Kate nodded and went out of the back door to return a few moments later with a large beige blanket that had red and black stripes along its length. It was still in a plastic bag, which Kate quickly removed it from. She gave the blanket to Matt who told Jacko to stand while he wrapped it round the boy's shoulders. Jacko sat back in the chair, clutching the rough cloth close to his skin.

Matt turned to Kate. 'Have you got somewhere we can put his clothes to get them dry?'

'Here, give them to me. I'll put 'em in the spin dryer.' She gathered up the sodden pile and walked to the door leading into the utility room.

Seconds later, Kate appeared in the doorway and beckoned to Matt. He went over to ask if there was any problem and was surprised to see her holding up a red T-shirt with GAINSBOROUGH HOUSE stamped in large white letters on the back. Neither of them said anything for several seconds until Kate said quietly, 'I'm afraid we do have a problem. He's from the manor and I heard yesterday they were out looking for someone.'

Matt thought for a moment. 'Okay, we'll deal with that once we've got the lad back on his feet. In the meantime, I'll find out what I can about him, then we'll decide what to do.'

For some reason, Kate liked the *we'll decide*. She nodded and put the T- shirt into the spin dryer. She came back into the kitchen and placed a chocolate bar, some coins and a crumpled ten pound note on the table.

Jacko looked at them, shook his head and burst into tears. It was Kate who stepped forward to put her hands on his shoulders. 'Don't worry,' she said softly. 'We'll take care of you. I'll get you a hot drink and find you something to eat, but in the meantime,' she picked up the chocolate bar and gave it to him smiling, 'you had better finish this up.'

She turned to find Matt watching her. 'You're in good hands, young man,' he said quietly. He touched Kate gently on the arm. 'I'll leave you to it. I need to get myself dried out a bit. Okay if I use your bathroom?'

It was only then that she noticed his bedraggled appearance and realised he also must be soaked through. 'Help yourself, Matt, you know where it is,' she paused for a moment. 'If you need to change, I could find some of Dad's old clothes if you like.'

'No, I'll be alright, thanks, just need to get these boots off and have a rub down. Probably put my stuff in the spin dryer once the lad's are dry.'

Kate did not like to think what he might wear while his clothes were drying. She put the kettle on and went to the kitchen cupboard. 'Would you like a hot chocolate drink?' she asked, looking towards Jacko.

He nodded and muttered, 'Yes, please.'

She noticed his stutter had gone and he was sitting more comfortably in the chair. 'Feeling better now?' she asked as she stirred the chocolate powder into a mug.

The answer, 'Yeah,' came as she offered him the mug.

'My name's Kate Lethbridge, what's yours?'

There was a long pause before he replied in a whisper, 'Jackson Williams.'

'Well, Jackson … '

'It's Jacko, actually.'

'Well, Jacko, how would you like eggs on fried bread and baked beans, followed by bread and jam?'

'Yeah, great, thanks.' Jacko cupped the mug in both hands and took his first sip: it tasted good. Hot chocolate was a new experience for him.

Kate closed the oven door. 'You warm enough now?'

He nodded.

'Good. If you go and sit at the table, I'll get things started.'

She had just finished cooking when Matt appeared in the doorway with the wet bundle of clothes under one arm. He was completely naked except for the bath towel round his waist. He had made sure it stretched down to his ankles so that it concealed his badly scarred left leg. He nodded towards Jacko. 'Do you think his stuff is dry yet?'

Kate tried to look unconcerned as she placed the meal in front of Jacko. 'Your guess is as good as mine,' she told him and could not resist a smile as he clutched at the towel to prevent it slipping to the ground. 'I couldn't say, but I suggest you don't put your woollen sweater in the dryer. It'll probably shrink to half its size.'

'Yes ma'm.' He gave a mock salute and disappeared into the utility room to return a few minutes later with Jacko's clothes. 'Near enough dry, I reckon, so the lad … '

'His name is Jackson, or Jacko.'

'Okay, so Jacko can get dressed as soon as he's finished eating.' Matt became aware that Kate was eyeing him with a look of restrained amusement on her face. He was suddenly embarrassed and hitched the towel tighter round his waist. 'Sorry about this,' he said, pointing to the towel. 'Couldn't think what else to do.'

Kate gave a broad grin. 'You don't need to worry, it suits you.'

He smiled back. 'Good. In that case, I'll wear it when I take you out.'

'Huh! Don't think your girlfriend Serena would approve.'

'She's not my girlfriend. I've only taken her out once.' Matt was pleased Kate had noticed his liaison with Serena and, for a moment, entertained a hope that her interest might be tinged with jealousy.

They both watched Jacko tuck into his plate of egg and beans before Matt indicated that they should go next door out of earshot. In the living room, Kate perched herself on the arm of the sofa, while Matt decided that his present attire dictated that he should remained standing. 'We'll have to take him back,' he told Kate.

She was looking at him and suddenly burst out laughing.

'It's no laughing matter, Kate.'

'I know, but you are.' She tightened her lips and tried to look serious. 'Sorry, but you look as though you've just got out of the bath and can't find your trousers.'

Matt glanced down at the towel and tightened his grip; he was not amused. 'I'm sorry if you find it distracting, Kate, but this young man appears to have absconded from a government detention centre, and he could be in big trouble.'

'You may be right but I think we should try and find out why he has done this. He must be desperate to attempt it wearing only a T-shirt and with less than twenty quid in his pocket. He can't be more than fifteen or sixteen, still a child in my books.'

The humour had gone from her voice and Matt realised that she was genuinely concerned. 'Okay, let's get him back into his clothes and see what we can find out. In the meantime, since you think my present garb is hilarious, I'll get back into mine, dry or not.' Matt was tempted to put his tongue out but decided against it. Instead he hitched up the towel and disappeared into the utility room.

He returned a few minutes later dressed in a check shirt and jeans but barefooted, explaining that his socks were not yet dry enough to put on. Together they went back into the kitchen where Jacko was finishing a second jam sandwich. The blanket was now off his shoulders and wrapped around his waist. 'You feeling warm enough now?' Matt asked.

Jacko nodded and, with an embarrassed look towards Kate, asked where his clothes were. She picked them up off the chair where Matt had put them and placed them on the table.

At the same time, Matt stepped forward and pointed to the red T- shirt. 'This time, you wear that one on the outside, young man,' he told him.

Kate went back into the living room while Jacko got dressed. He did so slowly and Matt could see that the youth was very reluctant to wear the red shirt. It was several seconds before he eventually pulled it on over his head and turned to look at Matt, who immediately put a hand on his shoulder. 'I'm sorry, Jacko. We'll have to take you back to the manor.'

'No, no ... not there. Can't go back there.'

This took Matt by surprise. 'All right, lad,' he said quietly. 'Come through into the other room and you can tell us what's troubling you and why you tried to run away, if that's what you were doing.' He took hold of Jacko's arm and guided him into the living room, where Kate had stocked up the wood burner to warm up the room. She pointed to the sofa and told him to make himself comfortable while she and Matt chose the easy chairs.

For several minutes, they sat in silence before Jacko eventually began to talk. He told them about the abuse he had suffered at the hands of Beaky Andrews, the threats to his mother, and the need he felt to get home to protect her.

Kate was the first to speak. 'Why not just phone her up and warn her?'

'Naah, what good would that have done? She couldn't do nothin', neither could the bloke she's with, if he's still there.'

Kate raised an eyebrow. 'Surely the local police could do something.'

'In your dreams. They ain't got time to do nothin' for the likes of us.'

Matt had been listening intently. 'So what do you think this Beaky chap could do?' he asked.

'Not so much Beaky as his mates. I've seen 'em put the frighteners on people just by hanging round and getting 'em to pay a bit towards their habit, and my mum won't have anything to give 'em, so … I dunno.'

'Would you like me to contact your mother? Would you like her to come down and see you, give you a chance to explain what has happened?'

Jacko shook his head. 'She can't come, got a little 'un and it costs too much.'

'Okay, I understand, but if you could give me her phone number, I'll let her know what's happened and see if we can arrange something.'

'I don't want her to know.'

'Alright then, I'll just see if I can make some arrangement for her to visit and you can decide whether to tell her or not. What about that?'

Jacko said nothing and seemed to be studying the intricate pattern in the carpet. Eventually he looked up, gave a long sigh and shook his head.

Matt looked at Kate and shrugged. She beckoned to him and told Jacko to stay where he was while they went back into the kitchen. She closed the door. 'What do you reckon we should do?' she whispered.

Matt considered for a moment. 'There's no doubt he's a very troubled and confused young man, and equally there is no doubt we'll have to take him back to the manor,' he told her. 'What they do from then on is up to them, but my guess is that if the claim of physical violence is true, they might try to hush it up.'

'So we just take him back and leave it there?'

'Any better suggestions?' asked Matt.

'What about reporting it to the police?'

'And get the boy into even more trouble? Not a good idea. I think we have to take him back to the manor. Perhaps he could plead that he got lost in the fog and couldn't find his way back. If they wanted to keep it low-key, they might well accept that. Come on, let's get the job done.' Matt opened the door into living room to tell Jacko what they intended to do, but the room was empty. He looked into the small office area, but he was not there. Matt thought he might have gone upstairs to look for the bathroom. It was then he saw that the window onto the front drive was open. 'Come on, Kate,' he yelled out. 'I think our friend has scarpered.'

CHAPTER 22

Matt ran back into the kitchen and began pulling on his damp socks and sweater. 'Where are my bloody boots?' he called out to Kate, who had already put on her coat and was heading for the back door.

'In the utility room on top of the spin dryer. We'll go in my car.' The door slammed as Matt hurried to retrieve his boots and pull them on.

The Fiat was already ticking over as he ran over and opened the passenger door. 'He can't have got very far,' he said as he got in and slammed the door shut. 'The problem is, which way?'

'My guess is he'll go towards the village.'

'You're probably right. I can't think he'll want to go back in the direction of the moor after what he's been through.' Matt though for a moment. 'Yes, I reckon he could be on his way back to the manor. The lad's not stupid, he knows if he goes back of his own accord, they are more likely to be lenient with him, and I think I've got a bit of leverage that will ensure that they do. So let's see if we can find him and give him a helping hand. Do you reckon?'

Kate nodded as she turned out of the gateway towards the village.

It was not long before they caught a glimpse of Jacko's red shirt at the T-junction. As Matt had predicted, he turned left in the direction of the village.

Kate put her foot on the accelerator and pulled up just in front of him while Matt opened the passenger door and got out to bar Jacko's way with outstretched arms.

The youth stopped in front of him and, without being asked, announced that he was going to give himself up at the manor. Matt lowered his arms and smiled. 'Well done, young feller. I'm sure that's the right thing to do. Come on, get in, we'll give you a lift.'

Jacko hesitated. 'Don't wanna trouble you no more. I … '

Matt took hold of his arm and gently eased him into a back seat. 'That's alright, lad,' he told him, 'I'll have a word with whatshisname.'

'Burford,' Kate interjected.

'Oh, yes, Mr. Burford. I'm sure he'll understand.'

Jacko gave a grunt of disbelief as he settled in the back seat with his arms folded and eyes closed.

As they drove through the manor gates, Matt told Kate to park in her usual spot beside the gate to the stables. 'I think I should take him in on my own,' he told her. 'You work here, so it's probably best that you are not seen to be involved.'

'Why? I don't mind being involved if it helps.'

Matt gave her a big smile. 'It's just that I might have to tell a few fibs,' he said quietly. He turned to the passenger in the back seat. 'I'll tell them that I found you wandering on the moor and you asked the way back here. Is that okay?' Jacko gave a brief nod as Matt continued. 'I don't think you need to say much more. You got lost, slept in a barn and met me, that's all; so come on, Jacko, the sooner we get this over and done with, the sooner I can get out of this wet clobber and get something to eat.'

Together they walked round to the front of the manor and went on through the main door into the lobby. Matt could hear the clink of utensils coming from the dining room and the smell made his mouth water; it was lunchtime. Jacko indicated towards the front office where he knew Mrs. Gazeley would be sitting eating her meagre sandwiches.

'I'll do the talking,' Matt told him as he knocked on the door and, without waiting for a response, opened it to push Jacko through.

Mrs. Gazeley looked up and almost choked when she saw who was standing in front of her. 'I found this young man wandering on the moor. He said he was lost and couldn't find his way back,' Matt told her.

She put down the sandwich she was eating and reached for one of the phones on her desk. 'I'll tell Mr. Burford you are here. He's having lunch at the moment but I'm sure he'll come straightaway. Would you both like to take a seat?' There was a brief conversation on the phone during which the voice at the other end seemed to reach a high pitch. Mrs. Gazeley was nodding. 'Yes, it's him, and the gentleman from Coombe Cottage.' She had recognised Matt as soon as he came through the door. 'He's on his way,' she told him.

A few minutes later, the door opened and Burford walked in. Matt and Jacko stood up. Matt sensed the youth was tense and put a hand on his shoulder. He repeated what he had told Mrs. Gazeley. Burford looked briefly at Jacko, but seemed more interested in Matt. He held out his hand. 'Don't think we've met, Mr. … '

'Winsford, Matt Winsford.' He shook the hand, but did not smile.

'Come with me please, both of you.'

He led them out down the corridor and into his own office, indicating for them to sit while he settled himself behind his desk. He picked up a pencil and began to twirl it between his thumb and forefinger while looking intently at Jacko. 'Right, Williams, what's your story?' He asked sternly.

Jacko stood up. 'I got lost in the fog.'

'You got lost yesterday, so where the hell have you been since then?'

'Dunno, it got dark. I slept in a barn.'

'And you were trying all that time to get back here?' Burford's voice echoed his disbelief. He slapped the pencil down onto the top of the desk and leant forward. 'All right, Williams, go and get yourself sorted out, and come back and see me at two o'clock.'

Jacko gave a slight nod and walked to the door, pausing briefly to look back at Matt. 'Thanks,' he said quietly, and went out, closing the door behind him.

Burford sat back in his chair and picked up the pencil again, and began to twirl it. 'I don't believe a word of that,' he told Matt. 'I haven't the slightest doubt he was bent on getting away from this establishment for good. It's something that has only happened here once before and, in that case, the lad was caught and sent to a more rigorous establishment. That is what is going to happen to our friend, Williams.'

'I don't think that would be very wise, Mr. Burford.'

Burford sat up. 'I don't think you understand, Mr. Winsford. I have already reported this incident to the authorities, and they will do as I suggest.'

Matt drew his chair closer to the desk. He folded his arms and looked steadily at Burford. 'There are things in this establishment that, to my mind, don't add up, Mr. Burford. Firstly, that lad told me he was physically abused by one of your staff. I noticed the bruises and I believe him. Secondly, he knows, from previous contact, that his abuser is not only into drugs, but has done time for it. Thirdly, if that is so, how come he works in a place like Lidstone Manor?'

Burford shifted uncomfortably in his chair. 'This is all hearsay, Mr. Winsford and, I can assure you, there is not an atom of truth in any of it.'

'Well, in that case, if I do pass on the facts to the authorities, you will have nothing to fear.'

There was a long pause before Burford replied. 'I will certainly investigate any accusations of physical violence, Mr. Winsford, but as to the drugs issue, I can tell you that we have a strict anti-drugs regime here.'

'I'm sure you do, Mr. Burford.' Matt tried to sound convinced. 'I have no doubt you keep a close eye on the inmates, but it is a member of your staff we are talking about, which brings me to another matter I would like to discuss with you: the stables.'

'They are nothing to do with me, Mr. Winsford. They are the sole responsibility of my wife.'

'I am aware of that, but I'm sure you know what goes on there.'

'What do you mean what goes on there? It's a stable that takes liveries and does some horse trading.'

'Then why are they so interested in me? I get the feeling I'm being watched all the time.'

'That's ridiculous.'

'Maybe, but the fact is on several occasions, I have seen one of the men there watching my cottage through long-range binoculars, and I would like to know why.' Matt was getting to the issues he wanted to confront Burford with. He watched the man's reactions as he continued. 'I wondered if you might have any idea who might have trashed the cottage soon after I moved in?'

Burford shook his head. 'I don't see what that has to do with me or the stables. Why are you asking me these things?'

Matt sensed the man was getting agitated and angry. He pressed on. 'Then there was the attempted mugging.' Matt paused and watched the man intently. 'I heard one of the muggers call out the name Ken, or it might have been Kev. So I would be looking for a Kenneth or Kevin. Any clues?

'I'm afraid not.'

Matt felt sure he was lying. 'In that case, I'll just have to keep digging, not that it would necessarily turn up anything I could prove. I guess I'm just curious by nature.'

'So, what has all this to do with Jackson Williams, Mr. Winsford?'

'Quite simply that if you take his case up with the authorities, I will have to tell them all I know … about Williams, I mean.'

The inference was not lost on Burford. 'Alright, Mr. Winsford, I will do what I can to keep the incident "in-house", but I am curious to know why you are taking so much interest in this young man?'

Matt considered for a moment. 'I don't like to see any young person victimised by institutional bullying.' He thought it sounded a bit pompous, but it was true; he had seen it happen to young recruits and knew the results could be disastrous for some individuals.

'I don't think this a case of institutional bullying, Mr. Winsford,' Burford sounded defensive, 'but if there is any evidence of individual bullying, I will certainly look into it and take appropriate action.' He had a feeling he already had and was relieved that Kevin Andrews was no longer a part of the organisation. In a few days, he would be able to tell Winsford that the matter had been resolved and the perpetrator dismissed. Sounding more confident, he invited Matt to come back in a week's time when he would be able to tell him what had been done.

'I would like to see the young man then, if that is possible.' Matt knew from experience that things "brushed under the carpet" did not always end satisfactorily as far as the victims were concerned. He wanted to check.

Burford hesitated. 'If you feel that is necessary, I can arrange for you to see him on a Sunday at normal visiting time. His family never bother to come so it won't clash with anything.'

'Good, we'll leave it at that then.' Matt stood up. They shook hands.

As soon as Matt had left the room, Burford picked up the telephone and tapped in the number for head office.

*

Kate was sitting in the Fiat listening to Radio One. She had phoned the stables on her mobile to briefly explain that she had been delayed and would be late back after lunch. She knew that Greta would not be too worried as the riders did not normally return from the hunt until mid-afternoon at the earliest and she would be able to cope until then. She told her that Ivan, as usual, was away "on business".

She sat back and contemplated the morning's events. It had been interesting, to say the least, watching this guy deal with the half-conscious youth. It seemed almost as though it was a routine he had been through before, and she wondered if he was some sort of paramedic. Whatever or whoever he was, the more she thought about it, the more she became convinced that there could be nothing sinister in the background of someone who could behave like that. Perhaps Matt Winsford was just an ordinary bloke who was recovering from a nasty accident.

Matt could hear the *thump thump* of the drumbeats as he approached the vehicle. The latest pop would not be his first choice of music. At school, he had been a member of the school choir and music lessons had concentrated more on the classical side; he liked Elgar, Pomp and Circumstance, of course, and Vaughan Williams' The Lark Ascending reminded him of home, walking the stubbles with his dad and the birds rising up in front of them.

Kate turned the music off as Matt opened the passenger door and got in. 'Sorry to keep you waiting,' he said as he clicked the seat belt.

'That's alright. What did Burford say?'

Matt grinned. 'He was going to recommend the lad should be sent to what he called a more rigorous establishment, but I think I said enough to put him off that. With any luck, our friend Jacko will end up with just a ticking off. I'm going to be allowed to see him in a couple of weeks and I'll get to know what Burford has done about the staff bullying issue.' He turned to look at Kate. 'Thanks for your help,' he said quietly. 'Couldn't have done it without you.'

187

Kate smiled and told him she hadn't done anything much and it was only a case of being in the right place at the right time. 'Come on,' she added, 'let's go home and get something to eat'.

As the Fiat turned out of the manor gateway, they were suddenly aware of a red-coated horseman coming up behind. Kate lowered her window and pulled over to let him pass. As he did so, he peered down and stopped his big grey horse alongside. 'Hello, young Kate. I thought it was you. Not out today then?' The voice had a slight West Country burr.

Matt leant over and looked up to see the flushed face of a middle-aged man; like many red-coated hunters, he wore no chinstrap and his ample grey sideburns came halfway down his cheeks. He was smiling broadly at Kate, then shifted his gaze to Matt and, with a nod, asked if they were following.

Kate shook her head. 'Not today, Bill, got too much on.'

The man's smile got even broader as he looked at Matt. 'I can see you have,' he said. He touched the grey with his spurs and trotted on down the road as several more riders appeared, many of whom waved to Kate.

'Who was that?' Matt asked.

'That was the one and only Bill Bowden. Quite a character in these parts. He has a small farm and large holiday caravan complex near Torquay. He's been a joint master for over twenty years now, and I've no doubt will continue as long as he keeps putting some of his hard-earned cash into the hunt.' Kate stopped talking and was listening. 'Hark!' she suddenly cried.

It was a term Matt had heard many times before: it meant she could hear the hounds. Sure enough, when he lowered the window on his side, he heard the sound that took him back to his boyhood.

'They're speaking in the copse the other side of Long Meadow,' Kate told him.

Matt knew that hunting hounds did not bark, they "spoke" or "gave tongue". It was more than ten years since he had heard a pack of hounds in full cry but it still raised the hairs on the back of his neck. 'They're onto a fox,' he said.

'No,' Kate corrected him. 'We can't hunt foxes now. They will be following a laid trail.'

'Oh, yes, I had forgotten. In fact, the last time I went hunting was over ten years ago, just before the ban.'

'So you've been hunting?'

'Done a bit.'

'Where have I heard that phrase before?' Kate glanced sideways at him. 'There's nothing to stop you having a day with these,' she said casually. 'I'll find you a suitable horse and you can pay a visitor's cap; I'll have a word with Bill.'

Matt smiled; he had often wondered why they called the day subscription a "cap". Perhaps because in the old days it would have been collected in the secretary's hat. He thought for a moment. 'No, thanks, I'm not sure that I'm up to it yet.' He did not want to elaborate but the fact was he dare not risk further damage to his leg; the possibility of it being crushed against a gatepost by eager riders anxious to get through, or catching his foot against the trunk of a tree by riding too close were the sort of things he had experienced as a boy.

'Ah, well, perhaps another time.'

Matt was pleased she sounded disappointed. 'Anyway, what's it like following a man-laid trail instead of a fox?'

'You probably wouldn't notice the difference,' Kate told him as they drew into the yard. Mary Lethbridge's grey Skoda was already parked by the back door of the house. 'What on earth's been going on here?' she asked as they entered the kitchen. She had the bathroom towel in her hands and was looking at the dirty plate and crumb-strewn table.

Kate picked up the plate and knife and fork and put them into the sink. 'It's a long story, Mum, so let's go into the sitting room and Matt can tell you all about it.' They went in and Matt recounted the morning's events.

'That explains it,' Mary said.

'Explains what, Mum?'

'Melissa Thompson was out with some of the liveries yesterday and she said she'd seen a young coloured lad running up past Colspit Wood. I suppose she noticed him because we don't get many of that sort round here. She thought he was just out training for the Plymouth half-marathon or something.'

'I hope that doesn't go any further,' Matt said. 'I've told Mr. Burford that the boy was lost on the moor, which he was, not jogging round the lanes looking for a way out.'

Mary smiled. 'I think you've both done very well. I'd hate to think of that poor lad getting punished after what he'd been through.'

Matt closed his eyes. There it was again, Mary Lethbridge treating him like a good little boy due for a lollipop. The lollipop came in the shape of an invitation to lunch.

*

Jacko was sitting on his bed when Clayton and Wiggy came through the door. It was Clayton who spoke first.

'Wow, man, what happened?' Jacko took the money out of his pocket and threw it down on the bed.

'I fucking cocked it up,' he said, and told them most of what had happened, leaving out the episode where he was found half-dead on the moor.

Clayton sat down beside him and began to pick up the coins. 'So this guy found you wandering about and brought you back here?'

'Yeah, an' there was a bird what took us in her house. I felt bloody awful. She gave me some grub. I think she works in the stables.'

Wiggy walked over and picked up his ten pound note. 'That'll be Kate,' he told him. 'She's alright, gave me a good time at the stables.'

'Wa-hey!' Clayton called out.

'Not like that, you twit. It's just that she seemed to make working there easy.' He watched Jacko take off his muddy trainers and begin to pick the mud off with his fingernails. 'So what happens now?' he asked him.

'Dunno, got to see Burford at two o'clock. What's the time now?'

Wiggy looked at his watch. 'You're late.'

'Shit.' Jacko quickly put his trainers back on and made for the door.

*

'I'm not used to waiting, Williams.' Burford was sitting at his desk, arms folded, when Jacko walked in.

'Sorry, sir. I ain't got a watch.'

'That's no excuse, Williams.' There was a long pause while Burford leant forward, elbows on the table and hands clasped.

Jacko could see he was angry and was afraid he was the cause; it meant he could expect the worst. He closed his eyes, waited and was surprised when he was told he would not be punished for what had occurred over the last two days.

'I have been persuaded,' Burford told him, 'that you were genuinely lost. I have therefore reported to the authorities that you are back and no harm has been done. However, I think it is right that you are put on extra duties and I will give instructions that you will be kept under close surveillance. Is that clear?'

Jacko opened his eyes and gave a sigh of relief. 'Yes, sir.'

'Right, you can go.'

Jacko thought the man looked very agitated. He was right. Burford had just received some very disturbing news.

CHAPTER 23

'I'm afraid it's only yesterday's leftovers,' Mary said as she served the portions of warmed up shepherd's pie with spoonfuls of freshly cooked swede. She sat down and watched as Matt immediately tucked into his meal while Kate picked at the mashed potatoes, seemingly deep in thought.

'So you two have been a couple of Good Samaritans this morning,' Mary commented as she started her own meal.

Matt shook his head. 'I wouldn't say that,' he muttered between mouthfuls.

'I would,' Kate said. 'Or at least, I should say that you were. I just happened to be around.'

Mary smiled. 'Doesn't matter, Kate. You were able to help Matt and that's what counts.'

'What's that supposed to mean, Mother?'

'Oh, just get on with your meal, girl.'

Nothing more was said until the dishes were cleared away when Kate suddenly announced that she had to get back to the stables and moved towards the door, pausing briefly to look at Matt. 'See you,' she said with a faint smile. He hoped so.

Matt had just time to settle into the driving seat of the Volvo before Bullet jumped onto his lap and began licking his face. The old dog had been sleeping on the passenger seat while his master had been otherwise engaged. 'Get down, you old fool.' Matt pushed him back, started the engine, sniffed and lowered the window to release the smell of dog fart.

The drive back to the cottage gave Matt time to consider more carefully what had occurred and what he had learned from the young man he had helped. There was something definitely not right at Lidstone Manor. How could they have employed a known drugs offender in a government sponsored establishment? How come it had been so easy to dissuade Burford from taking action against the young lad? What was he frightened of?

Then there was the question of the stables. Why were they so interested in him? As far as he knew, he had done nothing to upset them in any way, and yet he had the distinct feeling that he was under surveillance all the time. The biggest puzzle concerned the trashing of the cottage and the attempted mugging. Were they connected and, if so, what was the purpose? Perhaps he would learn a little more on his forthcoming visit to see the young coloured lad; it was one reason he had made the request, another reason harked back to his army career and his experience with young recruits – he just felt he wanted to help him.

A quick shower and change of clothes gave Matt the necessary buzz to think about other things and, in particular, the forthcoming supper with Spud Wannacott.

Half an hour later, he was driving down the steep, winding road to Bovey Tracey. Aware that he was not a great cook, he had decided that a couple of the excellent steak and kidney pies from the local butcher would fit the bill, together with a packet of frozen peas and a ready-made trifle from the small supermarket. Potatoes were no problem; he had a twelve kilo bag in the kitchen bought from the farm just down the road. He completed his shopping with two six-packs of John Smiths, which he put in the bottom of his backpack before carefully placing the other purchases on the top.

The cloud had dispersed leaving a clear blue sky as man and dog progressed through the open moor towards the tree-lined road that led to Lidstone. It meant there would be a frost and, following the recent rain, ice on most of the roads. He was glad it was not him driving that night. It was reassuring that Spud had a Land Rover so he should be okay as long as he drove carefully, particularly when he'd had a few beers. He glanced at his watch: there would be just enough time to do some work on Dot's portrait before he had to start cooking. How nice it would have been, he thought, if his guest had been Dot's owner. He dismissed the idea as a slight on Spud. In truth, he was glad the old man was coming, it gave him a chance to talk openly about the thing that dogged his past, and he felt very much at ease in his company.

As it happened, he need not have worried about Spud's driving. The old man arrived on foot just after seven-thirty. It was Bullet who heard the gentle tap on the front door, alerting his owner with a tirade of angry barking. With a yell to the dog to shut up, Matt opened the door and welcomed his guest with a broad smile. 'Come in, come in,' he said, stepping back to allow the old man in. 'What's it like out there?' Matt asked.

Spud shivered as he switched off his torch and stuffed it into the pocket of his thick brown overcoat, over which he wore a green reflective bib. 'Bloody cold,' he told him. 'Real brass monkey weather and like a skating rink at the bottom of the lane. I've been on at the council for months to get the drain cleared, but you know what it's like these days, drains and potholes don't feature in their budget.'

'So you decided to walk it.'

'Yep. Don't like driving on ice, especially after I've had a drink or two.' He handed Matt the long hazel walking stick he held in his left hand together with a large plastic bag containing something heavy. 'Thought you might like a bit of fresh venison,' he said with a grin as he took off the black woollen hat which came down over his ears.

'Thanks very much, Spud.' Matt opened the bag and looked in to see several large chunks of red meat. 'I'll look forward to that.' He helped him out of his overcoat and led him into the kitchen. 'I'm afraid you won't be getting anything as exotic as venison. It's just steak and kidney pie and mash. Come and warm yourself for a few minutes while I put them in the oven and get the spuds boiled.' He pointed to the chair nearest to the stove and noticed that the old man was wearing his regimental tie with his smart brown tweed jacket and grey cords. He wished he had put on something better than jeans and his old blue sweater, and made an excuse for his own rather dishevelled appearance, saying that he had been too preoccupied with his painting to notice the time and hadn't had time to change. Which was partly true.

As Spud sat down, he pointed to his rubber-soled army surplus boots. 'Okay with them, or should I take 'em off?'

Matt grinned. 'I think we are all better keeping our footwear on, particularly if you've just been walking. How far is it?'

'Barely a mile, I reckon. Hardly far enough to put on a sweat.' Spud grinned as he unbuttoned his jacket and settled back into the chair to watch his host trying to emulate Jamie Oliver.

Matt closed the oven door, checked the potatoes just coming to boil and poured the frozen peas into a saucepan of hot water ready to heat up just before they were ready to eat. 'I'll just lay the table,' he told Spud, 'then we can go into the sitting room for a noggin. How does that sound?'

'Okay by me,' came the reply as Spud loosened his collar and moved the chair further from the oven. 'Whew, I'm not used to this sort of temperature.' He took off his jacket and hung it over the back of the chair.

Matt grinned. 'You have to give it to old Spreyton, he's geared up this place for winter lets with the latest electric central heating. For a lot of folk, it would be more comfortable than back home. Come on, you'll find it cooler next door.'

And it was, but not much. The electric imitation fire produced a warming glow, in front of which Bullet was stretched out quietly snoring. Matt told Spud to make himself comfortable while he poured two generous glasses of Bushmills whiskey topped up with ungenerous amounts of water. The two men sat in silence, sipping their drink, until Matt eventually opened the conversation by asking Spud if he knew anything about the people running Lidstone Manor.

'What makes you ask that?'

Matt told him what had happened earlier that day. The old man fixed his eyes on the glass in his hand for several seconds before answering.

'So … you're telling me this young man was physically abused by someone he knew to be a drug dealer and who was employed by Lidstone Manor, which is supposed to be a juvenile correction centre? That all sounds a bit fishy for a start. Then the man threatens to take it out on his mother if he tells anyone?'

'That's about it. You can understand why a scared and probably confused youngster would attempt to get away home.'

Spud grunted. 'I've known young recruits, with a lot less reason, try and do the same.'

'Me too, but the question is, what do we do, if anything, about it?'

'That's a difficult one, but what you've told me backs up the rumours I heard coming from the stables recently, and there's something going on there I'd like to share with you … ' A pinging sound coming from the direction of the kitchen stopped Spud mid-sentence.

Matt stood up. 'That means the pies are ready, you'll have to tell me after we've eaten. Give me a minute while I mash the potatoes and heat up the peas. Would you like another drink?'

Spud shook his head. 'No, thanks, I'll finish this one then come through.'

Four empty beer cans and two half-full glasses stood on the table as the last of the dessert was finished. Spud leant back and patted his belly. 'Very nice,' he said. 'I enjoyed that. It's not often I get to eat in company. So cheers.'

Both men drained their glasses, after which Matt stood up and began to clear the table. 'I'll make some coffee. Milk and sugar?'

'Yes, please, just a small spoonful.'

'Okay, I'll bring it through to the sitting room. Help yourself to another tot.'

Seated once more in the comfort of the sitting room, Matt sipped his black coffee. He was curious to know what Spud had been about to tell him concerning the stables before being interrupted by the oven timer. The old man put down his coffee cup, picked up his glass of whiskey and took a gulp.

'It happened a couple of days, or I should say nights, ago, up in the woods at Haldon,' he told him. 'It must have been about two o'clock, pitch dark, and there it was, the big Scania horsebox parked up miles from anywhere, just off the road.' He took another gulp of whiskey. 'And that's not all. As I was watching, another vehicle turned up. Couldn't see what sort but it was white, and then I heard horses stamping and the sound of people talking. A few minutes later, all went quiet until the Scania started up and drove off towards Exeter.'

'Very interesting.' Matt poured himself a small whiskey and grinned at Spud. 'And what is equally interesting is what you were doing in the forest at two o'clock in the morning.'

The old man said nothing for several second, then looked up at Matt. 'I hope you enjoy your venison.'

Matt grinned. 'I'm sure I will, but let's get back to the Scania. What do you think it was doing there in the middle of the night?'

'Your guess is as good as mine. All I know is it was there, not broken down because it started up without any problem, and there were several people. Couldn't say how many, but definitely more than two.'

'And the horsebox was still loaded?'

'Yes. I distinctly heard the thump of hooves.'

'I still can't understand why a horsebox, loaded with horses, is parked up in woodland at two o'clock in the morning; and then there's the other vehicle.' Matt thought for a moment. 'Do you think the drugs chap is mixed up in this and they are, in fact, drug dealers?'

'Well, there's one thing. No sniffer dog is going to find anything with four or five horses stomping around, and it would need a brave man to go through that lot to look for suspect packages. No, the only way would be to unload the animals, and I can't see them doing that in a busy terminal.'

'You're right, Spud. Jesus, do you reckon we should tell someone?'

The old man paused before speaking. 'Yes, as long as you don't let on that it was me what saw 'em.' He smiled and took another gulp of his whiskey.

'Okay, I think Jim Lethbridge has a contact in the local police, so I'll mention it to him and we'll see what turns up.'

Spud nodded and held up his empty glass for Matt to replenish. 'Talking about turning up, I see your girlfriend's back.'

Matt poured himself a small amount of whiskey before replying that as far as he knew, he did not have a girlfriend.

Spud chuckled. 'I'm talking about the gal with the white van. It was parked up on the grass verge just past the manor gates yesterday.'

'Oh?'

'Yep, didn't see me, too engrossed in her mobile, probably contacting her customers and taking lots of orders.'

Matt was disappointed; she had not contacted him. 'I suppose so,' he said lamely.

The conversation turned back to the question of the abused youth and how best to help him. Matt told Spud he had permission to see the lad in a couple of weeks.

'If I were you,' Spud told him, 'I'd just make sure he's alright and leave it at that. There's not much else you can do.'

'I don't know. I'd like to think there is something better for him when he's finished at the manor. What about an apprenticeship of some sort?'

'You'll have to talk to the lad about that and find out what he would like to do. There's always the possibility of an army apprenticeship, and you might be able to pull a few strings.'

'Hadn't thought of that. I might suggest it to him.'

Spud looked at Matt and nodded. 'Good, so when you've sorted out the lad's future, I'd like to suggest you start thinking about your own.'

Matt gave a long, thoughtful sigh. 'I know, Spud, you don't have to lecture me. I've been thinking about it a lot recently, and I've come to the conclusion that I'll be going home for Christmas at the latest. I'm feeling okay now and, I have to say, much of that is due to you.'

'So, are you going back to the army?'

'Haven't made up my mind yet.'

'I'll miss you, Matthew Winsford.' The old man's voice sounded croaky. 'You'll be the only one.'

Spud shook his head and smiled. 'I don't think so, young man.' He looked at his watch. 'It's been very nice, Matt, but time's getting on and I should be making my way back before it gets too late.'

He stood up and Matt noticed he was not very steady on his legs. 'Are you sure you'll be alright?' He asked him. 'You could stay the night if you like and I can make a bed up in the spare room.'

'No, thanks, I'm fine, and anyway, old Jen will be expecting me back. She's been cooped up inside long enough already and God knows what she'd do if I left her there all night.' He began to put on his jacket. Matt helped him on with his overcoat and fetched his hat and stick.

Outside it was bright but cold and the old man's breath hung in the air. Matt clasped his hand and shook it. 'Thanks for coming, Spud, and thanks for, you know, helping.'

The old man smiled. 'That's alright, boy, everyone needs a shoulder to cry on at some time in their lives. I'm only too pleased it was mine.' He turned to go when Matt took hold of his arm.

'Hang on a minute, Spud.' He went back into the cottage and returned with a slip of paper. 'Here's my mobile number; give me a call as soon as you get back or I'll not sleep tonight.' The old man nodded, folded the paper and stuffed it into his overcoat pocket, then he took out his torch and walked up the drive towards the gate. 'Take care,' Matt called out and listened to the *tap-tap* of the stick getting fainter along the road.

Less than an hour later, Matt's phone rang and he was relieved to hear that it was Spud on the other end. 'You okay, Spud?'

'Yea, fine, and guess what? It's just as well I didn't take the old Land Rover 'cos there was a police car parked just up on the top road about a hundred yards from your gate. Looking to catch anyone driving from the pub, I suppose.'

'That's odd. Can't be many going that way. They must have got more coppers on the beat than they let on.'

'That's not all. It seems your girlfriend works late. Her van passed me going like the clappers in the opposite direction.'

'I suppose she's pretty busy this time of year, just coming up the Christmas.' Matt did not sound convinced. 'Anyway, you got home alright and that's the main thing, so take care and I'll probably see you sometime next week.' Matt switched off the phone as Bullet came over to put a wet nose on his hand. Matt gently stroked the grizzled head. 'It seems it's all go out there tonight, old chap,' he told him.

CHAPTER 24

'They've picked up Kevin Andrews.' Burford was sitting at his desk, nervously twirling the familiar pencil, while Greta and Ivan sat, stone-faced, watching him.

It was Ivan who spoke first. 'How did they know?'

Burford shrugged. 'Your guess is as good as mine. All I know is he was arrested at his mother's house in Tottenham a couple of days ago.'

'Who told you, William?' Greta leant forward to put both hands on the desk.

'A chap called Chalky White phoned. Said he reckoned they must have been followed from the station, but worse than that, apparently Chalky had been instructed to take Kevin to Hampstead so he was probably followed there.'

'Whew!' Ivan let out a long breath. 'That does mean big trouble.'

'What I'd like to know is how the bloody hell did they find out he was going there?' Burford raised his hands in a gesture of exasperation.

Ivan was watching him intently. 'You always use landline phone?'

'Yes, of course. I'm perfectly aware that mobiles can be tapped so we never use them for business.'

Ivan thought for a moment. 'You have any visitors recently that you did not know?'

Burford thought for a moment. 'Only that chap from Coombe Cottage. Why?'

'You could have been bugged.'

'Good God, how the hell could that have happened? No, there's no way he could have put a chip anywhere. He sat just where you are now, where I could see him all the time.'

'No one else you do not know has been to this office?' Ivan moved his chair closer to lean forward and put his elbows on the desk.

'The only one I can think of is the copper who came about the late night movements of the Scania.'

'He sat?'

'About where you are now, didn't move except to lean forward and put some papers on the desk for me to look at.'

'Ah.' Ivan eased his chair forward and, with his fingers, began to explore the underneath of the desktop which overlapped a few inches beyond the solid wooden front. It took him only seconds to dislodge a tiny black plastic box, less than an inch square and a quarter of an inch deep. He slapped it onto the desktop with an angry growl and said something in a language Burford did not understand before dropping it on the floor and crushing it under his boot. There was a long period of silence before Burford swallowed hard and muttered something to himself which was inaudible, except for the last word, which was a long drawn-out 'Shit!'

It was Greta who spoke first. 'So what happens now?'

Ivan was picking up the pieces of plastic and wire. 'How long ago he was here?'

Burford shrugged. 'Must be a couple of weeks or more. I could look it up if you like.'

Ivan shook his head. 'Not necessary,' he told him. 'Bug only good for two, three days at most, then battery run out. Important is what you said in those days to anyone.'

There was a long silence before Burford spoke. 'You remember, I had a word with Kevin that afternoon about his habit and then you and Greta came in and we discussed what to do about the changes we would have to make to satisfy the complaint made by the copper.'

'You tell him to see his contacts?'

'Yes, then a couple of days later I bought his ticket and told him he would be catching the eight-thirty from Exeter.'

Ivan gave a groan and threw his hands in the air. 'That is it then. Let us hope they are only interested in him and not us.'

'He does have a past record in drugs.'

'That is the worry.'

'So what do we do now?' Burford's voice indicated his rising panic.

It was Greta who answered. 'Shut down as from now. Get the Scania back to a normal horsebox and forget about anything else.'

Her husband nodded in agreement. 'We've got too much at stake here at the manor to risk any more of your little deals.' He was looking intently at Ivan.

'Deals not so little,' the ex-jockey retorted angrily. 'You both will miss the results.'

'Not so much as you, my friend.' Burford was beginning to lose his temper. 'You got us into this, now you can bloody well get us out.'

Ivan raised his hands, palms towards his accuser. 'Just calm, please. Alright, we stop now, wait for things to calm down, then we see.'

'The problem is,' Greta said quietly, 'there's a consignment on its way as we speak. What do we do about that?'

'Just keep our bloody fingers crossed and hope they haven't sussed us yet.' Burford looked anxiously at his wife as he dabbed his forehead with his handkerchief. 'Could we abort?'

Greta shook her head. 'No chance. You know full well contact en route is verboten. We cannot use mobile phones.'

Ivan stood up suddenly. 'They must not come here so I will go and meet them. I know first stop. I go now. Will get there before them and make arrangements. I take Land Rover.'

Burford leant back in his chair and nodded. 'Okay, let's hope to God you can sort something out before things turn really nasty.'

'I do my best.' Ivan called over his shoulder as he went out of the door.

When he had gone, Burford and Greta sat looking at each other, both deep in thought. It was Burford who spoke first. 'We should never have got mixed up in this business.' He shook his head slowly, picked up his pencil and began to twirl it nervously.

His wife grunted dismissively. 'Too late now, William.' She stood up and gazed out of the window. 'The best we can hope for is that Ivan gets to the Scania before anyone else.'

Anyone else being the Border Control Agency?'

'Precisely.'

'How would they know? I mean, we never discuss consignments except in private, just the three of us, and certainly never on the phone. Kevin knew what we were doing but never the details of routes or timings until the day of departure, and that goes for the rest of the crew.' Burford joined his wife at the window and as they watched a line of red T-shirted young men walk from the garden to the main house, he turned to face her and put a hand on her shoulder. 'I came into the other business because of you, Greta. I wanted the best for you and we've come pretty close to the nest egg I was hoping for, so let's cut our losses and get out while we can. I'll send in my resignation, you can find somebody to take over the stables and we'll say goodbye to all this and head for Spain, Malaga, or anywhere. What do you say?'

Greta shook her head and looked up at him, close to tears. 'If only it was as easy as that, William but you know as well as I do that you might be able to drop out but I cannot, not while you know who is still around.'

'That bloody man,' Burford said between gritted teeth. 'I wish to hell you had never got involved with him.'

Greta sighed and began to wipe her eyes with her handkerchief. 'What is past is past, we cannot undo. Ivan is my curse and I must live with it.'

We must live with it, my love.' Burford put his arm round his wife and gave her a hug.

*

'Guess what, man,' Clayton flung himself on his bed and laid down, hands under the back of his head, gazing at the ceiling.

'What?' Jacko was sitting, trying to clean some of the mud that still stuck to his trainers.

'It looks as though your worries might be over, Jacko.'

'What are you talking about?'

'It seems our friend Beaky has been picked up by the fuzz somewhere in London.'

'How do y' know that?'

Clayton sat up, tapped the side of his nose with his forefinger and winked. 'Let's just say I got my contacts.'

'You mean Mrs. Gazeley told you., Wiggy said as he threw a damp towel at Clayton's head.

'Don't matter how I know, man, it's a fact.'

Jacko stopped what he was doing. If it was true, it meant his worries were over. Beaky was taken care of: his mother was safe. He reached into the drawer of the bedside cupboard and took out her latest letter to read again. It told him she was well but expecting again; her latest boyfriend Andy had gone the way of all the others and she was living alone again. There was a long screed about the change in benefits and how that was going to make life more difficult; finally, she implored him to "be a good boy", make the most of his time at "the school" and concentrate on getting a job at the end so that he could come home and help.

He carefully folded the letter and placed it back in the drawer. Hopefully she would never know what he had tried to do. He thought about the two people who had helped him. It was the first time he had experienced that sort of kindness from strangers. He realised they were not complete strangers; he had recognised the girl from the stables and he was sure the man was the guy who lived in the cottage at the top of the hill. Burford had told him the man was coming to see him sometime next week; the thought made him feel uncomfortable. Why did he want to see him? What did he want? Why had Burford let him off so lightly when he had obviously attempted a bunk.

Jacko closed his eyes as he turned over the questions in his mind. It was a dig in the ribs from Wiggy that brought him back to full consciousness.

'Come on, Jacko, the supper bell's gone.' Jacko sat up and shook his head.

'You go on, I ain't hungry.'

Clayton grinned. 'Don't bother him, man, he's still knackered from the run.'

Jacko said nothing as he watched them go out into the corridor.

CHAPTER 25

The news that Serena was back had come as a surprise to Matt. He was disappointed that she had not contacted him yet, in spite of the fact that it had been two days since Spud had seen her van.

The sighting had prompted him to get on and put the finishing touches to the portrait of her dog. Now he stood back and studied his work, pleased with the result and hopeful that Serena would feel the same way. He now had a good reason to get in contact. He took out his mobile and tapped in her number: the voice at the other end told him that she was not available and he should try later. He put his phone back into his pocket and walked through into the kitchen where Bullet was noisily gnawing a large bone. He sat down at the table, feeling depressed. He began to realise how much he missed the comradeship of fellow soldiers; the only person he could really talk to was Spud, and he was not there.

It was a long time since he had felt so fed up. The half-empty whiskey bottle on the shelf looked inviting but he decided against it and instead reached for his walking boots. 'Come on, Bullet, let's go walkies.' The old dog immediately abandoned the bone and, tail wagging furiously, waited at the door and watched his master put on the familiar wax jacket. Matt glanced at his watch: it was just gone four o'clock; plenty of time before it started to get dark. He decided he did not need to take a stick this time; his leg felt good and there had been less pain recently, which made him more determined to get back to walking as normally as possible.

Outside a pale winter sun hung over the ragged moorland skyline. The sky was a clear blue and Matt knew there would be a hard frost by the morning. He pulled the zip of his jacket higher as the cold air bit into his lungs, then he felt for the old flat cap which he had stuffed in his pocket the previous day. He crammed it on his head and, with a yell to Bullet, set off across the lane and onto the familiar track that led onto the moor. Overhead a flock of crows cawed noisily as they glided towards their roost in the fir plantation in the valley below, while a lone buzzard mewed plaintively high above them as it soared on the last thermals of the day.

He walked briskly for half an hour up the steep incline towards the distant silhouette of Hound Tor while Bullet hunted through the gorse that grew to the left of the track. On the right, a drystone wall stretched into the far distance; now in disrepair, many of the stones had fallen onto the track, creating an additional hazard for walkers as Matt discovered when he almost tripped over a stone that had rolled into one of the many ruts. It jerked his left leg and caused him to stop and massage the limb until the pain subsided and he felt he could continue. He walked slower now, wishing he had brought his stick and trying to ignore the discomfort until it eventually forced him to stop and lean against the wall so that he could take the weight off the leg. He watched Bullet dig at a rabbit hole in the dead bracken while his thoughts turned to his possible future. It was obvious the leg was not going to be normal for a long time, if ever, so decisions had to be made.

Matt turned and looked back at the woods and green fields of Lidstone Coombe. He could just see the church tower and some of the houses through the bare branches of the oak, ash and sycamore trees that lined the road to the village. He realised he had grown very fond of this part of Devon and it was going to be very difficult for him to say goodbye to it, but there was little chance of staying indefinitely. What would he do? There was no way he could make a full living out of painting; he would have a small pension from the army, but that would not be enough. He was not certain the army would have him back, but if it did, he knew he would be relegated to some sort of desk job, and after serving on the front line, he knew he could not accept the job of a pen-pusher. It was then he saw a rider coming down the track towards him.

Matt looked up and smiled. 'Had a good day?'

Kate was dressed for hunting and the dried sweat on Harry's flanks indicated a good gallop at some stage. 'Yes, thank you.' She returned his smile and patted the horse's neck. 'We ran right across Hameldown and into Sousons Wood, which is why I'm a bit late getting back.'

Matt was not sure how far that was but he had seen the massive hump of Hameldown on the horizon and realised it must have been very demanding to gallop over the top of it and on to the woodland beyond. 'Someone must have laid a good trail,' he said.

She grinned. 'You bet.' The horse snorted and began to fidget. 'Better get on,' she said and paused. 'The offer of a day's hunting is still on if you are interested.'

Matt thought for a moment then shook his head as the pain in his became more acute. 'Don't think the old leg is quite up to it yet but I would be happy to come to a meet on foot one day. It would be like old times when I was a boy, except I don't think I will be able to run as well as I did then.'

'You could follow in the car; lots of people do.'

'You mean over the top of Hameldown?'

She laughed. 'You know what I mean. Why don't you try the meet at Dunscombe House next Saturday? It will be all in-country and old

George Bourne makes us very welcome: a glass of whiskey or port, pasties, sandwiches and, if you're lucky, roast potatoes followed by cake.'

Matt knew that in-country meant that it would be in a farming area where it would be easier to follow in a vehicle. 'Where is Dunscombe House?'

Kate thought for a moment. 'It's not easy to find but have a word with Spud, he will almost certainly be going. There is no way he would miss the goodies handed out there.'

Matt nodded. 'Okay, I'll do that.'

'Good. See you.' She waved a hand as she nudged Harry into a walk.

Matt watched them make their way down the track and his immediate impulse was to follow, but then realised there was no point: there was no way his damned leg would let him catch up let alone walk at the rate Harry was going. Seeing Kate at that moment brought his thoughts back to the possibility of staying on at the cottage at least until Christmas; and then there was the question of Serena: she was the dark horse and he had no idea where he stood with her.

Come to think of it, he had no idea where he stood with Kate. He had been impressed by the way she had reacted when they were helping the young coloured lad; there was sympathy and kindness in what she did. It showed a genuine desire to help and he had the feeling that the episode had somehow eased any tension between them: perhaps next time he asked her out, she might agree.

Serena and Kate – no, Kate and Serena – it had been a long time since he had been in a relationship and that had ended mainly due to the pressures of army life: his regular absence on duty, moving house from one posting to another, and the constant worry of whether or not he would return from active service in one piece. It took a certain type of woman to put up with all that, and he would hesitate to inflict it on either Kate or Serena, even if they were willing, which seemed highly unlikely at that moment.

An orange sun now hung above the western skyline. Soon it would dip below the ragged tors. It was the time of day known locally as dimity or dimpsy: not completely light, but not yet dark. Matt shivered; he was stiff and getting cold. Reluctantly he pushed himself away from the wall to stand upright, and at the same time putting his weight on the injured leg: the pain had lessened, he felt ready to follow Harry's hoof prints down the track. He moved to the patch of bracken where he could see one hind leg protruding from the rabbit hole. Bullet was still scratching and growling as Matt grabbed hold of the limb and pulled him out. 'Come on, you old bugger. Leave it! Time to go home.' The dog snorted, shook the soil from his coat, and fell in behind his master.

By the time Matt reached the lane above the cottage, the daylight was fading and he could see the lights of the village beginning to come on. As he turned the corner, the first thing he saw was the white van parked in the cottage driveway with Serena standing beside it, her back towards him. The sound of his boots on the gravel startled her so that she turned round abruptly, giving a sigh of relief when she saw who it was.

'Whew, just in time,' she said. 'I was just about to leave.'

Matt noticed she was wearing a smart black trouser suit, not the sort of garb suitable for selling horse tack. Serena walked towards him and gave him the cheek-to-cheek hug that was the accepted greeting between close friends. He breathed in the heady scent of her perfume before reluctantly allowing her to step away.

'Great to see you,' he told her. 'What have you been up to since I last saw you?'

If he was hoping for an explanation of Spud's sighting of her in the middle of the night, he was doomed to disappointment. She merely shrugged and told him the run up to Christmas was always a busy time and that she had finished her business in the area and would be leaving for home in the morning. 'I just came to see how you were getting on with Dot's portrait,' she added.

Matt was gutted. 'So … so you're going off tomorrow?' He had hoped their brief liaison might lead to something more permanent, but it would appear that was not to be.

'Yes, I'm afraid so.'

At least she sounded as though it was not of her choice, which gave Matt some small comfort. He led her into the cottage and turned on the lights in the studio. Dot' portrait was displayed in a prominent position in the centre of the room. There was a brief moment's silence during which time Matt stepped behind, his fingers crossed.

'Brilliant!' The exclamation came suddenly and Matt hoped his sigh of relief was not audible. Serena walked over to pick up the painting and hold it at arm's length. 'You've got her to a tee, Matthew.' Matt wished she hadn't used his full name, it sounded a bit too formal. She placed the canvass back on the easel and turned to him. 'So how much do I owe you?' The question came suddenly and Matt was caught off guard; the fact was, he could not remember how much he had suggested; that day was still a blur in his memory. She noted his hesitation. 'I think you said a hundred and fifty quid.' She felt in her pocket, pulled out a roll of notes and gave then to him. 'Worth every penny,' she told him.

For a moment, Matt hesitated to take the money, then he reached out, took the notes and put them straight into his pocket. Serena smiled. 'Don't you want to count them?'

He shook his head feeling slightly embarrassed. 'Thank you, I'm sure it's all there.' He put his hand into the pocket and felt the notes: for the first time, he realised that it might be possible to make at least part of a living out of his erstwhile hobby. 'It's still a bit tacky,' he told her. 'I only finished it a couple of days ago so you'll have to watch it doesn't get smudged.'

'Don't worry, Matt, I'll take good care of it for both our sakes.'

That sounded better.

'So will I see you again?' He hoped it did not sound like a plea.

She smiled. 'How about having a bit of supper, on me, at the Lidstone Arms tonight? That is if you've got nothing else arranged.'

'Well … er … yes, thank you, and no, I haven't.'

'That's fixed then. How about half seven. I'll meet you in the bar.'

Matt could not help thinking that it ought to be him organising things as he carried the painting out to the van and carefully placed it in the back, well out of the way of Dot who was fast sleep curled up on the passenger seat.

Serena was standing by the driver's door when Matt decided to take the initiative: he stepped forward, took her in his arms and kissed her full on the mouth. To his pleasant surprise, she made no attempt to resist; on the contrary, she returned the kiss and gave him a hug before turning and getting into the driving seat. Neither said a word as she switched on the lights and drove out onto the lane.

Matt went back into the cottage, a bedraggled Bullet at his heels. The old dog went straight to his bed, turned round three times and, within a few seconds, was snoring, while his master switched on the fire in the sitting room, took off his boots and collapsed into an easy chair.

After the encounters with Kate and Serena, he was even more confused: should he go, or should he stay? At least if he stayed, he could remain just a chap with a gammy leg; no big deal and no one was going to make a fuss. Only Spud knew the truth and he had promised to keep quiet. Perhaps he could find a job locally, augment his income with his painting, and who knows? He sank back, closed his eyes and dozed.

*

When he woke, he could see that it was pitch dark outside. He looked at his watch: half past six; just time to shower and change. He would walk to the pub, which would give him the option to have a glass or two of wine with the meal. Dress would be informal – he had learnt that lesson – open neck, no tie, twill trousers and a sweater. For the latter, he considered his favourite dark blue; high-necked would be just right.

He had been right about the frost. The ground felt hard as he started out   down the track and the air had a bite which caused him to zip up his jacket as high as possible; he wished he had brought a pair of gloves, and put both hands in the jacket pockets. The sky was clear, and although there was no moon, there was enough light to allow him to comfortably find his way down the track without the use of the small torch he could feel in his right-hand pocket.

There were only three people at the bar of the Lidstone Arms when Matt walked in to hang his coat in the small cloakroom area. Two, he recognised as locals, while the third was a stranger, about his own age, fair-haired and dressed in a smart grey suit, white shirt with no tie. The man nodded towards Matt before finishing his pint and walking out towards the door that led to the upstairs rooms. Matt ordered a pint of the local ale and, by way of conversation, asked Tom Slater if the man was staying at the pub. The landlord replied in the affirmative. 'We've had one or two new faces about recently, mostly business types,' he grinned. 'Good for trade, though wish we could see more of 'em.'

At that moment, Serena appeared through the same door. She was wearing a blue and white flowered dress with a short black jacket, her hair hanging loose to her shoulders. She gave him the customary peck on the cheek before settling on one of the high stools next to him. 'You stole a march on me,' she told him. 'I was going to pay for the drinks; it's my treat, remember.'

Matt grinned. 'Too late. So what would you like?'

'Just a small glass of red then please, Matt.'

They took their drinks to Matt's favourite table in the corner and sat where they could both see the other customers in the dining area. 'Always makes it more interesting,' Serena had commented as they say down. Matt agreed as he handed her the menu. The decision not to have a starter was mutual; she chose the roast duck while he went for the special chilli, a dish he had enjoyed several times before. The young girl who took the order smiled at Serena, said hello and asked when her pony's head collar would be delivered. Serena smiled back and told her she would drop it off next Thursday.

'I thought you said you were off back to wherever tomorrow.' Matt sounded surprised.

'I've had to change my plans, which is just as well as I had quite forgotten that young girl's order.'

'Good thing you were here tonight then, otherwise you would have had a very disgruntled customer.'

Serena shrugged. 'It happens, but fortunately not often.'

Matt was going to ask her what she was doing swanning about in the middle of the night, but at that moment the man he had seen earlier came back into the bar wearing a blue overcoat and a bright red scarf, which was wrapped round his neck with the ends hanging loosely down the front. He briefly glanced their way before saying something to the landlord and making his way out. Matt watched him go before turning to Serena to ask her if she knew who he was. Her reply was a brief and succinct, 'No.'

'Strange, he seemed to know me when we were in the bar earlier. You must have passed him on the stairs.'

'Yes, I did.' Serena picked up the wine menu. 'What do you fancy to drink with the meal?'

The abrupt change of subject caused Matt to hesitate for a moment. 'Er … I don't mind, you choose, it's your treat after all.' He grinned and sat back with folded arms while she perused the list, eventually deciding on a South African Merlot. Matt nodded. 'Suits me, I'll need something with a bit of body to go with the chilli, it'll cheer me up a bit. And talking about cheering up, look at those two, they look as though they could do with cheering up.' He was looking at the table where Burford and Greta were just about to sit down.

Serena followed his gaze and grinned. 'They don't look very happy, do they? I expect it's because their horsebox is a day late coming back.'

'How do you know that?'

'Your girlfriend in the stable yard told me.'

'She's not my girlfriend.' Before Matt could say any more, Serena beckoned to the waitress and ordered the wine. He was beginning to feel uncomfortable; the evening was not going the way he had hoped, and he had the distinct impression that this was turning out to be more of a farewell party than a happy reunion. He was glad when the wine arrived and the waitress poured two generous glasses.

Serena was still watching the two at the far table. Burford's agitation was obvious as he leant forward to speak in a hoarse whisper while his wife sat motionless, staring at some point above his head until eventually she raised both hands in a 'That's enough' gesture.

'Cheers!' Matt raised his class and took a sip.

The word brought his companion's attention back with a jerk. 'Sorry, yes, cheers, Matt.' She turned towards him, lifting her glass and smiling.

'You seem very interested in those two,' Matt nodded towards Burford and Greta.

Serena took a sip of her wine and, after a long pause, told him that it was only because Mrs. Burford was a very good customer and, like any good salesperson, she was interested in all her customers. 'I suppose I'm a bit nosey,' she added. 'I like to know what's going on.'

At that moment, the food arrived. The young waitress asked whose was which before putting the plates carefully on the table. Dishes of vegetables for the duck came a few minutes later. 'Can I get you anything else?' the girl asked. Serena and Matt both shook their heads. 'Then enjoy,' she told them as she turned to walk away.

'They all say that now,' Serena commented as she helped herself to the vegetables.

Matt grunted. 'Probably comes from the States.' He took a mouthful of the chilli and nodded in appreciation.

'Ever been there?'

'No. Been to Canada.'

'On holiday?'

Matt hesitated. 'No, work.' The subject was beginning to get too close to home and he tried to think of a way to change it, but the next question came before he could speak.

'So the company you work for is international?'

'Yes.'

'Doing what?'

Another pause. 'Transport. Can I top up your glass? This wine is very nice. Have you had it before?'

Serena nodded between mouthfuls. 'Thank you, and yes, it's one of my favourites.'

Matt was relieved that the questioning ceased as they continued the meal. He had the uneasy feeling that if the interrogation continued, he would be forced to tell her more than he wanted at that stage. If their relationship developed further, he would eventually tell her the truth, but at that moment, he was not hopeful that would happen.

As the waitress took their orders for dessert – strawberry trifle for her, cheesecake for him – a low buzzing noise, which seemed to come from Serena's small black handbag, made her look up with embarrassment. 'Sorry, it's my phone. I switched it to vibrate,' she said as she reached into the bag. 'I should have switched it off.'

'You'd better answer it,' Matt told her with a grin. 'You never know, it might be the order of a lifetime, make your stay here really worthwhile.'

She shook her head as she studied the phone to check the caller.

Matt had the distinct feeling she wanted to take the call. He pushed back his chair and stood up. 'I'll just pop to the loo while you take it,' he told her.

The desserts had arrived by the time he returned. Serena seemed to be studying the trifle with a serious expression on her face. She brightened up as Matt arrived back.

'Okay?' he asked.

'Yes and no,' came the reply, then after a pause, 'I'm sorry, Matt, but I'm afraid we'll have to cut this evening short, something has cropped up.'

'Not family, I hope.' Matt sounded concerned.

'No, no, just business.'

It was obvious to him that she was not going to elaborate any further. 'I hope you'll have time to finish the meal.' He tried not to sound too disappointed.

'Oh yes, of course, Matt.' She reached across and took his hand. 'I'm sorry, I didn't plan for the evening to end like this, but … '

'I know, I know, business is business.' He shrugged and began to eat his chees-cake. *Bugger, just my luck.*

Serena ate her trifle slowly, deep in thought. She considered returning the call to say the deal was off, but knew she could not, the consequences would be too great. Instead she finished the trifle, slowly drank her glass of wine and waited for Matt to indicate that he was ready to move.

Reluctantly he stood up and moved towards her. 'Thank you for the dinner,' he said rather lamely.

She got up and reached across to take his hand. 'I'm so sorry, Matt. I was really looking forward to this evening.' She gripped his hand and led him back to the bar. 'If you would like another drink, it's all on me.' She leant forward and kissed him on the cheek.

'Will I see you again?' he asked.

She gave him a wide smile. 'I'll be in touch, and when this business is finished, perhaps we can continue where we left off tonight.' She gave him another peck on the cheek, nodded to the landlord and disappeared through the door that led to the stairs.

Matt watched her go with mixed feelings. He very much wanted to develop their relationship, but deep down he had the distinct feeling that was not going to happen.

'Would you like another drink, Matt?' Tom Slater had been listening as he polished glasses behind the bar.

'No thanks, Tom, not just now. Guess I'll make my way home.' Matt walked slowly over to retrieve his coat before making his way to the front door.

Outside was bright moonlight. He paused to take a deep breath before turning to cross the car park entrance just as a large black Audi jerked to a halt in front of him. It turned onto the main street and disappeared at speed towards Bovey Tracey. Matt stood gazing after it, trying to understand what he had seen. The glimpse of a bright red scarf indicated the identity of the driver, but it was the dim outline of his passenger which disturbed him most: he was sure it was Serena.

CHAPTER 26

'I don't understand it.' Burford was standing by his office window, looking anxiously towards the manor gates. He turned to face Greta who, dressed in a white polo-necked sweater, buff riding breeches and black riding boots, was perched on the edge of his desk. 'It's been over two days now and not a word from Ivan. God knows what has happened to the Scania and its load. How many?'

'Horses, four.' Greta eased herself off the desk and came to stand next to her husband. 'As for the rest of the consignment, your guess is as good as mine since we are not involved with that side of the business.'

'So what's happened to those animals? Where are they and who's got them?'

Greta shook her head. 'Should have heard something by now if there has been an accident, even if it happened on the other side. It's true the horses were not worth a lot, but the worry lies elsewhere, as you well know.'

'And we don't have Kevin around anymore to sort out that side. I know he was a pain in the arse, but at least we could rely on his contacts to keep us in the picture so that we knew what was going on.' Burford returned his gaze to the manor gates. 'So what do we do? Never mind those other buggers up in the smoke, let's concentrate on us.'

'I think we do nothing for now.' Greta sounded emphatic. 'We can claim to have done no more than provide transport for something we know nothing about.'

'Don't think that'll wash, my dear, and there are others involved, don't forget.'

'Well, let us just wait and see. I cannot afford to cross Ivan, you know that, and as for the other person, I do not think we have to worry.'

Burford gave a long, deep sigh. 'Okay, okay, I hear you. So we carry on as normal.' He was about to say that he would find that very difficult when the conversation was interrupted by a knock on the door. 'Come in.'

Mrs. Gazeley appeared in the doorway. 'Sorry to butt in,' she said, 'but there's a phone call from a Mr. Winsford asking when he can come and see Jackson Williams.'

Burford glanced up at the ceiling. 'All right, Mrs. Gazeley, I'll take it in here.' He waited until she had left before walking over to the desk to pick up the phone, keeping his hand over the mouthpiece. 'That's all I need,' he said shaking his head, 'that bloody man poking his nose in again.' He paused for a moment before putting the phone to his ear. 'Hello, Mr. Winsford. How can I help you? … Yes, I remember, I suggest … ' he glanced at his diary, 'I suggest … let me see. What about next Thursday afternoon at, shall we say, three o'clock? … Right, see you then.' Burford slowly replaced the phone, moved to the padded office chair behind his desk and sank into it with a prolonged groan. 'I can't work out what that chap is up to,' he told Greta. 'Apparently he wants to see Jackson Williams to discuss the boy's future. Why he has taken such an interest in Williams, I just can't fathom, unless … ' Burford leant forward, elbows on the desk, 'unless he's using it as an excuse to pump the lad for more information.'

'Information about what?' Greta frowned and shook her head.

'Well, you know, Kevin and all that, his connection with us and what else Williams knows about him.'

'You still think this man Winsford is some sort of undercover agent?'

'I don't know what to think, Greta. I wouldn't be surprised after what's happened over the past few days.'

'Don't get paranoid, William. I think you begin to jump at threats that are not there.'

'It's all right for you to say that, Greta, You're used to this sort of thing, I'm not.'

'What do you mean I'm used to this sort of thing? I am not a criminal.' The indignation was evident in Greta's tone.

'Come off it, old girl, you know damn well what bloody Ivan holds over you. Sword of Damocles comes to mind.'

'That was all a long time ago and far away from here.'

'But he could shop you nevertheless, which would mean deportation back to Germany, and I couldn't take that, Greta.' Burford got up from his chair, walked across and put an arm round his wife's waist. 'I will do anything to make sure that does not happen, you know that.'

Greta took hold of his hand, looked up and kissed his cheek. 'I know that, William,' she said quietly. 'Whatever happens, we will see this out together.'

*

'So what's this guy want with you, man?' Clayton was sitting next to Jacko at breakfast.

Jacko shrugged. 'Dunno, something about what I could do when I'm finished with this place.'

'Why's he picked on you?'

'Your guess is as good as mine.'

'You don't reckon he fancies you then?' Clayton grinned.

'What do ya mean fancies me?'

'You know, man. Is 'e looking for a young boyfriend?'

Jacko shook his head. 'Nah, had 'is girlfriend with 'im, and anyway I would have known. You forget I've been there, Beaky Andrews for one. No, the bloke seemed straight enough, just seemed to want to help me, that's all.'

'Lucky old you. Take my advice and see what you can get out of 'im. You never know, he might be going to give you a job or something.'

'Could be, I suppose, but more likely I'll get the usual crap about pulling meself together and going straight, and all that stuff. I expect he's one of them do-gooders what goes round schools and that, telling us what we should be doing.'

Clayton put a hand on Jacko's shoulder. 'I'm telling you, man. Don't you be scared to get what you can out of this guy.'

Jacko took a gulp of the now cold tea in his mug and grimaced. 'Yuck, dunno what they put in that bloody tea urn but it tastes fucking awful.' He stood up, pushed his chair back and turned to walk away.

Clayton grabbed his sleeve. 'Hang on, man, I ain't finished me breakfast yet.' If he expected a reply, he was due for disappointment. Jacko shook his arm free and walked out without saying a word.

*

On Thursday afternoon, the phone on Burford's desk rang twice. He picked it up to hear Mrs. Gazeley's voice tell him that Mr. Winsford was waiting.

'Tell him to come in, Mrs. G.'

Seconds later, Matt was ushered into the office to be met with a brief handshake from Burford, who had come from behind his desk to greet his visitor. 'Good afternoon, Mr. Winsford. I take it that you have come to see young Williams, as we agreed.'

Matt nodded. 'That's right, Mr. Burford.'

'Could I ask the purpose of this meeting and why you feel you should be involved with this particular inmate?'

Matt did not like the sound of the word inmate but let it pass. 'It's simply that I think I might be able to help this young man. I am sure you recall that I met him when he was in a very distressed condition. I felt sorry for him and wanted to help, that's all.'

'So what makes you think you can achieve something we cannot?' Burford was getting annoyed.

'I'm sure you do a very good job here, and if my visit can help that, I shall be satisfied. I do have some experience in training young men.' Matt had no wish to elaborate further and was glad when Burford turned to walk back to his desk and pick up a phone.

'Mrs. Gazeley, could you ask Mr. Griggs to send Jackson Williams to my office at once please?' He looked at Matt and nodded towards one of the chairs. 'Take a seat, Mr. Winsford. Williams will be with you shortly. I'll leave you to it, but please remember, this is a secure training centre. Inmates have to serve their time and cannot be released until that time has been served.' He left the room before Matt could reply.

A few minutes later, the door opened; Jacko stood in the doorway, looking bewildered and apprehensive.

Matt stood up and smiled reassuringly. 'Come in, Jacko, this won't take long. I just wanted to have a chat about things you might like to do when you leave this place.' He indicated the chair next to him and invited Jacko to sit down, conscious of the fact that the youth was looking very uncomfortable. There was an awkward silence before he continued. 'Have you got any idea what you would like to do in the future?'

Jacko shrugged. 'Dunno, never thought about it much.'

'What do you like doing best, I mean, while you're here?'

'In the workshop, messing about with them old cars and the tractors.'

The answer came without hesitation and Matt smiled. 'Anything else?'

Jacko thought for moment. 'Yeh, the mornin' run.'

Matt's smile turned into a chuckle. 'I seem to remember you are fond of running, young Jackson Williams, and let's hope you're sticking to the official route these days.'

For the first time, there was a faint smile on Jacko's lips. 'Don't need to bunk off no more.'

'I'm glad to hear it, Jacko, and my advice: keep the slate clean while you are here, and don't let them chalk up anything else against you.'

Jacko said nothing. He waited to hear what else was to come and watched as Matt took out several brightly coloured leaflets from his inside pocket and gave them to him. 'Look through those when you have a bit of spare time. They're about apprenticeships and, if you are interested, I suggest you talk to your mother and social worker and either of them can contact me if they want to discuss anything further.' He handed over a slip of paper. 'That's my mobile number, don't lose it.'

Jacko looked confused. 'Is that it?'

'Yep, that's it, Jacko. Sorry if you expected more.' Matt stood up and watched a thoughtful Jackson Williams leave the room.

After calling in Mrs. Gazeley's office to say that he was finished and asking her to thank Mr. Burford, Matt left the manor and began to walk to where he had parked the Volvo, then halfway to it, he suddenly changed his mind and turned towards the gate into the stable yard.

At first there seemed to be no one about, then he heard a familiar voice coming from one of the loose boxes. When he walked over to investigate, he found Kate bending over in front of a tall bay horse. She was putting a wet bandage onto the near-foreleg while speaking comforting words to calm the animal.

Matt watched for several seconds before announcing his presence with a slight cough.

Kate looked up, frowned and then, to Matt's relief, smiled and said, 'Oh, it's you.'

He returned the smile. 'Yep, I'm afraid it's me.'

'What brings you here on a Thursday afternoon?' She stood up, patted the bay's neck and turned to face Matt.

'Just been to see the coloured lad we rescued the other day.'

'Not sure that rescued is the right word but I know what you mean. How is he?'

'It looks as though they have done what that Burford chap promised me and have dropped any disciplinary action against him.'

'That's good. I really felt sorry for the boy, he seems to have had a pretty rough time as a kid, and I'm glad you helped him.'

Matt looked intently at her, taking in the pleasing face, the blue eyes and wisps of blonde hair that fell across them; not as glamorous as Serena Brent perhaps but … 'I'm glad we helped him,' he told her, putting due emphasis on the *we*. 'It was a joint effort, remember.'

'I suppose so.' She slipped the bolt on the loose box door and came out into the yard.

Matt was thinking of something else to say. In the end, he nodded towards the bay horse. 'Tendon trouble?'

'That's right, just a bit of heat. Should be okay in a few days.'

Matt peered into the box. 'Nice looking sort,' he told her.

She grinned at him. 'He's the horse I was going to let you take out hunting with me, but … '

Matt asked if she minded him going in and having a closer look. 'Be my guest,' she said, opening the door and following him inside.

He stood back to get a better view. 'Very nice,' he said, trying to sound professional. 'Who does he belong to?'

'At the moment he belongs to Greta, but he's up for sale and she would like someone to ride him while she looks for a buyer. He's quiet and I've hunted him a couple of times so I can vouch for his good manners.'

It suddenly occurred to Matt that a day in the company of Kate Lethbridge might not be such a bad idea after all, and if he banged his leg in the process, so be it. 'Am I allowed to change my mind?' he asked, and was pleased to see her face light up when she replied that he certainly could and she would fix it for him to hack out with her as soon as George's tendon had gone down.

'Is that his name? George?'

'No, but that's what we call him. His proper name is Windsor Boy but that's a bit of a mouthful so we had to think of something shorter and Mother came up with that.'

'Your mother has a good sense of humour,' Matt said as he patted George's neck. 'When do you think he will be ready to ride?'

'Shouldn't take more than a couple of days for that swelling to go down, so if we give it seven days, we should be okay. The meet at Dunscombe is a week on Saturday so we've got plenty of time to get you both settled.'

'Thanks, I'll look forward to it,' Matt said as they walked out of the loose box and into the yard. I'll give you a ring just to make sure everything has gone to plan,' he told Kate as she closed the top and bottom bolts of the door. He paused for a moment and then said, 'I hope I don't mess it up, Kate. I mean, I wouldn't want to embarrass you by coming off at the first fence or having to knock off because of my leg.'

She looked up at him and smiled. 'Don't worry, Matt. I'll look after you.'

He quite liked the sound of that.

CHAPTER 27

The trial ride on George had gone well, as far as Matt was concerned. The horse had proved to be easy to handle and, for an animal of nearly seventeen hands, remarkably agile and fast – a very different beast from the smaller, placid Molly he had become used to. Now he could ride beside Kate without having to look up whenever he spoke to her. That had given his ego a modest boost.

The day of the meet at Dunscombe dawned cloudy, reasonably mild for the time of year, and with a slight drizzle. Matt looked out of the kitchen window as he drank his second cup of coffee; he could see no further than the far end of the lawn and hoped that the old saying 'rain before seven, clear for eleven' would prove to be true.

At nine o'clock, after giving Bullet a quick walk in the field below the cottage, he started to get dressed in his new breeches and well-polished boots, then he brushed off his tweed jacket, picked up his hat and the old riding crop his mother had sent him, and made his way out to the Volvo. He was not required to turn up at the stables until ten o'clock as Kate had told him she would get George ready, but he knew from past experience that it often took longer than expected so he planned to get there by nine-thirty to give her a hand.

When he arrived in the yard, he found it a hive of activity. Kate and Greta were busy preparing three livery horses, including the solicitor Peter Ridley's bay. Greta herself would not be riding as it was more important on a Saturday to look after the paying customers. In addition to Greta and Kate, there were three teenage girls busy preparing their ponies, and a plump blonde woman in faded jeans was helping a boy of about eight or nine, who was wearing a tweed jacket that was too big for him and a pair of jodhpurs that were also too large, groom a fractious dapple grey pony that was tied up outside its loose box. It reminded Matt of his own experience as a child and he could imagine the young boy's excitement tinged with apprehension as the pony was saddled up ready for the ten o'clock departure.

The two-mile hack to Dunscombe would take them about half an hour. Peter Ridley's bay led the group at a steady walk, while Kate on Harry and Matt on George took up the rear so that Kate could watch the young riders in case there were any problems. She was particularly concerned that the boy on the dapple grey was having some trouble controlling the animal. 'Should have somebody with him,' Kate said. 'His parents don't ride so he has to cope on his own. I suppose I'll have to keep an eye on him.' Matt thought of his own childhood and how glad he had been to have his parents with him out hunting.

'That's good,' he said. 'What's his name?'

'His name is Robert, Robert Dawe. His grandparents farm between here and Bovey, or at least they used to; it's on the market at the moment. Robert's father is not interested and the other brother is working abroad, so I suppose it was inevitable.' As Kate stopped speaking, there was the sound of a vehicle coming up behind. She looked back and called out to the riders. 'Single file please!'

Matt watched as the black-coated riders eased their mounts as close to the road hedge as possible to allow it to pass. It was then that he realised he and young Robert were the only ones wearing ordinary tweed jackets: he hoped they would not be the only ones at the meet dressed 'rat catcher', as it was known in hunting circles.

The vehicle approaching them was a quad bike driven by large red-faced middle-aged man wearing a black waterproof jacket, his flat cap crammed well down on his head so that he had to keep his head up to see where he was going. Behind him sat a younger man, similarly dressed but hatless, his long blonde hair flowing back in the breeze. They slowed down as they passed the riders and the young passenger waved at Kate and gave her the 'thumbs up'.

'What was all that about?' Matt asked.

'Oh, that's Charlie Brimblecombe and his son, Max. They're our trail layers and it looks as though they've finished the job and are ready for the start.'

Matt shook his head. This was all new to him.

More riders joined them as they trotted up the long drive that led to Dunscombe, and Matt was glad to see that several were dressed like himself or wore waterproofs of various colours. They came into a gravelled courtyard which fronted a large thatched house which, Matt surmised, had once been a traditional Devon longhouse but had been modernised in recent years. Here they joined another score or so of riders who were already enjoying the hospitality of the host as he passed among them with a tray of plastic cups with a choice of either port or whiskey.

George Bourne looked to be a man in his seventies, medium height, lean, bow-legged and with a bald pate that glistened in the damp air. He was booted and spurred and wore a blue waterproof coat that looked as though it had seen better days. Eventually he came up to Matt and offered up the tray. Matt chose the whiskey while Kate went for the port, then with a bright 'Good morning, sir, don't think I've had the pleasure … ' he turned to Kate.

'Ah, young Miss Lethbridge! Perhaps you would introduce me to your boyfriend.'

Kate refrained from telling him he was not her boyfriend but duly introduced Matt as a fellow hunter from 'up country.' The old man nodded and, with a smile, said he hoped they would have a good day.

The drinks were followed by an assortment of food comprising sausage rolls, egg and cheese sandwiches, small pasties and roast potatoes. These were followed by slices of currant cake and chocolate biscuits carried round by a number of helpers, some of whom, Matt assumed, would be family members. In addition to the riders, Matt counted more than twenty foot followers, which included Spud who was chatting to the scarlet-coated huntsman in the corner of the courtyard while the hounds milled around him, eager to get started. There was a second similarly dressed rider, a young man in his late teens, who was endeavouring to keep the pack together. The inexperienced whipper-in was having trouble with one black and white bitch that was getting too interested in the food that was being handed out.

It prompted Spud to grab her by the scruff of the neck and bring her back to the rest of the pack. In doing so, he noticed Matt and Kate on the far side of the courtyard and went over to greet them. 'So you decided to do it then,' he said, grinning at Matt.

Matt feigned a puzzled expression. 'Do what?'

'Why, come trail hunting, of course.' Spud patted George's neck as he looked up at Kate.

'Take care of him, young Kate,' he said nodding towards Matt. 'Don't find his sort around here very often.'

The look of embarrassment on Matt's face was genuine. 'Don't take any notice of him, Kate. He hasn't a clue what he's talking about.' He raised the plastic cup in his hand. 'How many of these have you had, Spud?'

'Not enough, sir.' The ex-sergeant major made a mock salute, turned abruptly and walked unsteadily to where the helpers were still offering the stirrup cup to the hunt followers. He helped himself to another tot and stood talking to a glum-looking Charles Spreyton who, Matt thought, did not look very happy.

'Why did he call you sir and do that?' Kate asked.

Matt grunted. 'Because he's half-sloshed and hasn't a clue what he's saying.'

The next person to approach them was a middle-aged woman in full hunting kit carrying a small cloth bag. Kate leant towards Matt and whispered. 'Hunt secretary.'

Matt nodded and fished in his pocket to find the fifty pounds visitor's 'cap' while for Kate, being a full subscriber, it was fifteen pounds. The secretary smiled at Matt and asked if he was likely to hunt with them regularly. Matt shook his head and told her he would only be in the area for a few more weeks. Kate wondered how many weeks that meant as she watched the secretary move to the next rider. 'She was hoping for another subscriber,' Kate whispered. 'Always on the lookout for more dosh.'

At that moment, the general chatter suddenly lessened as a scarlet-coated Bill Bowden eased his horse towards the house and near to the front door as George Bourne emerged, now wearing his black hunting coat, his hunting crop in his hand. The master stood up in his stirrups and turned towards the assembled followers. There were calls of 'Hold hard', aimed at people still talking until eventually the chatter ceased completely.

Bill cleared his throat. 'Mornin' all,' he looked up at the sky. 'We must have done something right 'cos it's stopped raining.' He waited for the laughter to subside before continuing. 'We have to thank our host George Bourne and his family for an excellent and generous meet.' This was interrupted by more applause and clapping. 'And I can tell you that our trail layers Charlie Brimblecombe and his son Max have done us proud by all accounts, so we can look forward to a good day's hunting.' The last remark was greeted with applause and some laughter as Bill waited for George to mount his horse; it had been brought down from the stables behind the house, led by his granddaughter, who was riding a young chestnut thoroughbred.

Max watched as their host struggled to mount a nice-looking bay mare, helped by one of the foot followers. Once in the saddle, there was no doubt the old boy was perfectly at home. He gathered up the reins and, with a nod to the master, took his place at the head of the waiting riders. The huntsman gave a short blast on the horn and they were off, following the pack down the drive towards the woodland opposite.

Within a few minutes, the hounds were off at full cry along a wide track that led through the wood to the open grass fields beyond. The riders followed the master at a fast gallop, many urging their mounts on to get to the front as the huntsman blew a series of quick blasts on his horn to encourage the pack.

Matt decided to stay at the rear until he was sure of George's response to the general noise and excitement. He need not have worried; George proved manageable and well-behaved in spite of the riders galloping past.

Kate had gone on in order to keep close to the grey pony which was pulling hard so that its young rider was experiencing great difficulty in keeping the animal under control. The gate at the end of the track had been opened so that hounds and riders could go through without stopping. Matt held George back, the growing pain in his leg prompting him to avoid the inevitable crush that was bound to occur in the narrow gateway. When he did let George go, he was agreeably surprised at the big horse's agility and speed as they galloped along the track and through the gate to join the rest of the riders.

Now confident in his mount, Matt urged him forward to join Kate. The speed lessened to a steady canter, and eventually a trot, as the hounds fell silent. Bill Bowden raised a hand to indicate they should halt to enable the huntsman to cast the pack to find the scent once more.

Kate smiled at Matt as he rode up. 'How's he going?' she asked.

Matt paused to get his breath. 'Brilliant. How about you?'

'I'm okay but I'm not so sure about young Robert there. He's having a job holding that pony. Think I might have to take him home if it doesn't settle down.'

'That would be a pity just as things are getting going.' Matt looked around. 'Exactly where are we? Don't think I've been this way before.'

'See those trees over there?' Kate was pointing to a dense clump of oak and ash trees two fields away. 'That's the edge of Colspit Wood and the old stone quarry, and the other side of that is the lane that goes down into Lidstone.'

'Ah, yes, now I know roughly where we are, I can find my way back if you have to leave early.'

'You'd stay on then?'

Matt grinned. 'You bet, as long as the old leg holds up.'

At that moment, the pack found the scent once more and they were off at a steady canter towards the field gate, which was being held open by Spud Wannacott. 'Get away on,' he yelled with a grin as Kate and Matt went through.

The next field sloped steeply to the far hedge where the hunt had made a low rail jump. Kate suggested they used the gate but had to change her mind when she saw Robert on the grey pony heading for the jump. 'Oh God,' Kate muttered, 'he'll never make it.' She turned Harry to follow the pony and yelled at Matt to carry on to the gate. He ignored the command and went with her.

There was the inevitable queue of half a dozen riders waiting their turn to jump as the grey pony barged through, its rider obviously not in control. Cries of alarm were muted as the pony and rider sailed over the fence.

Kate could hear the boy yelling 'Whoa!' on the other side as he tugged on the reins. 'Let me through please,' she called as she steadied Harry to take the fence. The other riders obliged, except one: Matt dug his heels into George's flanks and followed her.

The pony was now about a hundred yards ahead of them, its nose touching its chest as the young boy leant back to haul on the reins in a vain effort to check the animal's wild gallop.

'They're heading for Colspit and the old stone quarry,' Kate called out as Matt came alongside.'

'It must be fenced,' Matt yelled back.

'Only an old post and rail, and if the bloody pony tries to jump that, we're in real trouble; it's steep and rocky the other side.'

Matt did not reply but dug his heels into George, overtaking Harry in a few strides and, jockey-like, crouched forward to urge the horse to maximum speed. The pony was only a few yards from the quarry when Matt overtook it. He pulled George over abruptly to get in front of the bolting animal to turn it away from the fence. In this he succeeded, but in doing so, one of George's front legs buckled, sending Matt through the fence to tumble, head first, down a steep, boulder-strewn, slope.

The pony galloped back towards a group of alarmed riders who endeavoured to stop it. The animal skidded to a halt, sending the unfortunate boy over its head onto the grass, then it turned and galloped off to disappear through the field gate the riders had just come through.

'Leave it,' Kate said, as she dismounted to pick up Robert and brush him off. 'I expect someone will catch the damn thing.' She was gratified to see that although Robert was obviously shaken, he was apparently unharmed. Satisfied with the boy's condition, she looked around for Matt, unaware of what had happened at the fence, and was alarmed to see people rushing over to where a riderless George was quietly cropping the grass.

Leaving Harry in the care of one of the girls from the stable, she ran over to find out what had happened. She stepped over the broken rail and half-ran half-skidded down the slope to where Matt lay on his back unconscious, his head resting against a jagged piece of rock. Peter Ridley and Spud were already there, discussing what to do.

'Don't move him,' Spud advised. 'We don't know if his back has been injured. It's a job for the professionals.'

'Right, I'll call the air ambulance,' Peter Ridley said as he clambered back up the slope.

Kate knelt down next to Matt to undo the chinstraps and remove his hat, then she took off her coat, rolled it up and placed it under his head. 'That was a pretty hairy thing to do, Matthew Winsford,' she said quietly as she gently stroked his brow with her handkerchief, and when there was no response, she closed her eyes and turned her head away to hide the tears.

A sobered Spud put a consoling hand on her shoulder before loosening Matt's collar and wiping the smear of blood from the side of his face.

A minute later, Peter returned. 'They're on their way,' he told them. He was studying the prostrate figure on the ground when he noticed a slight flicker in the eyes. 'He's coming round,' he said with a note of optimism in his voice.

As he gradually opened his eyes, Matt realised there were people around him. The images were blurred and his first thought was that it was another of his nightmares, but different: no grinding noises, no blackness, no blue staring eyes, but the pain was there. He heard himself groan, a hand touched his face and it was then he knew it was no dream. He closed his eyes as the pain intensified. It was a different pain from the one he was used to. He tried to move but could not, then everything clouded over once more as a familiar sound penetrated his consciousness: the whirr of helicopter blades.

CHAPTER 28

As Matt slowly regained consciousness, he became aware of people talking.

A man's voice: 'Good, I think he's back with us. Keep up the morphine until he's completely conscious, then we'll reassess the situation.'

Then a female: 'Right, Doctor.'

Matt looked around. He was enclosed by pale blue curtains, which parted as someone walked away. His eyes were beginning to focus as the nurse attached something to one of his fingers; she was looking intently at a screen by the bed. Apparently satisfied with what she saw, she turned to Matt and smiled, the whiteness of her teeth accentuated by the dark-brown colour of her skin. Matt was comforted by the genuine look of concern in her eyes and he felt he was in good hands as she checked the drip tube in his left arm. It was then he realised that his right arm was in a sling. He tried to move it and felt a sharp pain in his shoulder. The nurse lifted her hand in a restraining gesture. 'I should try to keep as still as possible, er … ' she looked up at the noticeboard above his head. 'Matthew, isn't it?' Matt tried to nod and it was only then that he felt the pain in the right side of his head. The nurse picked up the clipboard at the foot of the bed and wrote something on it. 'Don't try and move on your own,' she said with another smile. 'Just press the button and someone will get to you as soon as possible.' He raised his left hand in acknowledgement as she drew back the curtains and moved to the next bed.

Matt could now see the patient in the bed opposite: an elderly man with his plastered arm in a sling. He slowly moved his head to the left and could just make out the other two beds in the ward.

The man opposite smiled. ''How's it going, young man?' he asked.

Matt returned the smile. 'Not too bad. How about you?'

'Okay, fell down the bloody stairs. Missus says I should take more water with it.' His grin widened. 'No, I just tripped, sign of old age, they say.'

'Where are we?'

'Torbay Hospital'

'What day is it?'

'Tuesday. I came in on Sunday and you were spark out then. Good to see you back in the land of the living.'

'Thanks.' The conversation was interrupted by the arrival of a tall, fair-haired man in a white coat with a stethoscope hanging round his neck. He looked pleased as he studied the details on the clipboard. Matt thought he looked too young to be a specialist – not much older than himself – but he was wrong. He stood watching Matt for a few moments without saying anything, then he drew up a chair and sat down facing Matt. 'Good,' he said, opening the file he was carrying and looking briefly at its contents. 'It seems that we are making progress. That is very satisfactory.'

Matt detected a foreign accent but could not place it as the man continued. 'First, the fracture in your collar bone is not complicated and should heal in a few weeks. Likewise the wound to your head is not serious, thanks to the protective headgear you were wearing, although it has caused concussion which we will keep an eye on. Any pain in the chest will be caused by bruised ribs and should ease in a few days.' He paused and studied his file before continuing in a more serious tone. 'We have kept you sedated because of the injury to your spine.' He pulled back the cover from Matt's feet. 'Could you please move wiggle your toes?'

Matt closed his eyes and it took several seconds but eventually he was able to move both big toes slightly.

'Good, that is enough. The X-ray showed two crushed vertebrae but no damage to the spinal column. We will send you for a scan to make sure there are no other complications.' He smiled, stood up and tucked the file under his arm. 'I think you are now stable, so by tomorrow you can receive visitors,' he said as he replaced the chair and moved to the bed opposite.

Matt mulled over the facts and wondered how long he would be kept in hospital, and a sudden thought came to him: who was looking after old Bullet? He felt certain Spud would get the duplicate key from Spreyton and take care of him. If not, there was always Kate and, of course, her mother. He relaxed and drifted into a troubled sleep, to be woken by a nurse and two porters with a mobile bed to take him down for the scan.

When he returned to the ward, the rest of the day seemed to pass very slowly. In the afternoon, visitors began to arrive in ones and twos to chat quietly with the other three patients. A plump grey-haired woman was talking to the man opposite, obviously the wife, Matt concluded. He tried to ease himself up into a sitting position but the pains in his shoulder and back were too much and he was forced to abandon the attempt. A nurse arrived with a glass of water and three pills. He swallowed them slowly, one at a time; almost immediately, the world went blank.

When he awoke the next morning, the coloured nurse was by his bedside, with the same bright smile and twinkling eyes; he immediately felt better. She helped him into a more upright position and, although the pain was still there, it seemed more bearable. She presented him with more pills and told him that she expected him to eat all his breakfast. It arrived ten minutes later and, for the first time since being admitted to the hospital, he felt like eating the cereal and scrambled egg.

The afternoon visiting hour found Matt propped up on his pillows, dozing contentedly after consuming most of his shepherd's pie at lunchtime. He had almost fallen asleep when he became aware of two people standing by his bed. He opened his eyes to see the plump woman he had seen in the stable yard and a stocky, shaven-headed man who had the ruddy complexion of someone who worked outdoors. They introduced themselves as Rosemary and Roger Dawe.

'We wanted to thank you for what you did on Saturday,' Rosemary said.

Her husband nodded and added, 'If it hadn't been for you, it would probably be our Bobby in that bed.'

'I just happened to be in the right place and on the right horse at the right time,' Matt croaked. 'How is the little lad?'

Rosemary smiled. 'Oh, he's fine. Wanted a day off school to come and thank you, but we told him that wasn't on and we would do it for him. Believe it or not, he actually wants to keep that wretched pony, says we should get another bit or something. I told him we will have to see what Kate suggests before we do anything,' she glanced towards the entrance, 'and talk of … here she comes.'

Matt managed to turn his head to see Kate, in a short, flowered dress, walking towards them carrying a small plastic bag and with a newspaper tucked under her arm. She smiled broadly at the Dawes, asked how Robert was and, when she heard he was okay and back at school, told them that she thought he was a brave little chap and she would do her best to help him if he wanted to carry on riding.

Rosemary expressed her thanks. 'We won't stay,' she said, turning to Matt. 'Just wanted to thank you for what you did and wish you a speedy recovery. So take care and we will look forward to meeting you again.' Her husband nodded in agreement and gave a 'thumbs up' as they turned to leave.

When they had gone, Kate opened the plastic bag and took out a bunch of grapes. 'Mother's idea,' she said with a grin as she placed them on top of the cupboard next to the bed. She drew up a chair and sat looking at Matt for several seconds without saying a word.

Eventually she took his hand and placed the newspaper on the bed in front of him. 'Why didn't you tell us, Matt?' she asked quietly.

'Tell you what?'

She slowly unfolded the paper, the latest edition of the local daily, and turned to the centre page. It took a little while for Matt to focus on the print but there was no mistaking the headlines: AFGHANISTAN WAR HERO SAVES BOY RIDER. "Captain Matthew Winsford suffered serious injury during a trail hunt saving nine-year-old Robert Dawe from certain disaster when the boy's pony bolted uncontrollably towards Colspit Quarry." It went on to describe the incident in detail and, to Matt's horror, there was a picture showing him on George at full gallop chasing the pony. There was more detailing his injury in Afghanistan (they called it a wound) and the reason for his stay at Coombe Cottage.

Matt could read no more. He closed his eyes and lowered the paper onto the bed with a groan. 'Oh my God. Spud, it could only have been bloody Spud. I'll kill him next time I see him. Who took the photograph?'

'That would have been Peter Ridley. He's always ready to snap anything that might be useful for PR purposes.' Kate gave a slight grin. 'It wouldn't surprise me to see it in the *Horse & Hound* and *Hounds* magazines.'

'Oh no … no, that's the last thing I want.'

'Why not, Matt? Whether you like it or not, you are a hero round these parts. I can't see why you had to keep everything about yourself so secret. You must know the folks around here would be only too pleased to help you if you would only let them.'

'You don't understand, that's the trouble. The last thing I want is people thinking I am something I am not and fussing around me. I am not a war hero. I did a straightforward mundane job and got blown up due to my own bloody stupidity and … ' He stopped abruptly. He could not tell her the rest. 'I came to Devon to be on my own, to get away from all the hoo-ha I was getting at home. Now, I might just as well go back there because it's going to be the same here.'

Kate did not know what to say. She took the newspaper, folded it and placed it on the bedside table. 'You can read the rest of the paper when you are feeling better. There is only one thing that might interest you: it looks as though the manor might be closing down.'

'Good Lord, that's a bit sudden. Why is that?'

'Nobody seems to know at this stage. Even the paper only quotes it as a rumour. All I know is there have been a lot of strangers in smart suits wandering about and I haven't set eyes on Greta nor Burford since yesterday morning. I've had to cope with everything in the yard on my own.'

'Probably some sort of inspection, I shouldn't wonder. You know how rumours get about when that sort of thing happens.'

Kate shook her head. 'No, I think it's more serious than that. I was interviewed by a chap who said he was from the Border Force, grilled me about the horse trading business, who organised it, what places they travelled to, what part I had in the business. I told him I only looked after the stabling and helped find buyers, that was all. I told him I didn't know what this was all about … but I don't think he believed me.'

Matt could see she was upset. He took her hand and squeezed it. 'Don't worry, I believe you,' he said with a smile. Then he closed his eyes as the pain in his back kicked in.

'Are you alright?' Kate asked anxiously.

Matt grimaced. 'Just the old back. I'm all strapped up but it still gets me now and then. Nothing to worry about, same with the shoulder, I'll be right as rain in a week or two.'

Kate stood up. 'I think you should get a bit of rest now. I'll look in again tomorrow.'

Matt watched her walk away and, as he noted the movement of her buttocks, he realised he was feeling much better.

*

The evening visitors began to arrive at six o'clock, and it was not long before Matt saw Spud Wannacott walking towards him, a guilty look on his face.

Before Matt could say anything Spud raised his hand in a calming gesture. 'I know what you're going to say, Matthew, and I'm sorry about what has happened. I … ' He was abruptly interrupted by an angry Matt.

'So you bloody well ought to be, Spud Wannacott. What the hell do you mean by telling everyone?'

'I didn't tell everyone, Matt. It was that chap, Ridley.'

'So you told Ridley everything I wanted to keep just between you and me.'

'Not everything, Matt, just the bits I thought … '

'Why, for God's sake?'

'Well, Ridley thought it would be a good idea to get something in the press – he does all the PR for the hunt, you know. He asked me if I knew you and what you did for a living. What could I say? Should I make something up or simply say I didn't know you? Most folks there would know that was a lie.'

'Was it him who took the photo?'

'Yes, he does that sort of thing when we get the antis out, especially if there are hunt saboteurs around looking for trouble.'

There was a long silence while Matt looked blankly up at the ceiling. Spud shifted uneasily in his chair and waited for him to say something. Eventually Matt turned to him and said, 'You know what this means, don't you?'

'No, but I can guess. You'll be moving on.'

'Right. Much as I've enjoyed my time here, or most of it, I might as well go home now and sort out my future, and when I have, who knows, then I might come back.'

'Would a certain Miss Lethbridge have anything to do with your coming back?'

Matt did not answer. Instead he pointed to the folded newspaper. 'Bin that bloody thing.' There was a note of resignation in his voice. 'I ought to be angrier with you, Spud, but I suppose it was probably inevitable that it would get out sooner or later.'

'I still don't see why you have to desert us.'

'Don't you? Have you got any idea what it would be like to have people like Mary Lethbridge fussing around you, not to mention the various official organisations now that would soon be knocking on the door of Coombe Cottage? No, I'll be much better out of it.'

'Well, I for one will be very sorry, but I'll wish you well and hope that things turn out alright.'

'I'll let you know, Spud.'

The old man nodded and sat studying his fingernails in silence for several seconds before suddenly telling Matt that he had taken Bullet home. 'Which reminds me, when I went down to the colonel's for the key to your cottage, he seemed pretty upset about what was happening at the manor. Apparently he had been interviewed by some bloke about the goings-on there.'

'Yes, Kate mentioned something about being interrogated by a man from the Border Force. Wonder what that's all about.'

The news that Kate had visited the patient brought a smile to Spud's face. 'She'll get to know more about it, but if you ask me, I reckon it's something to do with that chap what was rumoured to be into drugs.'

Matt recalled what Jacko had told him. 'Do you think they'll close Lidstone Manor down?'

'Dunno, your guess is as good as mine.'

Matt closed his eyes and relaxed back onto the pillow, giving his visitor a good hint that it was time for him to leave. 'Thanks for coming, you old bugger,' he said with a grin. 'We'll get together when I get out.' He opened his eyes and raised a hand as Spud picked up the newspaper, waved it at him and made his way to the door.

Somewhere, a bell sounded and, within a few minutes, the visitors had departed, the ward fell silent and the lights were dimmed.

*

As he dozed in the half-light, Matt began to think about what Kate and Spud had told him. He wondered what would happen to Jacko if Lidstone Manor closed.

CHAPTER 29

Two days later at ten o'clock in the morning, Kate's Fiat was parked in the hospital car park while she walked beside Matt down the slope from the hospital main entrance, conscious of the fact that she had come straight from the stables in her jeans and sweater and smelled very horsey.

At his request, she had borrowed the key from Spud and found a pair of brown corduroy trousers in his bedroom, together with shoes and a canvass bag to carry his mud-spattered breeches, his riding boots and hat. He wore his tweed jacket with the right side draped over his injured shoulder as he walked steadily towards the little car.

'Are you okay?' Kate asked for the third time since they left the ward.

Matt wished she would stop saying that. 'Yeah, I'm fine, thanks. My shoulder seems to be getting there, the back support has stopped itching, and I can laugh without my damn ribs giving me gyp. So, all in all, yes, I'm okay.' He suppressed a groan as he lowered himself into the car seat.

Travelling along the new motorway towards Newton Abbot, Kate seemed preoccupied with her driving and said nothing until Matt asked her if she knew anymore about what was going on back at Lidstone. She gave a slight shrug. 'All I know is the Burfords have disappeared. There's a new chap in the office and I don't know if I'm going to get paid this month.' She reached for a handkerchief under the dashboard and blew her nose. Matt thought there might have been a tear and did not know what to say and so said nothing until they arrived at the cottage.

'Thank you very much for the lift, Kate. Would you like to come in for a coffee?' He reached across to his right-hand jacket pocket to find his keys.

'Thanks, but I must get back to the yard. I'm expecting the farrier and he'll want to know which animals are to be shod.' She went to help Matt out of the car but was waved away as he swung his legs out and pulled himself up with his left hand. 'Mother thinks you should come and stay with us until your shoulder has mended,' she said as she pushed car door shut.

Matt straightened himself with a grunt and told her to thank Mary very much, but he was sure he could cope, though he would be grateful for the occasional lift into town. Kate assured him that all he had to do was ring her mother and she would no doubt jump to the occasion.

Matt stood and watched in the lane as Kate reversed the car out. He smiled and waved to her and, as the car moved off, she waved back before accelerating towards Lidstone.

An hour later, Matt was relaxing by the fire in the sitting room when he heard the rattle of Spud's Land Rover pulling up outside and, almost immediately, an ecstatic Bullet leapt onto his owner's lap and tried to lick his face.

Spud stood in the doorway with a wide grin on his face. 'How's it going, Captain Winsford?'

'Oh, shut up, you old bugger.'

'Is that all the thanks I get for looking after that daft little mongrel of yours?'

Matt turned to him. 'It's all the thanks you get for letting the cat out of the bag – and he's not a mongrel.'

'Well, I've brought this for you as a token of recompense,' he pulled a bottle of Bushmills whiskey out of his overcoat pocket and waved it at Matt, who gave a sigh of resignation and pointed to the kitchen.

'You'll find a couple of glasses on the shelf and I'll have water with mine.'

Spud took off his coat and did as he was asked, returning with the glasses and a jug of water. He poured the drinks and sat down opposite Matt.

Nothing was said as the two men sampled the whiskey until eventually Matt put down his glass and got up to stand looking out of the window towards the manor. 'So what's the latest on the saga of Lidstone Manor?' he asked as he stretched backwards to ease the pain in his spine.

'I've told you all I know, except that I saw a coach coming out of the gate as I was coming here. Reckon they were taking the lads away, by the look of it. A couple of "men in blue" with them, so it looks as though that's it as far as Lidstone Training Centre is concerned.'

'Do you know what's happening down at the stables?'

'A bit of a mystery there. I'm told the Burfords were taken off in a large black car and haven't been seen since, and that Ivan feller has disappeared completely, so what's going to happen there, I don't know. Poor young Kate has been landed with the whole caboodle to sort out on her own.'

Matt shook his head. 'And I'm not much bloody use to anybody as I am, just when she could do with a bit of help.'

Spud drained his glass. 'Tell you what, I'll treat you to a bite at the pub, it'll cheer you up a bit. What do yer say?'

Matt smiled. The idea was appealing; perhaps Serena would be there. 'Okay Sar'n Major Wannacott, you're on.'

There were very few people dining in the Lidstone Arms when they arrived and, as they moved towards his favourite table in the corner facing the bar, a quick survey told Matt that Serena was not one of them. He turned to Spud. 'I'll buy the drinks.'

'Thanks, mine's a pint of Dartmoor Ale.'

Matt nodded and went back to the bar to order two pints of the local brew. 'Quiet today,' he commented to Tom Slater as the latter placed the full glasses on the bar.

'Should have been here earlier in the week,' the landlord told him. 'It was chaos; police, bigwigs from London, not to mention all the staff from the manor when they closed the canteen,' he smiled, 'but you were somewhere else, of course. I read all about it in the local rag; you're a bit of a hero, Captain.'

Matt said nothing as he reached for the glasses.

'Can you manage with that arm in a sling?'

Of course I can bloody manage, Matt thought to himself. But it hurt when he picked up the glass with his right hand.

Back at the table, Spud was perusing the menu card. 'What are you having?' he asked as Matt carefully placed the beers on the table.

'Cod, chips and peas for me please.' Matt made the choice not only because it was one of his favourites, but also because it was the least expensive. Spud decided on the same and went to the bar to make the order, then both men settled back to sip their beer while waiting for the waitress to serve them.

Matt was looking at the other diners. 'Tom Slater just told me they've had a lot of police around this week.'

Spud nodded. 'That's right. A lot seems to have happened in the past few days. No Burfords, no Ivan and, incidentally, no one has seen your Posh Tack friend around recently so that makes four AWOL.'

'You can't lump Serena in with those other three, Spud. She's probably gone away on her sales round.' But the vision of her being driven away, also in a large black car, on the night of their date, caused him to wonder.

The meal arrived, carried by the usual young waitress, and Matt set about it with vigour – it was the first decent meal he had eaten in almost a week. Neither of the men spoke until the last chip had been consumed and then they both sat back and watched as fresh customers came through the door; one caught Matt's attention and he leant forward to get a better view. The man was dressed in what looked like a police uniform, and his face was vaguely familiar as he walked to the bar and perched on one of the stools. It was when he took off his hat to show a mop of fair hair that Matt recognised him as the man who had come into the bar the evening he had dined with Serena, the man who had driven her away. As Matt watched, he realised he was being scrutinised and, eventually, the man gave him that slight nod of recognition, the same as on the eventful evening two weeks ago.

'Looks as though the fuzz are still around,' Spud said, 'and that one seems to know you.'

'Well, I don't know him.' Matt turned away to study the menu card.

'He's coming up here,' Spud told him, as the man left the bar and walked towards them.

'I'm sorry to interrupt, Mr. Winsford. My name is Richard Carter, Border Force.' The man held out his hand and Matt stood up and shook it left-handedly as Carter continued. 'I wonder if you could spare a few minutes when you have finished your meal. I would like to have a few words in private if you are agreeable.' The tone was polite and the accent from the north.

Matt was glad he had not called him Captain Winsford. 'What is it about?' he asked.

Carter glanced at Spud, who immediately got up and made a hasty retreat, saying he needed the loo. 'You don't have to go,' Matt called out.

'Yes I do,' Spud said with a grin.

The Border Force officer watched him walk away then turned to Matt and said reassuringly, 'It's not urgent, but I understand you have been involved in some unfortunate incidents relating to the activities of the organisation operating from Lidstone Manor, and my colleague and I feel that you should be put in the picture regarding the latest developments.'

Matt could not think what to say and, for a second or two, sat in silence trying to work out how the man knew who he was and who had told him of the ragging of the cottage and attempted mugging; he wondered if Spud had something to do with it.

His thoughts were interrupted when Carter asked him if he would be available that afternoon. 'We have a private room at the back of the hotel,' he told him. 'Would it be possible to meet up there sometime this afternoon? You say the time.'

Matt considered for a moment before telling him that he could come at two o'clock as soon as they had finished lunch. The fact was he found the situation intriguing and looked forward to finding out what really was happening at the manor.

Carter smiled, 'Great, we'll see you then,' He returned to the bar and Matt saw him order a pint of lager and a packet of crisps.

When Spud retuned to the table, he sat in silence until Matt told him what Carter had said. He then asked him if he had ever spoken to the man. Spud shook his head. 'Never seen him before, let alone speak to him.'

Spud ordered coffee and suggested a whiskey to go with it but Matt declined, saying that he wanted to keep his wits about him if he was going to be interviewed by the men in blue. They talked nostalgically about their army experiences until the clock above the bar showed five minutes to two.

'You'd better get going,' Spud said as the waitress came to clear the table. 'The bill's mine so you can toddle off and see those blokes, then you can tell me all about it.' He grinned and followed Matt towards the bar where Tom Slater directed Matt to the reserved room. 'I'll wait here for you,' Spud called out.

'Don't forget, you're driving.'

'I'll just have a shandy.'

'That'll be the day,' Matt said to himself as he went out through the lobby to find the door marked 'private'. He gave a single knock and went in.

Richard Carter was sitting at a large oval table in the middle of the room. On it there were four glasses of water and the same number of note pads: it was obviously being used as some sort of conference venue. Carter stood up as Matt walked in and, with a smile, indicated to the chair next to him. 'Please take a seat Mr., or, should I say, Captain Winsford?'

Matt gave a sigh and shook his head. 'I would prefer it if you dropped the formalities, Mr. Carter, and called me Matt. That's how most people know me round here.'

'Excellent, Matt, and it's Richard please.' Carter settled back into his chair, rested his elbows on the chair arms, and clasped his hands against his chin. 'First of al,l may I say that I … we … hope your injuries are recovering well. It was … '

At that point, Matt interrupted with a brief, 'Thank you.' Already embarrassed enough, he did not want to hear any more about the incident in the hunting field.

There was a short silence before Carter continued. 'I expect you will be wondering why I have asked to meet you here in private. The fact is, I think my colleague will be able to explain more fully the results of our investigations.' He took out his mobile and tapped in a number. 'Hi, are you finished out there? Good, see you in a couple of minutes.'

While they were waiting, Carter told Matt they had something in common: he was also an ex-serviceman, Royal Marines. 'A lot of our people have been in the military,' he said and went on to explain the duties of the Border Force: drug trafficking, illegal immigration, visa checks and, of course, security.

He was about to say more when there was a tap on the door.

'Come in,' Carter stood up and Matt looked round.

Standing in the open doorway, dressed in a smart blue uniform, was Serena Brent.

CHAPTER 30

Serena smiled nervously as she walked towards a stunned Matt, who had started to rise out of his chair, only to slump back in surprise, sending a shock of pain to his shoulder. He grimaced, prompting Serena to ask if he was feeling all right. 'Yea, I'm fine, it's just that … '

'I know, I'm sorry, that's why I'm here. We thought it had better come from me personally rather than you find out later when this business is wound up.' She glanced at Carter, who touched her gently on the arm. 'I'll leave you to it,' he said as he walked towards the door.

Serena drew up a chair and sat down opposite Matt. Her hair was drawn back into a bun and her make-up was subdued. Even so, he thought she looked stunning. At first, he could think of nothing to say to her and he sat in silence weighing up what she had just told him; it meant that he had been deceived, that the evenings out together and the pretence of getting her dog painted were a sham.

'You were just bloody sizing me up, weren't you? he said angrily. 'You wanted to know if I was part of that drug dealing organisation and so you decided to check me out. Isn't that the truth?'

'No … well … er, yes. Oh, it's difficult for me to explain, Matt, but the fact is, I am attracted to you and much of what happened was for real, but … ' Serena shook her head and Matt had the impression that she was close to tears. She reached out to touch his hand. 'But I had my orders, Matt, and I knew it was going to hurt you. I'm not proud of that.'

Matt gave a long sigh. He knew what being under orders meant and that it was not always easy to carry them out. He closed his eyes and said quietly, 'Okay, what is done is done, but I wish you had been straight with me.'

'Perhaps when this is all buttoned up, we could get together again.'

Matt opened his eyes and thought for a moment, then shook his head. 'No, Serena, I'm afraid it's once bitten, twice shy,' he said quietly as he withdrew his hand. 'So tell me about this drug dealing then.' There was a tone of resignation in his voice.

Serena raised her eyebrows as she said, 'Oh, didn't you know? Not drugs. People.'

'Sorry, I don't understand.'

'They were bringing illegal immigrants into the country and exporting people who desperately wanted to leave without being noticed by the authorities. As simple as that.'

Matt still looked puzzled. 'Is that worth the risk? I mean, how much cash is that sort of thing going pull in?'

She smiled. 'You would be surprised how much some people are prepared to pay to get to the UK. It can run into anything up to three or four grand a piece, and there are plenty of customers anxious to go the other way, particularly criminals who have had their passports confiscated and want to leave without being noticed. They might well offer two or three times as much, and our friends could carry anything up to eight each trip.'

Matt gave a low whistle. 'So they could make fifty thousand or so on some occasions? Wow! But why use a horsebox?'

'Two reasons. First, in the vehicle they used, it was easy to block off the two front stalls to make a compartment with access only through a door in the driver's cab, a door that would normally be used to check the welfare of the animals. It meant that any casual inspection would detect nothing unusual, and in any case, what harassed inspector is going to barge through four or five large animals to check? Second, as you probably know, we use sniffer dogs to detect humans in vehicles, but in this case, because of the horses, they were ineffective, likewise the carbon dioxide detectors. Incidentally, it was Kate Lethbridge who mentioned that she did not know why they never loaded more than four horses and possibly a small pony in a vehicle that was designed to carry six large animals. The fact she told me that gave me the first clue that she was not involved.'

'So you were sussing her out too?' Matt sounded annoyed.

'That's my job, Matt.'

'You were spying on us, and all that blurb about the Posh Tack business was just a load of crap.'

Serena closed her eyes for a moment. 'Yes and no, Matt,' she said quietly. 'Yes, I had orders to investigate any possible suspects, and no, what I told you about the business was true. It does belong to my parents. I did used to work for them, and incidentally, this was not the first time they agreed we could use it as a cover.'

Matt shook his head. 'I can understand your need to check out everybody down at the manor, but why me?'

For the first time, there was a faint smile on Serena's lips. 'Simple. They thought you were one of us and we thought you were one of them.'

'It's nothing to laugh about. My paintings were ruined and I was mugged.'

'That was their way of checking you out. I suspect they reckoned that if you were just a holidaymaker, you would pack up and run after they trashed the cottage. When you didn't, the next move was to try and get hold of your mobile phone so they could hack into it and get the information that way.

To some extent, that put you off the radar as far as we were concerned, but I still had to make sure.'

'So you strung me along into believing that you were attracted to me, just so you could cross me off your list.'

Serena shook her head. 'As I told you, Matt, it wasn't like that … '

'I know, I know,' he interrupted in a tone of disbelief, 'you found me irresistible so had to get me to paint your dog and take you out.' He made a move as though to get up and Serena held up her hand.

'Wait please, Matt, don't go yet. There is more you ought to know,' she felt in her pocket, took out a small notebook and began to flip through the pages. When she eventually found what she was looking for, she looked at Matt and said, 'Jackson Williams. Kate Lethbridge told me you had helped him at some time.'

At the sound of Jacko's name, Matt sat up and began to take more interest. 'That's right. He was being bullied by one of the staff, but what has Jacko got to do with all this?'

Serena smiled. 'Your friend Jacko, as you call him, was the key, the key that unlocked the door of the whole conspiracy. It was Jackson Williams who recognised that Kevin Able, as he was called at the centre, was in fact Kevin Andrews, a man who was a convicted drug dealer and known paedophile. He told his friend Wiggins, and Wiggins told Kate, who thought it was very strange that a secure training centre should employ such a person, and discussed it with her father, who passed the information on to the local police. That's how it got to us.'

'So what happened next?' Matt was beginning to be intrigued by the whole process.

'That is when I got involved. My job was to find out as much as possible from the locals and to try and verify the identity of the man Kevin Andrews.'

'So you chatted up Kate … ' he paused, 'and then you took photographs of the diners in the Lidstone Arms. I remember wondering what the hell you were doing. You told me afterwards that you were taking them to send home to your mother. I thought it was a bit of a daft reason at the time but I wasn't going to say so.'

Serena grinned. 'I thought so too, but it paid off more than we had bargained for. It turns out the man they called Ivan is in fact a certain Ivan Bukowski. He, as I think you know, is a former jockey where Greta worked as a groom. Apparently they were both involved in horse doping scams at a number of racecourses throughout France and Germany. Bukowski was caught, convicted and did time while she managed to avoid the police and escape to England by marrying Burford, who was a British army major stationed in Germany at the time. She is still wanted by the police in Germany, and we suspect Bukowski was blackmailing her into helping run this people trading business. That knowledge gave us the incentive to try and get a bug into the establishment, which we did with the help of the local police.'

'Jesus, you make it sound like something out of a James Bond movie.' Matt seemed genuinely impressed, which gave Serena's ego a boost as she continued.

'We knew there was only an outside chance of picking up anything of use in the short period the bug would function, but we got lucky and heard Burford discussing the red herring we had concocted concerning the noise of the vehicle at night. It became evident that there was something fishy going on. What, we were not sure at the time, but it was clear that Bukowski was in charge and that Andrews was some sort of go-between, connecting the stables with a larger organisation. We decided to put a tag on Andrews and see where it led, and again we got lucky because it led to a man called Sandor, a man we suspected was the boss of an international organisation dealing in drugs and people smuggling. At that time, we did not know which applied to Lidstone. Eventually we picked up Bukowski on his way to the Channel Tunnel and, incidentally, that's why I had to cut short our date. I had to go to Dover to positively identify the man.' Serena relaxed back into her chair. 'That's all I can tell you, Matt. I hope you can forgive me for misleading you, it was not something I did lightly.'

Matt said nothing. He stood up and stretched to ease the pain in his back, then he nodded. 'Okay,' he said quietly. 'I understand. I guess it was all in a good cause, but that doesn't mean it doesn't bloody hurt.'

'Oh, Matt!' Serena got up, stepped forward and kissed him on the lips. 'You really are a one-off, Matthew Winsford. If only we had met in different circumstances, then … '

'Don't live in the land of "if only",' Matt told her. 'It only leads to grief. Believe me, I know.' He walked towards the door, paused and looked back. 'And you are one of the best-looking bits of crumpet I've ever been out with,' he said with a wry smile.

Back in the bar, Spud was just finishing his second pint. 'So what was that all about?' he asked as Matt joined him.

'I'll tell you on the way home, Spud, but just now I'm completely knackered, so if you don't mind, I'd like to leave this place.'

The light was fading as the Land Rover drew up outside the cottage. 'You going to be alright?' Spud asked as Matt got out.

'Don't worry about me, Spud. I've been in worse places than this.' The old man nodded. 'Me too, but I'll pop in tomorrow just the same.'

Matt waved as the Land Rover departed, then he went to the back door to let an eager Bullet out onto the lawn. When the old dog had done his business, he called him in and they went into a cold sitting room where Matt slumped into an armchair and sat with the dog on his lap.

It was getting dark when he took out his phone. 'Hello Mother, it's me. Just to let you know there's a change of plan. I'll be home before Christmas ... '

Matt sat in the dark for several minutes before getting up and switching on the electric fire. His phone conversation with his mother had been brief: she was unaware of his recent injuries and what caused them. He had long ago ceased bothering his parents with details of his personal life, particularly things that might cause his mother to worry or get upset. That they knew about his injuries in Afghanistan was inevitable – he had been posted home and the only place he could go was home, but he had made the stay as brief as possible and a casual remark about their holidays in Devon had brought back memories of the open moorland and quiet countryside. It had prompted him to seek the solitude he felt he needed. Now it was coming to an end. He sat back in the chair, the events of the day drifting through his mind, until he fell into an uncomfortable doze.

*

A knock on the door woke him. It was pitch dark outside but he could just recognise the face peering through the window: it was Kate.

He got to his feet and nearly stumbled over Bullet, who was asleep by the fire. 'Come in, Kate,' he called out. 'The door's not locked.' He switched on the light as Kate pushed the door open and came in holding a carrier bag. She was wearing close-fitting jeans and a tight blue sweater; both did much for her figure, Matt thought.

'How's it going?' she asked.

He grimaced and said he was a bit sore, but otherwise he wasn't too bad.

'I need to take this through into the kitchen,' she said, pointing to the bag. 'Mother thought you might need a little sustenance after what you've been through.'

Matt led the way and turned on the lights to see her take out a dish covered in foil and place it on the table. Whatever was in the dish smelled good and he realised how hungry he was. The removal of the foil revealed a generous slice of homemade steak and kidney pie, potatoes and peas, all with a rich, brown gravy: it made Matt's mouth water.

'It might need warming up,' Kate said as she put the dish into the microwave oven. 'A couple of minutes should do it. I'll find a plate.'

'Don't worry, I'll eat it out of the dish; saves more washing up.'

Kate grinned. 'Typical,' she said and sat down at the table to wait for the microwave to do its work while Matt took a knife and fork out of the drawer.

He paused and looked at her. 'Would you like some?'

'Thanks, but I had mine before I came out. Mother told me I've got to wait to take the dish back, so I'll stay until you've finished.'

Matt drew up a chair to sit opposite her. 'It's very good of Mary to do this and I'm grateful, but please tell her that I can cope and I'll get down to see her in a day or two and thank her personally.'

'Would you like a lift?'

'No, thanks, the walk will do me good.' Matt said as the microwave went ping.

Kate gave a grunt of disapproval as she got up to retrieve the dish and place it in front of him. 'Why won't you let us help you, Matt? She sat down, folded her arms and watched while he set about the meal with great gusto with just a fork in his left hand.

He gave the occasional nod between mouthfuls but did not speak until the dish was empty, then he put his fork down, sat back in his chair and gave a grin of satisfaction. 'Haven't had anything as good as that since I was a kid,' he told her.

'I asked you why you won't let us help you?' Kate said as she picked up the dish and walked over to the sink. 'You know, you are quite a hero in these parts after the business out hunting, and folks will be only too pleased to do what they can to make sure you are looked after.'

Matt closed his eyes and slowly shook his head. 'I'm not a bloody hero. I did what had to be done, that's all, and now I just want to stay here quietly until I'm fit enough to go home.'

'You're leaving Lidstone?' There was a note of disappointment in Kate's voice as she began to rinse the dish.

Matt looked at her. 'As soon as I can drive safely. It's been great being here and much of that has been due to you and your mother and … ' There was a faint smile, 'and Molly, of course, but the time has come for me to sort out my future, and when I have … ' he looked up and smiled, 'who knows?'

'Are you going because of what has happened at the manor? I heard that you were interviewed earlier today by a certain Border Force Agent.' There was a note of disdain in Kate's voice.

'I confess I was more than a bit shaken, Kate. It's not nice to know that you have been taken for a ride, and that's putting it mildly.'

'We're both in the same boat, Matt. She fooled me too, although I did wonder why she spent so much time at the stables when there were so few customers.'

'Well at least the mystery has been cleared up. I suppose you know all the details?'

'No.' She wiped the dish and put it back into the carrier bag.

He recounted what Serena had told him, carefully omitting the more personal items.

Kate said nothing until he asked, with concern in his voice, what she thought was going to happen to her job at the stables. She replied that Colonel Spreyton had told her she could carry on as usual, keep any livery money, and he would make up the difference between that and her normal wage until he found someone to take on the lease. He had told her he wanted to keep it as a going concern until then. 'He seemed quite a bit brighter than he did during investigation,' she added.

Matt grinned. 'That's because he's been let off the hook, but I wouldn't be surprised if the old devil knew what was going on and got a cut somehow, probably a cash backhander that no one could trace,' he paused, 'but I'm glad you're not out of a job; you deserve better than to be chucked on the scrap heap because of a bunch of criminals.'

Kate studied his face for a moment, then bent forward and kissed him on the forehead. 'That's for caring about other people,' she said softly.

Matt did not know what to say. He felt slightly dazed. This was the second kiss in twenty-four hours from two different women, something of a record as far as he was concerned. 'What did I do to deserve that?' he croaked.

'As I said, you care about people, not just me but that young lad, Jackson, Jacko, or whatever his name is. You went out of your way to try and help him, a complete stranger.'

'You did too, Kate. Like me, you did what you thought was right for the lad.'

Kate thought for a moment. 'I wonder what's going to happen to him now the centre is closing?'

'Oh, he'll finish his time in another institution somewhere, then I hope he'll do what I suggested.'

Kate smiled. 'Don't tell me, I can guess.' She stood up and reached for the carrier bag. 'Time I was going,' she said. 'I'll pop in tomorrow if that's okay, see if you need anything.'

'Thanks,' Matt struggled to his feet, 'and thank Mary for me.' He went to open the door for her and, as she turned to thank him, he put out his good arm, pulled her gently towards him and kissed her on the mouth. She did not resist and gave him a wide smile as she went out. He walked with her to the car, neither spoke: it seemed there was nothing to be said.

CHAPTER 31

He's gone then?' Mary was preparing the evening meal as Kate came through the kitchen door.

'Went this afternoon in a puff of Volvo exhaust fumes. He ought to get that car seen to before it conks out completely.'

'His shoulder was okay?'

'He reckoned so, although it has only been three weeks since he broke it.'

Mary concentrated on the dish of roast potatoes she was turning before putting them back into the oven, then she asked tentatively, 'Did he say anything about coming back?'

'No, just said he wanted to get home before Christmas and that he'd keep in touch.' Her mother snorted and said the best she could expect was a Christmas card.

Kate had a feeling she might be right but didn't say so. 'Young Robert Dawe was asking about him,' she said. 'He wanted to thank him in person for what he did. I told him he was too late and he asked for his mobile phone number so he could text him. I ask you, a nine-year-old kid.'

'I know, I've seen them on the school bus, completely oblivious of anything else around them, just totally occupied with those damn smartphone things. Sign of the times, I suppose.' Mary shook her head as she walked to the dining room to lay the table.

Kate stood with her back to the hot Aga. It had been sleeting on and off all day and her backside was numb with cold. She thought about what her mother had said about only getting a Christmas card and wondered if she was right.

*

The Christmas card had duly arrived a week after the festivities. In it, Matt had written that he was feeling fit again and had been busy in the weeks before Christmas sorting out his discharge from the army. He sent his regards, but no love and no kisses.

That was two months ago and Kate had heard nothing since. She had considered emailing him but thought better of it. Perhaps he wanted to forget her; if so, she was damned if she was going to try and crawl back into his life.

In the meantime, she had her work cut out dealing with the new arrangements at the stable. Colonel Spreyton had kept his word and made up her income to a satisfactory level but had hinted that he might have a buyer for the whole estate, including the manor and the stables. He had been very upbeat about the possibility of a sale; it would make him a millionaire, of course, but for Kate, it meant the possibility of being out of a job.

*

It was the end of March. The trail hunting season was almost over and Kate could look forward to a less hectic time when the horses could be turned out to grass and work in the yard would ease a little. The period since the Burfords left had been very hard. Apart from the extra work, the thought that she might be out of a job at any time was always at the back of her mind, and the latest news confirmed that threat.

On the first of April, April Fool's Day, Kate received an email from Matt. It was brief, but it told her that he had got a job and that he had been away on a course overseas. He did not say where but he went on to apologise for not contacting her sooner. He said he would explain everything when he came down to Devon, which would be within the next week or so, depending how soon his contract was finalised. The receipt of the email gave Kate a boost, but the contents did not. It obviously meant he was leaving the UK to work abroad. So where did that leave her?

That evening, just before Kate and Mary were about to sit down to supper, Jim came in, a knowing grin on his face. Mary got up to fetch his plate, which was being kept warm on the stove.

'You're looking very smug, Jim. What has kept you this time?' she asked, a note of resignation in her voice.

'I had old Colonel Spreyton in this afternoon. His Retriever bitch is in whelp and he wanted me to check her over,' he said as he sat down at the table and picked up his napkin.

'What's so marvellous about that, Dad? It's the sort of thing you do every week.' Kate said between mouthfuls.

Her father's grin widened. 'It wasn't the examination, twit. It was what he told me while I was doing it.' He paused as the plate of chicken stir-fry with rice was placed in front of him. He took up his fork and began to tackle it without speaking.

Kate stopped eating and looked at him: news from the colonel might be about the manor, and that would almost certainly affect her. 'Come on then, Dad, what did the old boy say?'

Jim took his time before answering. 'He told me that he had just come from his lawyers and they had finalised the sale of the Lidstone Estate – lock, stock and barrel.'

'Wow!' Mary said. 'So who's bought it?'

Jim put his fork down and relaxed back in his chair. 'You remember I told you that Bill Dawe's boy Steven works for a real estate company in Canada? They've bought it. Apparently they had been looking for a suitable investment in the UK and, with the drop in the value of the pound after Brexit, this seemed the right time. I assume Steven got to know it was on the market from his brother, Roger. They are a close-knit family, and I heard Bill say that they regularly talk to each other on Skype, so you can bet all the latest from Lidstone gets across the pond pretty quickly.'

Kate gave an anxious glance in the direction of her father. 'Did he say what they were going to do with it?'

Her father smiled. 'Apparently they told him they wanted to turn it into something they call an activity venue: an up-market hotel with facilities to take part in various things like guided walks, countryside activities and such. He couldn't elaborate any further but he did say that they wanted to offer equestrian activities: riding instruction, pony-trekking, that sort of thing, and he has recommended that you should take care of that side of it, so with any luck, my girl, you'll still have a job.'

*

The May blossom was full out in the apple orchard behind Lidstone Manor as Kate finished brushing the stable yard. At the far end, a youth was tidying the muck heap and two of the DIY livery girls were making sure the tack room was neat and tidy: they were expecting the first visit of the new estate manager that morning.

Kate nervously looked at her watch. It was only a week since her appointment as stable manager had been confirmed and she was keen to show that everything was in good order when her new boss arrived.

Five minutes to go before he was due to arrive, and she heard a car door slam shut: he was early. She quickly went into the tack room to give her hair a quick comb before making her way to the gate.

Outside, a new silver Land Rover Discovery was parked on the drive and, standing beside it, in a smart brown sports coat and cream-coloured cords, stood Matthew Winsford.

The gasp from Kate was audible. 'What … oh … er, sorry, Matt, I was expecting the new manager,' she looked nervously towards the front gate of the manor. 'He's due to arrive any minute, so if you don't mind, could you hang on until he's been?'

Matt seemed highly amused about something. She was at a loss for words and eventually muttered something about it being a nice new car.

'Not mine,' he said cheerfully. 'Goes with the job.'

'What job?'

He laughed. 'Why, manager of Lidstone Estate, of course.' He stepped forward and gave her a hug. 'That's right, the bad penny has turned up again.'

'I never thought of you as a bad penny, Matt. Well, not after I realised who you really were.'

'That's a relief,' he said as he took her hand and squeezed it. 'So let's inspect your domain, Miss Lethbridge.' He turned to let Bullet out of the vehicle and, as the little dog scampered ahead, he led her through the gate and into the yard. 'Excellent,' he said.

Kate chuckled. 'You haven't looked round it yet.'

'Don't need to. I know it's excellent without looking.' He glanced towards the muck heap. 'I seem to recognise the lad over there,' he said.

Kate smiled. 'You should. It's Wiggy.'

Matt waved. Wiggy grinned and raised a hand in reply. 'How did you get hold of him?' Matt asked as Kat steered him towards the tack room.

'I knew I was going to be short-handed,' she told him, 'so I got Wiggy's mother's phone number from Mrs. Gazeley and gave her a call. Wiggy had just finished his time under supervision and was keen to come back and work with me so I persuaded him to take up an apprenticeship in Horse Care.'

Inside the tack room, the two girls had done their work and all was clean and tidy. Kate picked up the old electric kettle from the shelf and grinned at Matt. 'Okay, you can tell me how you came to be my boss while I make us a mug of coffee.'

'It came out of the blue really. I'd had a couple of interviews for jobs, neither of which I was very keen on, and then I had a phone call from a man who said he was Steven Dawe. At first the name didn't ring a bell, until he told me he was young Robert's uncle. I thought at first that it was going to be another embarrassing "thank you" call and was preparing myself to be polite but brief, so it came as a relief as well as a surprise when he said nothing about the Robert incident but told me he was ringing from Canada on behalf of the Newton Brook Real Estate Company and that he had heard that I was seeking employment and could I meet up with him on his visit to the UK in two weeks' time as he had something I might be interested in. So that's how it all started.'

Kate handed him a coffee, then sat down in one of the chairs. 'And then you went off on this course. What was that about?'

Matt took a sip from the mug and put it down on the table for it to cool off. 'Well, first of all, the meeting was at their London office. It was only then I learned that he was one of their top executives: it turned out to be more like a job interview than a personal chat. Anyway, the long and the short of it was he offered me the job which, of course, I accepted and the next thing I was off to Newton Brook, which is just outside Toronto, and was sent to see one of their so-called activity venues near Calgary. I had a terrific time, riding cowboy-style on a ranch, fishing, trekking on foot, and there were classes on writing, public speaking, drawing and painting, and more. All to give me an insight of what they expected here. I must say, I was impressed, and told them I thought that sort of thing would go down well in Devon. They stressed they wanted to give overseas visitors a taste of the traditional English countryside which, of course, means hunting, shooting and fishing – that's where old Spud will come in – and then there are all the other activities I mentioned, although I'm not sure riding cowboy-style would fit in.' He gave her a broad smile and drained his coffee mug.

Kate said nothing but sat calmly looking down into the liquid swirling in her mug. 'So where does that leave us?' she asked softly.

He did not reply but stood up, took her by the arm and told her to come with him. 'I've got something I want you to look at,' he said. He led her out of the yard to the adjoining stone-faced lodge. 'Nice old place, isn't it?'

'Yes, very nice.'

'Have you ever been inside?'

'No I haven't.'

'Would you like to take a tour of it?'

Kate was puzzled. 'Why should I want to do that?'

Matt gave her a broad smile and squeezed her hand tightly. 'Because, Kathryn Lethbridge, that is where *we* are going to live.'

*

Two hundred miles away, Jacko sat on a bench inside a large gymnasium. Dressed in a blue tracksuit, he was bending over to tie his new trainers, a smile on his face as he contemplated the forthcoming run.

His thoughts were suddenly interrupted by a shout from the open door.

'Williams! Git your arse out here … Now!'

Jacko grinned, stood up and straightened his tracksuit top. 'Right, Sarge, I'm coming.'

Reviews

This is a first effort that was long in the making, and I don't u
ally go for romance stories, but both my wife and I particularly lil
this one.

★★★★★ **By Bob Goı**

I have never been to Bermuda but have always been interested
going. "Reunion In Paradise" provided very good word pictures frι
someone who obviously knows the place very well.

While I think this is a story best appreciated by women, the ε
ventures of the five women having the reunion supplied a uniq
backdrop for a guided tour of the island and its attractions.

As the author developed the personalities of the characters
volved it made me fantasize about how fun it would have been to
one of he males in the story.

My interest in Bermuda has been rekindled and if I ever make
trip there "Reunion In Paradise" will be my tour book.

★★★★ **By Don Kʲ**

It's such a delight to read this fine work, written by my close p
sonal friend. For a good number of years I've been aware of her wɾ
and am thrilled it's finally available.

The level of detail of Bermuda came only from her having liⱱ
there, but her recall of locations is truly remarkable.

This is a delightful read. Well done!

★★★★★ **By Michael Gustavs**

This novel is a "love" novel with some manly bits in it. I enjoy
the story line and thought it was well researched and written.

★★★★ **By Hercu**

Reunion in Paradise

M. J. Hinds

Reunion In Paradise

By M. J. Hinds

First edition, published 2017

Cover Images from iStock license numbers 517666930; 533455904

Copyright © 2017, M.J. Hinds

ISBN-13: 978-1-942661-67-2

Published by Kitsap Publishing
P.O. Box 1269
Poulsbo, WA 98370
www.KitsapPublishing.com

Printed in the United States of America

TD 20170801

50-10 9 8 7 6 5 4 3 2

Acknowledgments

I did not pen this book on my own. The Holy Spirit gave me the verbiage as we met daily. In editing my notes there were several occasions that I did not recognize a word and would have to look up its meaning.

I truly hated for this adventure to end. I loved going to Bermuda in my thoughts and being with my dear friends, Claudia, Barbara, Vivian and Stephanie (Some of the names may have been changed). Thank you all for portraying my beloved characters . . . a special thanks to my daughter-in-law, Susie, who found me my publisher.

Also, in loving memory of my mother Marjorie, a dedicated English teacher and avid reader, she taught me the love of reading.

Last but not least my husband, Bruce who tolerated me through this whole process as well as being my continuous editor and best friend.

M. J. (Melanie)

Barbara: The flamboyant, gregarious reddish blonde, with great legs and a sexy, husky voice that drove men wild, was still nursing the wounds of an earlier divorce. She discovered that the love she thought she had long ago discarded, was merely lying dormant, but still relevant. The news of her former major league baseball player-husband's sudden firing from the club, could only mean one thing--the end of his career. Overpowered by her emotions, she knew she had to find her way back to him.

Dr. Stephanie: A vain, tall, willowy brunette having gone under the knife more than once for cosmetic purposes, wreaked of sophistication. Always attired in the latest of fashions, she commanded the attention of everyone when entering a room. Her title of "Dr. Psychologist" added to the statement she desperately wanted to make; always so serious and so dedicated to her advancement in life. Certain prerequisites had to be met; there were no choices for her. Things were either black or white. She chose money over love when she married. Now, she had to live with that choice--or did she?

Stephanie's premeditated life takes an unexpected detour due to a disturbing turn of events. Her mysterious daily disappearance at ten o'clock arouses the suspicions of her comrades. Evolving themselves into the "Snoop Sisters," they follow her. But to their dismay, they discover they weren't the only ones on Stephanie's trail. Confronted by her friends' discovery, she realizes that her husband may have discovered her affair. Was her politically hungry husband having her followed? Her greatest fear might materialize--the loss of her status. The statuesque female's highly revered position in society was now in jeopardy. She had clawed her way to her pivotal pedestal and sacrificed true love for it. Would her power driven husband expose her, and dispose of her as a result of her unfaithfulness? Would she be returning to a marriage on the mainland or a sensationalized divorce? Her startling past catches up with her.

Melanie: Everyone's vision of the California girl--slender, blonde, bronzed skin and electric blue eyes whose

biggest fault was trusting. Her amiable nature and vulnerability led to disastrous affairs of the heart. Subsequently, she never commanded the respect from her peers that she would finally achieve elsewhere, after her departure from "the group." Her heart broken so many times; could she ever trust a man again?

Melanie meets the tall, handsome Bruce who has fled to the enchanted isle to nurse his wounded pride and his heart. A victim of the best friend stealing the fiancée scenario, it is more his pride that hurts than his heart. Surprised at his feelings of relief, and the intensity of his attraction towards Melanie, his destiny begins to take an astonishing new course. Though, it is a rocky road to romance filled with life's detours awaiting him. The love triangle that evolves between Bruce, Melanie and the determined Sandra, is not the only triangle they must deal with. The infamous Bermuda Triangle sets the stage for Melanie's love's disappearance, and shattered dreams.

Claudia: a stunning black haired beauty with sable brown eyes was nicknamed "Rocky," for her obsession with jewels. She clung to her self proclaimed independence, as though it would flee on the next gust of wind. Distant, yet a member of the once infamous "Lakes Ladies," she always attended all their social gala festivities. Two bad marriages clouded her past. The scar tissue surrounding her heart was impregnable, or so she thought.

Did she dare allow herself the indulgence of love in her structured life? Unsure if the new relationship she left behind in the States was the real thing or just another decoy, she questioned her future with the involvement of the younger man. Claudia's dreaded fear of discovery of her May-December affair has a surprising outcome. To her delight,

time had mellowed her peers' opinionated critiques, and her relationship is uncharacteristically well received by her companions, while
Vivian's abusive husband is condemned.

Vivian: A pint sized Italian with big emerald green eyes and swoop-
ing eyelashes was so reserved, so cautious of all who entered her life.
Each would be sternly scrutinized with a leery eye before being given a
pass for entry into her world. Married to an alcoholic, she knew it was
time to take charge of her own life--but was she capable?

Dear petite Vivian, who lived dutifully to the matrimonial vows
she had taken fifteen years earlier, was defiantly ready to change the
previous set course of her life. Did the debonair John Pendleton have
anything to do with her decision? This would be so out of character for
her, but she was struggling for her survival. The air was being choked
out of her day by day. The realization that no one was going to save her
but herself, finally took hold! To her dismay, the shocking arrival of her
drunken, abusive husband on the island put her to the test. Faced with
her most significant life's decision, she could no longer taunt with her
future, but rather orchestrate it!

Bruce: The tall, dark, handsome stranger, jilted by his fianceé for
his best friend, flees to the tropical isle to nurse his betrayed heart and
shattered ego. Fate steps in by uniting him with the beauty, Melanie.

Chapter One

Not even the Coast Guard had the answer as to the disappearance of the yacht, *Enchantress*. After all this time, Melanie could not dismiss nor accept the phenomenon of the Bermuda Triangle. Had it claimed her love, Bruce, as the newspapers reported? The distressed beauty had read every written word she could find on the subject but found no peace of mind. Repeatedly she awakened drenched in perspiration from the harrowing nightmares that haunted her. As Melanie readied herself, her bags packed and waiting conveniently by the door for the airport limo driver, she could not believe it was almost Christmas. It did not seem that long ago that she was departing for Orcas Island to complete her novel, "Lost Love," but it was nearly a year to the day. The reflection from the antique mirror imitated an older vision of the slender blonde. Straightening several straggly hairs while fumbling with the can of spray, "Damn these hairs. And, damn these lines!" The tears shed over the past year had left indelible souvenirs around the corners of her pretty blue eyes. She was sure they had not been so apparent before she lost her love, and all their dreams shattered, the result of a heartfelt tragedy that afflicted her life.

Drifting off in thought, she realized the enormity of the legacy he had unknowingly left her. "Lost Love" had gyrated her life into a whirlwind during the past year. Now, she could put to rest the once nagging, fearful thoughts of her demise as a bag lady in her senior years. The profits from the book and the motion picture were substantial. Since sales were down a bit, her publisher arranged a signing tour to generate more revenue during the holiday season in the New England states ending up at the Thatcher Inn for Christmas in Vermont with her family.

Feeling pangs of guilt for ignoring everyone in her personal life for so long, she decided that she'd call the other members of her intimate group, The Fabulous Five, to wish them a happy New Year and announce her return to the living; anxious to share with them the unbelievable previous year she had experienced. Melanie doubted if they were aware of her success, since she wrote under a pen name. With the zillions of romance novels on the market … .

A subtle knock and it was back to reality. Holding the door, the young driver followed with the waiting bags. Yes, she was looking forward to these holidays.

Once settled in the comfortable leather seat, the seasoned traveler enjoyed the first of her traditional three in-flight drinks she had become accustomed to when flying. Not normally a heavy drinker, or in need of alcohol because of a fear of flying, to the contrary, she adored being aloft. It made her feel flighty, free from the confines of earth and its relentless pressures.

With just the right amount of horseradish to add the zip to her Bloody Mary, though, the stalk of celery was a bit overwhelming. Giggling as it tickled her small nose, she thought it resembled a miniature palm tree with its leafy headdress. A flurry of activity in the airplane's galley verified that the flight attendants were wasting no time pampering their elite passengers with their specialized service. Melanie loved the first class treatment.

"Hot towel, Ms. Pearce?" Nodding and lifting the slightly scented cloth from the silver tray, she proceeded to gently wipe her hands. It was touches like this and the superb meal that followed that spoiled her from ever considering flying any other way.

Offered several choices of wines, the stunning blonde seated in 3A selected a fine chardonnay to accompany her breast of chicken, delicately bathed in a delightful champagne sauce. Fortunately, no one was occupying the seat next to her, the way she preferred it. This was a time of solace.

"Excuse me, would you like that Bailey's with your coffee now?" asked the tall steward.

Beginning to feel slightly melancholy from the Bloody Mary and wine, this would supply the final touch. Cocking her head back against the cushion, "Yes, that would be perfect."

There was something about that combination, the rich roast of coffee beans and the sweetness of the Bailey's. Now, her favorite time had arrived. All the formalities out of the way, she followed the Captain's instructions and sat back and relaxed while staring out the window. The majesty of the clouds reminded her of another flight she had taken a year and a half earlier, before her whole world changed. Who would have imagined landing in Bermuda that day, reuniting with her four best friends in life and meeting her Prince Charming would have changed her own course forever. Nestled snugly in her seat while adjusting the pillow, she closed her eyes and allowed the flood of memories to envelope her consciousness.

A satisfying smile inched across Melanie's face as the airplane made its final approach to the tiny enchanted island. The low flying swoop allowed her eyes to take in the majestic views in almost their entirety. The sparkling crystals of the infamous pink sand reflected off the shimmering turquoise-blue waters, while the cheerful pastel colors of the gaily painted houses with their pristine whitewashed stair stepped rooftops, did not look real from the air. The beautiful scenery brought back vivid memories of the year Melanie and her three year old son had spent as residents of the British colony.

Anxious to land and drink in the intoxicating fragrances of the lily fields, oleanders, and vibrant bougainvillea, she knew it wouldn't be much longer now. Grateful that the others had welcomed her suggestion of meeting here, she could take charge since this had once been her turf. Two decades had passed, but how much could an island of one mile by 21 miles change? Feeling confident of her touring knowledge and her capabilities of playing host from her innkeeper days, she felt more than ready to take on the challenge of entertaining the "vixens." The "vixens" was how she affectionately envisioned her friends of the past decade.

Making her way through customs, she glanced around the familiar terminal. It had not changed in the twenty years, except for a fresh coat of paint on the walls. It would be thirty minutes before the first of the other four arrivals, time enough to collect her luggage and meet Claudia's flight. How long had it been since seeing her dear friend,

"Rocky," nicknamed for her love of jewels? Impossible to believe, but it had been five years. Though it seemed like one, maybe two, since she had attended Claudia and Bill's wedding. Too bad it ended in divorce a year later.

Relieved to see her familiar luggage, Melanie unconsciously exhaled a sigh of relief. "No lost bags, so far so great," she musingly thought to herself. The distant sound of jet engines alerted her to the approaching plane. The butterflies were starting. "Yes, this is going to be a memorable ten days," she muttered under her breathe.

The door swung open and the first of the passengers began to disembark. There she was, looking gorgeous as ever. The years had been kind. Of course, Claudia would fly first class.

Waving frantically, Melanie caught her attention, and they ran to embrace one another.

"God, it is so good to see you!"

"Same here. Am I the first?" Without waiting for an answer, Claudia scanned the immediate area. "When are the others arriving?"

Melanie pulled back and flipped her long blonde locks over her shoulder. "Stephanie and Vivian arranged to fly in together, and they should arrive in 45 minutes. That will give us time to collect your bags and have a refreshing tropical drink to get us in the island mood," leading the way as they walked. Her sophisticated demeanor and striking looks attracted the attention of the flock of taxi drivers anxiously awaiting their next fares.

"Sounds delicious! What about Barb?"

Melanie tilting her head, "Knowing our compatriot, if she didn't hold up the airplane's departure, she should be arriving about twenty minutes after Stephanie and Vivian."

"Perfect, I can't wait till we're all together so the fun can begin!"

The rum punch just hit the spot as the two friends chatted a mile a minute to catch up on the previous five years, intermittently interjecting mutual compliments to one another on how well they each looked. Right on time, the plane settled onto the runway and approached the terminal with its waiting welcomers.

The four females outdid themselves all talking at once, but this would be nothing compared to when crazy Babs made the scene. Of course, her flight was late, and all four gals were sure she had something to do with its tardiness.

At last it arrived, just as the sun started its descent. The door barely opened when a flurry of activity closely behind it appeared. There she was, arms laden with a gigantic carry-on, a huge straw picture hat, chandelier earrings that reflected the last of the sun's disappearing rays, and a purse that could be mistaken for a small trunk. The bits and pieces of her that were attired glowed with fluorescent, multi-colored geodesic symbols. One could not miss her!

"Are we ready for this?" Claudia asked questioningly.

"I'm not," sighed Vivian as she stood on her toes to see for herself. "Well, in all these years, nothing has changed. Barbara is still Barbara."

"That may be true, but would we want her any other way? Don't answer that!" Melanie said with a twinkle in her eye. "Ready or not, ladies, here we go!"

The ear piercing screeching, kissing, and embracing caused quite a commotion at the gate arrival area. So much so, that a uniformed airport official ushered the five to a less crowded spot. Barbara wheeled around on one foot and bellowed to one of the passengers who looked lost and forlorn.

"Bruce, over here! I met this gorgeous guy on the plane, and I promised to introduce him to my dearest friends.

Melanie, I told him you could tell him where to stay, since he didn't have time to make reservations." Barely taking a moment to pause for air, she breathlessly continued with her lipstick smudged from all the greetings. "Apparently, it was a spur of the moment decision. He was dumped by his fiancée, poor thing, and was feeling really low. Realizing the need to get away, the first brochure he picked up described Bermuda. One quick call to the airlines, and within an hour the darling was headed for paradise. Can you imagine anyone letting a hunk go that looks like him? Anyway, I assured him that we would take good care of him."

"Oh, no you don't, Barb. This is to be just the five of us. We all agreed...NO husbands, boyfriends, or lovers on this trip. In layman's terms, that means NO MEN!!" Vivian protested. All the gals agreed, but it was too late. Not a moment later, before anything else could be discussed, a tall, dark, curly-haired, handsome man with the saddest blue-green eyes joined them. Barbara immediately grabbed his arm as if he were her own private trophy and began the introductions. Melanie's small delicate hand slipped into the engulfing grasp of the tall stranger, and their eyes locked for a instant. Awash with feelings of lightheadedness, she reveled in the moment. Then, as if an involuntary reflex took over, she instinctively dismissed the flood of emotions she was experiencing. She snapped herself back to reality. Once all the formalities were out of the way, Melanie recognized the need to take charge.

"Okay, Bruce, give me an idea of just what kind of accommodations you're looking for. There's always the Princess Hotel, one of the finest large hotels on the island. If you're a golfer, they have a world famous course. It's very pricey, but first class all the way. Then, there are a number of smaller, affordable guest houses. Which will it be?"

The girls all looked at one another, as such abruptness was not the norm for Melanie. Barbara, perceiving her friend's annoyance at the intrusion of this outsider, decided to step in.

"How about a nice guest house near the place we rented. That way, if he gets lonely, he can stop bye."

"Oh, great," Vivian mumbled so only Stephanie noticed. "Here we go again."

"Look, Barbara," the handsome intruder now feeling like a snake at a garden party, "I am not here to rain on your girls' parade. As I told you on the plane, I needed to get away to think and to heal some wounds. A tiny island in the middle of lots of ocean seemed ideal. So, you all go ahead with your plans."

A twinge of guilt tugged at Melanie's heart strings, as she knew only all too well just the kind of pain this poor fella was going through. "Wait a minute," her voice having returned to a softer tone, "I know of a darling place nestled in a small cove right on the beach. They only rent out a few rooms, and it is secluded and private. How does that sound?"

"That may be just what the doctor ordered," Bruce responded with a gleam in his eye, and a hint of a dimple appeared on his flawless olive cheek.

"Perfect!" squealed Barb. "Let's get this show on the road. Lead the way, Miss Social Director."

Melanie glowed inwardly, sensing the power she held over them and liking it maybe just a little too much.

The poor taxi driver didn't know if he would survive the slow, congested drive to the south shore of the island. The speed limit, normally a mere 20 m.p.h., was slow enough, but at 5 m.p.h. it was going to take every bit of 45 minutes to cover the 16 mile drive. The decibels of noise in the cab reached a deafening pitch, with all competing to be heard over each other. Bruce and the driver exchanged sullen glances and rolled their eyes.

"Mm, excuse me folks, but I'd be happy to introduce you to our lovely island," realizing he must take charge or lose his hearing.

As if by magic, the occupants of the taxi ceased their chatter and fell silent to the cab driver's heavy English accent.

"Bermuda is made up of 150 islets and islands, a chain of isles, you might say, giving the illusion of one long strip of land. Only twenty of the islands are inhabited." Swerving to miss an obviously confused tourist who was driving on the wrong side of the intersection, "Bloody Yank, they're going to kill us all!" Regaining his composure, the neatly attired elderly man picked up his narration. "Now, where was I? Oh yes, the seven largest are connected by bridges and causeways, creating a 21 mile fish-hooked shaped strip." Clearing his throat the driver continued, "Our widest point is only two miles." Several surprised gasps could be heard. "I guess you could say, we are about the size of Manhattan, though not quite 21 square miles." Sensing a restlessness from his passengers, he spoke more rapidly, fearing he was losing their attention. "At points, the island is so narrow, that the blue-green sea is never more than a mile away and rarely out of sight."

Bruce, more fascinated with learning the facts about the enchanted island than the other passengers in the cramped cab, asked how near they were to Nassau in the Bahamas.

"Well, governor, we're about 900 miles from Nassau and 700 miles from New York. We are quite proud of the fact that we're the oldest existing, self-governing British colony. Our barristers still wear the traditional powdered wigs."

With that statement, Barbara could no longer maintain her silence. "Tell me, sir, do they wear those wigs to bed? I can just imagine all that powder everywhere, if things were to get *intense*, if you know what I mean?"

Vivian blasted Barb before the driver could answer. "You know, Barbara, I'd forgotten just how crass you can be!"

As if embarrassed, the cabby ignored the confrontation and continued his factual dissertation.

"We have nine parishes, which resemble your counties in the states. Our original capital was St. George, founded in 1612, but the present is Hamilton. The stocks and pillories still remain in the town square of St. George."

"Bear that in mind, Barbara. You may end up in one before our stay has ended," Vivian retorted.

Obviously attempting to hold back a chuckle, in a quivering voice, "Our population is about 60,000 and.... Oh, here we are." The driver exuded a huge sigh of relief.

After what seemed an eternity, the overloaded taxi came to a grinding halt. Then, to everyone's sheer terror and morbid silence, it careened down a steep, ruddy driveway picking up an unsettling fast pace. The driver repeatedly pumped the brakes but to no avail. Beads of perspiration formulated across his dark skinned brow. One slid down his wide brimmed nose and teetered on a wild hair in his mustache. Now pumping with a determined intensity, he brought the faltering vehicle to a screeching, sand crunching stop.

"You're here, sir, Misty Cove Guest House."

"Thank God, and not a moment too soon for me," sighed Bruce. "Thank you, ladies. Have fun catching up with each other. That is if there is anything left to find out."

"Are you kidding," babbled Barb, "This will take all ten days. Come by, and don't be a stranger. We've all got shoulders for you, if you need'em. You know where we'll be, The Enchanted Isle Cottage."

"Yeah, got it. I will stop by one day just to see if your tongues have worn out."

Almost in unison, all chimed together, "Not a chance!"

The car surged forward as the girls stopped their incessant chatter only long enough to take in one of the many breathtaking views Bermuda was famous for. Two minutes later, they were descending down another long winding drive. Unlike the previous one, this one gently curved its way down ever so gradually to what truly lived up to its namesake. Tucked in an English garden off to one side was a white colonial sign etched in gold trim with elegant black lettering "The Enchanted Isle Cottage...welcomes you. Hosts Millicent and Bernard Lombard."

What could have been a movie set was an authentic vision. The pale yellow and white shuttered house with its Victorian charm and gingerbread trim over its rooftop pinnacles, almost looked out of place. This was not typical of the Bermudian architecture. The pastel stone walkways were surrounded by manicured shrubbery, and oleander bushes brimming with flowers. The bougainvillea was neatly climbing pristine white trellises against the house. The exquisitely hand carved door accented by a rainbow of stained glass was breathtaking. This gemstone set among nature's jewels of emerald green waters, sapphire blue skies with billowy opalescent clouds lazily drifting amongst the heavens, caused the gals a momentary lapse in conversation. Each was taking in every detail of this storybook setting.

The elaborate front door opened wide, and a tiny matronly English woman in a floral print and lace dress welcomed the gaping mouthed group.

"Welcome to The Enchanted Isle Cottage, ladies. Let me introduce myself. I'm Millicent Lombard...your hostess."

Melanie stepped forward and gingerly shook hands with this gracious woman. "Millicent, I am Melanie. We've spoken on the phone several times." Mrs. Lombard acknowledged the fact in her British accent.

"Leave your satchels. They'll be taken to your appropriate rooms.

Come, I'll give you the grand tour of E. I. My husband, Bernard, and I built our home 35 years ago after we made our way across the seas from our homeland of Great Britain. We had visited this tiny paradise on our first anniversary and made up our minds that one day we would become residents. Fifteen years later, we bid farewell to our family and friends and started to build our dream. My sweetheart, Bernie, oh, I am the only one to call him that. To everyone else, he is Bernard. Now, where was I? Oh yes, Bernie is a shipbuilder. Bermuda is one of the world's sailing capitals. Betcha you did not know that," the older woman said with such pride. "Anyway, he immediately started his own business, and we designed our regal home. We imported just about everything. Needless-to-say, we are very proud of it.

"Listen to me carry on. Some hostess I am. There'll be plenty of time to rattle on about Enchanted Isle during your stay. Let me show you to your rooms. Then, refreshments served on the verandah. There still will be a bit of light yet for you to enjoy our magnificent views but don't dally."

Quickly settled in their prospective quarters, each of the five literally flew down the grand winding staircase of rich pecan woods, wishing in their hearts they could be sliding down the banister instead. Melanie promised herself that she would do just that sometime before they had to depart.

The view from the wrap-around porch was truly like none other any of them had ever seen. The green hills in the distance were laced with colorful flowers leading down to the pink sand beaches, only to be offset by the reflections of the bright blue and turquoise seas. It was magical. As a matter of fact, The Enchanted Isle was just that... enchanting. Nestled amongst numerous brochures of things to do and places to see was an old well worn album. It was a pictorial history of the inn from its conception. A pin could have dropped in the abnormal silence of these particularly chatty females, as they were mesmerized by the photos of the early stages of the inn. Then, as if on command, the oohs and ahs collided together as they viewed the sensual forms of Victorian architecture taking shape. Mrs. L. tiptoed in carrying a lacy wicker tray of refreshments.

"Here we are ladies, some tantalizing island punch to welcome you." As she poured each a glass, including one for herself, she raised the Waterford crystal glasses and toasted her new house guests. Following the initial clink of goblets, each felt compelled to make her own salutation to the group. Hence, a barrage of questions for poor Mrs. Lombard all having to do with the inn and its heritage. The echoing of the grandfather clock in the hallway brought the moments of nostalgia to an end.

"My goodness, girls..."

Claudia wasn't the only one who picked up on Millicent's referral to them now as "girls."

"It's too late for you to dine in town. Most places close down tight early week nights, so I'll whip up some tea sandwiches for you. That is, if that will be agreeable with you." Each nodded yes wearily, as the anxieties of their traveling, accompanied with the wallop of the infamous house punch were taking their toll.

"Hey, why don't we all get into our robes and meet back here for our late evening snack," suggested Melanie.

"Sounds good to me," sighed Stephanie. "Somebody wake Vivian up. Talk about some things never changing."

Claudia challenged Barbara to rejoin them in ten minutes and not a minute longer. She was notorious for always keeping them waiting. That first evening resembled an old fashioned slumber party. The sandwiches were delicious, the English tea biscuits paired with the Earl Grey tea made for a perfect palatable match. By midnight, each exhausted from their enjoyable day nodded the others good night, and immersed themselves into the delicate solitude of their finely decorated rooms.

The sun rose bright and early as did each guest, filled with anticipation to see every inch of this glorious island...all 21 miles of it. After a superb British breakfast which included Millicent's famous scones, Bernard offered to drive them to the moped livery on Hamilton Street. During the short journey, he must have answered no less than 102 questions regarding the "must sees" in Bermuda, all coming at him simultaneously. With a sigh, a wipe of his brow, and a wave, he wished them all good luck and cautioned them one last time to remember to drive on the left side of the road.

The clerk at the cycle shop must have thought the navy had landed. These five females could fluster even the most tranquil person. His insistence that they take and *wear* the helmets that accompanied the motor-assisted bicycles seem to be his nemesis. Repeatedly, he warned the Americans that it was Bermudian law. "Hairdos or no hairdos!" At his wits end, his final gesture pointed to a large, weather beaten sign that hung unevenly over the entrance. *"Keep left and don't look back."* Nearly an hour later, which seemed three times that long to the bewildered shopkeeper, each gal with her own cycle headed off to see their paradise. Melanie led the "Hell's Angelettes" to their first stop, Devil's Hole, a natural grotto occupied by huge sea turtles, gray sharks, groupers, and hogfish. Some of the inhabitants were hundreds of years old. Tourists stood on a wooden bridge above the grotto dangling baited lines, hoping an ancient turtle or other specimen would swipe it away.

Anxious to get to town, the ensemble walked back to their parked bikes. "Perhaps, you've noticed the darling names on the houses we've passed. They don't use house numbers, only names," Melanie commented.

"You mean the sign that said "Bacardi on the Rocks" was not an advertisement but the name of someone's home?"

"You got it. There are some great names, too. You'll notice them as we explore. Pumpkin Patch, Wreck Hill House, Shalom, and Swingle Trees, we lived in the last two I mentioned. And, my son attended Strawberry Hill pre-school.

I would drop him off on my way to the King Edward VII Memorial Hospital, where I was a volunteer Pink Lady. He had his own little seat on the back of my moped and a basket on the front for groceries. It was a different way of life, one I learned to appreciate."

Their next stop was the town of Hamilton. Of course, Barbara, her firm, tanned body mostly exposed in her halter top, short shorts, and her signature visor holding back her strawberry blonde locks was immediately entranced with the "Bobby" directing traffic from his caged structure. Drawn to his Bermudian shorts that bared his knees, she parked her moped and ran in front of oncoming traffic to place herself right under his nose.

"Miss! Miss! What are doing?" he questioned in an authoritative British accent. It didn't take but 60 seconds to have him under her spell. Meanwhile, horns were honking, and a traffic jam materialized.

Vivian trying to be heard above all the commotion, "She's at it again! Somebody do something about her!"

"Who might that be? You know no one can control Babs," Claudia rolled her eyes and motioned they park the bikes and start discovering the intimate shops. Barbara would eventually find them.

Up one side of the street and down the other, they entered each doorway—Triminghams, Smith's, Calypso—until finally they were beginning to run out of steam. Even the long legged brunette, Stephanie, who had an insatiable taste for expensive trinkets, was ready for a break.

"It's time, ladies, to visit the Tea Cosy on Burnaby Street for lunch. Unless, of course, you want to go to the Irish Linen Shop first?" Melanie knowing all too well that the consensus of opinion would be rest and nourishment.

A delightful meal consumed and recharged with energy, the "Lakes Bunch," a term referring to themselves having all been residents of The Lakes years earlier, headed to Horseshoe Bay Beach, one of the most popular and most photographed beaches on the island and a delightful place to explore its cave-like formations. After a refreshing swim and more touring of the narrow bougainvillea-lined winding streets with their pastel colored houses, it was late afternoon when the five weary tourists stopped at Henry VIII's, an English pub across from the splendid Sonesta Beach Hotel on the South Shore in Southampton.

"Now, how's this for a view?" asked Melanie of her companions.

"I could sit out here all day and watch the surf crash against those rocks," murmured Claudia between sips of a chilled White Zinfandel.

"Barb, we thought we had first lost you to that policeman this morning, but we were sure you were a goner when you went the *wrong* way in the roundabout. They can really confuse a person. I'm glad there are only two to contend with on the island. I had some close calls myself when I lived here. The one thing you cannot allow yourself to do is daydream when driving. It's so natural to find yourself on the right side, which is the wrong side of the street," Melanie concluded.

"Thank God, our intersections at home aren't like these, Vivian sighed.

"Hey friends, I had that Bobby cop handled once he straightened out that slight traffic congestion."

"Slight?" said all four in unison at the top of their lungs!

"Okay, okay, it was a bit of a mess, but I ended up with a date with him, so it was worth it," Barb said pulling at her halter top.

"Well, he probably figured it was the only way to get you to leave him alone so he could do his job," bellowed Vivian.

"Hey girls, how's it going?" a male voice coming from behind their patio table. Barb puffed up her chest, as if a peacock in full bloom, and jumped up to plant a glossy red lipstick imprint on Bruce's tanned cheek.

"Hi, handsome! How's the healing of your broken heart coming along?"

"Well, if any place can heal it, it's this one. I've been all over this island, and it is one gorgeous place! Have you made it out to St. George's yet on the other end? That's where they have the stocks and pillory in the town square. They make for great pictures. I was told that the Peppercorn Ceremony at Market Square will be held tomorrow evening. Apparently, the governor receives the annual rental of one peppercorn from the uh, oh, yeah, I think they're called the freemasons, for use of the old state house."

Stephanie answered, "No, we haven't made it there yet, but we have been to...," and she rattled off a number of stores. Bruce shook his head in disgust.

"Ladies, ladies! Don't tell me you've come all this way to go shopping, when there are a million great places to explore!"

"We are exploring!" Vivian defensively slammed back. "We're just starting at the opposite end of the island. We have plenty of time to take in all the sights."

"Well, just don't miss touring Fort St. Catherine."

Before he could expound upon his reasons for the suggestion, Claudia quipped, "Why on earth would we want to spend our precious time in a musty old, rat-infested fort?"

Overcoming his annoyance, Bruce displayed a sincere desire to share his day's discoveries with his less than interested audience. "Claudia, correct me if I am wrong, but I detect that you have an appreciation for beautiful jewelry."

"You are accurate in your judgment. My nickname just happens to be Rocky, but what does that have to do with an old fort?"

Feeling confident that he piqued her interest, he continued. "Fort St. Catherine has a noteworthy exhibit of replicas of Britain's crown jewels, as well as historic dioramas, you know, three-dimensional scenic displays." Observing that he hadn't gained the reaction he expected, he decided to abort the mission and queried, "Do you mind, if I join you?" As he didn't wait for an answer and pulled up a chair next to Melanie. "And how are you surviving all these females, pretty lady?"

"You forget, I'm one of them."

"No, you're not. You are different," he whispered in her ear.

Barb caught the gesture and immediately moved her chair closer to the only male amongst the harem. Melanie, feeling frisky, decided to counter strike with, "Babs, tell your friend, Bruce, how you already managed to finagle a date with an authentic Bermuda Bobby *and* cause a hell of a traffic jam in Hamilton this morning."

"Now, why doesn't that surprise me!" laughed Bruce before the strawberry blonde had a chance to answer. "And, you've not been on the island 24 hours yet."

That was all that was needed to start Barbara off on a 20 minute hilarious accounting of the morning's encounter. Bruce bought them all another round as their laughter reigned on. With the sun starting its descent, dinner plans were discussed.

"Fine, then it's settled. I'll meet you all at your place in an hour, and you can follow me to the Princess Hotel. I hear the food is fabulous and expensive, so don't be typical females and conveniently forget your wallets, ladies," he chuckled.

"Cheapskate," mumbled Melanie under her breath. "Barb, you'd better get started, we know how long it takes you to get ready."

Not about to take anymore criticism for one day, she snapped back, "Hey, I've changed!"

"Oh, sure." Stephanie knowing her fiery friend longer than the others, threw her head back. "Actually, it wouldn't hurt all of us to start operation clean up. We need it after today."

Mrs. Lombard's bathrooms were a flurry of activity for the next hour. She giggled to herself as the women were skittering in and out of each other's rooms borrowing paraphernalia from one another. It took her back to her own college days to the dorm she shared with fifty other females.

Chapter Two

Bruce toweled dry the remaining droplets of water off his deeply tanned body. Just one day back out in the sun's rays was enough to stimulate his Italian skin to produce a copper haze. As he checked out his new shade of color, he sized himself up in the full length mirror on the bathroom door.

"Not a bad shape for a guy approaching the big five-0," he gleamed into his reflection. The soft slapping of the bay's water against the boat dock was music to his ears and redirected his thoughts from his own vanity to a deep rooted dream. Oh, how he loved the water and had since childhood, growing up on the north shore of Long Island. One day, yes one day in the near future, he was going to live on the water preferably on a boat. He had been designing his dream craft for ten years. Determined more than ever to make it a reality, now that Debbie was no longer in his life. She did not share his love for a nautical life-style but rather wanted a banker's nine-to-five stable life. Well, that's what she chose when she threw him aside for his best friend, Dick.

"More power to her! I hope she gets bored with it all, as I know she will!"

Bruce heard himself echo the words out loud and then shook his head as if he could shake the thoughts free from his mind. A glance at his watch told him he would have to hustle to meet the "foxes" on time. What an erroneous thought, to think they would be ready. If he were wise, he'd make himself a drink and soak up more of the incredible views and mosey over there thirty minutes after the agreed hour. After a slight tussle with his conscience, a mutual agreement of twenty minutes tardiness was acceptable. That would still enable him to enjoy one stiff drink before taking on five of the most frustrating, beautiful, and yet beguiling women he had ever encountered...all at one time.

The inward warmth from the dark rum and the slight outward burning from the sun that day caused him to change shirts at the last moment before closing the bungalow's door. "Yes, the aqua floral (Tom Selleck shirt) should bring out the green in my eyes. I wonder if other guys get as hung up as I do on what to wear. I know I have my mother to thank for this. Lucille is the biggest clothes horse there is," he muttered aloud. He grabbed his off white sports jacket and was on his way.

Millicent answered the melodic door chime, another import from England. "My, you look handsome, Mr.?"

"Just call me Bruce." He gingerly took her hand and gently placed a delicate kiss upon it, releasing it and staring into Millicent's soft blue eyes. She was mesmerized from that moment on with this Tom Selleck look alike.

"That's it!" she sputtered loudly, shocking not only herself but Bruce as well. "Has anyone ever told you, you look like that actor, Tom," but before she could finish the last name, Bruce cocked his head coyly, knowing it had come up a lot more often than he cared to admit. At first, he felt flattered, but now it was almost an annoyance. He resented being someone else's clone.

The hurried footsteps and commotion was indicative of a flurry of activity upstairs that broke the spell, as it was obvious the girls were not quite ready. "Dear sir, come sit on the porch, and I'll see what I can do to hurry your "five" dates along. They've been scurrying about up there for well over an hour."

"Why doesn't that surprise me? Mmm, that's the second time today I've made that same statement."

It was not two minutes after he seated himself down on the overstuffed polished cotton cushion, that Melanie appeared at the doorway. Her crisp white, short sun dress accentuated her bronze tan. She allowed her long blonde tresses to drape over her shoulders. Her exquisite blue eyes sparkled with her enthusiasm as she spoke. "You look tanfastic...I mean fantastic, though I may have been correct the first time."

"Cute play on words. Speaking of looking great, may I say you're a gorgeous lady." Their gazes locked into one another's but only momentarily. Vivian popped into the room dressed in a deep fuchsia outfit, followed by Claudia wearing a stunning black jumpsuit. Stephanie descended the staircase in a flamboyant island print wrap around skirt and Danskin top revealing her cleavage.

"Well, we're almost all here. I could have predicted who wouldn't be ready on time." Vivian turned and asked Stephanie to call up to Barb. "Tell her we are leaving in three minutes!"

Ten minutes later, racing out the front door, Barb in a red mini dress which almost entirely bared her thighs, joined her compatriots who were already mounted on their cycles, helmeted, and engines revving. Avoiding the glares, she quickly readied herself and surprising all, blasted past them in an uproarious passing of the gears. Bruce was not to be outdone, since driving fast was his specialty. In a flash, he pulled in front of Barb and assumed the role of leader of the pack. It was a glorious evening, and the scenery was embellished with beautiful scents from the lilies. It was an adventure of the best kind. Every moment would become a cherished memory.

The luxurious Princess Hotel, one of Bermuda's finest, majestically sat on a hilltop overlooking the sea. Amazingly, all six arrived without incident. Although, it was a unified consensus of opinion, that they should double up on the cycles for future night rides. Why take six bikes when they could buddy ride and get by with three? It would be safer, especially on the trips home after indulging in potent tropical drinks. Remembering to stay on the left side of the road and maneuvering motorbikes in dark, unfamiliar territory was a challenge for them all. Practically speaking, two heads would be better than one to be mindful of staying left.

The maitre d' looked with envy towards Bruce and his gorgeous harem. It was obvious that the distinguished salt and pepper haired man was entranced by the bevy of beauties surrounding him. After seating the entourage, he bent down and in a low voice volunteered his services, should Bruce need them. His shift was due to end on the hour, and he would be available. Bruce chuckled and suggested that he check back with him. He very well might need a recruit by then.

The elegance of the posh dining room wreaked expensive. One glance at the menu supported the notion. Sensing the notable discomfort, Melanie offered the suggestion that they celebrate their first official evening out on the town royally and proposed a toast. "To the friendships that are represented here. May they continue to grow in sincerity and flourish in the years to come."

"Here, here," they all chorused. The tinkling of crystal commenced an unforgettable evening.

Bruce was tuckered out after twirling five females across the dance floor. Though, other men with the obvious permission of their wives, took pity and cut in to give him a respite. The only time he politely refused their offer was when he and Melanie were together. She seemed to be custom made to fit into his arms, unlike his recently departed fiancée. She was a larger built girl and not much of a dancer.

When all the wining, dining, and dancing ceased, naturally, the bill of fare was presented to the gentleman at the table. It was a dead give away when Bruce's tanned face paled as his eyes focused upon the amount. "Well, ladies, I fully intended to pay for the pleasure of your company, but $587.50 is just a bit too steep. I'll go as high as $400.00, if you don't mind kicking in the rest." This was his way of testing them. Would they stick him with the check? All too often, that happened when a group of females were together with one male.

To his delight, each agreed they should pay their fair share. After all, Bruce really didn't know them, and why should he have to cough up such an exorbitant amount of money. What they were not aware of until moments later was that he had done just that. He had paid the full amount and even added to the already included gratuity, totaling an even $600.00. They argued all the way to the parking lot trying earnestly to reimburse him until he shrieked, "Enough! It was my treat. If it will make you feel any better, you can buy me an after dinner drink at Tom Moore's pub. But, let me suggest we take a cab and leave the mopeds here." He was impressed with these ladies. They genuinely wanted to play fair. What a refreshing change from the women he was normally subjected to. These gals could actually be real friends. Perhaps Melanie's toast could apply to him as well, though, he hadn't thought it would at the time it was proposed.

Six bodies plus the driver's made for a tight fit in the taxi, but

Bruce didn't mind a bit. As they piled in, he stood back a moment and grabbed Melanie's hand. "Wait, how about if you sit on my lap? We cannot possibly all fit in."

"Smooth, Blue Eyes, real smooth. Sure, why not." The taxi weebled and wobbled with its over-capacity load. In a wonderful British accent, the driver had kept them laughing hilariously the entire ride, knowing it usually paid off with a fat tip, as it did when he had delivered them to the Enchanted Isle.

"Here we are, Govenor...enjoy yourselves."

"Arthur, come join us. It's late, and you probably won't have any other fares tonight. Besides, we'll need you to drive us home."

"HOME! But what about our cycles? They're back at The Princess."

"Vivian, my dear, it's a hell of a lot safer to have Arthur here drive us home. I'll make arrangements to get the bikes tomorrow. Now, relax. Loosen up a little and try to enjoy yourself."

Vivian knew Bruce was right. For some reason, she had always had some difficulty in that department. More serious than the others, she wondered why she fit in with them at all. Sensing Vivian's mood, Melanie coaxed her inside to join in the merriment. The nightly regulars had teamed up with a group from one of the annual golf tournaments. The piano player responded as best he could to all the requests ranging from a tourist favorite, "The Big Bamboo," to reggae and The Beatles.

"Vivian, what's wrong? I can tell something is really bothering you."

"Melanie, it's Frank. I just can't get him off my mind. We quarreled bitterly before I left for the airport. He didn't want me to come. He hates to share me with anyone or anything. He's driving me away, and I cannot seem to make him see what he is doing to us."

"God, Viv, I remember him doing that to you years ago. So, nothing has changed then? How's his drinking problem?"

"Worse than ever. I can't take much more. Melanie, I'm seriously considering leaving him. I promised myself I would make up my mind while I was on this trip."

"Okay, Viv, but don't decide tonight. Have fun this first week. You look as though you could use some. Chances are that you've forgotten how. We'll spend time talking about your options later. If need be, we'll stay a few extra days after the rest have left and figure out your life. But you have to promise me to put Frank out of your thoughts. THINK...*Vivian*, THINK...*Bermuda*, THINK...*good times with your closest pals*. Who knows when we'll get another reunion together."

"You're absolutely right! Starting this evening, NO, starting now, I am going to enjoy every moment of this paradise!"

"Amen! Now, let's join the chorus and make total fools of ourselves. You and I have been too straight laced for too long." Melanie ordered them two White Russians. The real fun was about to begin.

It was the wee hours of the morning when Bruce decided to become "father hen" and gather up his chicks. He had to literally pry Vivian out of the arms of a dashingly handsome, mature British yachtie. He looked as though he belonged in the House of Parliament and the type to wear a white powdered wig. The two White Russians must have taken effect. She was giddy yet powerfully seductive in an almost school girl way. Bruce hadn't seen this side of her. All her guarded defenses were down. He decided he liked her much better this way. He had seen Melanie talking to her earlier. They both looked so serious. But, after they made a private toast, neither was the same. They both seemed to shed their inhibitions and took over the party. They sang and lured guys away from their bar stools to dance with them. They were very entertaining to observe. That was all Bruce got to do, since he ended up cornered in a booth talking to Stephanie, who had decided to hang out her shingle and critique the different personalities. With each drink, she spilled more delicious information in Bruce's ear about each of her comrades. By the end of the night, he had a good fix on each of his new acquaintances. Well, if it took booze, preferably White Russians, Bruce decided to keep them plied with alcohol. After all, this was a special time for all of them. Stephanie had filled him in on the extraordinary circumstances that surrounded each of their lives with the exception, of course, of her own. She claimed all was copacetic in her life. It couldn't be better. Only she knew that copacetic could not be farther from the truth.

Arthur, a bit tipsy, assured his passengers that he knew those roads with his eyes closed, and that they were a few times. Claudia took over the responsibility of keeping Arthur alert enough to get them safely back to the Enchanted Isle, which he did. They all gave him a kiss on the cheek and prearranged another driving date. They had decided to make Arthur their designated driver for their evenings out and about the island. Claudia volunteered to chaperone "Artie" and keep an eye on his consumption. She found him innocently attractive and safe! Unless, of course, her attentions were distracted elsewhere. But, until then, they could count on her. Poor Arthur would have some explaining to do to his wife with getting home so late, to say nothing of being covered with all shades of lip imprints on his cheeks.

He roared off up the driveway, just after they all agreed (Arthur included) to be quiet and not wake up the Lombards.

"It's a good thing we are their only guests."

"Shh!" The others whispered in unison. Each tried to be as quiet as a mouse, but the moment one started to giggle it was all over. Barb accidentally snorted a laugh and simultaneously *fluffed* a tiny gas bubble, and that was all it took. Gales of muffled laughter echoed on the wide stairway. Each found a step to perch upon, and that was as far as they got. In a few moments, the inevitable happened. Millicent appeared like a nightingale in a beautiful Irish cotton nightgown with a delicate satin collar.

"Such a sight. I must say you remind me of teenagers sneaking home after curfew."

"Well, we are, aren't we? At least it feels that way. There is something about being here, in your home and you. You seem like our mother, and we've reverted back to our youth," Melanie said sheepishly.

Millicent loved what she was hearing. She was beginning to feel the same way. She knew now that the next nine days were going to be extremely special to her. She was grateful that she had only five bedrooms for guests, and that each would be occupied by one of these beautiful, ephemeral "adopted daughters." She would have the large family she had always dreamed about. Even if it was only temporarily with strangers she barely knew, but was already becoming attached to.

The elegant lady joined the girls on the gracious stairway as each gave an accounting of their fabulous evening. When the grandfather clock struck three chimes, she bid them all good night. Following each one to their rooms, she made sure they were tucked in. Once back in her own bed next to her Bernie, snoring ever so softly, she smiled from her heart. Never had she felt this way, so fulfilled. As fleeting as it would be, she was going to love and cherish every minute the girls were under her roof.

Chapter Three

The next few days were heavenly spent. Each of the gals agreed to do her own thing for the first half of the day. At one o'clock, they would meet on the porch to decide the rest of the day's plans. Stephanie, an avid reader, enjoyed a gentle swing in the hammock with a good novel. A treat for her, since the majority of her reading included the latest psychology journals. Vivian, born to shop till she dropped, sought out each and every boutique and retail store from one end of the island to the other. Claudia accompanied her on several of the missions. Her specialty was the jewelry shops. She then begged off so as to include some sunbathing time. Barb, well, who knew what she was up to. She vanished after breakfast. Though, once she did admit she was meeting her "bobbie," the traffic officer before his shift began. Melanie combed the beach taking long walks after breakfast. A writer at heart and by trade, she was never without her notepad and pen.

It was on her second morning walk that she encountered Bruce, who was also strolling along the coastline. Misty Cove's beach elongated into Enchanted Isle's. He needed time to think, he said, to decide what direction he wanted his life's journey to follow. He hadn't much luck in the romance department and thought he should concentrate fully on a dream he had been entertaining since childhood.

"What dream is that?" Melanie asked cautiously, not wanting to appear too nosy. "Is it something you'd like to talk about?"

"Sure, why not. I have been designing boats on napkins, place mats, scraps of paper for years. It is my life long ambition to be a boat builder. To custom design boats for clients and then oversee every detail until their christening day."

"Ohh, sounds terribly creative and challenging. Where would you like to launch this dream of yours?"

"That has been the question. I checked out the west coast a few years back, but costs were prohibitive there to start up an operation and existing ones are out of my financial pocket. Logically, my next search took me to the east coast, but again, I only ran into dead ends for one reason or another. But, since arriving here, I've been obsessed with my dream...more than ever before. I am seriously considering talking to Bernard Lombard. He's been a shipbuilder all his life. Granted, his operation here is small, but he seems happy and content. Besides, who needs all the stress of a large enterprise?"

"Bruce, I am sure Bernie, um, Bernard would love to discuss this with you. I even overheard him say to Millicent that he is contemplating retirement one day in the not too distant future so they could travel and experience the world, while they still had their health and working genitals. Then, he described some romantic situation he fantasized for them to find themselves in, and Millicent blushed a deep crimson. Who would have thought he was such a romantic? Perhaps, he would consider a partnership with you. That way you could learn the business and capitalize on all his years of experience."

A light sparked inside his head, and Bruce leaped forward and picked up Melanie, swinging her around in the warm Bermuda breeze. "You are one terrific lady and with brains, too! You have good insight, and yes, I am going to take your suggestion and talk to Bernie!"

"Hey, guy, one more little suggestion..." He stopped all movement and froze holding her slightly above his head. "I suggest you don't call Bernard, Bernie. Millicent commented that only she is allowed to call him that, but we girls do behind his back. A form of rebellion, I suppose. You certainly wouldn't want to get off on the wrong track."

"You're right!" Then, with a long intense look, Bruce stared into her electric blue eyes as he lowered her feet to the sand. "You are right, maybe more right than either of us has realized." With that, he pressed his lips against her soft, moist mouth, and they kissed long and intensely. They both knew that something was happening between them. Was it that they were vulnerable? Though, it had been months since Melanie's last disastrous affair and only days for Bruce. Were they both on the rebound, each longing to find real love? As if they sensed what the other was thinking, they released their embrace and began walking down the beach. Bruce broke the long silence.

"I know my heart is still wounded, but to be honest, I don't think it is as much my heart as it is my pride. I knew I wasn't really in love with Debbie, but I cared deeply for her. I was tired of the dating scene and thought it was time to give in to all the family pressure and settle down. I am still steamed that I didn't notice what was going on behind my back. I am just too damn trusting!"

"Oh, tell me about it. I've always believed in the golden rule. Do unto others and all that good stuff. I have taken pride in dealing honestly and fairly with all I meet. My only reward has been a consistently broken heart."

"It seems we can really relate. Let's let that be the foundation of our relationship and build from there. Don't misunderstand me, I am not looking to replace Debbie right away in my life, but you've stirred some real emotions in me, lady, and I haven't felt anything quite like them before. If you are game, I'd like to see how they stand the test of time. That is, however many days you have left here in paradise, could we spend the majority of them together?"

This was coming a little too fast for Melanie's comfort level. She'd had a whirlwind romance once before that left her with a severely scarred heart. The memory of that and the wisdom of the effects that a tropical paradise can have on two lonely people could spell disaster when it came time to part. When the tropical nights drenched in romance ended, where would that leave them. Reality does have a way of returning to lives. What would it do to theirs? Melanie didn't feel she could take such a risk. Not now...she was still recovering from the last.

Finally, finding the words she spoke. "I can't just run off and leave my friends. After all, this is our reunion." She emphasized the *our* and realized she wanted to protect and defend this special time they had all sacrificed to make possible. Now, this intruder, a male, wanted to interrupt this time of theirs!

Bruce snapped back from his romantic fantasy of the two of them discovering each other's secrets and bonding together over the next days to the tone of Melanie's voice and reality. "Oh, hey, no problem. I understand completely. Well, I've enjoyed our chat and thanks for the advice about Bernard."

Melanie realizing too late what she had done to this poor soul, tried to reach out, but Bruce darted off down the beach. "Great going, you idiot! The nicest guy you've met in eons and you slam the door in his face!" She ceased mumbling out loud as people on the beach began to look at her peculiarly.

Once back at the house, still with pangs of guilt, she called to leave Bruce a message. "How about joining me for an apology drink at Henry VIII's at four o'clock. Hope you'll be there, because I will be." This way she could apologize and still be back in time to do whatever with the girls that evening.

By four forty-five, Melanie knew she was being stood up. She finished her second rum punch, paid the tab, chatted to the noisy parrot, Henry, on her way out, and revved up her motorbike to its highest r.p.m. Peeling out of the gravel driveway onto the pavement made more commotion than she had intended. Everyone on the patio looked up, and she instantly blushed from head to toe. She decided that she could not return for a few days. She was too embarrassed.

At five thirty, the clan gathered on the Lombard's porch for their traditional sunset cocktail hour. Melanie, two steps ahead of them with her rum punches, nursed her white wine. Matter-of-factly, she asked if there were any messages for her.

"No, should there be?" Claudia, the first to respond.

"Oh, I ran into Bruce this morning on the beach, and he mentioned he might call to see what we were doing this evening." How she hated to lie, even a small white lie. He must be royally "p.o.'d" with me, she quietly thought to herself. "Anyone up for a moonlight walk on the beach after dinner?" She asked the group, hoping she might catch Bruce doing the same.

"Sounds like a plan. Can't get enough of the sheer beauty this island has to offer," responded Claudia. The others all nodded in agreement. Vivian said she could use the exercise to walk off dinner.

Following their scrumptious meal at a small casual outside cafe, the motorcycle brigade descended down the driveway and parked their bikes. They ran inside to change, meeting ten minutes later down on the beach. With the exception of Melanie, they were chatting up a storm. When they sauntered by Bruce's cottage, of course, Barb had to notice that he was at home but not alone.

"Looks like our Prince Charming is entertaining a female on his porch swing. I'm glad to see his heart is recovering. I was beginning to worry about him. He ignored all my passes."

"Maybe you aren't his type, Barb!" Melanie sarcastically flipped back.

"Hiss, hiss," the other girls echoed in unison. "Is it the full moon, or are you just being bitchy?"

"I apologize. That certainly didn't come out right. Sorry, Babs. I just meant..."

"Hey, don't worry about it. I do detect a touch of jealousy. Am I right?"

It must have been the moon, for normally Melanie kept her feelings to herself. She was a good listener, but rarely divulged her own secret thoughts. In the next few moments, she commanded everyone's attention as she relayed the conversation earlier that morning with Bruce. Each friend offered her lovelorn advice. The final consensus was for her to open up the doors of her heart. He wasn't your ordinary kind of guy. Each felt he was special and worth some effort. They would gladly trade places with her.

Now, Melanie was sure she had been a jerk with him. All her pals had just confirmed it, but how was she going to undue what she had done? "Mimosas on the beach tomorrow morning! What do you all think? I'll head out at the usual time but with chilled champagne and o.j.. Cross your fingers that I run into him."

Awake at dawn with high expectations for a new beginning with Bruce, Melanie counted the hours. At the proposed time with an ice bucket in hand, she started down the beach. In the distance, she could see the familiar outline of the six foot four stud she searched out. "Perfect," she said aloud. Followed by, "Not perfect...damn!" He was not alone. His company from the previous evening must have spent the night!

Melanie's head started reeling. "I can't deal with this. Why do I care if he is with someone. I hardly know him!" Her thoughts pounded at her temples. "That could be me with him this morning. You fool, you stupid fool! You can't just give up. You like this guy too much. Do something about it!"

Shaking her thoughts loose, she continued her steps closing the distance between Bruce and Ms.? and herself. Once upon them, she politely made conversation.

"Hi, you two. The girls and I noticed on our walk last evening that you had company, Bruce. Taking a chance you might still be here," as she shot the brunette invader a glance. "I thought you would enjoy some Mimosas to start your day off, after a long, busy night."

Bruce decided not to cut Melanie any slack by purposely not divulging that they both had too much to drink the night before, and neither was in condition to drive. They had not made love. Actually, they met while snorkeling at Horseshoe Bay, and both in need of companionship decided to have dinner together. There was no chemistry between them, at least not for Bruce, but he was not about to let Melanie know that. He had not received her message until he and Sandra made their way back to his cottage for a nightcap.

Sandra's father had been in the shipbuilding business all his life, until he died two weeks earlier. Extremely close to him, she was having difficulty accepting his death. On the advice of friends, she decided to get away to Bermuda. She and Bruce hit it off conversationally, although, she would have preferred it to go further. He barraged her with questions pertaining to the business, since she, too, was involved in it. Being no dummy, she realized this was her hook to reel him into her life. It was obvious to Melanie that this girl had fallen prey to Bruce's charismatic charm.

Bruce put two and two together and realized why Melanie had shown up on the beach with the bucket brimming with delightful morning eye openers, and it was not for the reason she gave. He decided to further torment her and let her believe the conclusion she already had deduced, at least for the time being.

"I must say, what a neighborly gesture. Sandra and I thank you for being so thoughtful." With that, he accepted the bucket and took Sandra's arm to lead her towards his cottage.

In total disbelief, Melanie turned on her heels not believing that he wouldn't suggest sharing the container's contents with her. Her stomach filled with acid and her eyes with tears. "Damn it! I don't want to feel this way here! I came to enjoy my friends, and this a__hole is ruining my stay. I must get a handle on this and snap back. This is ridiculous! From now on, it's just the girls! NO damn men!!" Half crying and still talking to herself, she returned to the house.

Chapter Four

Melanie's wasn't the only heart feeling troubled. Vivian's husband had been calling and leaving numerous messages for her to return home at once. Apparently, he could not deal with her flagrant display of independence from him. With each day, the calls increased. Poor Millicent had run out of excuses to give him as to why Vivian couldn't take his calls. Finally, out of desperation, Vivian accepted the phone from Millicent. She couldn't ask her to lie for her anymore. It was noticeably disturbing to Millicent. Deceit was not part of her makeup. Millicent's character appeared to be as pure as newly fallen snow.

Tears, angry words, long pauses, and finally a slamming of the receiver in its cradle, broke the awkward silence they had all succumbed to on the porch that quiet balmy afternoon. Everyone had decided to take advantage of the languid summer day and read the books they had brought with them. Since their arrival, they had been on the go too much to read. The hammock was in great demand. So, utilizing Millicent's suggestion, her guests selected a number from a wicker basket and drew their sequence for hammock time. As Millicent so succinctly put it, "It's the only democratic way." They overwhelmingly agreed, and each one hugged her tightly. They were becoming so attached to this jewel of womanhood. The group all confessed how they wished they could just stay on for an indefinite time. None were anxious to return to their stressful lives off the tiny island they referred to as their paradise.

Vivian refused to disclose her personal problems, but then she had always been a very private person. Though Melanie knew that when the two of them could find some privacy away from the others, Viv would open up. She was trying valiantly to put up a good front, but Melanie saw through it. "That damn Frank!"

Claudia's nine-year relationship had dissolved six months before.

After nearly a decade with the same person, there was an adjustment period returning to the single's world. She had sworn she would never remarry after two disasters. She and Howard had never married. But, with each passing year, the pressure was on them from all their well meaning friends. Under the circumstances, everyone was glad they had not given in to their insistent prodding, or Claudia would have been 0 for 3.

Those first months after Howard's departure from her life, Claudia buried herself in her business. She owned a children's' shop where she devoted an incredible amount of hours each day. Those close to her began to worry about her substitution of work life smothering any chances of a personal life. Thanks to dear Babs, who put a twinkle back into her eyes following an introduction to a very tall, good looking former pro basketball player. He was just what Claudia needed. They made a dynamic entrance whenever they walked into a room together. He stood a full six foot eleven inches tall, and she a petite five foot three. It was always good for starting tongues wagging. More than once they had been referred to as Beauty and the Beast purely because of the contradiction in their physical statures.

The gals were quite amazed when Claudia accepted their invitation to join them. They all felt certain she would never leave the new love in her life. Her reply to Melanie was, "Why should I give up a golden opportunity to be with all you catty bitches? Besides, you'll just talk about me if I'm not there!" Melanie reassured her she was correct in her judgment and was thrilled she would be coming along. More than once she had been observed day dreaming, and all knew who it was about.

It was Stephanie, though who piqued everyone's curiosity. Every morning she would take off on her moped at ten o'clock sharp. By the fourth day, Barb couldn't stand not knowing the motive behind Stephanie's daily disappearance. Nor could she tolerate her friend's evasiveness. The most outspoken member of the group insisted that she was going to join Stephanie on her mystery jaunt. But, that was not to happen. Stephanie turned abruptly and let Babs know that in no uncertain terms she was not welcomed to accompany her on her ride.

"Barbara, did you ever think that maybe, just maybe, I would like some quiet personal time to myself?!"

Barb taken aback by Stephanie's abruptness, shook her head, and walked up the steps to the inviting porch to rejoin the others. "What the hell is her problem?"

Vivian, the first to answer, "You know, it could be for the reason she stated."

"I suppose. No! I don't suppose. I bet she has someone stashed away that she is rendezvousing with right here under our noses!! Yes, that's got to be it." Without another word, she raced across the driveway and literally jumped on her motorbike, as though she was an old time cowboy hopping onto his horse. She tore up the driveway in record time.

"I don't believe her," screamed Vivian. "She can't ever respect anyone's privacy. She feels compelled to meddle into everyone's business! I'm glad she knows better than to bug me about mine. I'd bite her head off!!"

"Trust me," Melanie interjected. "She knows that, Viv. I'm sure we'll get a full report when she returns."

Claudia quietly taking in all that had just transpired. "I hope Stephanie doesn't catch Babs following her. Mad won't begin to cover her reaction. I'd hate to see her get really miffed and leave early. Hopefully, Barb will be cautious in her spying."

Nearly an hour had gone by when the sound of a moped engine was heard coming down the drive. "Well, let's hope there aren't fireworks," Claudia casually said while glancing up from the novel she had been glued to all morning.

Barb ran up the steps two at a time. Totally out of breath, "You'll never believe where she's been going."

"You're right. Are you going to keep us in suspense or share your super sleuth findings with us?" asked Melanie.

"Stephanie has a post office box! Apparently, she is sending someone love letters and receiving the same. Why else would she insist upon going by herself to the post? I saw her mail a letter and then go open a box with a key. And, ladies, there was a letter inside."

"Now, how do you know it was a love letter?" asked Claudia.

"It must have been, because she had a strange smile on her face when she found the letter and immediately walked across the street to sit on the pier to read it. If it was a letter from her husband, she wouldn't need to be secretive about it. His letters could be sent directly here to the house."

"You've got a point, Babs, but let's not pry into her business anymore than you already have." The words barely out of Melanie's mouth when Stephanie had turned off the engine of her cycle.

"Hi! What are you all up to?"

"We were discussing...the day's plans. Have any suggestions?"

"Why don't we accept Barb's friend's offer to go sailing on his boat. It's a perfect day to be on the water." Stephanie's words brought Babs back into the conversation. It seemed her mind had drifted off to the mystery evolving around Stephanie's daily thirty minute absences. She realized it was Stephanie's way of an apology for her shortness with her earlier.

Barb had struck up a conversation with John, a resident bachelor, while enjoying a sunset rum punch at Henry VIII's during one of their outings to the infamous pub. "Yes, I'll call John and see what time he's planning on sailing. I hope he hasn't changed his mind." Moments later, Barbara returned to the porch with a wide grin. "It's all set. He'll be by in an hour to pick us up at the dock over where Bruce and his date will be waiting. He mentioned the more the merrier." Barb glanced over to see Melanie's expression. She thought she detected a slight sadness in her eyes. "Well, this should be a jolly day for us all, commented Barb."

Each of Melanie's friends picked up on her exaggerated cheerfulness. "Babs, what should we bring?" Melanie asked.

"I told John we'd pack a grand lunch and not to worry about food. He said he would take care of the beverage department."

"Ms. Summers, how on earth are we to pack a grand lunch and meet him at the dock in less than an hour?" Vivian's annoyance observed.

"We'll just have to hustle, my dear." Millicent, their guardian angel, had stepped out onto the porch moments earlier just in time to overhear their plans. "Lovies, I happen to have some ham and part of a leftover roast chicken in the fridge. If we toil about, we can toss together a lunch fit for the king himself. One of you go to the garden and fetch a bunch of fresh lettuce and tomatoes. Also, grab that pitcher of sun tea sitting on the far ledge, in case this fella's idea of beverages are only alcoholic. One must always have tea available, whether it be hot or chilled."

"That's your British coming out. You *Limies* think you must have your tea. It is your answer to everything," Barb teased following up with a sincere hug for her gracious hostess.

"Don't be disrespectful. I'm proud of my heritage." Millicent tried to sound stern, but they all saw through it. In her best English accent, she scurried them off to the kitchen to make the luncheon preparations. It was a flurry of activity for the next forty-five minutes. When the entourage entered the bright yellow and white room, it was as neat as a pin. When they departed, they left more than a mere mess. It was as though a bomb had hit it. Drawers and cupboards left ajar, the cutting board table in the middle of the beautifully tiled floor was filled with opened containers, knives, plastic wrap and a ton of crumbs from cutting the different kinds of delectable breads that Millicent had so generously supplied.

"We hate leaving you with all this mess," the whimsical women chimed in unison, almost like a choir.

"Never you mind. You'll need to gather your things for your boat trip. So skedaddle, if you are ever going to make it to the pier."

"You are too wonderful, and we all love you."

Each of them pecked her on her rosy cheeks. She noticed her reflection in the chrome strip on the refrigerator and giggled at the five sets of lip imprints. Millicent never wanted to wash them off her face, for they represented so much love to her. Though, she knew it was not practical, she had decided to let them wear off on their own. At least she'd leave them on to proudly show her Bernie. They were like trophies of love to her. Bernie and she would have a great chuckle over them. These were the happiest days of her life. She, too, never wanted them to end. She was painfully aware of how quiet and lifeless the house would be after their inevitable departure. A knock at the back door brought her back to reality and to the state of the kitchen.

"Mrs. Lombard," the stout Bermudian woman looked aghast. "What on earth, woman, happened here, and your face?" Millicent scurried around the room with a dish towel in her hand wiping at anything that came her way, trying to hide her flushed cheeks. "Oh, my guests and I prepared a picnic lunch, and they had to hurry off to catch a boat."

"Well, mum, it's a good thing I come to work this afternoon."

"Oh, you can't know, Hattie, how pleased I am to have your help."

Hattie appraised the damage as she scanned the holocaust. "Yes, mum, I think I have a pretty good idea. Now, just where would you like me to start?"

"My dear Hattie, we'll tackle this together before my hubby comes home for lunch."

The two women both so different in their walks of life, and yet no one could have mistaken the amount of respect and affection each held for the other.

Chapter Five

John and Bruce were growing impatient as their passengers were now twenty minutes past cast off time. Bruce's date didn't seem to care, as she looked quite content sunbathing on the trampoline between the two bows.

"Bruce, are you upset that I invited your friends along? Barbara seemed to feel you would be delighted. I spoke to her this morning."

"I don't know that delighted would be the word I would use, but no, John, I don't mind." He was not exactly being truthful with his host. He had been dreaming about sailing on John's beautiful 47' catamaran since he first saw it moored in the picturesque harbor. He had made several inquiries about it around town the day before. He was compelled to locate its master. To Bruce's good fortune, one salesclerk was a friend of the owner. He took Bruce's phone number and told him he would relay his message to Mr. Pendleton, the boat's skipper. As Bruce was leaving the marine shop, he heard the salesman call him back. "Mr. Hinds, the chap who owns that boat just walked in. John, this fella has taken a fancy to your vessel and wanted to talk with you about it."

The clerk introduced Bruce to the tall, lean man with sandy colored hair. They seemed to hit it off instantly, the common denominator being their mutual love for catamaran sailboats. It was late afternoon, so John suggested they take their conversation to his favorite local pub where they could delve into the depths of sailing boats.

Three large pints each of Watney's ale under their belts, and they seemed like old school chums. John invited Bruce to go sailing the following day. Just as Bruce was about to pounce on John's offer, they were rudely interrupted by a mutual acquaintance, the effervescent Barbara. Barbara greeted them in her sexiest voice.

"I thought I recognized you two gorgeous guys. You know, John,

I really expected to see more handsome men on this fabulous island of yours, but they all look so English. You know what I mean, pale... lanky...no muscle men. Don't the British like a tanned, muscular physique?"

"Miss Barbara, I am English, and I am proud of my countrymen. We are not to be compared with your California beach boys."

A wave of embarrassment flushed across Barbara's face. "Oh, dear John, I certainly didn't mean to offend you. As a matter fact, I was shopping across the way, when my eyes were attracted to the two most attractive men on the island. So, I just had to come over to say hi. I'm truly sorry. Well now, how do you two know each other?"

"Bruce and I met about an hour or so ago. He has expressed an interest in my boat."

"To buy?"

"No, no," Bruce interjected. "I'm big on cats, and John's *Mistress* is a beauty."

"Forgive my ignorance, but what do cats have to do with John's boat, and what's this about his mistress?"

Both men nearly blew the foamy heads off their freshly poured mugs of ale. Bruce briefly explained that "cats" was an abbreviation for catamaran sailboats. And "Mistress" was the name of John's yacht.

"I've just invited Bruce to go for a sail tomorrow."

"Oh, John, would I be too forward if I asked to come along? I would so love to go sailing and see your beautiful island from the water."

John gave Bruce a quick look. "I'm not even sure if Bruce is going. You arrived before he could give me an answer."

Bruce in the middle of a swig of beer, gulped out an affirmative "yes" accompanied by a helacious burp. All three broke out in gales of laughter, and Bruce, obviously flustered, apologized. "So much for a nice informative sail with Captain John," Bruce mused to himself.

When John maneuvered the large sailboat masterfully into the dock, Bruce stood at the stern helping the ladies aboard. Sandra had perched herself up on the trampoline which stretched across both bows. It was obvious to the five pairs of scrutinizing eyeballs that had just boarded, the black one piece bathing suit did justice to her round stomach and full thighs by compressing them with its spandex strength. Cleverly, the attention of the suit was drawn away from her problem areas and attracted to her main asset...her cleavage. The plunging v-shaped bodice dipped down to her navel. Sensing a sudden burning feeling and wise enough to know it was not being directed from the sun's rays, Sandra swiftly dispatched an invitation for them to join her. "I've got the best place in the house, rather on the vessel for sunbathing. There is plenty of room, and I'd enjoy your company."

She didn't have to ask twice. Claudia, Stephanie, and Barb hastened to grab their spots, while Melanie and Vivian lingered. It was obvious why Melanie lagged behind, hoping to talk to Bruce. Vivian, on the other hand, surprised all by planting herself next to Captain John, who was commandeering the helm, an aggressive move for her.

Bruce was too busy for chatter with Melanie, as he was encompassed with his first mate responsibilities. He cast off the lines and was literally jumping all over the boat hoisting the large sails. It became glaringly apparent to Melanie that she was not going to receive any of his attention. Disheartened, she decided to fraternize with the others. Purposely, she settled nearby Sandra. She wanted to acquaint herself with the competition for Bruce's affections. Assuredly, she felt she had the best over-all body, but the major deficit was in the upper portion. Perhaps Bruce was a boob man, and if that were the case, there was nothing she could or would do about it.

Melanie's opening inquisition began with the usual questions. Sandra enthusiastically answered each one, though, aware of Melanie's ulterior motive. Surprisingly, she liked Sandra. She was genuinely interested in her replies. Melanie sensed an inner sadness about her. When Sandra revealed the recent loss of her father, tears of compassion swelled in Melanie's eyes. She then shared her own loss of both her parents, and they both sobbed.

Bruce had been too intensely involved with his ship's duties to notice Sandra and Melanie talking so intimately to one another, until he caught a glance of them wiping their eyes with their towels. Wondering what on earth they could be crying about, he made a mental note to inquire about it later.

The day went gloriously well. The balmy breezes were perfect for sailing, and Bruce was auspiciously in his element. He and John made sublime sail mates. Anchoring in a secluded cove, they all jumped overboard to enjoy the tepid, aqua, crystal clear waters. Each with snorkel gear on, they swam for nearly two hours. Bruce and John spent most of the time diving below scouring the white sandy bottom. The females floated lazily on the surface fascinated by the multi-colored fish. Little did the ladies realize that the fellas were doing more than just observing marine life. In fact, they were busily catching lobsters. Their fish net bag filled, they surfaced with eight of the spiny crayfish. Once aboard the boat, John and Bruce placed their live catch in a deep ice box and announced to the remaining swimmers that they were invited to a lobster boil on John's beach that evening. "This is my favorite way of entertaining, as you will see," John commented.

It was nearly two o'clock before the last of the luncheon feast had been devoured. Sandra and the men repeatedly complimented the ladies on the lovely spread they had prepared with such short notice. They confessed they had a fairy godmother help them. These were the terms in which they referred to "their" Millicent. She was growing in endearment and becoming a kindred spirit to each of them. Individually, they wanted to adopt her and keep her in their lives long after they departed from this Atlantic haven. She had that kind of affect on people.

The setting sun provided a majestic backdrop as the graceful yacht sailed into Hamilton Harbor. A leisurely sail along Front Street docks accompanied by John's narration of Bermuda's history had all passengers enthralled. As they sipped their rum punches, they listened intently to the knowledge John shared with them. He adored his Bermudian isle, and it was apparent he regarded it with a great deal of pride. "Bermuda's motto is "Quo Fata Ferunt" which translates into "Whither the Fates Lead Us." John continued, mentioning that the nine parishes each had its own coat-of-arms taken from the distinguished family names of the original directors of The Bermuda Company. "From east to west they are: St. George's, Hamilton, Smith's, Devonshire, Paget, Pembroke, Warwick, Southampton, and Sandys. Actually, the town of

St. George was settled in 1609 or 10. From 1612 until 1815, it was Bermuda's capital city, subsequently and until the present day, it's Hamilton." It was at this point that John took in a deep breath and waving his hand towards the beaches he beamed. "Our beaches are world famous for their fine pink coral-studded sand, which I might add, never burns your feet!

"You know, we former Britain's brought along our afternoon tea accompanied by scones. It's a tradition here, too. I'm happy to say. The English love their tea."

"Yes, so we've heard. We were alerted to this when Melanie insisted upon taking us to the Tea Cosy on Queen Street...such a quaint place."

"Tell me, Stephanie, did you like the scones?"

"Too heavy for me, John, but then I'm always conscious of my figure."

"Mm, somehow I thought that might be your answer. Do you ever lift your self imposed restrictions? Being a psychologist, I'd imagine you live a rigid, disciplined life."

Barbara pouncing on John's statement, "That's why we all need to get her to let her hair down and loosen up. You know, dear, you've been unusually tightly wound, even for you, since you arrived. Is everything all right in your life?"

"Barbara! Stop looking for an excuse to go poking into my affairs."

"Affairs. Interesting you should use that word..." Before a cat fight erupted and spoiled the beauty of their sail, Claudia inquired about the stepped roofs on the pastel colored homes.

John's acute perceptiveness to Claudia's cue, swiftly replied noting that the steps were tiered in order to catch rainwater that was stored in cisterns under the houses. "That is why all island residents are water conservationists. Oh, there, look up on the hill on the starboard side, I mean on the right. You see what looks like miniature houses with pyramid shaped roofs and topped with balls. They are called butterflies, or cooling houses which were ancestors to refrigerators. You'll notice the buildings are constructed of limestone, coral, and cement blocks, and of course, our beautiful Bermudian cedar."

Just as John said the word cedar, Bruce announced they were coming about. The wind had shifted, and they needed to change course.

"John, are cricket and football still the national pastime?" Melanie asked.

"Well, you realize that our football is the twin of your soccer. And, to answer your question, yes, they are. We also have a number of equestrian horse shows and naturally, numerous golf tournaments. Bermuda boasts several world class golf courses. Say, Bruce, do you play? I can get us on the beauty at the Princess Hotel."

Bruce stopped for a moment from his duties of securing the ropes and enthusiastically grinned from ear to ear. "Just let me know the tee time, and I will be there."

Once docked at the pier of John's home, the group disembarked laden down with the carry-ons they had brought aboard. All were in agreement upon seven thirty to resume the gaiety of the day they had enjoyed thus far. Lobster, moonlight, and splendid company, what more could anyone ask for?

Chapter Six

Back at The Enchanted Isle, the gals reminisced every detail of their day to Millicent. She hung on each word uttered to her, which was a feat, considering five chatter boxes all engaged in conversation simultaneously. Her ears still buzzing and her mind whirling with the avalanche of information it had absorbed at a deafening pace, Millicent collapsed on the porch glider to collect her wits. Out of breath from their elaborate dissertations, her guests disappeared to shower and change for the next event on the agenda.

The ringing phone snapped Millicent to attention. It was Bruce inviting she and Bernard to the lobsterfest. After describing the charming couple to John, he mentioned he knew the Lombard's casually and would enjoy their company that evening. Millicent explained that she had planned one of Bernard's favorite meals, roast beef and Yorkshire pudding. It was not the kind of meal that would hold well to serve the following night, but they would love to join them all later for dessert, which she insisted upon bringing.

What a night! The star studded sky and the nearly full moon reflecting off the tops of the rolling surf with gentle seaside breezes were perfect ingredients for a delightful beach party. John and Bruce had gathered enough driftwood to keep the bonfire aglow until the wee hours. The massive cast iron lobster pot had a permanent home suspended over a sunken deep hole with a grate across to hold it. The fellas had also filled the mini cavern with enough firewood to bring the water to a bubbling boil. It was obvious that John was accustomed to entertaining this way and had it down to a science.

"John, you have provided me with one of the best days of my life. It was damn lucky for me to have run into you yesterday. Sailing today made me more aware than ever that *this is the life for me!* You know, there may be some truth to the old adage about every cloud having a silver lining."

"Really, how so, Chap?"

"Well, I came here under adverse circumstances. My fiancée ran off with my best friend, and I have to admit my heart and my pride were temporarily wounded. But, after today, I've made a complete recovery! I am realizing that things have worked out for the best...at least for me. I wasn't really in love with Debbie, and marriage would have been a mistake."

John now listening intently to Bruce's tale of woe asked, "Would Sandra have anything to do with your realization that your Debbie would have been a mistake?"

"No, actually, I've met someone else who has captured my attention."

"Let me guess again then. It must have been one of the lovely ladies we spent the day with, am I right? Though, I am not sure which it would be, since I noticed you hardly spoke to any particular one all day."

"John, old man, today was my day...mine...with the wind and the sea. Your beautiful *Mistress* was the only mistress that I was interested in courting today. There's time to work on the other later."

"Later, you say, as in tonight?"

"Possibly," Bruce answered coyly.

John rather intrigued, "Tell you what, don't divulge the name of your mystery heartthrob. I want to figure it out for myself. As of now, I don't have a clue, except I strongly suspect Barbara is *not* your love interest."

"You're damn right about that!" Bruce emphatically retorted. "Don't get me wrong, I think she's a great gal and certainly one of a kind...just not my kind. She needs a guy who can keep up with her, and my laid back Libra nature could never cut it. She'd be bored with me after forty-eight hours."

"I'd have to agree with you. I too, would be no match for that siren, but I think she's a hell of a woman. Life with Barbara would never be dull...probably more of a roller coaster ride. My British stuffiness would bore her to tears."

"Who would be bored to tears?" Startling both gents, Barbara had sneaked up on them while they were engrossed in their conversation.

"Well, speak of the devil," said John.

Barbara tickled that they had been discussing her, probed each of them for details. Both, slightly embarrassed, were quick to change the subject. John took the initiative and inquired, "Where are your lovely compatriots? Surely, you didn't come ahead on your own?"

"Now, John, love, why would that surprise you? Perhaps, I wanted to steal some time with you two handsome chaps for myself," giving each a flirtatious wink.

"We're here!" The four remaining members of the quintet assembled around Barb and her escorts.

"My, you ladies can sure dress up a beach. You look lovely, each of you."

"John, you are so gallant. Are all Englishmen so charming?" asked Vivian.

Melanie seized the opportunity to respond and remind all of her association with the British. "Vivian, every male I've ever met here is a perfect gentleman. They are taught early on in life to be well mannered, polite, and courteous at all times. It's in their blood, their heritage. My son attended the fine English pre-school, Strawberry Hill, here on the island. At the age of three, he and his other pint-sized classmates were little ladies and gents. I was so impressed with their behavior. I hated taking Stephen back to the States to enroll in an American school where the emphasis was placed on the rights of the pupil, rather than on teaching manners and respect of their elders."

The loud bang of John's screen door interrupted the moment. Sandra walked out carrying a large tray of colorful glasses, a pitcher of rum swizzles, and an ice bucket with a bottle of chilled Parducci white wine. Bruce spying her as she headed towards the beach, initiated a brief hello to Melanie, and excused himself to go assist Sandra.

Melanie thinking to herself, "This guy is tough to hang on to for more than a fleeting moment. You fool, you blew your golden chance to have all his attention. You may as well face the fact you may not ever have that opportunity again. He has just gone through the ultimate rejection of marriage, and then he allowed himself to be vulnerable again...and you cut him off at the knees! Two rejections back to back will cause the creation of protective barriers and probably a moat around his heart." While staring off into the rippling sea and ensconced in thought, Melanie nearly jumped out of her skin when she felt someone tug on her arm.

"Hey, lovely lady, come join the party. We've been calling you, but you seemed to be lost in an ocean of thoughts." She was surprised and delighted to be face to face with Bruce.

"Boy, have you got that right! The rolling surf has a way of capturing my mind and its fantasies."

"Fantasies," Bruce quipped back. "How intriguing. Care to elaborate on them?" he asked with a devilish grin.

"Possibly...that is if we can ever find some private time together," she answered with an annoyance in her voice. As if breaking the spell, she instantly realized that she had done it again.

Bruce's hand quickly recoiled from her arm as if burned. He responded gruffly, "Let me remind you that it was you who made it quite clear that you intended to spend these precious days with your friends!" Barely finishing his sentence, he turned and walked away briskly. Ready to voluntarily place herself in front of a firing squad for her stupidity, Melanie stomped through the sand kicking up a spray as she hiked back to join the others.

Sandra had apparently been observing the entire confrontation. An opportunist by nature, she gleefully perched herself beside Bruce on the arm of the wooden Adirondack chair, seizing her good fortune that the barricade of "Melanie" in Bruce's future plans had just been removed by Melanie herself. Bruce had confided to her the evening before that he longed to pursue Melanie and secretly felt in his heart that she was his soul mate. Feeling drawn to him and mutually sharing a love interest in the boating business, Sandra was disillusioned and gravely disappointed with his confession. But now, all that seemed to be behind them, and it would be clear sailing ahead, pardon the pun. She was setting her course straight for Bruce's heart. He was more than vulnerable now, and she knew just how to handle him.

With the exception of Melanie for obvious reasons, all were enjoying the merriment of the moonlit evening. The lobster was tender, cooked to perfection. As was the corn on the cob roasted in its husks, the tasty salad John had prepared, and the warm French bread. His selection of wine seemed to cap off the culinary tastes.

As if that was not enough, John's fingers gracefully plucked the strings of a family heirloom guitar, while entertaining all with his classical renditions. Vivian was moonstruck with John, and it was becoming evident to everyone who sat in observance, even to John. The gals had never witnessed her blatantly showing an interest in anyone other than her husband. It just wasn't Vivian's style. She was loyal and faithful, even to the point of her own demise. Her bouts with Frank and his alcoholism were not merely frequent these days but constant. They had definitely taken their toll, and it was evident to her dear friends. Each was tickled to see her truly enjoying herself, for it had been years since she was a happy person.

John switched gears to liven the pace, as he could see that his guests were illustrating signs of fatigue. After a day in the sun and wind followed by a filling feast, the melodic sounds of the guitar was causing everyone to yawn and be on the verge of sleep. In his limey accent, he jolted them with a fast paced sing along. As they entered the third chorus of the tune, Millicent and Bernard arrived with an exquisite dessert.

"Good evening to you band of merry makers. I've brought you an English trifle." As if poked with a cow prod, each jumped to their feet to see this pièce de résistance. The sudden movements also seemed to give them a second wind. Following the divine last course of the luscious delights came dancing around the campfire. Sandra was determined not to let Bruce out of her reach, except when she stooped down low to mimic doing the limbo.

Distraught could hardly describe Melanie's emotions during the utterly festive activities. This should have been one of the best nights of her life, but instead, her stomach was filled with acid. Her entire trip was now clouded over, and she found herself anxious for it to end. Ironically, just several days before, she had been worried that the days would speed by too quickly, and it would all be but a memory. To take her mind off Sandra's enticing antics with Bruce, Melanie plunked herself down on a blanket next to Millicent and Bernie.   Somehow, she felt comforted just being in their presence. She induced a conversation that took them back to their courtship and through the past decades of marriage and their life in Bermuda. Without realizing that the group had tuckered out, she noticed them picking up the remaining dishes and making trips up to the house.

Melanie muttered softly, "I have so loved hearing your stories." It was as though she lived each one with them and had removed herself from the present. Millicent keenly aware of Melanie's broken heart patted her arm, reassuring her that everything would work out in her favor. She just needed to give it time, and the results would be more favorable if she did.

"Patience, my dear, is something we all need more of," she whispered lovingly. Melanie kissed her sweetly on her velvety smooth cheek and then rose from the Tartan plaid blanket to assist with the clean up. She could not help but notice Vivian clinging to John's side.

"Good for Vivian. She needs a wonderful man in her life. I do, too, but I guess I'll have to wait longer for mine and learn to muffle my mouth," she pondered.

Millicent and Bernard escorted their house guests home walking along the beach. The mystique of the late evening had them all spellbound, and ne'er a word was spoken. Bernie, in disbelief, piped up, "This is the most quiet these five chatty females have been since they arrived on our island."

Millicent put her finger to her lips, "Luvey, I think they're just plain pooped. Let them enjoy their silence. Lord knows it is rare."

Bruce and Sandra lagged behind the group. Aware of this, Melanie fought off the overwhelming desire to sprint towards the house, and finally let the tears she had held back all evening flow behind closed doors. Feeling thoroughly frustrated for allowing another male to mess up her life, she knew she needed to get a grip on herself, once and for all! Relating to Scarlet O'Hara, she would think about it tomorrow. She was just too weary to take control of her emotions until then.

Chapter Seven

The next two days were spent touring hidden havens of the island and sunbathing on secluded beaches. True sun worshippers, they reveled in the intoxicating rapture of the beaches. Having mastered their mopeds and remembering to drive on the left, they rode in single file up hill and down dale giggling all the while. They were having the time of their lives. Melanie had actually succeeded in filing Bruce away to the back of her mind to be reckoned with at a later time. She rose to the occasion of enjoying her dearest friends, the sole purpose of the trip. That was true until exploring one of the tucked away hideaways, when she recognized two familiar bodies sunbathing in the nude behind a mammoth rock. Not wanting to be noticed, she quickly changed the course of direction she and the others were headed.

"Damn, and I was doing so well not dwelling on him," she thought to herself as she and the girls climbed another rock. Unfortunately, the rock's elevation allowed for a bird's eye view of Bruce and Sandra. Barbara, as if on radar, beamed right on to them. Not being able to control her spontaneity, she blurted out, "Hey, you two! Catching rays, we see. Mind if we join you?"

Melanie, trying to muffle Barb's mouth, snapped at her. "Of course, they mind, you idiot! Why would they be hidden from view if they wanted the world to see them?! Disregard, you two. We were just leaving. Enjoy your day."

Quickly, Melanie escorted her friends down from the rock to their cycles. "Sometimes, Babs, I just can't understand your gall!"

"Hey!," she retorted. "I wasn't serious. I didn't want them to do anything in front of you, dear pal. We are not blind, you know. We are aware you are hurting inside because of that clown. You're good at camouflaging your feelings, but you forget we know you too well. We're all experiencing your pain."

Melanie astonished to hear Barb's words grabbed her in a bear hug, squeezing tightly. She sobbed, "You are all the best. I'm so touched."

"We know that, but if you're going to get anything cooking between you and the Italian stallion, you have to get busy. Time is running out. Remember, you have us to assist you in any and all ways."

Vivian, Stephanie and Claudia joined them offering their suggestions on how to win Bruce away from Sandra. Vivian mentioned that while dining with John the evening before, he discussed a conversation he'd had with Bruce. Bruce confided to him that he was interested in one of them, and it was not Sandra. Melanie's eyes widened and she immediately began pumping her for more information.

Claudia breaking into the discussion, "What I can't figure out is why then is Bruce spending all his time with Sandra, if he is really infatuated with Melanie. We know his interest does not lie in any of us."

"Oh, I don't know about that. His attraction might very well be in my direction," Barb said in jest.

"Sure, Barb, if you want to delude yourself, but I hope you're not serious," Vivian responded with an edge in her voice.

"Relax, relax, I am teasing."

Hesitantly, Melanie eluded to the confrontations that had taken place between her and Bruce. "It's my fault. I did not want him, a male, *any* male for that matter to interfere with our time together. We've planned this reunion for years, and we all agreed NO MALES included."

"Well, that may be true, but how do you think we would feel if we stood in the way of you finding Mr. Right? Granted, we agreed not to bring any males, but we never said anything about not meeting any while here."

"Good point, Barb."

"Why, thank you, Vivian, I appreciate that."

Stephanie, with her analytical mind, suggested they come up with a plan to get Sandra out of Bruce's life and Melanie into it. "Vivian, do you think we could get John to go along with us and lend his help? Since you two have been spending time together, you know him better than we do."

"I honestly don't know. He's so British, and that defines proper with a capital P. He would probably relate himself to Benedict Arnold, if he became involved. He and Bruce have developed a friendship, as they've spent much time together lately discussing the shipbuilding business. They have gone so far as to approach Bernard Lombard regarding formulating a partnership. Thus, allowing him to retire and travel the world with Millicent. According to John, Bernard does not want to sell his business. He has had his eye out for just the right partner to take over for him for some time now. He and Bruce have really clicked. John thinks he regards Bruce like the son he never had. Bernard proposed to John that he be the silent third partner. With John's knowledge of English laws and a Bermudian citizen, he could guide Bruce along the way. It would expedite the leadership transition, and Bernie and Millicent could get on their way sooner. Otherwise, it may take several years before Bruce knows all the ropes and legalities involved."

"So, as a silent partner, I take that to mean that John would not be associated with the day-to-day operations of running the business but rather as a consultant?" Melanie asked.

"Yes. According to John, his banking business takes up most of his time. He is vice-president of the Barclay Bank, in case you did not know."

"Excuse me, you two, but we've gotten side tracked. We need a plan to get these lovebirds together," Barb attempting to focus the conversation on their obvious mission. She rallied to causes of the heart.

"Melanie, why don't I suggest to John that the four of us have dinner. That way you and Bruce could try to connect again?"

"I don't know, Viv. He's definitely turned off me. You know, this all has a familiar ring. It reminds me of high school days, plotting with girlfriends to get the guy. Can life be that recyclable?"

"That may be true. Perhaps back then was our preliminary training for the real thing later in life," Stephanie interjected.

"Well, I am meeting John for a sunset drink in an hour. I'll make my suggestion to him then."

Barbara was too impatient to settle for Vivian's methodical plan and decided to devise one of her own. Aware of the sands slipping through the hourglass, time was of the essence. She was determined to get Bruce and Melanie together ASAP, if not sooner! It was a self proclaimed goal before departing the fantasy island.

Chapter Eight

She momentarily drifted back in memory to her relationship with her former college sweetheart, turned professional baseball player husband. How had she let all they shared slip away?

Barb and Lance had been each other's best friend until the Big Leagues entered their world. Too much fame, fortune, and women. The baseball groupies throwing themselves at the players after every game, waiting outside the locker rooms, following them to the bars and propositioning them in the hotel lobbies and elevators. It was too much temptation for some, and her husband was one of the some.

How many times she had looked the other way. A callous formed over her heart for each indiscretion she became aware of. Finally, when her mate no longer respected her enough to at least be discreet about his affairs, she struck him out of her life. He believed all the fanfare written about himself, and his ego became increasingly inflated. Along with the bolstering of his self image, came the drugs. His personality degenerated into a "Jekyll and Hyde" due to the influence of the cocaine and booze. Accompanying these changes that took place in her former lover, came attacks of abusive behavior. He had fits of rage, including taking a baseball bat and smashing the windshield of her Corvette as she attempted to save herself late one night. Then, there was the time in their swimming pool when he was so drunk, he tried to drown her! Barb physically shuddered at the memory, and it snapped her back to reality. She hated when she would flashback to her unpleasant past.

Bab's plan called for immediate action, and that meant a visit to Bruce. She was a firm believer of straight forwardness and not pussy-footing around. She excused herself, giving the premise of showering and getting ready for whatever dinner plans that transpired. Only instead of ascending the elegant staircase, she slipped out the kitchen door. Though, she did not go unnoticed. Millicent happened to glance up while picking peas from her hillside garden and observed Barbara running through the small grove of lush bougainvillea, which bordered between Lombard's and the Misty Cove property.

"My, that's curious behavior," she thought to herself. "I must inquire about it when I return to the house." But, before she could, she watched Barbara return only moments later. "Well, that was a quick visit to Bruce's," she mused, sure that that was where she had gone. "He must not be home. Millicent Lombard!" she reprimanded herself. "Stop being a busybody." Gathering up all the peas in her calico apron, she headed back towards the house, but not before stopping to select the plumpest red tomato off the vine for their dinner salad.

Realizing the possibility that Bruce may not be in his cottage, Barb had the foresight to grab a pen and slip of paper from the grocery list pad Millicent left on the counter. She had quickly scribbled a message for him to call her the moment he arrived home and then adding "P.S. It's urgent that I talk to you."

The shampoo bubbles were running down her tanned face just missing her eyes when there was a knock on the bathroom door. "Barbara, dear, you have a phone call from Bruce, and he says it is urgent he speak with you." Barb could detect the concern in Millicent's sweet voice.

"Tell him I'll be there in a minute. Thanks, Millie." Only the tenacious strawberry blonde dared to be so brazen as to refer to the matriarch of Enchanted Cottage in such a manner.

Wrapped in a floral silk robe, which the inn provided for their guests, and a towel tied turban style around her head, Barb dashed out of the ivory and peach decor of the lavish bathroom. Clumsily, she picked up the French phone receiver laying on its side, nearly knocking over the small Queen Anne table in the hall. Out of breath, she huskily asked Bruce point blank if he had any interest in seeing Melanie again. She then quickly prefaced it as a date. Bruce stunned at Barb's abruptness, remained silent for a moment.

"Well?" she questioned.

"Uh, Barb, tell me what brought this on, and is this what you referred to in your note as urgent? I hate to think of how you'd relay a real emergency.”

“Look, green eyes, unless I’m dead wrong, you both really feel a connection, but you’re not giving it a chance to blossom, *and* time is running out. That is why I said this was urgent!”

“Hey, Babs, I tried to get close to Melanie, and she shut the door in my face!”

“I know, I know, and she deeply regrets that now. But, Bruce, be honest. You would have to be blind not to see that she has tried to make up for that. For starters, delivering champagne to your door, and then you had the audacity not to invite her to share any of it with you and Ms. Bimbo.”

“Wait a minute! Sandra is not a bimbo!”

“Maybe not, but you have thrust her in front of Melanie’s face every chance you get. Are you serious about her?”

“Ms. Barbara, that’s a very personal question.”

“Don’t give me that, Bruce. Are you or aren’t you? If the answer is yes, I’ll hang up now and won’t bother you further.”

Again a long silence, and the bewildered male on the other end of the line finally spoke softly. “Barbara, I could fall in love with Melanie, if she’d give me the chance.”

“Good. Better yet, that’s great! I was afraid for a moment there that my gut instincts were wrong about your feelings for her, and that would have blemished my perfect record. The others and I have been trying to come up with a plan to get you two together before we all are kissing good-bye. Vivian, believe it or not, actually suggested asking John to invite you both out to dinner and make it a foursome. As a matter of fact, she is probably asking him as we speak. They were to meet at Henry VIII’s for drinks. Could you get over there now and just run into them by happenstance? We need to get this plan in motion.”

“Sure. I suppose I could. I was contemplating going over there myself for a sunset brew. Actually, it has damn near been a daily ritual.”

“Now, listen sweet lips, don’t blurb a word to anyone that I’ve talked to you. Those friends of mine would tar and feather me before sunrise tomorrow.”

“You got it, babe. Mum’s the word. And, Barb, thank you for interfering.”

Barb quietly opened the large walk-in closet door. Afraid of being overheard, she had slipped in amongst the lavender scented linens, grateful that the phone cord was long enough as she conducted her conversation from within. Now, she had to make sure that no one saw her coming out, for there would be questions. The coast clear, she swiftly replaced the antique phone back onto the lace doily and returned to finish her shower. She felt quite proud of herself for taking the initiative and intervening in cupid’s department.

Ten minutes after Bruce had hung up with Barb, he casually strolled across the flagstone patio of his favorite pub and ordered a Watney’s beer. “No, on second thought, please make that a double rum swizzle.”

One of the waitresses seemed to be transfixed on the tall American stud, as she loved to refer to him, at least to her fellow waitpersons. She started to make conversation with him when his eye caught Vivian waving him over to her table.

“Oh, say, would you please send my order over to that table. I am going to be joining some friends.” Perturbed that Bruce just cut her off, the waitress with her off the shoulder peasant blouse, an unconventional uniform, turned on her heels and steamed off towards the bar.

“Greetings to you both. It’s nice to see familiar faces at my favorite haunt. John, are you a regular here at Henry’s?”

“This and Tom Moores attract most of my business. Now and then I find myself at The Hog Penny Pub. Have you found that one yet?” John asked while winking at Vivian.

“Speaking of business, have you come to a final decision regarding Bernard’s boat operation?”

“There’s only one hitch that I can see, and that’s my overwhelming desire to design my own cats. If Lombard will grant me the freedom to build one prototype for possible manufacturing, I’m definitely in. I realize his concern that I am a novice, and I lack the many years of experience he has, but I’ve been researching catamarans since my twenties. I wouldn’t dare disgrace the fine reputation Bernard has earned.”

“Listen, chap, Bernard is one hell of a man. He remembers what it is like to be green in this business. After all, he was too when he started here three decades ago. I'm sure you'll impress him with your designs and earnestness. Besides, Bermuda needs more industry."

"Hmmm, excuse me, gentlemen, but may I get a word in here?"

"Oh, Vivian, luv, I am afraid we've been terribly rude."

"No, no, John, not at all. But, if you have completed your business discussion, I'd like to ask Bruce if he'd care to join us for dinner later. Melanie and Barb are joining us, too. Claudia and Stephanie, believe it or not, are taking in a show. Some foreign movie."

Bruce already clued in, thanks to Barb, smiled coyly and accepted with pleasure. Somehow, though, he had a strong premonition that Barb would not be showing up with Melanie.

As the sun, a magnificent fireball, began to set, the blue moped whined up the driveway to the parking lot. Vivian obviously on the lookout for the girls, turned in the direction of the sound of scrunching pebbles. "That's funny, but I don't see Ms. Barbara. Usually, one cannot miss her making an entrance."

Melanie, looking fresh as a daisy, seemed to float across the terrace. Her smile was bright and yet warm. Her eyes sparkled as she approached their table. "Greetings to you three. Looks like you only get me. Barb wasn't ready and had her nose glued to the sports page of the USA Today. She never lets a day go by that she doesn't look for anything written about her former husband. I truly believe she's still in love with him. Though, she would never admit it to us, much less to herself. It was an ugly divorce as he parlayed affair after affair under her nose. It left some deep scars, I'm afraid. That's why she toys with men the way she does, to get even."

Bruce anxious to change the subject, offered to pour Melanie a rum swizzle from the large pitcher on the table.

Smiling, she accepted the drink. "Well, stranger, how's your lady love, Sandra? Will she be meeting you, or is she here in the ladies room?" Instantly, she wanted to bite her tongue. Why did she always allow her mouth to spoil anything that possibly could develop between this handsome hunk and herself.

Ignoring the urge to reciprocate the pretty lady's sarcasm, he answered intently, "Actually, I simply stopped by for my sunset swizzle and ran into John and Vivian. They've invited me to join them for dinner."

The foursome drank the mammoth pitcher of rum concoctions and ordered another. By eight o'clock, they decided to give up on Barbara joining them and adjourned to the romantic inside dining room. The heavy dark woods, candlelit sconces on the walls, and amber glow from the fireplace created a mood for romance. Of course, the rum had a hand in it, too.

Everyone but Melanie knew that Barb was not going to rain on their parade. They just kept up the charade for appearances. When Vivian and Melanie excused themselves to go to the powder room, Vivian confessed that they had prearranged the evening. Melanie smothered her with hugs and kisses along with nonstop *thank you's*. Vivian revealed that it was not only she that was concerned, but that the group of them had a pow-wow. The objective being how to get the two together before their trip came to an end. "I came up with this plan. We couldn't very well leave it up to you. You seem to have an uncanny knack for saying the wrong thing to that darling man out there. You almost did it again two minutes after you arrived!"

"I know. I know. Thank God he let it go by this time."

"Melanie, do all of us a favor, and let this relationship flourish, even if you don't know that this is the right guy for you. Trust your dearest friends...we know! Now, we'd better get back, or they'll be sure we deserted them."

Dinner was followed by dancing out on the terrace. A reggae band had set up all their equipment, and it was not long before they had captured most of the lingering diners from the inside dining room. It was there under the canopy of the stars that the magic spell of the evening was cast upon the two destined lovers as they danced. The sweet scent of the oleanders mixed with the smell of the sea catching rides along the breezes was captivating to the two people who adored the tropics. It was as if they had finally found one another. All the barriers vanished, and cupid was set free to play havoc with their hearts.

As Bruce held Melanie in his arms, he knew that she belonged with him. He felt as though he had found his soulmate. Almost as if reading his mind, she felt *at home* next to the warmth of his body. Feeling compelled to search out an avenue that would allow her to be with him, her mind wandered. He lived in Rhode Island and she in the Rocky Mountains. Lost in her thoughts and emotions, Bruce brought her back to the present with a soft kiss on her nose. As if a dam had let go, she blurted out apologies for her past snippy remarks. She wanted desperately to clear the slate and start anew. She confessed her jealousy regarding Sandra, and that it brought the worst out in her. Had it not been for her deep commitment to her friends, she never would have turned away from his affections when he first displayed them towards her. Since they unanimously approved of her relationship with him, it was as though she had the green light to forge ahead with no guilty strings attached.

"Melanie," Bruce trying to get a word in. "Your friends love you and want what is best for you. Fortunately for me, they think I fit that bill."

Finally, tuckered out from dancing, the anxious couple wanted to find a secluded beach and talk. There seemed to be so much they needed to share with one another. They returned inside in search of their companions to bid them a good evening and go on their way.

John and Vivian had retreated earlier to the massive mahogany bar and were enjoying a nightcap. Vivian, normally not much of a drinker, was definitely under the influence. "Vivian, in all the years I've known you, this is only the second time I have seen you like this, and both times have been on this island with me! What do you suppose that means?"

Slurring her words while valiantly trying to come up with an answer, John cut her off by placing a kiss tenderly on her lips. "I think I will take this little lady home with me tonight, if that's agreeable with her and you, Melanie. I don't know that she could make it up the Lombards' staircase without causing all kinds of commotion and disturbing the household. I promise to behave as a perfect gentleman. Though, I wish I did not have to," his voice trailed off.

"You are so gallant, Sir John. I think that you have a fine idea. Though, I'd love to see Viv's face in the morning when she awakens and wonders where on earth she is. Somehow, I don't think she will remember this conversation."

Stumbling off the bar chair and into John's arms, Vivian tried to defend herself and her condition. She was definitely under the impression that she was just a bit tipsy. She also thought it a wise decision to spend the night at John's and not embarrass herself in front of Millicent. None of the girls wanted to disgrace themselves, for Millicent held a place of honor to each of them.

Saying their good nights, Melanie followed Bruce on her moped to his cottage. He grabbed a blanket, a bottle of chilled Perrier, and glasses deciding that they had had enough alcohol for one night and wanted their talk to be with clear minds, considering the circumstances. Off they sauntered down the beach, feeling the cool sand between their toes, until Bruce lead them to a tiny remote, secluded cove.

"Is this where you would take Sandra?" Melanie's jealousy rearing its ugly head. "Oops, I'm sorry," she retracted in a softer tone, squeezing Bruce's free arm.

"For your information, the answer is no. I discovered this special spot my first night here. It is where I come to think...and...pray."

"Pray?" Melanie's voice surprised.

"Yes, I do believe in the power of prayer. Especially now, since your being here is a definite answer to mine. I can't tell you how many times I've stood in this spot, staring up at the sky and asking that He show me how to get you into my life."

Tears rolled down Melanie's cheeks. She was so choked with emotion she could not speak but stared through her tears into Bruce's eyes. She had always had a strong faith, but no one other than her son to share it with. They spent the next hours star gazing, lost in its glittery darkness. They spoke of every desire for the future and shared their pasts until the first hints of sunrise began to break the evening spell.

"Oh, Bruce, my precious Bruce, I must get back. I don't want the Lombards to think I've been out all night."

He understood but had to laugh. "You know, sweetheart, they're not your parents. You are an adult."

Even Melanie broke into laughter. He was right, but somehow they felt like parents. After all, her parents had died nearly a quarter of a century ago, and she loved feeling as though she belonged to Millicent and Bernard, even if it was only temporary. Bruce walked her home and kissed her passionately good night. Their only passionate kiss of the entire evening, but they both sincerely wanted to express their feelings by talking this first night together. They knew the passion would follow.

Having safely crept up the winding stairway with no creaks to give her away and locked behind the ivory paneled door of her Victorian bedroom, Melanie fell onto the lace bedspread dreaming of her Prince Charming.

Chapter Nine

A loud banging on the front door and the chiming of the door chimes abruptly awakened Melanie from the sound sleep she had drifted into just after dawn. Quickly putting on her robe, she ran out of her room to see what all the commotion was about in the entry hall. A quick glance of the bodies present immediately alerted her of oncoming trouble. Barb, Claudia, and Millicent were trying desperately to calm down the intruder. Noticing Stephanie's absence and then seeing the time on the grandfather clock in the hall, Melanie realized how late she had slept. It was 10:15, and that meant Stephanie was on her secret mission to the post office. Except, it really was no secret since self appointed special agent, Barbara tailed and tattled on her to the rest of the group. It didn't take but another moment to recognize the voice at the end of the stairs.

"Oh my God! It's Frank!" she mumbled to herself. No longer obscured from view, all eyes turned to Melanie as she descended the grandeur of the stair case. Barb, first, then Claudia and Millicent in chorus, "Do you know where Vivian is?" Then Claudia adding, "It doesn't look as though she slept here last night. Her clothes from the beach yesterday are still laying on her bed. No one has seen her this morning either."

Melanie's mind was racing to come up with any other explanation than the real one. How would it look to Viv's husband that she spent the night at another man's home? Without further hesitation, she quickly answered that Vivian had decided to spend the night at Joanna's. Hoping the girls would catch on and play along with her made up story, she continued. "You remember the gal we met who is going through the terrible divorce and is a basket case? She has evidently adopted Vivian as her mentor. We ran into Joanna at Henry VIII's, and she was a real mess, drinking too much and hanging onto any guy that came within five feet of her. Viv took charge, shooed away the sharks and offered to take her home to pump coffee into her, accompanied by some well meaning advice. It probably got late, and you know Vivian, she doesn't like driving the cycle late at night. She's terrified of the dark winding streets, and the drunks inherently are on the wrong side of the roads." This seemed a perfect time to address Frank and inquire as to why he was there. That way Claudia and Barb's bewildered expressions wouldn't give away the yarn Melanie had so eloquently spun.

"Frank, why are you here? You knew this was to be just the girls' reunion," Melanie's tone cool and short. "Vivian didn't mention you were coming."

The gray and dark stubble of beard appearing through his ruddy complexion and tousled hair reinforced his unkept appearance. Through his apparent anger he finally found his voice, "That's because she didn't know. She won't take my phone calls, and I want her home. Damn it!"

Millicent puffed right up and informed Frank that there would be no swearing under her roof. In fact, she did not like his demeanor and politely suggested that he leave. When Frank refused, she literally inflated herself a foot higher and ordered him out of her home in no less than a harsh authoritative tone.

Melanie advised him to either find a place to stay, for he was not welcomed there or, better yet, leave the island. She would be sure to have Vivian call him at home that evening. Frank, not buying Melanie's later advice, elected to find himself some lodging and would attempt to reach Viv from there. Turning on his heels, he slammed the heavy oak door so hard the gals shuddered in fear the stained glass panels would shatter.

"Well! My word. That was no way to start a lovely day. What a grim character poor Vivian is married to. He looks to me like a man who indulges too much into the bottle," Millicent said while shaking her head. "Why don't I fix us all some tea, and Melanie you can fill us in on the real story as to Vivian's whereabouts."

"Millicent, if you saw through my lie, do you think Frank did?"

"No, luv. He's so obsessed with himself he couldn't see a freight train heading straight at him. I'll fetch the tea, and perhaps you had better warn Vivian that tropical storm Frank has hit our melancholy island. I'll meet you all on the porch."

Melanie fumbled through the pages of the phone book nestled on the hall table in search of John's phone number. She dialed clumsily and was relieved to hear his soothing voice. She minced no words and elaborated on the urgency of the situation. John offered to drive Vivian home immediately.

Once upon the porch with tea in hand, Melanie unraveled her home spun yarn. She reiterated the entire prior evening's events including her sneaking up the stairs at dawn. The looks of approval on each of their faces regarding she and Bruce were worth everything to her. They were sincerely happy for her.

"Melanie, my dear," Millicent queried, "How do you think Vivian feels about John?"

"To be honest, I would love to see her with John. Frank has brought nothing but heartache to her life. He's a drunk and totally unfaithful. She knows it too, but it takes some of us longer than others to realize the vows we exchanged on our wedding days were meant for both parties."

The scrunching of pebbles on the driveway presaged Viv's arrival. John opened the front door, and together they went inside joining the others on the crowded porch. Vivian was visibly shaken at the reality of Frank's presence on the island. Fear and anger were uppermost on her mind.

"I refuse to see him! This is *my* time...MY TIME!! He may not spoil this for me!" One could not help wondering if she was referring to her time with her friends or her time with John.

John put a consoling arm around her shoulder and comforted her. "Vivian, why don't you call me later. If you need a friendly male ear, you've got mine."

Her eyes were pleading with him to stay, but her common sense dictated her words. "John, I don't know what to say to you. I just know that I don't want you to leave. I feel safe with you."

Millicent gently trying to reassure her of her safety, insisted she would call the constable, if Frank returned displaying inappropriate behavior. "Viv, I think it best you confront your husband. If you honestly believe in your heart that your marriage cannot be salvaged, then perhaps it is time to close that door and get on with your life. Please don't think that I advocate divorce dear, but life is a precious gift given to us to make the best use of it. It is obvious to me that yours is being shamefully wasted on a man who does not appreciate you. And, that is a sin in my book, and in the good Lord's, too. Now let me think of the quote in the Bible...."

Just then Vivian completely broke down with tears streaming down her olive skinned cheeks, sobbing uncontrollably. "I've tried for fifteen years to honor my vows. I can't find the strength to continue on this course of devastation and destruction. I am Catholic and my church, along with my mother would disown me. She is Old World Italian, and you honor your vows till death do you part, no matter what. I feel so trapped! My life is a living hell, and I can't seem to change it!"

Barbara, not a fan of Vivian's or vice versa, surprisingly put her arm around Viv's shoulder. In an unusually soft spoken voice exuding sincere warmth, she tried to console her. She quoted a scripture and then asked Vivian if Frank was a Christian.

"He pretended to be when we got married, but it didn't take long for me to see through his act. He knew I would never marry him otherwise."

Again shocking the small intimate group, Barbara's uncharacteristically soothing voice repeated the quote ever so succinctly, "1 Corthinthians 7:15...*But if the husband or wife who isn't a Christian is eager to leave, it is permitted. In such cases the Christian husband or wife should not insist that the other stay, for GOD wants his children to live in harmony.*"

Vivian reacting almost childlike responded in a tiny voice, "But I'm the one who wants out, and I am the Christian!"

Babs looking directly into her eyes, "Do you honestly think you can be the person our Creator planned for you to be, if you're living in misery all the time? He cannot work with you, if all your thoughts and emotions are sabotaged with pain." This was too profound to be coming from the wild and crazy friend. She was revealing a gentle side of herself that only Melanie had observed on one other occasion during her divorce. The others stood in dead silence with looks of utter disbelief on their faces. These pearls of wisdom could not be falling from Barb's lips. It was so out of character for her.

As if snapped out of a trance, she released her embrace on Vivian and stepped back. "Sorry, I don't mean to preach to you. It's your life." The abruptness and tone was obvious to all that Babs had reverted back to her normal self. But, neither Vivian nor any of the others would ever forget those precious moments when she cast aside her suit of armor and revealed her fragile soul. Vivian knew in her heart that she would view Barbara in a different light from that point on.

John issued his farewells and left quietly. Vivian, as if still in a trance, heard her friend's words echoing and remained stoic until her peace was obliterated by the sudden interruption of the phone ringing. It was Frank demanding to see her. He had taken a room at Sommerset Cottages. Vivian could tell by the inflection in his voice that he was not alone in his accommodations. His dearest companion in all the world was with him, his mistress... Veronica *Vodka*. Vivian had named this paramour years before. She claimed that she felt compelled to refer to the vixen in her husband's life, even if it did not exist in human form. She was certain she could compete for Frank's affections, if she thought of it as an adversary. Though, her theory was destroyed after several years of diligent efforts to win back her mate. It had been nearly three years since she had conceded to Veronica. She was certain that his suitcase carried more liquor than clothes, and his tone confirmed it. His insistence that they meet gave Vivian no other option but to comply.

They agreed to meet on the Sommerset Bridge, the only wooden working drawbridge left in the world. After hanging up the receiver, Viv instinctively realized that her choice of meeting places was probably not a wise one. In Frank's frame of mind, she suddenly feared for her safety. He could push her off the bridge knowing she could not swim and profess it to be an accident. She knew he had them both heavily insured. The color drained from her richly tanned face and was replaced with the ashen tint of fear. She found herself trembling from head to toe. She decided to call John and enlist his advice. Her fingers fumbled as she dialed his number on the European phone. By the seventh ring, now crazy with nerves, she started to replace the receiver when she heard a man's out of breath voice.

"John, John, please say that it is you!" She literally half crying and half screaming shouted into the phone.

"Vivian?" He answered with grave concern reflected in his voice.

"Yes, John, I've just done a very stupid thing." She explained about the impending rendezvous with Frank and expressed her anxiety. John insisted upon accompanying her, but in such a way that neither she nor Frank would notice his presence. He opted not to share with her his plan, so that she would not seem conspicuous to Frank. But, he assured her that she would never be out of his watchful eye. Feeling somewhat better, she thanked him profusely and also apologized for dragging him into her domestic nightmare.

"My dearest Vivian, you have invaded my heart, so I must look after you. It is my duty, and you know how we English are about our duties." Touched by his words, she gently asked if they could meet after the crisis was over. "Of course, luv, call me when you return to the Isle."

Such a potpourri of emotions were running rampant throughout Vivian's being. John had just shared an intimate expression of feelings towards her, whose affect surprised her by the involuntary thumping of her heart. It angered her that she could not devote the time to process the sensations she was experiencing, for she had to deal with Frank, and she was not quite sure just how to handle him. A tug of war had emerged between what she wanted to do versus what was the right thing to do. It was at this point, Melanie interrupted her internal conflicts.

"Viv, are you all right? You look as though you've seen a ghost, and you are trembling. What can I do to help?"

Grabbing Melanie's arm, Vivian steered them into the dining room away from any listening ears. She explained the events that had just transpired between she, Frank, and John. Vivian's concern for her own safety aroused Melanie's.

"Viv, I would never dream that Frank would do anything to harm you. I have to give the bastard the benefit of how in love he is with you."

"That may have been the case but no longer. I did not want anyone to know how abusive he has become after he's been drinking. The years of alcohol have really turned him into a "Jekyll and Hyde." Melanie, I've learned to fear him, and I'm frightened most of the time anymore."

"Damn it! That's it! How, Vivian, how could you even consider going back to live with that monster? Vows or no vows, you must concede to the fact you don't live in a marriage. You are living in hell. It's up to you to end it! It is your life we're talking about."

Vivian's head perked up after listening to these wise words spoken by her dearest friend. Was this the sign from above she earnestly sought? Her inspiration was interrupted by Stephanie's entering the dining room.

"Sounds as though you're the shrink." Stephanie shooting an icy glance at Melanie, and her tone accompanied the cold stare. "You know, Viv, I am the professional here. People pay me for my advice. But for you, there is no charge. Unless, of course, you prefer to base your life decisions on some amateur psychology. I can remember when you and I were the best of friends. You shared your every thought with me."

Melanie now understood the cynicism of Stephanie's sarcastic statements. She, the professor with the PhD, was jealous! Jealous of the closeness that had developed over the last few years between Vivian and herself. Stephanie was so busy hobnobbing with the "who's who" of society and constantly out of town attending medical seminars, that she had basically dumped Vivian along the way never stopping long enough from her own personal quests to realize how deeply she had hurt her best friend.

Melanie, cocking her head back, looked Stephanie straight in the eyes, "Take over, doc. The patient is all yours. But, remember these words and apply them to your behavior of the last several years, what goes around, comes around." With that Melanie confidently sailed past the two and headed out the front door.

Stephanie obviously shocked, "What the hell did she mean by that?"

Vivian, looking at her watch and noting the time, excused herself and said she had to go meet Frank. Her parting words to Stephanie were, "Think about it, doc."

Chapter Ten

Stephanie decided to "think about it" later. For right now the steamy letter that was causing condensation in her secret P.O. box was burning an imaginary hole in her pocket. She had quickly reviewed it on the pier, just as she had the others she had received, but now she wanted to delve between the lines. The worldly woman found herself a secluded spot in the rose garden out of view from the house. Not wanting to be disturbed, she lazily allowed her mind to drift back to her most private memories of her love and how they met. It was one of the indulgences she embellished when time would permit, which was not often in her hectic life.

Stephanie's secret love was the total opposite of her husband. He was a man of limited means. This attribute was not to her liking, but the rest of him more than made up for the lack. As a manager of a local construction company, he lived in a different world than Stephanie's. He adored her and brought out of her a side she was unfamiliar with herself. Sean, a rugged Scandinavian, had a heart of gold and loved the simpler things in life. His love and appreciation of nature was beginning to rub off on her. He had taken Stephanie on picnics that provided her with the finest of memories. Their outings were not only sensual but educational as well. He would taunt her with his obliging sexuality and, at the same time, point out a rare butterfly or a bird indigenous to the region. It was not only his incredibly sexy body that intrigued her, but his intelligence tweaked her curiosity. At first, she wondered why a man with his brains and high IQ had not achieved more for himself. He was surely capable of owning his own construction company, and yet as she later learned, he turned down an opportunity to do just that.

Sean had come from a large family, and his tastes were pure and simple. To him, life was an event. It took center stage everyday and was a show for all the world. His philosophy was you could either sit back and miss it all or take an active part as a player. He chose the latter. Which was why he was adamant about handling just enough responsibility to keep it in check. When he closed his office door at the end of the day, the business hours were in the past, and the hours left were all his to enjoy. And, enjoy he did! Life was a precious gift, and he was keenly aware of never taking it for granted. He came close to death in a skiing accident when he was 21, and the scars on his right shoulder and knee were an ever constant reminder he was truly blessed to be alive.

Actually, it was those scars that introduced Sean to Stephanie. Both found themselves enjoying an aprés ski Jacuzzi at a posh resort in Aspen. Normally, such a ritzy place would not have been Sean's cup of tea, but since the weekend stay was a gift from a very satisfied client, he thought he would indulge himself. He had his crew work night and day to finish the job by the deadline. This was his reward for the many headaches his client was solely responsible for, with tirades at all hours of the night. Perks of this kind made his job more manageable.

Easing himself slowly into the hot steamy water, quite a contrast from the thirty degree temperature of the outside air, he could not help but notice through the vapors of steam a willowy silhouette immersing herself. It was instant gratification to every muscle in his perfectly toned body. He involuntarily released a huge sigh, which caused a muffled giggle from the other occupant. Too relaxed to respond, he closed his ice blue eyes and began to reminisce about his fabulous day on the exquisite Rocky Mountain slopes. Twenty or so minutes later, he hurriedly walked to the inside spa area to shower and dress. Stephanie, preceding him by only a moment, held the door as he swiftly slithered by barely brushing against her statuesque form. Instantly tantalized and aroused, she stole a long glance at the stranger towel drying his masculine physique. She found herself staring at his eight inch scar stretching from his collar bone across to his shoulder. Sean caught her intense glance.

"Ugly, isn't it?"

"May I ask how you attained such a trophy? An old war wound, I suppose?" Stephanie blushed slightly, an emotional reaction rather foreign to her.

Sean bellowed a hardy laugh. "Fortunately, no. I came by this and the one down here," he pushed the long towel aside to expose the nasty remnants of stitches permanently affixed to his knee, "as a result of a skiing fiasco some years ago. But, it has never kept me off the slopes. Though, it is like having a guardian angel with me at all times, reminding me of how well loved and protected I am. It's symbolism has given me a sincere appreciation of every day I'm alive."

"How profound. I could use some of that sincere appreciation for my life. Somehow, it seems shallow and empty."

Sean zeroed in on the disillusionment in Stephanie's voice and asked if they could meet for a drink in the lounge after dressing.

Stephanie, seated on an overstuffed wing back chair enjoying the warmth of the fireside, was taken aback when she glanced up to see a vision that looked like an ad for the hotel, a ski god dressed in a gorgeous Norwegian sweater and tight fitting jeans that topped an expensive pair of gray alligator boots. His bronzed tanned face set off his shimmering blue eyes and his golden curly locks. Stephanie was spellbound by the radiance of his magnetic smile and perfect white teeth. He reminded her of a Greek statue that came to life in ski country.

Sean's purity of mind and heart were soon apparent to Stephanie. So unlike Charles, he opened up and told her all about his growing up in Sweden, his wonderful family, and his love for the United States. Though, when Stephanie asked him what brought him to America, he suddenly looked sullen and a mist encompassed his beautiful eyes. His voice mellowed while he sat down in the accompanying chair. "First, before I get into that, I promised you a drink." Waving to an attractive cocktail waitress, he asked Stephanie if he could order for her. As if under a hypnotic spell, she nodded her head slightly.

As they sipped their brandy, the handsome man proceeded to share a tragic love story gone awry. Having just graduated from college, he took a holiday in Monte Carlo. It was there that he fell deeply in love with a lovely young exchange student from the U.S. They were inseparable. When the time had come for her to return to her homeland, they decided to marry, and Sean would relocate to the States. Sean reached for his drink as the fire crackled behind them. The spicy smell of the burning pine cones wafted through the air.

Stephanie, hanging on every word that flowed out of his incredibly sensuous mouth, asked, "I can't stand the suspense. What happened?"

Taking a breath and slowly exhaling a deep sigh, he continued. "Stephanie, to this day I am still not quite sure what happened. Once we settled in a cute one bedroom cottage on Whidbey Island near Seattle, things started to change. So slowly at first that I did not notice. Jennifer just appeared to be falling out of love with me. She had received a promotion at her place of business and seemed to have less and less time and interest in us." Half choking on a sip of the aged brandy, he cleared his throat.

"I had landed a position in a construction company framing houses. My boss took a liking to me and asked me to be his apprentice, so I could learn the business from the bottom up. I loved my job, but my first priority was Jennifer and our marriage. She felt differently. Her career came first. After a miserable year of hurts and fighting with one another, I came home one night after an exhausting day to find a note on the mantel and all her things gone. She had accepted the manager's position of their branch office in Seattle. It was a golden opportunity, and she could not afford to pass it up.

The next day I hopped the ferry to go find her and try to talk to her. I found her all right. In the arms of her boss, whom I had met at the company Christmas party. She then confessed she had been having an affair with him for some time and followed him to Seattle where he was transferred. We both decided then and there a divorce was our only solution.

Stephanie having finished her second Brandy, kept thinking the same recurring thought. What a bitch! How could anyone treat this hunk and yet fragile man that way?

"Stephanie. I've bored you with my story, and I deeply apologize. It has been a very long time since I've told anyone."

"Oh, Sean, on the contrary. I simply cannot believe a woman could do such a thing to you. Just for the record, we American females are not all like that. So, may I ask, did you remarry?"

Half chuckling, Sean answered, "No. Once was enough for me. I could never go through that heartache again. How about yourself?"

Stephanie had removed her wedding ring earlier after she fastened her seat belt on the flight. She wasn't quite sure why she had. Was she hoping to have an affair on her ski retreat? She did not have that answer either but subconsciously must have wanted to leave the option open. Now, how should she respond to this honest man? Her mind urged one response and her heart another.

Squirming in her comfortable chair, she finally found the words. "Sean, I have to admit that I am so tempted to lie to you, but..."

"Oh, please, Stephanie, I cannot tolerate lies, no more lies for me!"

"I can see that. The only reason I would even consider being untruthful to you is because I am terribly attracted to you. I don't want this to end before it even starts." Sean feeling uncomfortable fidgeted in the wide chair. Stephanie continued, "Yes, I am married. But not happily." She proceeded to share her "C'est la vie" marriage to the attentive listener for the next hour. Dining together that first night was to establish the foundation of their friendship. They talked endlessly for the next two days, whether they were on the ski lifts, stopping for a hot toddy break on the slopes, or at dinner. It was not until their third evening together, literally talked out, they consciously decided to make love. The chemistry between them was reaching a crescendo that was impossible to hold back any longer. They could not stop pawing one another.

It took some coaxing on Stephanie's part to convince this man of ethics to sleep with a married woman. He swore he'd never do such a thing, remembering the stinging truth when he learned of his wife's adulterous affair. But, Stephanie had a way of always getting what she was after... especially men!

So, the beautifully sunny days on the majestic mountain slopes evolved into the warm fireside evenings of nonstop lovemaking. Thus, their torrid affair began. Being geographically undesirable actually worked in their favor. They would never have been able to keep it confidential, if they lived in the same locale. It was too hot! Stephanie scheduled more out of town seminars than she had in the past.

She knew Charles wouldn't care, since her absence usually went unnoticed. Her real concern was his finding out about Sean and her. Charles would never tolerate a cheating wife. His ego wouldn't allow it. On the other hand, she could not face losing all that she had sacrificed to attain. She knew in her heart she loved Sean and he loved her. He had a melting affect upon her that no other human achieved. When in the presence of her Scandinavian lover, she experienced a glacial warming. Putting her in touch with innermost feelings that were foreign to the analytical doctor.

Perhaps, it was the combination of aging and being in love that attributed to the softening of her nature. Her comrades had noticed it but dared not to mention it. But even Stephanie, had sensed a newness about herself...and liked it. Being hard and callused had attained her the goals she demanded, but inside, the temple of her being had always been cold and drafty...until Sean. But, they both knew Stephanie too well and were wise enough to accept the fact that she was incapable of living Sean's middle class lifestyle. Things had to remain status quo. It was the only acceptable way for them.

How she missed her mystery man. How long could she keep their affair a secret from her powerful husband? So far, she gave herself an "A" for the juggling act she had been performing the last year. But, it would only take one slip, and her whole world could collapse like a house of cards. Was it her imagination, or did she really detect a hint of suspicion from her real estate tycoon hubby. He was seriously considering running for the office of mayor. All she needed was a snooping reporter to leak her affair to the media. If she cost her husband the election, he would make her pay dearly. So much was at stake. Too much to gamble and yet, she was addicted now to her "other" lifestyle. Her frequent getaways had become a way of life. It granted her the tolerance to put up with the barbaric ways of making love that she was subjected to as the Mrs. Charles Winston. What a person will do for money. She had no choice if she was to complete her doctorate program. She had run through her divorce settlement from her previous marriage and her mother's savings. Nothing, not even her two children were going to get in her way. Stephanie was obsessed with the prestige and recognition that came with hanging out her shingle. She had to prove to everyone she was brighter and smarter than them all.

Perhaps marrying Charles wasn't the only alternative, but no other suitors had presented themselves at that particular time in her life. And, time was becoming her enemy. She was in her mid thirties and still a part-time student. She and her elusive sheepskin were beginning to show signs of wear. Her marriage to Charles Winston opened all the once locked doors. She could pursue her destiny without interruption, for Charles promised her that when he gave her a three carat Marquis diamond ring. He was wise to know if the gift of her paid tuition was not enough to clench him a "yes" to his marriage proposal, he was certain she could not resist the dazzling ring. Impressing her friends was an integral part of her complex personality. After pursuing Stephanie for nearly eight months, he had learned a great deal of what made her tick. He was perceptive about people and that contributed to his vast success. His intuitiveness knew that when Stephanie accepted his offer, it was not out of a great love for him. But then, he did not love her either. Charles decided after their second dinner date that Stephanie could fit the bill as the suitable kind of woman to represent Mrs. Charles Winston. He required someone of intelligence and class, an independent woman who would not cling to him or ask a lot of questions about his activities. He knew that if he set her up with her own practice, she would be too elated and too busy to interfere in his private world. In addition, it certainly enhanced his image to have a bright, successful psychologist for a wife. Everything Charles Winston did in his life was well thought out with the inevitable ulterior motive. He and Stephanie had that in common.

No decisions were ever based on emotion. He had decided as a young man he was lacking in sensitivity and feelings. His parents, both successful political attorneys obsessed with their own careers, merely had a child to carry on the Winston name. Murielle Winston resented the morning sickness she endured the first three months of pregnancy. Though, she never missed a day of work until she went into labor to deliver Charles. She was willfully trying to delay his entrance into the world until she finished the most important case of her career. Just moments into her closing arguments presentation to the jury, which Murielle masterfully based the outcome of her defense, Charles could not and would not wait any longer to appear. Resisting the rigid cramps of early labor hours before, the driven attorney was more than determined to have this baby when it was convenient for her, and that meant after this highly publicized trial. Winning this case would set her apart and literally be her triumphant claim to fame. Her name and reputation would be the topic of discussion amongst the right Washington circles. She had clawed her way to get this far, and this was the case that would catapult her to success.

But unfortunately, baby Charles was enroute, and all the will power his mother could muster up was not going to delay his delivery. During her much rehearsed speech to the jury, at a climatic point, she gasped, grabbed her rotund stomach, and shrieked. The judge who was acquainted with and also immune to Muriell's courtroom theatrics, darn near toppled off his bench hearing her shrill voice. She was immediately rushed to the hospital after the judge called for a twenty minute recess. Being wheeled from the courtroom on a gurney, Murielle begged for a postponement until she could resume her final arguments. But, the judge denied her request and ordered her associate to continue on her behalf. The trial had lingered on for months and all were weary, yet anxious to end it.

As the sirens whirred through the busy streets, Murielle cried tears of deep despair. Her cries were not from the pain she felt, that just infuriated her all the more. They were not tears of joy for awaited motherhood. She knew in her heart that her associate could not possibly deliver the defense's final dissertation with the same impact that she could. She felt robbed of her golden opportunity. This had been her fight for months and now some young....

It was while drifting in and out of sleep in the recovery room after having given birth to a healthy 9.2 pound son, she heard the dreaded words on a radio at the nurses' station. The prosecutor was jubilant with joy having defeated Murielle Winston, the self proclaimed nemesis of all prosecuting attorneys. "Now, perhaps, Mrs. Winston will stay at home being a new mama and out of the courtroom." Murielle oblivious to the pain and ordeal of childbirth was wracked by a different kind of pain. She decided then and there that she wanted little to do with her newly arrived offspring. As far as she was concerned, he had cost her the victory of her career. She produced an heir to her husband at the expense of her job.

In spite of all her efforts, the loss of that precedent case did paralyze her career goals. She enjoyed a monetary success, but she never attained her ultimate position amongst her peers, and she blamed her baby for it.

Charles Winston III hardly knew his mother, and the lack of maternal nurturing was representative in his coldness towards the people around him. Children truly are the products of their environment, as he was the end result of his. He was incapable of loving anyone, and Stephanie was painfully aware of this fact. A shudder came over her, as a renegade branch from the fragrant rose bush brushed up against her. Realizing the time, she swiftly walked back to the house.

Chapter Eleven

Vivian nearly drove off the narrow road several times as she approached the designated meeting spot she and Frank had agreed upon. Her hands were trembling on the cycle's throttle, and she was having difficulty in her concentration to stay on the left hand side of the road. She parked the bike in some weeds on the side of the bridge. Frank was there, standing in the middle of the structure. A sudden fear grasped her heart. She definitely did not relish the idea of walking out there to meet him. She would have felt far more at ease not being on the bridge. Frank knew that, too. Already experiencing a build up of stomach acid, she commenced the walk.

"Come to think of it, Frank never has accommodated my desires," she muttered to herself. "Frank," her tone controlled as she approached him. "Must we stand out here in the middle of nowhere?"

His voice tight, "Yes, Vivian, we must. I am comfortable out here, and frankly, I don't give a damn if you're not!"

"Well, I can see this conversation is going to go far. Frank, why the hell are you here? You made a scene at the inn and embarrassed me in front of my friends."

"Surely, you don't expect me to give a crap about that bunch of bitches. This may be news to you, but they are *not* your friends!"

"You may think what you want, but I happen to know better. Anyway, this has nothing to do with why you are here trying to ruin the only happy moments I've enjoyed in years! I want you to leave immediately. I wouldn't dream of interrupting your golf retreats."

Realizing their verbiage was getting them no place and defeating his purpose to get his wife to return home with him, Frank decided to try a new tactic. With a softened voice now filled with false warmth, he moved closer to Vivian. "Listen, sweetheart, I just can't function without you by my side. I need you to come home."

Vivian now feeling contempt and disgust snapped back, "Frank, where on earth did you come up with that garbage? We both know you want me home, because you can't stand your own company. I'm not there to receive your verbal abuse and sometimes worse! You miss your galley slave to make your meals and clean up after you! Some marriage I have! It's so one sided it makes me sick!"

Sensing the loss of that round, he threw out the old one-two punch that usually abruptly ended one of these confrontations, "Well, you vowed for better or worse, remember? Nobody promised you a rose garden."

"Hey, Frank, that isn't going to work anymore! There's even a passage in the Bible that..."

"The Bible! Who has been filling your head with Bible stuff?" he angrily shouted. He knew that someone must have informed her of this revelation, or she would have mentioned it before to him. He was well aware of the fact that the only hold he still had on her was to throw up her vows. She always reacted in the same manner when he did. She'd become very quiet and sheepishly walk away, resuming her wifely role, until the next time they squabbled. Remind her of her vows, she would tuck her head, and all would be well for a time. He recognized that it was a monotonous cycle, but he had grown to rather enjoy the sport of it. He thrived on the power of control over his betrothed. It was all a game to him, like hunting. Only this time something was definitely out of the ordinary. For the first time in fifteen years, she did not react normally. He was sure that by now they would be returning to get her things, and both be on the next available flight home.

"Frank, cat got your tongue? You haven't said a word for over three minutes."

"I want to know who told you about some Bible verse."

"You wouldn't believe me, if I did tell you." Vivian knew all too well that if she told him it was Barbara, he'd laugh in her face and dismiss it as B.S. Right now she knew he was concerned, for her religious beliefs dictated her life. This could be powerful knowledge to her, if what Babs told her checked out. She was anxious to return to the Isle and research Millicent's ivory Bible held in its own stand in the parlor room.

"Frank, we aren't getting anywhere. Just get it straight that I am not cutting short my time here with the girls. I have waited years for this reunion, and nothing, not even your death, is going to ruin this for me! So, you might as well go home. I will not be accompanying you!" With that, she turned and walked back to her moped smiling and feeling better than she had in such a long time. Glancing over her shoulder briefly to see Frank had not budged an inch. She speeded back to the Lombard's thinking, "Barbara, you cannot be wrong about that scripture. If anything you have ever said was true in your life, please may it be what you told me. You actually sounded sincere. You..." The scrunch of the pebbles on the driveway brought her thoughts back to reality. She parked her bike and ran into the house. Within minutes of her arrival, the phone rang. Millicent stepped out from the kitchen to inform Vivian of her caller, surprised to find her leafing through the Bible.

"For me? It couldn't be Frank, I left him on the bridge," she mumbled. "Hello."

"Viv, are you all right?" John's voice sounded so comforting to her. "I saw you leave the bridge and had to call. I couldn't tell if you were upset or not. Actually, you appeared as though there was a spring in your step, but I must have imagined that."

"Oh, John, I completely forgot you were going to be nearby. Incidentally, where were you? I didn't see a soul on the tiny inlet beach or near the bridge."

"That, my dear, was because I wasn't in either of those places. I was anchored off shore in the dingy portraying an avid fisherman."

"That was you in that ridiculous looking plaid hat? I remember looking away from Frank at one point, and almost breaking out in laughter when I saw what appeared to be an old fisherman in such a peculiar chapeau. But, I was too angry to laugh then, but I can chuckle now," and she did.

"Hey, madam. Don't make fun of my disguise. It worked didn't it."

"Oh, my precious John, how can I ever thank you for all you've done for me?"

"First, I like being referred to as *your precious John*. You can call me that anytime. Second, I haven't done all that much for you, and third, why don't we meet so you can fill me in on why you sound in such good spirits. I expected to find you hysterical or at least in tears."

"Yes, that sounds perfect. I do owe you that. You name the place, and I'm treating. After all, it's the least I can do for my personal body-guard."

John suggested an out-of-the-way pub frequented only by the locals. It was off the beaten path and rarely did a tourist ever find it. It was the only establishment on the island that did not want to cater to tourism. It was a well kept secret, so the residents had a place to flee to and could avoid the often loud and sometimes obnoxious visitors.

The girls had decided to sunbathe on The Enchanted Isle's beautiful beach. They reached the halfway mark of their vacation and were all dreading when the last day would come. There was already talk between them of the possibility of extending their stay for a few extra days, though, Claudia wasn't as anxious to linger, since she had a new love waiting for her back home.

"I am dying to know how Viv is," Melanie said while applying more lotion to her legs. "God, if Frank has done anything to her, I'll..."

"Don't make idle threats," Stephanie snapped.

"Stephanie, get off my case. You are the one who dumped Vivian's friendship. This is not a contest between us. I value both your friendships. Viv could use your support and caring about now. She would open up to you in a second. She admires and respects your every opinion. And, I'd gladly relinquish my consolation couch and let you take over. As you so succinctly put it earlier, you are the professional," Melanie paused and then added, "shrink."

"As much as I hate to admit it, I was out of order before. You're right, Melanie. I have not been a good friend to Viv for a long time. My own life has become so complex."

"Well, the same goes for you as it did for Vivian or any of you. If you need to talk, I'm here for you. That's what a good friendship means. It goes deeper than just sharing meals, laughter, shopping, and gossip. At least, it does for me."

Stephanie looked touched by Melanie's words and uncharacteristically reached over from her towel and patted her friend's arm. In merely a whisper the words, "I'm sorry," came out of her mouth. Melanie was surprised but delighted at the gesture, for she hated any kind of conflict. She nodded her head in acknowledgment.

At about that moment, Claudia announced she was baked enough and planned to return to the house. Also, her curiosity was piqued to find out about Vivian and Frank's situation. She half feared they would find Viv's room empty and Millicent explaining her return to the U.S. One by one, the attractive foursome picked up their beach towels and trekked back to the manse silently, each concerned what they would find. All four were elated when Millicent informed them of Vivian's rummaging through her Bible, her date to meet John, and the happy smile she displayed. Millicent noted that it was the happiest expression she had seen upon Vivian's face since she arrived.

"Babs, can you blame her for wanting to check out your Biblical reference? You're not noted for quoting scripture. Besides, do you realize you may have single handedly given her the key to her life?" Melanie looked at her friend staring into her hazel eyes. "You are undoubtedly responsible for the big smile she was wearing when she left."

Barb rarely felt like a heroine, but she liked what she was experiencing...a warmth inside. She had always wanted Vivian to like her, but she knew they were both so different. She constantly seemed to rub her the wrong way. The only thing they had in common was their motherhood.

"Oh, Barbara dear, I put the sports page on the wicker table for you," Millicent slipping her a wink.

Thinking to herself, "That Millicent is one sharp lady. I know she knows why I want to keep track of Lance. I can't get that rat out of my system. I don't want to love him! I've been with a dozen guys since our divorce, and yet, no one has that kind of magnetism for me."

Turning the page, there he was smack in the middle of another brawl, and of course, the headline read, "Troubled Winter in troubled waters again!" Barb sighed with concern for her former husband. His temper was his downfall. His tantrums undermined his irresistible charisma. At times, one would swear he was a toddler in a grownup's body. If baseball gets fed up with his antics, what would he do? The possibility existed that the end may not be far off. His drinking, drugs, and escapades had caused him to be bounced around the league from team to team. By now, his bizarre and unpredictable behavior preceded him wherever he went. He consistently added fuel to the fire of his irrational reputation, and he didn't seem to care. Barb was genuinely concerned for his survival aprés the baseball life. She knew he was already on a self destructive course, but at least he had his world of the big leagues. Once that was stripped away, and it was only a matter of time now, she truly feared for his life. She knew the headlines would read an accidental overdose, but she would know the truth. Realizing it was no longer her business did not stop her from watching over him, even it was from afar.

Chapter Twelve

In hopes of catching Bernard, Bruce arrived at the The Enchanted Isle ten minutes early for his date with Melanie. He had wanted to strike up a conversation about Bernard's boat building business. They had met several days before with John to discuss Bruce's involvement with the business, but nothing concrete had transpired since then. Bernard had informed both men that he would be in touch with them, but neither had heard from him. Finding Millicent tending to her impeccably groomed "English" garden, he approached cautiously, so as not to startle her.

"Ahem. Good day, Millicent." Having not heard his steps on the stone path, she whipped around sending the carefully selected snapdragons and periwinkles she had collected in her basket all over the lush green turf.

"Oh my, I didn't hear you, Bruce. E-gads, look what I've done!"

Bruce stooped down to help pick up the beautiful array of flowers. "Millicent, I was hoping to catch Bernard at home. I had driven by the boatyard earlier, but he was not there."

"That's true. Today is Wednesday, and he always goes to St. George's to portray his role in the Peppercorn Ceremony. He dresses in costume and has been doing so for the past ten years. And I might add, he's never missed a ceremony. I know he will miss it, if we ever leave our island home."

"Actually, Millicent, that was why I had wanted to talk to him. We met a few days ago regarding my buying into your business, and..."

"Dear Bruce, I know all about it." Having refilled her straw basket, she motioned him to sit on the garden bench. "My Bernard is struggling so to make his decision to leave his life long dream. He feels he is betraying the good Lord, since he was already blessed and granted his dream of the ship building business. Yet, now he has another dream for us to travel and see the world. Bernie is experiencing remorse for allowing these emotions to affect his judgment. He sees himself as a greedy sinner. He's been tussling with his conscience since he came from your meeting together. My poor hubby has hardly slept a wink."

"Millicent, he could come back anytime. He wouldn't be closing the door."

"I see it that way, and I said the same thing to him. But, he must come to terms with his final decision. You must not hurry him, Bruce, or I know he'll not make the decision you are hoping for. That's the advice of an older woman who really knows her husband."

"Believe me, young lady," Bruce emphasized *young lady* with a twinkle in his eye, "I appreciate your words of wisdom. I won't bring up the topic for at least 24 hours, but after that I'll go crazy. I'm running out of days to be here."

Millicent put her lily white hand on his leg and looked deeply into his aqua green eyes, the color they took on when the sun shone directly on them, "What is meant to be will be. Now, I must put these flowers, one of God's loveliest gifts to us, in water before they wilt."

Bruce felt a conflict of emotions. On one hand, disappointment having not talked to Bernard, yet on the other hand, encouraged by his lovely wife. A quiet voice from within comforted him, "Patience, patience will win out."

Melanie observed Millicent and Bruce chatting together in the garden from her bedroom window. She had been ready nearly an hour for their date. She could think of nothing else, since the bright, warm sunlight kissed the panes of the bay window and awakened her early that morning. She decided to forfeit the usual half hour that she was religiously committed each day to exercise. But not this day. She was eager to commence with her daily ritual of personal grooming. Being as nervous as she was since awakening, she knew today would require extra time for perfecting her makeup.

It was finally happening for her. She knew she must use caution, and mentally attach an imaginary muzzle on her mouth. She had made it through their wonderful evening together the night before and not once said a derogatory statement. Though, she almost slipped when her determined rival for Bruce's affections sallied forth to their table at the Rum Runners Pub on Front Street. They had been discussing the ornate ironwork that enclosed the outside balcony high above the street. Apparently, Sandra had been trying to track him down the entire day before. She so obviously used the excuse of wanting to discuss—more like dangle the bait—his becoming involved in her deceased father's business. Melanie half expecting Bruce to leap at her offer, shocked her and Sandra. Bless his gorgeous heart, he politely told her he was otherwise engaged for the evening and did not want to discuss any business plans other than his proposal to Bernard.

Taken aback, but only momentarily to regroup her tactics, Sandra apologized to both of them for her interruption. Unable to leave matters where they were, the devious she-devil added that before Bruce made his definitive decision he owed it to himself to hear her out. Being the gentleman that he was, he agreed to meet with her soon. Ignoring her next attempt to pin him down to when that meeting might take place, he graciously excused both he and Melanie so they could dance.

On the dance floor, Melanie about to blurt out something she surely would have regretted, impulsively kissed Bruce instead. "Now, if I can only remember to do that each time my mouth is tempted to get me in trouble."

Bruce stopped her by placing his own kiss on her soft petal pink lips. "Yes, I prefer this approach to the other," he whispered to her.

They danced into the wee hours, until the band announced their final song, neither wanting the spell of the evening to end. Their attraction was so strong for one another that they knew if left to their own devices, they would be all over each other. Somehow, as tempting a thought that might be, they wanted to become better acquainted. Their beginning had been rather choppy, and the last thing they both sought was a quick affair. Once they crossed that threshold, the whole relationship would take on a different perspective. They sincerely desired to wait until the time felt right. Basically, they were two people who met only days before, and the better part of those days were emotionally upsetting to them both.

A light tapping on the door to her elegantly decorated room, brought

Melanie back to the present. Bruce's soft voice called her name from the other side of the hand carved pecan door. She swiftly opened it and invited him in.

"You look as refreshingly beautiful as the first day of spring," he complimented her, his smile allowing his dimples to show.

"And you, sir, look more handsome than a man should be allowed to," she swoonedstaggered as she took a step back to visually encompass all six foot four of him.

"You realize, of course, this is probably not a safe place for us to be, due to our mutual admiration society for one another."

"That may be, but before we leave, look around at this splendid room. All of Millicent's special touches are everywhere. I realize this is ultra feminine for a man's tastes, but it is so me."

Bruce surveyed the Victorian bedroom with it's ruffled lace curtains tied back at the appropriate points in the bay window, the fragile porcelain doll collection strategically placed on the floral tapestry window seat, the collection of fine miniature china in an European styled curio cabinet, all set off by the richly appointed Queen Anne furnishings. No magazine had ever featured a more beautiful room.

"So, this is you? You're right about it being feminine, but even I have to admit it is breathtaking. I'm sure some of these pieces are priceless."

Eyes bright and words effusively escaping her mouth, "I love it all so. I just wish I could stay here forever!"

"Well, my princess, one never knows which wishes may come true."

"Oh, Bruce, can you imagine living in this incredible home?"

"Just think, if all goes well with my taking over Bernard's and if I can sell some of my original cat designs, perhaps I'll be in a position to buy this one day. Then again, I doubt if the Lombard's would ever sell their home. It wouldn't hurt, I suppose, to make mention of it to them. I certainly would like to have the first right of refusal, if this property ever did go on the market."

Millicent peeked her head into the room, as she was passing by with a mound of towels in her arms. One had to wonder how she could see where she was going, since the towels towered above her head. She knew every inch of hallway and seemed to have no problem navigating her load of linens around them.

"Good morning, again," her soft voice muffled by the obstruction in front of her mouth.

"Oops, an embarrased Melanie caught by the mistress of the house. Actually, Millicent, you saved me just in the nick of time. Your guest here was about to entice me over to your elegant lace bedspread, and then who knows what she had planned in that lovely head."

Melanie gasped at Bruce's insinuations, and Millicent totally rattled, sent the leaning tower of towels all over the floor. The two ladies were beet red as they scampered to pick up the scattered wash cloths and towels. Bruce completely amused at the sight, bellowed with deep laughter, and bent down to lend assistance to the duo on the floor. It was a comical sight, and all three broke out into gales of giggles. Finally, Millicent righted herself regaining her composure and dignity, taking the Irish lace hankie from her apron pocket, and attempted to wipe the tears from her cheeks.

"I haven't laughed this hard in...I can't recall. Laughter is so good for the soul, you know."

"Dear Millicent, I do apologize for making such a statement. Melanie was merely showing off this lovely room to me. I do think you should be aware, though, that she is not planning to ever leave it."

Melanie swabbing her own tears from her eyes, admitted she wished she could stay forever.

"Well, my luv, if we actually follow my Bernie's dream, I will want someone to care for Enchanted Isle. Someone who will love and cherish it the way we do. But, you are young and have a career of your own, and..."

Melanie busting at the seams to respond interrupted her, "Millicent, remember I am a writer. I can write from anywhere."

Tossing back a fine strand of silver-gray hair wisping across her forehead, "Oh my, so you are. Well, then, we might have something to talk about one day. Now, I must put these away and get on with my chores. Have a delightful day together, children."

Once again with all towels stacked, she proceeded out of the room and down the hall to the double door linen closet.

"Hey, cutie, I know you love this room, but I have a day's activities awaiting us."

Off they drove on their mopeds, racing each other around the curved bends on the flower lined roads. The Golden Shower and Poinciana trees along Middle Road in Southampton Parish were magnificent. They wound their way down to the south shore in Warwick Parish to Jobson's Cove. To Melanie's astonishment, he had packed a picnic lunch and led them to the secluded beach she had witnessed he and Sandra on the day before.

"Is this where you take all your dates?" she asked with an edge in her voice.

Bruce surprised by her tone, inquired as to what she meant by that. She mentioned having seen him there with Sandra, but before she could ruin his plans, he grabbed her and kissed her hard. "Don't do this, Melanie. You know how I feel about Sandra. We've never been intimate. She happened to show me this spot one day, and at the time, I was wishing I could be here with someone I truly cared about. Now I am. I've been dying to get you here all morning. I was unaware you had ever been here, much less saw me here with Sandra."

Feeling about the size of a pea, Melanie hugged him as hard as she could. Without another word, they carried their snorkeling gear, the picnic basket and blanket down the rocky steps to a gloriously private cove. Silently, they set up camp unfolding the blanket and laying it down on the warm coral sand and then placing their belongings on it. Each, struggling with their thoughts, decided to remain speechless for the moment. Melanie disrobed her beach cover-up displaying her beautifully fit, tanned body. Bruce catching a glimpse out of the corner of his eye as he put on his snorkeling gear, gasped with excitement. This woman had him spellbound. He could hardly contain his arousal and knew he must make his way to the water immediately or be embarrassed.

A long extending jetty stretching far out into the tepid waters provided a superb snorkeling spot. Once safely in the water, he called for her to join him.

Helping to adjust her mask he whispered in her ear, "I've got a treat in store for you. Look over there," he pointed to a flurry of activity on the reef. The multi colored fish darted in and out of the rocks. Bruce motioned to Melanie to open her palm. He then took out a white plastic bag from the fish net carrier attached to a waist belt and poured a handful of peas into her hand. The fish went crazy. They adored peas and were entertaining to watch snatching up every one she held. Bruce decided to throw a bunch out knowing he'd be creating a feeding frenzy. He swam closer, grabbing her hand as they observed some of mother nature's exquisite creatures make piglets of themselves. A barracuda swam lazily by seeming undisturbed by all the commotion. Melanie gulped in surprise to see the long slim fish. Knowing the first half of it was all teeth, she began to choke on the sea water. Bruce assisted her by taking off her mask and snorkel while she regained her composure. "They usually won't bother you. They are attracted to shiny, metal objects like a ring or pendant." His eyes quickly scanned her body and was relieved she was not wearing any jewelry. "They can be nosy and want to investigate, but they normally don't attack a diver or swimmer."

Still a little out of breath, she said, "Actually, that is one piece of marine trivia I am aware of. I must have learned it in biology or Earth science class."

They continued to snorkel and hold hands pointing out to one another an occasional sea urchin or sting ray passing by. Melanie was concerned with meeting up with a shark, as they were known to inhabit those waters. Whereas Bruce seemed totally at ease and thoroughly enjoying himself not aware of the possibility of imminent danger. He noticed her uneasiness and signaled they surface and take a break.

"What are you so uptight about? Your head looks like it's attached to a swivel joint. You're turning it constantly. What are you looking for?"

The blonde beauty feeling slightly embarrassed told him of her fears.

"Sweetheart, I wouldn't worry about sharks. The word would be out all over the island, if any were spotted lurking in shallow waters. Now look, this is supposed to be fun!" He pulled her close to him and tried to kiss her, but their masks clunked together making it awkward. "Let's go up to the blanket where I can properly kiss you. And, if it's a really pungent kiss, I'll reward you with lunch."

"Melanie tingled from head to toe in anticipation of the forthcoming encounter. No one had ever affected her this way before. That one kiss led to many more, and the idea of lunch was becoming a blur. Between the heat of the sand rising through the blanket and the rising body temperatures, they both simultaneously broke apart to come up for air. With perspiration dripping down his forehead, Bruce reached for his towel, "I can see this is getting out of hand. How would you feel about that, my sweet?"

"Very tempted, but I am not an exhibitionist. It'd be my luck to have Barb and the group witness our first coming together, if you know what I mean."

"Yes, I do know. I want it to be the perfect setting when we make love. I suggest then that we get our minds onto other things...like food!" He set out a small checkered tablecloth on top of the blanket. Next came plates, wine glasses, a bottle of chilled chardonnay, a wedge of brie, a loaf of French bread and a huge cluster of seedless grapes. "It's not fried chicken, but I thought with swimming, we'd rather eat lighter."

Melanie's delight at the array of goodies was apparent. Her smile radiated as her eyes danced with joy. She pulled out the cork on the wine bottle moderately filling their glasses and proceeded to make a toast. "To my Prince Charming, who has thus far orchestrated one of the best days of my life." Their glasses clinked, and they sipped the refreshing wine.

Unbeknown to them, they were not alone. Sandra had made it a daily ritual to sunbathe on that very same stretch of sand. Only this day she moved her spot to a ridge just above the pair of lovebirds below. She felt sick with envy to be in Melanie's place. After all, she had been there when she and Bruce had first met. Deciding not to interrupt their lunch, she would wait before making her presence known to them.

Their lunch was not a hurried affair. They fed each other grapes one at a time, made constant toasts, and talked of how life should be.

After putting away the food and folding the tablecloth, Melanie nestled her head on Bruce's shoulder, as they both now felt sleepy from the wine and blissfully happy. It was then, that Sandra decided to drop in on them.

"Well, you two look content."

Recognizing the voice and peering through a squinted eye, Melanie saw Sandra towering over them. Bruce had either drifted off immediately or was pretending to be asleep. In either case, Melanie went along with him hoping it would dissuade the interloper from staying. Gingerly, she rose to her feet, motioning they move so as to not disturb Bruce. But, it was obvious that that was Sandra's intent. She had no interest in talking to Melanie, so she ignored her gesture and stood firm.

In a louder than normal voice she asked, "So how is the snorkeling? Did Bruce share my secret of the peas to feed the fish?"

At that point, Bruce could see it was no use to pretend to be asleep and acted as though he had just awakened from a nap. "I thought I heard voices. I must have dropped right off. Wine and sun does that to me."

"No dear, you only heard one rather loud, inconsiderate voice, and it wasn't mine." The perfect moments earlier now shattered, Melanie decided to return to the water so Sandra could get what she came for... Bruce! She grabbed her snorkel, fins, and mask and briskly excused herself.

"She obviously believes three is a crowd," Sandra said in a triumphant tone.

Bruce, embarrassed by his date's pettiness and her abrupt departure, asked Sandra what she had been doing the last few days.

"Researching the boat building business here, of course. I would have thought you were doing the same."

"Actually I have, in several meetings with Bernard Lombard and John Pendleton."

"And," she asked with enormous curiosity, "what kind of a deal have you put together?"

"So far, we've just laid the ground work and aired our desires."

"Well, my handsome friend, apparently I've accomplished a bit more than you have. I've had my father's staff of lawyers look into Lombard's Shipbuilding, and it is as solid as a company can be."

Bathed in gratitude and sincerity, "Thank you, Sandra, now you've saved me a ton of bucks to have it checked out, for which I am most grateful. I owe you."

"Grateful enough to take me to dinner, and I'll explain my interest in all this to you? Bruce, I'm prepared to make you your dream offer."

"Ooh, lady, you know how to tempt a guy. But, I have to be honest with you. I'd only agree to dine because of my interest in Lombard's. Would you mind terribly if we included Melanie? She has already expressed some invaluable advice regarding how to handle Bernard."

"I'm afraid that would be out of the question. I would not feel as comfortable talking about the deal with her present."

"Somehow, I knew you would feel that way. Where shall we meet and when?" he asked while his eyes shifted from Sandra's low cut suit to searching for a sign of Melanie's snorkel protruding from the emerald green waters. Oddly enough, he could not find a single snorkel, but rather two were evident swimming near a classic looking mahogany speedboat that was anchored near shore. Bruce thought he recognized the boat as one of John's personal fleet. The waves from a passing water skier caused the craft to shift around allowing Bruce to catch a glimpse of the name, "Mistress II." John must be snorkeling with Melanie he thought to himself and suddenly realized he resented Sandra's obvious pre-meditated invasion. This was to be a perfect day for him and his new love. Now she was enjoying the crystal waters with someone else. To top it off, he just made dinner plans but with the wrong woman. Bruce knew that once Melanie learned of his impending meeting with Sandra for dinner, it would be all over. She would never understand the reasoning behind it. Kicking himself for allowing Sandra to manipulate him, his mind raced to come up with a suitable plan to salvage the upcoming evening. An early dinner scheduled during the sunset hour when Melanie and the girls religiously met at Henry's for their rum swizzles would take care of Sandra and allow him to meet Melanie around eight o'clock. Knowing he would have to be tactful with Sandra, for if she caught wind of his deviousness, she'd never agree to it. It was imperative that he learn of her offer. His curiosity was killing him. Right before his eyes he could see his life changing, his dreams becoming a reality. Bruce knew if he played his cards right, he could have his ideal business and ideal woman, but getting them might induce an intricate juggling act on his part.

"Bermuda to Bruce. Where are your thoughts, as if I didn't know? Darlin, don't try to second guess my proposal. Just be patient until... say seven tonight?"

"Oh, Sandra," Bruce thought, "You've just provided me with my answer for tonight." Yes, he'd meet her early and then complain of an upset stomach and have to excuse himself about seven thirty.

"Sandy, you can't expect me to wait until seven! Let's meet around five and make it a long evening. There is so much to discuss."

Biting the bait unknowingly, "Five o'clock it is. Shall we rendez-vous at Henry VIII's?"

A sudden chill ran up Bruce's spine. They couldn't meet there. "No, to be honest I'm growing a little tired of Henry's. How about The Conch Beach Bar?"

"Perfect for me. I can walk to there, since it is right around the corner from my hotel. I'm off, big guy. I'll let you return to your ro-mantic lunch...except that you've lost your dining companion. Seems as though she's found a replacement for you already," Sandra quipped sarcastically.

Bruce's head whipped around and sure enough, Melanie and John were sitting in John's boat sipping a liquid refreshment. He could not show his anger towards Sandra and blow the possible opportunity she dangled before him, at least not until he heard her out. Swallowing hard, he forced a grin and acted as though Melanie being with John was not a problem for him.

"I'll just put away these glasses and take a swim out to join them."

"Well, in that case, I think I'll come along. Three's an odd number. Four is better."

Bruce realized he couldn't allow Sandra to be within ten feet of Melanie. Knowing her, she would surely want to tout about their din-ner date to Melanie. A brilliant thought had come to mind. "You know, on second thought, I think I may try to go back to sleep again. My stomach seems to be a little off today. I hope I didn't eat some bad fish, or worse, have a stomach bug." He grasped his stomach, as if he was in discomfort and laid down on the thin blanket.

"Perhaps, I can rub your back for you. That may help," Sandra reacting to him with concern.

Bruce feeling panicky to get rid of her and so far failing at all attempts, "No thanks. I'll never be able to fall asleep if you do that."

Her immediate comeback clothed in a sexual cloak, "Would that be so bad?"

Bruce realizing she interrupted him with her flirtatious innuendo, just made him want to strangle her. "Sandra, trust me. Sleep is the answer for what ails me. I want to feel better than this by five o'clock."

"Okay, I'll leave you, if you insist. I can't tell you how much I am looking forward to our evening." She pecked him on the cheek and finally walked back to her beach towel on the ridge above, where she perched herself once again never taking her eyes off of him.

Bruce suddenly sensed his entrapment. How could he swim to Melanie and John when eagle eyes observed his every move. Oh, this was a hell of a mess he got himself into. "By now, Melanie will think I don't care about being with her. Especially since Sandra has gone and I'm just lying here. Oh God, what a lousy predicament," his thoughts spinning so fast he was beginning to feel ill...a self imposed illness!

Melanie having noticed Sandra's departure was hurt and confused by Bruce's not immediately joining John and her. Then realizing he may not have recognized that it was John's boat she was on, she thanked John for rescuing a mermaid in distress and lending a comforting ear. She plopped over the side to return to the beach.

Thrilled to see her heading to the beach, Bruce decided to save his own hide and use his imaginary stomach ailment to bail himself out. At this point, he hoped he wouldn't end up with one, since lying was upsetting to his digestive system. Taking the initiative, he spoke first when she arrived at the blanket, using reverse psychology. "Hey, why did you run off on me and go pick up some other guy?" hoping to make her feel guilty for her actions.

Her first reaction of defensiveness was instantly replaced by guilt. "Some other guy! That was John out there silly," her voice softening. "I was so hot about Sandra invading our space and ruining our special time together, but John calmed me down."

Turning over on his side, "Well, I'm indebted to him. I felt you had abandoned me and left me for that great white shark to devour."

In nearly a whisper she leaned toward his ear, "Did she devour you."

"Not a chance, princess. The only devouring of me I will allow will be by the tiger shark that's next to me. And, if you ever run off and leave me to her again, I'll catch you and throw you over my knee."

"Ooh, sounds kinky," she purred. "You won't think so when your little ass stings from my hand."

"For my butt's sake, I'd better change the subject. What did Ms. Sandra want anyway? She sure hung around long enough."

"Of course, she did! You weren't here to intimidate her! Melanie, she wants to make me my dream offer. Apparently, she has spent the last two days making inquiries about the boat building business. She needs to meet with me to discuss her findings."

The warm sand sifted through her coral polished toenails. "You know, I liked Sandra when I met her on John's cat. She has been through a lot. I felt compassion for her, but it has evolved into an all out rivalry between us for your affections. It's too bad."

"Hey, listen, it doesn't have to be like that. She knows I am not interested in her romantically. She is aware it is *you* that I want!" he grabbed her face and kissed her. Out of the corner of his eye, he glanced up to the ridge to see Sandra's watchful eye. Relieved to see she had left, he now felt uninhibited to lavish his affections on Melanie. Already cheated out of part of their day, his desires were mounting rapidly. Melanie had stretched out next to him, the oil from her lotion reflecting the glow of her deepening bronze tan. It was easy to tell she meticulously cared for her body. But, it was her flat tummy and protruding hip bones that really started to stir the hunger of Bruce's loins. He couldn't help but envision himself lying on top of all that sensuality. He knew it would be worth the wait. He mustn't let Sandra interfere with the development of this relationship. He had never felt this turned on by anyone before.

Grateful that he hadn't had to use his ailing stomach excuse, one less lie to deal with, he did feel compelled to disclose his plans to her about his five o'clock meeting with Sandra. Hoping he would not regret what he was about to do, he treaded cautiously. Retreating back, he decided to smother Melanie with a bushel of kisses first.

Planting two dozen kisses all over her face, neck, shoulders, and midsection, he paused to look into her eyes. "Do I dare try to tell you once again that I am falling in love with you. Are you going to shut the door to my heart like the last time?"

Dreamily responding to his query, "No. Once a fool not always a fool, I would like to think. I don't want to repeat that kind of suffering. I love the feelings that you generate in me. I can't stop thinking about you when we're apart."

Delighted to hear her response, "Same here." Taking a deep breathe, "I have two obsessions now...my boat business and *you*, and not necessarily in that order. That brings me to a discussion I am not anxious to begin."

Melanie sat up looking worried. Her voice quivering, "Are there skeletons in your closet you feel the need to expose?"

Laughing loudly, "No, no. Nothing like that. But, I know you'll shut down on me once I disclose my plan."

"Will I have good reason to?"

"Not at all. You just have to give me a chance to explain."

"Okay, I will try to keep an open mind. Somehow I know this has something to do with Sandra."

"You're right. Her dad's staff of lawyers have done a thorough check on Bernard's operation. Melanie, do you realize how much money and time that has saved me? Sandra is willing to share all their findings with me. She has a proposal she wants to present to me at five o'clock today. I asked her if you could be there, but she said she would be uncomfortable."

Melanie stiffened at what Bruce had said but reminded herself to diffuse her emotions. "Does that surprise you, Bruce? That woman

wants you! She will resort to whatever tactics will attain the result...
YOU! She has her father's wealth and his business to tantalize you
with, which just happens to be your dream. I can't begin to compete
against that kind of collateral."

Scooping her into his arms, "Baby, you don't have to compete. You
are the one I'm interested in. I want our relationship to develop and
hopefully grow into a lifetime commitment. I want us to be *one*."

Her eyes filled with tears, and she impulsively hugged him. She
then placed a moist long kiss on his receptive lips.

"Oh, don't stop. You feel so good," he said as they broke for air.

"Believe me, I don't want to, but what time is it getting to be?"

"Almost four o'clock! Where did the day go?" he said shocked by
the hour. "I didn't finish telling you my plan for tonight."

"Yes, you did. You are seeing Sandra in an hour."

Bruce couldn't read Melanie's mood. Was she upset or not? "True,
but I moved the original time of seven to five, since I know that is when
you and your pals all meet at Henry's. By seven thirty, I am going to
complain of stomach pains and excuse myself. Whereupon, I will meet
you anywhere you say. Pulling her into his embrace so their oily skins
rubbed against one another, he looked intently into her eyes. "I must
find out what Sandra has to offer."

"Sweetie, that's easy. She's offering herself and throwing in a shipbuilding business to sweeten her chances of you taking the package.
Believe me, it will only be offered as a package deal. All or nothing.
No Sandra...no deal. So, my handsome stud, you are going to have a
heck of a decision to make. I don't envy you."

Rubbing his hand down the long curvature of her back, he softly remarked, "I'll cross that bridge when I get to it. Besides, I am interested
in Bernard's operation, not her father's."

Nuzzling under his chin, "She'll probably try to buy Bernard's and
then entice you with it. I don't see a chance for me with these kinds of
odds."

Spanking her affectionately on her derrière, "That's nonsense, and
I don't have anymore time to listen to it."

As they gathered their things, they agreed to meet at his place. That way in case Sandra followed him, he would not get caught rendezvousing with Melanie.

Surprised to find her cycle with a flat tire, but believing in the old proverb of things always happening for the best, she couldn't help but wonder if this wasn't the work of their intruder. She held onto him tightly as she rode on the moped's seat behind him.

Turning his head for her to hear, "You don't mind waiting for me at my cottage?"

Straining her voice to be heard above the whine of the cycle's engine, "Actually, I think it's intriguing, provocative, exciting. Shall I go on? Quite honestly, I will be anxious to have you come from another woman's arms." She felt him become rigid. Continuing, "I mean... charms, from another woman's charms to my awaiting arms...and lips and possibly other parts."

With that, he revved the motor, and the vehicle surged with a gust of speed. He dropped her off at The Enchanted Isle, embracing, kissing, and in agreement about their later rendezvous. Finally, he was feeling in sync with his beauty. He roared up the driveway so pleased that he had been honest about seeing Sandra. It would have been his luck that Melanie would see them together, and he'd never have been able to explain himself out of another mess.

It was ten past five when Bruce pulled into the parking lot of The Conch Bar. Located on an inlet cove complete with thatched roof and high back stools surrounding a U-shaped counter, it was an attractive place. Looking seductive in a low cut, yellow floral short dress, he noticed that each time he saw Sandra her appearance improved. He decided she must be spending time in one of those over priced hotel salons. After all, she was competing with Melanie who was top of the line. If Melanie hadn't been in his life, he felt he might be tempted to at least play Sandra's game, for awhile anyway. She had a great set of boobs, and the rest of her fixed up was looking good, money and a boat business, too. Strolling towards her, his devilish side made him question whether he should take advantage of this eager temptress who had so much to entice him with. His heart then sent him a shock impulse, and it snapped his mind into shape.

"It's going to be another beautiful sunset in paradise," he yelled as he was closing the distance between them. She waited to respond until he sat on the adjoining stool.

"How are you feeling?" she inquired.

Aware that he must not appear to be as well as he felt, "Fine for a spell, and then I seem to go downhill. Hopefully, I'll stay fine all evening," knowing he had no intention of it.

They ordered two Piña Coladas and a bowl of peel and eat shrimp. "Do you think the shrimp and cocktail sauce will settle well in your delicate condition?" she asked with concern.

"I hope so, as they're too good to pass up." Thinking this was going to be his excuse to leave when the time deemed right. "Sandy, I can't stand the suspense. Tell me what you have in mind. I can think of nothing else." That was partly true. Her business proposal and Melanie consumed his every thought.

"Why rush it, green eyes, at least this way I have all of your attention. We have the entire evening to get into it. For now, I just want to enjoy you and the sunset."

"This will never do," Bruce thought to himself. He had to get her to open up and soon, so he could fake his imaginary upset stomach and salvage a nice long night with Melanie. Sandra, looking engaging or not, was beginning to turn him off. They had two drinks consumed and about to order a third.

"Bruce, if I didn't know better, I'd swear you are annoyed with me."

Caught off guard and a bit embarrassed at being discovered, he shot back, "You could say that. We've been sitting here for over an hour, and you haven't given me a clue as to your plan." Aware his tone was too stern, he suddenly knew he must back off before he blew the evening. Inhaling deeply, he tried to soften his body language by half attempting to smile.

"Give me a chance, babe, the night is young, and I have every intention of showing you...."

Bruce could tell she was feeling the alcohol from her drinks. She was pushing her partially exposed breasts into his arm while rubbing her leg against his. When he felt her hand groping his lap, he sprang up, nearly toppling their drinks. Very sternly as though scolding a child, he announced that he was leaving. Her behavior was less than desirable and certainly not professional. He proceeded to tell her that he had agreed to meet to discuss her proposition...a *business* proposition and no other kind! He continued by accusing her of her actions being nothing more than a play to get him there. His voice rising even more so that others nearby were beginning to stare. "And furthermore, I don't believe you have a legitimate offer to make me!"

As if slapped across the face, Sandra assumed a position of attention and immediately replaced her sultry demeanor with a serious, no nonsense composure. She spoke softly trying to regain her poise and minimize her embarrassment. "Please, sit down and let me begin by offering you an apology." Pausing only long enough to sip from her water goblet, she added matter-of-factly, "And the position of president of Island Yachts."

Riveted by her words, Bruce pushed the stool back closer to hers and sat down quietly. He was to be her captive audience for the next hour and a half. She planned to set him up in his own catamaran operation. "Of course, you can name it anything you like, if the sound of Island Yachts does not suit you."

He knew that there had to be a major catch to this idyllic proposal. Being no fool, he knew what it was, but he had to be sure before he could commit his life to her scheme. "Sandra, all that you have unveiled represents a great deal of thought. Obviously, you and your father's lawyers have done your homework. But, I know there is something you are leaving out, and I strongly sense it has to do with you and me."

A long silence prevailed before Sandra cautiously reached for Bruce's hand. She took it and held it between her own, looking intensely into his deep pools of green eyes. Finally speaking, "Yes. I'll be honest with you. I realize what I am offering you is more than a magnanimous gesture. I want us to run Island Yachts together as a team, a couple, a..." she fidgeted on her stool. "Hopefully as married partners one day."

Bruce stunned by her words stammered, "But, but, Sandra, we

hardly know one another. I'm fresh from a broken engagement. I can't, I simply can't make a commitment like that. Especially so soon." Yet, in his heart he knew he could make a life long promise to love, honor, and cherish Melanie. There was no doubt in his heart how he felt about her. *Her,* he thought quickly glancing at his watch. It was 8:15 p.m. already, and he promised to meet her at 8:00. Realizing it would be too conspicuous to jump up and leave after looking at his watch, he tried to act nonchalant as each minute ticked heavily away. He was so afraid his awaiting beauty would give up on him and leave before he could get back to the cottage, and he couldn't blame her. How would he feel, if the situation was in reverse?

"Bruce. Bruce, did you hear what I said?"

"Uh, no, Sandy, I'm sorry. I am afraid I'm not feeling very well. Not quite sure what my stomach is going to do." An appropriate answer under the circumstances. Now, he could make his exit without alerting her curiosity. "I must be fighting one of those 24 hour bugs. Please excuse me, but I am going to have leave before I embarrass myself. I will call you tomorrow."

He settled the check with the bartender and beelined out to the parking lot. Sandra remained seated and somewhat dismayed by his sudden departure. The reggae band had been setting up their equipment and were now ready to make the place come alive. She had so hoped they would spend the evening dancing in each others arms. Excitedly talking about their new venture together, making plans for their future, and as a finale, awakening in the morning in her bed after a glorious night of lovemaking. She was still experiencing denial that none of this was going to happen that night, when a short, rather unattractive man asked her to dance. He had a divine Australian accent and without verbally accepting his invitation, she found herself being twirled about by this koala bear looking man. He certainly was a far cry from her dashing Bruce. But, he would do for now. She was in no mood to spend another intoxicating, romantic evening in paradise by herself. After several hot numbers, the band played a slow song request. Wally, Sandra's dance partner, introduced himself, and wedged his head right into her voluptuous cleavage. The aphrodisiac scents of the evening had made her horny for affection. She had spent hours in the hotel salon beautifying for a night of love with Bruce. Her disappointment could not be controlled. Therefore, she decided that Wally's head of red curls tickling her skin felt wonderful, at least for the present moment. And, it could stay right where it was nuzzled.

Bruce drove his moped like a maniac. Twice, he had found himself on the wrong side of the road. "That damn roundabout always throws me off," he thought as he swiftly sped over to the left. The headlight of a passing motorist showed 8:45 p.m. on his watch. "Oh, please, angel, still be there. I must see you tonight. Our time is growing so short." His words echoed in his ears as he descended the bumpy driveway to his cottage. Nearly spilling the bike over after he haphazardly put down its kick stand, he ran to his front steps. He stopped short in his tracks when he truly thought he saw a vision of an angel sitting on the porch swing. The reflection of the moonlight bounced off Melanie's filmy white, see through gauze dress, as it was fluttering like angel wings in the breeze. Her golden hair flowing with the movement of the swing.

"Hi," she said with a sweetness in her voice that brought Bruce almost to tears. He was feeling so guilty and so emotional. Without saying a word, he picked her up off the swing and gently carried her inside placing her on his bed. He started to kiss her passionately. He couldn't wait another moment to have her, unless, of course, she objected...which she didn't. They made beautiful love continuously until dawn. Exhausted and exhilarated, they lay in each others arms speechless.

Chapter Thriteen

It had been the wee hours of the morning when Vivian returned from her wonderful rendezvous with John. The small, out-of-the-way pub had provided them the privacy they desired to discuss Vivian's confrontation with her husband. John's genuine concern for her touched her deeply. She opened up and shared every detail of her life. Never once did he seem bored. To the contrary, he offered her a male's point of view of what avenues she might want to consider. She was spellbound by his gentle demeanor, so unlike Frank's impatient, macho manner.

Barb, Claudia, and Stephanie had planted themselves at the Elbow Cay Resort. They featured a terrific band, and the place was swarming with passengers from several of the cruise ships docked in Hamilton. They dressed to the nines and thoroughly enjoyed themselves mingling with people from various parts of the world. All agreeing, it was a definite highlight of their trip, and they must do it again before their imminent departure, but with Melanie and Vivian next time. "Perhaps for our final evening," suggested Claudia.

During the night, Stephanie had felt as though someone had been watching her. Once back at the inn, she mentioned it to Babs, but she excused it as paranoia. "You know, Barb, now that I think about it, I was sure that I was being followed yesterday when I went to the post..."

Before she could finish the sentence, Barbara completed it with, "Office?"

"Yes. How did you know?" Stephanie looking inquisitive.

Catching herself, Barb answered, "Well, it's elementary Watson. What word would you have said following post?"

Feeling ridiculous, Stephanie nervously laughed, dismissing her suspicions. "I guess I needed this trip more than I realized."

Barbara staring at her asked if there was anything she wanted to discuss. "I get the distinct feeling there is something heavy going on in your life, and I'd like to help, if I can."

Claudia sitting down on the porch chair pushing aside the plump floral chintz pillow, wanted to get in on the conversation. "Include me in on that. We've all noticed you have been tense, and we could almost accuse you of being secretive. We're supposed to be your best friends, comrades to go through life with...remember?"

Stephanie felt totally exposed. She knew they were too perceptive. That was what bound them together all these years. Was she being paranoid? Was someone really spying on her? She had to find out! The last two days she had become edgy, and the pressures of her affair being discovered terrified her. Stephanie was not willingly going to give up all she had plotted and schemed to acquire. But, what if it was out of her hands now? She could not face the humiliation her husband, Charles, would subject her to. He would paint her as the black widow, the villain to their friends, to the public. The adulteress. That would ensure his sympathy votes and catapult him into the mayor's office! "Oh my God!" she exclaimed out loud.

Barb and Claudia had noticed her long silence staring off into space. Her conflict of whether to open up and confess her secrets to them was evident. As if the valve blew off the top of a pressure cooker, in the ensuing moments she blurted out all the details of her affair and her estranged marriage. This was so uncharacteristic of Dr. Stephanie's behavior. Always in control. It was she, who under all circumstances remained composed and self assured. They all emphatically agreed she was incapable of ever climaxing to the breaking point. It was disturbingly refreshing to know she was just as human and as vulnerable as the rest of them. She wasn't super human, after all! Yet, to see her this way was unsettling. The dismantling of a shrine...a fallen idol.

Barb was entranced with every word that spewed out of her friend's mouth. This was right up her alley. Claudia poured them each a glass of ice water. Handing one to Stephanie. "Let us help you, for a change. Over the years you've advised us as to how to handle all the dilemmas we've found ourselves in, now it's our turn to lend you the helping hand."

Stephanie looking up at her through the tears in her eyes and slowly nodding her head. "Yes, I need the support of my pals." Hearing her express those words was a revelation in itself.

Barb was already formulating a plan to find out if Stephanie was in actuality being followed. "Tomorrow I will tail you but so discreetly that no one will notice. I'll have eyes in the back of my head, as well as the front."

Claudia unable to resist, "This I want to see. Why don't we take turns keeping an eye on Stephanie. That way it won't become obvious to the *spy?*" Deciding to go with Claudia's suggestion, they finalized their strategies and called it a night.

Meanwhile, Barbara was wrestling with her conscience about her deep concerns for her former husband. It was reported in that day's paper, he had been involved in another skirmish with an opposing team. She knew it was only a matter of time before he would be released. His batting average had been declining all season, and she was sure it was due to alcohol and drugs. If caught—and that too would be just a matter of time—it'd surely mark the end of his career. She truly feared for his livelihood, if that did occur.

Claudia, on the other hand, could barely get to sleep. She had received a phone call as she was preparing herself for bed. It was her new love requesting to join her for the weekend. He was missing her terribly and begged to come. Since Vivian was seeing John and Melanie's involvement with Bruce, she could not see why he could not spend two days with her. Yes, they had sworn *no men*, but the rules had taken a turn. Claudia told Derek that she would discuss it with the others in the morning and get back to him. Feeling warm and loved, she finally slipped off to dreamland.

A gorgeous day was on hand. At breakfast Claudia brought up the possibility of her guy flying in for the weekend. "I know we all agreed no males on this trip, but circumstances have changed with Frank arriving, and John and Bruce are very much on the scene. What do you gals think? I would love for him to meet you." The close knit group at first had mixed emotions but finally were unanimous in Claudia's sweetheart coming. "I'll see if I can get him a cottage where Bruce is staying. I would never impose his presence on the Lombards."

They each giggled at how pollyanna they were behaving. Claudia added, "I couldn't possibly be intimate with Derek under this roof. I just couldn't!"

"Okay, I have a suggestion," answered Barbara. "We recently discussed extending our stay a few days. With the introduction of several new developments, one being that Stephanie believes she is being followed...." Melanie and Vivian looked shocked at this piece of news. "Perhaps we can get to the bottom of it with a little more time. I'm in no hurry to get back to my aerobics studio." Each consented to do everything in their powers to elongate their visit to the enchanted island. "That way Claudia can enjoy her man, and we won't all be waving good-bye on Monday. We'll even agree to spend our last day together... just we females. All in favor say *aye*, no *nays* allowed." They were in agreement, it was decided.

Vivian's small voice piped in, "Ladies, we've overlooked one very significant point...our accommodations. Millicent probably has these rooms booked." And she did, as they were to find out.

Delighted at the prospect of enjoying her adopted daughters for an additional time, Millicent did something totally out of character. She phoned a fellow innkeeper to see if she had a vacancy on the extra days required. The answer was affirmative. She then asked her if she would mind terribly if Millicent sent her some guests. Millicent blushed from head to toe with her next statement. "Dearie, I've done an awful thing. I've overbooked myself on those days. A first for me in all these years."

The only first about it was that Mrs. Lombard had actually just told her first white lie, and the girls knew she had done it for them! Deeply touched, they each hugged, kissed, and thanked her profusely. It was decided then, that they wanted to take her to lunch on their final day, as a token of their sincere appreciation.

"That would be just ducky, my dolls. I'd love to be your guest for lunch. Now, I simply must call those folks to inform them of their change in lodging. Thank goodness, they've never stayed here before. If they were any of my regulars, I just would not have had the heart to send them elsewhere. We're fortunate in that a large number of our guests return to us every year like old friends visiting."

"We can certainly understand why they would want to. I'm sure, dearest Millicent, you can now add the five of us to your returning family of repeat guests," Melanie added. Melanie used the word *family* instead of friends, and Millicent was cognizant of the substitution. The older, refined woman beamed at them and hurried off, wiping a runaway tear from her cheek.

Several hours had passed before the guests of the Enchanted Isle had succeeded in making the necessary arrangements to extend their stay. Numerous phone calls back to the States had paved the way. As if granted a new lease on life, the gregarious group of women insisted on opening the bottle of champagne that Millicent had offered for their celebration toast. She, too, joined them even though it was only late morning. She loved the way they made her feel...young and frivolous. Millicent had always been so provincial all of her life. These rays of sunshine, each so diverse from the other, fascinated her. She loved all their differences and the bond that held them together.

Melanie could not wait to call Bruce, hoping he would be able to also stay longer. Vivian had had the same idea to call John. Though, she wondered how Frank would take the news. Speaking of Frank, she had not heard from him since their encounter on the bridge. She wondered if he was still lurking about the island. She would have to be extremely careful about seeing John. She had begun to feel terribly drawn to the proper English gentleman.

Just as she was about to leave a message, she heard Frank's voice. "Hello, hello." She proceeded to explain that she would be staying an additional few days. He was furious, as she knew he would be.

"I knew I should have stayed on that hell hole of an island, just to keep an eye on you!"

"Frank, don't be ridiculous!" Vivian blurted back into the receiver. "I'm here with my friends, and in spite of you, I am going to enjoy my- self. We'll talk when I get home." With that she hung up, smiling with relief that now she and John would not have to sneak around for fear of being seen by her peevishly disgruntled husband. She then immediate- ly called John to share her good news.

Claudia, deliriously happy, was changing into her Gottex swimsuit for some serious sunning. She wanted to be deeply tanned when her handsome, young Adonis joined her. "Oh my God!" she squealed. It never dawned on her in her delirium that the only flaw in her relationship with her new love, would become a golden opportunity for her peer group to pass judgment. She had always managed to avoid the center stage and played a low profile regarding her life and activities. Having been the target as a child of her step father's constant ridicule and satirical scolding, she became emotionally crippled. The result left her excruciatingly sensitive to others' judgment and approval. These females were highly critical and never held back voicing their thoughts of people, places, or whatever. Claudia knew only too well, they would have a lot to say to her once they saw Derek. Staring into the antique mirror at her reflection, she decided there was nothing she could do about it now. She would face them head on, and that would be that.

Bruce had adhered himself to Bernard's side, as if his shadow the entire day, badgering him with non-stop questions regarding his boat building business. His thirst for the knowledge was unquenchable. Bernard not only didn't mind answering Bruce's inquisition but thrived on it. Bruce reminded him of himself years before. During a lunch break, they switched topics from the operations of the business to more personal ones. The older gentleman shared the love and respect he held for his own father and highly respected him for guiding Bernard into his career as a ship builder. His dad would boast proudly that his son followed in his footsteps. "Like father like son," he would always say. Though, his father's shipyard had been in England. The only disappointment Bernard ever brought to his beloved parent was that he had not sired a grandson to carry on the family tradition and name. He and Millicent tried for years to have a child. She just could not conceive. By the end of the day, their camaraderie had taken on a deeper meaning. Bernard viewed Bruce as the son he had never been blessed with. Realizing that Bruce would be about the right age as his son.

That night Bernard shared his strong feelings for the younger man with his wife as they lay in bed, and the moonlight filtered through the sheer organdy curtains. "I think, luv, he might be our ticket to break loose and travel. I want so much to show you the world before we're too old," he said softly. He had built them a luxurious 55 foot catamaran yacht to sail the seas. The only time they had enjoyed it thus far, was when they had a respite between guests. And, that only happened on rare occasions.

Millicent, already smitten with Bruce's charisma, was his staunch supporter. She rattled on emphasizing his accolades, until Bernard sat up sternly, switched on the night stand lamp, and with concerned eyes asked, "Millie, it sounds as though you have a crush on this fella."

Caught off guard with blushed cheeks, she reassured her life's partner that she only had eyes and a dauntless love for him. "You naughty man. You stole my heart from me as a young maiden of seventeen, and you never gave it back. So how could I ever give it to anyone else? And...I've loved you for keeping it all these years." She kissed him tenderly and fell asleep tucked in his arms.

Bruce arrived at the back door after sunrise. He knew by leaving his cottage that early, he would not chance being there, if Sandra decided to stop by, as she had left numerous messages. Millicent surprised to see him, opened the door, and invited him in.

"Well, early bird, did you get the worm?" she asked in her delightful British accent.

"No, but that coffee surely smells good. May I have a cup?"

Scurrying over to the stainless percolator, she delicately poured him a cup. "Here you are, luv. What brings you by at this hour?"

Settling down in one of the cane back kitchen chairs, sipping the hot coffee, "Your champ of a husband, madame. Thought I might catch a ride with him so I can see how his day unfolds. I haven't missed him, have I?"

The kitchen door swung open, "Millie, darling, who might you be prattling with?"

Remembering their discussion in the night, Millicent decided to have some fun with her adoring husband. "Oops, we're caught. Thought you had left for the yard, my love," knowing he would never leave without one of her delicious breakfasts. She shot him a flirtatious wink.

Bernard glanced across the warm sunny room and saw Bruce, who was now sitting on the window seat in the alcove observing a hummingbird at the suspended feeder. A bit flustered by what Millicent had said to her husband, he quickly explained his presence. "Hope you don't mind, sir...my dropping by."

"Not at all, I admire your dedication. I'll enjoy having your company today."

They both polished off an enormous breakfast, gave Millicent a peck on the cheek (Bruce asked permission first), and off they went. She radiated in the already bright kitchen. "A son, he is just like a son," she muttered aloud.

The five guests of the Enchanted Isle finished their delightful breakfast of fruits, homemade muffins, juice, and coffee. They had informed their hostess the previous night before retiring, that they simply could not keep eating such extravagant breakfasts. She had to promise them to keep it light.

"Okay, now we need to plan our spy venture. Stephanie, you leave at the normal time, while Barbara and I will take off shortly before you. We'll plant ourselves at different intervals and pick up the tail from one another." Claudia sounded like an old pro at this sort of thing.

Melanie had to ask, "You speak as though you've done this before?"

"Me, heavens no. But years of television must have ingrained it in me," she responded. "We'll all meet back here with our report. Where will you gals be?" Claudia asked Vivian and Melanie.

"Right here, of course," replied Vivian between chews of her muffin. "We wouldn't miss hearing the results of your investigation." None of them really took the situation seriously.

At the appointed time, the first two mopeds took off up the driveway. Then Stephanie performed her daily ritual. She noticed Claudia parked behind a bushy Oleander on the corner of Potter's Wheel Road. She started to giggle to herself at how ludicrous "the plan" was. Claudia was good at portraying her detective role. She stayed far enough behind for Stephanie to periodically catch a glimpse of her in her side mirrors. Now, Barb was a bit more obvious dashing in and out of the traffic and on more than one occasion causing a motorist to squeal on their brakes. All seemed uneventful until the ride back from the post office. Just as Stephanie rounded a bend, a red cycle sped out of a driveway right in front of Claudia It startled her, and she nearly lost her balance. As if she instantly transformed into Nancy Drew, herself, she became keenly alert and mentally took note of every detail of the driver she was now following. She committed his license plate number to memory.

When Stephanie signaled her turn into The Enchanted Isle, the incognito pursuer drove past the driveway and then stopped along side of the road, obviously watching Stephanie's every move. Claudia had to drive on past so as to not draw any attention. When far enough away, she did a U-turn, and pulled behind a parked car on the opposite side of the road. She noted that Stephanie's observer was writing briskly on a notepad and checking his watch for the time. Then continued writing.

"My God," she thought to herself. "This is reality. Stephanie *is* being followed. I wonder by whom?"

Several moments passed and so did the motorist. Claudia was grateful that he was looking in the other direction towards the water. He had caught her off guard when he swiftly started the bike and drove towards her. Engaging her cycle she went back to the house, Barb pulling in behind her.

"So, it's a fact, isn't it?" Barb questioned. "Claudia, Stephanie is being followed, and I bet I know who is behind it!"

"Save it until we get inside with her," Claudia answered while running across the driveway.

Once inside the beautiful Victorian, the five ladies regrouped on the porch to decipher Claudia and Barbara's findings. As Claudia recounted her observations of the stranger, a look of grave concern fell over Stephanie's face. She had been thinking of nothing else all morning and arrived at the conclusion that her husband had to be responsible. Her stomach filled with acid which left a sickening sensation. She all but knew her life was about to take a drastic change of course. How could she prepare herself to face it head on?

Chapter Fourteen

Sandra was frantic with frustration. For two days she had tried numerous times to reach Bruce. Her female intuition informed her that he was not interested, but being the daughter of a stubborn German, she was not about to give up on him...not just yet. It dawned on her that she may not have been looking in the right places to find her dream man. She had simply assumed that he and Melanie would have been together, so she haunted the private beach spots on the south shore in Warwick Parish, sure she would find them at Jobson's Cove. When Horseshoe Bay and Henry VIII's proved fruitless, she continued the search as far as Sommerset.

"Ah, Lombard's Shipbuilding! Why didn't I think of that before?" Without another moment of hesitation, she pointed her moped in the direction of the boat yard.

Bruce and Bernard were in the middle of discussing a plan to take Bernard's 55' cat down to an island in the Bahamas. Some specially ordered parts for a custom boat needed to be picked up. They both agreed this would be the ideal opportunity to sail together, and for Bruce to display his nautical skills and knowledge to Bernard. Normally, one of Lombard's other employees would make arrangements to procure the necessary parts, but Bernard was as giddy as a child at the prospect of sailing his beloved boat with Bruce.

The whine of the approaching engine caught their attention, as they looked to see who was driving towards them. "Oh, no," Bruce said aloud. "I am not in the mood for this woman right now. She has been hounding me for days to come and run her father's boat building business. She's offered to set me up here to be your competition!"

"I know," Bernard said in a low voice. "Sandra's attorneys contacted me with a handsome offer to buy me out. Naturally, I politely refused, but they keep pestering me with higher offers."

Bruce looked angry. He felt she had gone too far! He knew her ulterior motive behind the enticing job proposition and was painfully aware of the strangling strings that were attached to it. He resented her and her father's high priced legal staff harassing Bernard. He had grown close to this man of great wisdom over the last few days. Bruce knew only too well that the last thing Bernard wanted to do was to walk away permanently from his life long dream business.

Stiffening his back, he excused himself from the elder gentleman and walked towards Sandra's parked moped.

"Hey, big guy, I've been scouring this island trying to find you. The last I knew, you were quite ill."

Responding half heartedly, "Well, I was, but I've been with Bernard the last few days discussing a future business venture together. Time is running out before I will have to leave, and I want to have made up my mind as to my destiny."

"Excuse me, but have you forgotten or just discarded the proposal I made to you regarding your future?"

Looking solemnly into her wide eyes, Bruce realized he could never accept her grand gesture and proceeded to explain to her. Overwhelmed with the urgency to set the record straight and be honest with her, he told her how he viewed her proposition and the commitment she expected from him in return. The cost was just too great. Knowing that he was possibly killing the chance of a lifetime, he continued to put all his cards on the table by professing his love for Melanie. As he expressed his deep feelings for Melanie he said, "I'm in love with her and have been since I first met her. I don't want to hurt you Sandra. But, I'm hoping to spend the rest of my live with her. What you're offering me is a dream come true. You can't buy my affections, they belong to Melanie. I wouldn't be honest if I led you on for the sake of business when my desire is for a lasting relationship bound by matrimony, with Melanie."

Feeling anger and humilitaion Sandra's voice broken with tears, "you can't do this to me," she cried. Involuntarily step by step sheretreated until she found herself standing by her cycle. With a crushed look of defeat and without a word spoken, she numbly slid onto the bike, started the engine, and slowly drove off.

Stunned at her sullen behavior, Bruce gave a huge sigh of relief having expected much more of a reaction from Sandra. He felt as if a monstrous weight had been lifted from his shoulders. With a broad smile and spring in his step, he returned to his waiting partner-to-be. Somehow, Sandra had unknowingly supplied him with the answer he was searching for regarding his destiny. Whatever changes he had to make in his life, this was where he wanted it to be.

Chapter Fifteen

Arriving along with the weekend came Claudia's love. The gals all teased her unmercifully at breakfast. Claudia had never exhibited her anxieties before. She had always seemed in emotional check, so in control until that morning. The thoughts of sharing such a romantic island with her lover nearly drove her wild. She was surprised at her anticipation of such all-consuming excitement. Her thoughts were scattered, her speech incoherent, and her actions downright silly. The girls were thoroughly enjoying her antics but thought she should take herself to the airport in plenty of time for Derek's arrival. Just in case she got lost along the way.

Derek's presence in the terminal area dwarfed everyone around him, standing nearly seven feet in height. Claudia's petite 5'3" emphasized his immense stature. Dying to show him off to her comrades, and at the same time apprehensive because of their age difference, she hesitated for only a brief moment before she scurried him off in the direction of their waiting mopeds. At least, she had had her wits about her enough to make prior arrangements for a motorbike to be awaiting Derek's arrival on the island.

"First, we'll stop by The Enchanted Isle so you can meet my friends. Then we will take your bag over to Misty Cove to your cottage, and you can change. Oh, sweetheart, I can't tell you how pleased I am that you are here." She added in a soft, sexy voice, "With me."

"Claudia, you don't have to. It is written all over you. Actually, I've never seen you like this before. And, I must tell you I am thoroughly loving it. The time you have spent here has worked magic on you. You seem so full of life. So carefree. So uninhibited. So..."

"I know, my love. It has had that effect on all of us. It will on you. So, get ready. Oh, I am most anxious for you to meet our fairy godmother, Millicent. She's truly angelic. You'll see."

Claudia had totally misplaced her former dire concerns when introducing her statuesque companion to all those she adored. Even the looks of surprise on their faces did not appear to cause a reaction from her. She was so caught up in her joy, and it was evident to all she was truly in love. Not even Barb would dare do or say anything to spoil Claudia's limelight. Only after she and Derek departed for his cottage, did everyone express their thoughts on the obvious age difference between them. It was then Barb made a comment on how popular May-December relationships had become the *in thing*.

Stephanie, always the analytical one of the group, voiced her approval. "I have never seen our friend this happy in all the years I have known her. I wouldn't care if she was in love with the man in the moon, if he could have this affect on her. He's okay in my book. Please, don't anyone even bring up the subject to her. And if she does, just play it down. Be supportive. Knowing Claudia, she has probably been a wreck worrying about our acceptance of her younger man."

Melanie contributing, "Yes, I agree with Stephanie. For once, let's not air our opinions unless they are positive. We owe Rocky that much for the sake of friendship."

All were in agreement. They had made great strides in perfecting respect for the sacred values of their kinship. This would never have happened in their earlier years together. Claudia would have been picked clean in front of and behind her back. It would have made for such a juicy morsel. Perhaps, not all things associated with age were negative and detrimental.

The weekend proved to be a beautiful memory for all. It was one big continuous party with John hosting the events from the mornings long into the nights: sailing excursions, picnics, beach parties, jaunts into town, more sightseeing, pub stops for liquid refreshment, and singing. It was a special time that none of them would ever forget. The bonding that took place during those few precious days would accompany each of them for the rest of their lives. A quilting bee of piecing the memories together in their individual life's tapestry.

Vivian, Melanie, and Claudia glowed from the passion each was experiencing from the presence of their prince charmings. Barb's thoughts often drifted to her former husband and wished she were sharing all the merriment with him. If only things could be different. Stephanie, on occasion, would become consumed with genuine concern of her husband's motives for having her followed. Had he discovered her affair? What could she expect once she returned home. Would her marriage be over? Catching herself becoming morose, she departmentalized her thoughts, did a mini psychoanalysis and regained her composure. At least for the present, knowing in a few short days, all this would be a fond memory. A memory of fun, laughter, and companionship, that might have to get her through a discordant ordeal awaiting her in the States. How she longed for her secret man to be with her in this romantic isle of love.

It was a crystal clear morning and all five of the 40ish beguiling beauties were up with the sun, this was to be their last full day on the bejeweled island and they didn't want to wast a minute of it.

Their reservation for lunch was at 11:30. Arthur arrived on the dot of 11 with a fellow taxi driver. "I thought we could use Jeremy here to give the 6 of you a proper lift to the Princess. We could never have fit you all in my cab."

"Oh Arthur, you're a mind reader, for I was wondering how we were going to do that," sighed Millicent.

"Okay gals, pick a vehicle and let's be off! Lunch is waiting," Barb jubiliantly professed.

Melanie saddened by the reality that their time was growing short, the departure was rapidly approaching. As they entered the meticulously groomed grounds of the Princess Hotel, Viv uncharacteristically bellowed, "this is a glorious day, let's be thankful for it." The others shocked by her sudden tribute all started to giggle. Once inside, then led outside to the famed patio the waiters dressed in sparkling white jackets dutifully took their orders.

After their first round of wine coolers their moods rose from melancholy to humorous with each trying to out-do the others with the reminiscent events of the past two weeks.

Claudia was the first to speak. "Remember Babs causing the traffic jam at high noon trying to finagle a date with the bobbie in the cage?"

The group roared with laughter.

While Mel was chuckling, "I've got one! How about our sneaking up the staircase, trying ever so hard to be quiet, until Barb fluffed and we had all we could manage to ascend the stairs to our rooms without causing a huge ruckus.

"Oh let's not forget our beloved moments at Henry VIII's enjoying our wine spritzers," piped up Claudia.

"Dear Millicent, only you could forgive us for nearly destroying your beautiful kitchen the day we put together that delightful picnic to take to John's boat," Vivian choked back tears.

"I can still taste the lobster we engulfed at John's lobsterfest along with Millicent's incredible dessert," recalled Stephanie.

The day sped by with laughter and intermittent tears until their final happy hour trip to Henry VIII's. Millicent caught up in the nostalgic moments tearfully thanked the girls for all the endearing memories. "From the moment you all arrived, my life took on a new meaning, both Bernard and I think of you as our daughters, I don't know what I'll do when you leave.

In a chorus all five in unison cried out, "We'll be back!"

Chapter Sixteen

The pungent aromas rose up to engulf the second story of the majestic Victorian structure. Vivian's dining senses were the first to intercept the redolence wafting from the kitchen below. She would miss awakening to the delectable culinary delights each morning. Life would no longer be enriched with the fulfilling experiences she had enjoyed on the island once she returned to her sullen existence with Frank. Well, that was going to change. She had concluded that her marriage was over, and she was determined to terminate it. Her time with John had shown her just how much her life was missing. Even if a long term relationship did not materialize between them, she would be indebted to him for opening her eyes to the riches life had to offer. She knew she had been merely existing not experiencing.

"Hey, sleepyhead. What time did you creep in?" Vivian peeking her head into Melanie's room?

"Good morning," Melanie responded in a groggy voice. "Only moments before I heard Millicent milling around downstairs. She certainly got an early start this morning. How about you?"

"I beat you by five minutes. Claudia and I nearly scared each other to death as we both crept up the porch steps. We were trying to avoid the front lantern lights. Can you believe how we are behaving? Like adolescents with curfews. More than once I've reminded myself that I am an adult, but since arriving at The Enchanted Isle, I have not felt like one."

"I know what you mean. In a way, it is almost like having a second chance at childhood. Not many people are as fortunate as we are."

"John wanted to wake up with me in his arms, but I told him I was not ready for that yet. I'm still married to Frank."

"Speaking of that, what are your plans regarding your marriage?" Melanie asked while wiping her eyes.

Vivian sitting on the edge of the bed sighed. "I am going to end it.

Melanie, John has awakened the life in me that I had thought died a long time ago. He has spent endless hours talking to me, cuddling me, and comforting me. He has respected my feelings toward my commitment to matrimony. Not many men would have behaved in such a gentlemanly manner and not taken advantage of me. Especially, on the several occasions I was completely intoxicated and all over him. I tell you, my dear friend, I could fall head over heels in love what that man."

"Personally, I think you already have, Viv." A knock on the door as it opened startled the two friends.

"I thought I heard voices. The heavenly scents from downstairs woke me from a dream I was having about Lance," Barbara said as she made her way into the room. Her tousled hair and no makeup gave her an entirely different demeanor. She flopped down into the ivory painted rocking chair with stenciled pastel flowers etched on its arms. "I checked on Claudia, but she looks dead to the world. I guess she got in pretty late. I must say I enjoyed dancing with John's friend, the colonel, last night. Wish I had met him a week ago!"

Curious about Barb's dream of her former husband, Melanie had to ask, "So, what did you dream about Lance?"

In a somber voice she answered, "I dreamed he was cut from the team. That his career was over. He was washed up in baseball with nowhere to go. He looked like a homeless bum. He was calling to me, and I was sobbing and sobbing for him. The funny thing was I discovered tears on my cheeks when I awakened. It all seemed so real."

"Dreams can be so realistic," Vivian commented sympathetically. "I suppose we should get Claudia up soon. The guys are coming for breakfast, and we still have to pack. I've dreaded this day for two weeks!"

"You're not alone. I have found the man of my dreams, and now I have to leave him," Melanie's voice quivered. "I want to spend the rest of my life with him."

Rocking slowly, Barb asked, "So what are your plans, little one?"

"Well, we have set a date to meet in Rhode Island when he returns from here. Of course, right now we don't know when that will be. He and Bernard will depart for the Bahamas after we leave this afternoon. Once they return, Bruce plans to stay a month, and then he'll go back to

Rhode Island to sell his home, officially resign from his job, and move his things to Bermuda. That is if everything works out well for him at Bernard's. He's asked me to consider relocating to Bermuda, and I am definitely giving it serious consideration. I adore Millicent and Bernard. If they do go off sailing about the world, I would love to house-sit The Enchanted Isle."

"Count me in to help you," volunteered Vivian.

"I guess I'll just have to come visit you both, and what a place to visit! You won't charge me, will you, girls?" laughed Barb.

"Seriously, Vivian, if you do go through with your intentions to divorce Frank, you'll have to come back here so you can cultivate your relationship with John. He is a wonderful man, and I think he is perfect for you. They don't make them any finer than John Pendleton.

"I completely agree. Only, I'm aware of my vulnerability right now, and God knows, I don't want to be impulsive. Time will tell a great deal. John and I discussed my entire situation until nearly dawn. He said he would give me all the time I need to heal. He wants me to come to him when I'm truly ready."

Barb looking at Vivian with an uncharacteristic sincerity, "God has answered your prayers. He has blessed you with your soulmate, Viv. I truly envy you."

John, Bruce, and Derek all arrived within moments of each other that final morning. Millicent had invited them to join her guests for a farewell breakfast. She planned an elaborate menu for the entire group. She had warned the fellas to bring their appetites with them. The jubilant lady was up before dawn making the necessary preparations. Cautiously, she moved about the dining room meticulously setting the table with her special Royal Doulton china. Having everything perfect was imperative to her. The Baccarat crystal reflected the light from the prisms of the elegant chandelier. Trying desperately to keep her mind off the reason for the lump in her throat. Never in all her years as an innkeeper had she felt so emotional about any of her guests departure. There were a few occasions when she actually welcomed their leaving The Enchanted Isle, but they were rare. Millicent loved nearly everyone that graced their home. That was her nature.

The dining room buzzed with conversation and continuous compliments to their hostess. Millicent beamed with delight at how appreciative her guests were with her culinary talents. As their final moments were slipping by, each clung to every word that was spoken, as if it were sacred. Under all the uproarious spurts of laughter and the exaggerated courteous behavior executed by the occupants seated at the long oval table, there lay a dense sadness. Soon they would be dispersing in different directions, returning to their familiar worlds.

In spite of Millicent's objections, it was a consensus of opinion that a mass effort would be initiated to clean up the measurable mess of the grand feast. Never had dish duty been so comical. The antics resembled adolescents with the slapping of the dish towels on derrières and hilarious joke telling. Laughing hysterically, Barb snorted, "This is positively too much fun!"

Afterwards, a walk on the beach was in order. The gals insisted Millicent join them and escorted her arm in arm down the porch steps. The fellas did the same with Bernard. The sound of the surf, the gentle breezes with the smell of the fragrant lilies, and the sheer beauty surrounding them were their final memories to take with them of their paradise island. Valiantly trying to be light hearted, Melanie quipped, "It's a good thing we took you to lunch yesterday, Millicent, and not waited until today. There is no way we could have eaten again before our departure after the sumptuous meal you prepared for us." The others all groaned in agreement.

"That was a jolly lunch yesterday. I want to thank you again for spoiling me that way. It is not often I get out for a luncheon engagement. I thoroughly enjoyed myself. I had forgotten how elegant the Princess Hotel dining room is, and the service...impeccable!" She quickly wiped a tiny tear off her rosy cheek. "I shall never forget it, or forget all of you. You've become so dear to me."

The time of departure had tearfully arrived for them all. This moment they had dreaded from almost the beginning of their marvelous adventure. The tears started sporadically at breakfast and continued throughout the afternoon. Millicent's apron pockets were bulging with tear soaked lace handkerchiefs. As the suitcases lined the entry hall, the inevitable would soon be taking place.

Plans for another reunion were being frantically made in haste for the following year. The Fabulous Five insisted Millicent register them in her booking ledger for the same time the next year. They all took a sworn oath that under no circumstances would any of them cancel out. No matter what!

The only member of the group that would not be accompanying them to the airport was Bruce. He and Bernard were setting sail for the Abacos Islands in the Bahamas. Bruce had taken a leave of absence from his job in order to work with Bernard and learn about his business. This was his dream coming true. He was elated! This was the way he wanted to live his life.

The familiar sound of Arthur's taxi could be heard as he descended the crushed stone driveway. Every other time his arrival was welcomed as he escorted them often on their evening outings, but this time would be different. The mood was somber. No gaiety, no laughter. He, too, shared in the sullenness. He hated to see his fun loving "fares" bid him farewell. Not only had it been a lucrative experience for him but one of his most memorable.

As Arthur loaded the taxi down and snugly secured all the luggage, the good-byes had commenced. As well as the recurring tears. Vivian promised to keep John advised of her status and return for another visit. Bruce and Melanie had been inseparable, but the time had come. It was a bittersweet parting. He dreaded seeing her go, but was most anxious to start his voyage with Bernard to the Bahamas. He and Melanie would reunite in Rhode Island in a month.

Claudia and Derek took the front seat, and the rest squeezed into the back, once they completed their thank you's, hugs, and promises to keep in touch with Millicent and Bernard. They "good-byed" for what seemed an eternity. Finally, the overloaded cab weebled and wobbled as it ascended the drive, just as it had on its original descent. Enroute to the airport, Authur commented about the article on the sports page of the paper that morning to Barb.

"Ms. Barbara, what do you think that former ballplayer husband of yours will do now that he's been released. Does that mean his career is over?"

Barb stunned by Arthur's remark, "I didn't see the paper today," tears running down her cheeks. Pulling the copy from his visor, he handed it back to her. "Oh my God! It happened just as I dreamed! What will he do now?" Between her sobs, she expressed how grateful she was that this situation waited to arise until the end of her reunion encounter. The ride to the airport was quiet as each reminisced the cherished memories of the past two weeks.

It was a traumatic day of farewells as the Fab Five kissed and hugged one another and boarded their respective flights, promising to honor their pledges to return the following year.

Back at the marina, Bruce and Bernard made the final preparations for their departure. The food for the voyage and the endless inventory of supplies were properly stowed. Each had a thorough checklist which he diligently inspected.

Millicent arrived breathlessly at the dock with an armload of her sweetheart's fresh baked favorites.

"Oh my, Bruce. Millie, bless her heart, has bestowed upon us another basket full of goods to be stored."

Upon smelling the warm shortbread cookies, soda bread, and scones, Bruce answered, "Not a problem, Captain. We can always find room for such palatable pleasures as these," he winked at Millicent.

"I wish I could be accompanying you two. The house will seem so quiet with the girls gone and you, my love," she said looking at Bernard.

"What about the new guests? They'll keep you busy. You certainly won't be alone."

"True. True. But, it just won't be the same," she retorted while wiping away a tear.

Bernard secured the dinghy on the aft deck while Bruce stowed the fenders and readied the lines.

"Well, my dearest, this is it. Unless you plan to sail with us, you had better disembark *The Enchantress*, for we are about to set the sails."

Kissing both men, she reluctantly made her way up the gangplank. She stood on the dock and waved them farewell until she could no longer make out the silhouette of the vessel.

Chapter Seventeen

Amongst the majestic mountains of Colorado, Melanie hurried home from the photography shop where she had just picked up the developed photos from her Bermudian trip. She made herself a cup of English tea and settled into her favorite wing back chair. A gentle breeze flowed through the open bay window. As she paused to linger over a picture of her and Bruce on John's yacht, *Mistress*, she closed her eyes and reflected back to that moment. Engulfed in its tenderness, the breezes touched her skin as if kisses from afar. Lost in her memories, she transcended back to the beautiful isle of Bermuda. Traveling faster than the speed of light, Melanie was catapulted from the past back to the present by the acknowledgment of her subconscious to the alarming words emitting from the television in the next room.

"Around the world in 30 minutes, this is Headline News. Another hurricane with sustained winds in excess of 150 m.p.h. continues to press towards the Florida coast and the Bahamas..."

The ringing of the phone brought Millicent running in from the garden, where she had been securing protective burlap wrappings over her plants. In hopes of saving them from the possible ravages of the impending storm. She was breathless and feeling anxiety from waiting for word from Bernard and Bruce. Radio contact with them had been lost for nearly 48 hours.

"Millicent. This is Melanie. Are they all right?"

"Luv, I honestly don't know," Millicent's voice quivered. "I thought you might be them calling. I've had no contact for two days now. I'm sick with worry."

"Have you contacted the Coast Guard?"

"Yes. Yes, of course. But, they have not spotted them. According to their last known position, they were expected to arrive in Marsh Harbor yesterday morning. The search is being hampered by the hurricane's high winds and treacherous seas. Bernard is a seasoned sailor, but even he is no match for the wrath of such a vicious storm." Both women broke into tears and sobbed into the open phone line.

That evening's news had picked up on the story of the missing two-some. Catching the tail end of the broadcast came the chilling words, "The Bermuda Triangle has mysteriously claimed numerous victims over the decades. Has the rapture of the deep been enchanted by the vessel *The Enchantress?*"

The following months were nothing short of pure agony for the devastated Melanie. The loss of Bruce was more than she could endure by herself. She immediately joined Millicent, but as time passed, she knew the inevitable outcome. Lost at sea. At first, she refused to leave the tiny isle for fear she would miss the return of her beloved. But when her daily inquiries to the Coast Guard regarding their search efforts were becoming an apparent annoyance to the uniformed dispatcher and the constant flood of memories that enveloped her every thought were becoming obsessive, she knew it was time to leave. There were just too many memories for her there. She could not get past them. She could never begin the healing process when constantly confronted with what had been and what was never to be.

As fragile as the delicate matron of The Enchanted Isle Cottage appeared on the exterior, Millicent's petite stature was a rock of strength for the bereaved Melanie. Her faith and sheer stubbornness in the belief that her beloved Bernie would never leave her life in such a manner was unwaverable. On only two occasions since the disappearance of *The Enchantress* had Melanie observed the older woman crying uncontrollably. She shielded her emotions as though embarrassed to reveal them. Perhaps, it was her British upbringing.

Nearly two months had passed since the incident. Millicent had canceled all the reservations again for the next month. She could not bring herself to exude a false air of cheerfulness, when her heart ached so. To emulate the role of a gracious hostess to her arriving guests was more than she could bear. The innkeeper in her knew that her patrons deserved the full treatment as honored house guests at The Enchanted Isle Cottage, and nothing less would be good enough. As the days beleaguered by, the impeccably groomed Millicent became increasingly aware that she had to do something about her life As if her adored one had intercepted her thoughts, she was convinced he had contacted her consciousness.

Melanie feeling the effects of a night robbed of sleep because of her recurring frantic thoughts of the perils that she could only assume now had been the fate of the occupants of *The Enchantress*, she noticed Millicent's upbeat composure. She was about to inquire, but her attempt was interrupted.

"My, it is an unusually beautiful morning, isn't it, my dear?" With almost a light headedness, she conveyed to Melanie what had transpired the previous night while pouring them both a cup of her Twining's tea at breakfast. "Melanie, my Bernie spoke to me in the night in a dream. His words were articulate and precise." As she continued, her soft blue eyes welled up with tears. One escaped down her porcelain cheek causing her faint pink blush to streak. "He said that you and I must return to our lives until he and Bruce sail back into Hamilton Harbor."

Melanie's eyes grew larger and stared intensely at the aristocratic woman sitting across from her in the sunny breakfast nook. "Oh, Millicent. Do you really believe they are alive? Do you know in your heart our loves will come back to us?" she pleaded. Tears now filling her large, questioning eyes.

Sensing the desperation in her warbled voice, Millicent consoled the waif-like girl, who over the past several months had become like a daughter to her.

"I do believe with all my heart that both of us will be reunited with our life's partners. And you, lovey, can take that to the Barclay Bank, my dear!"

Hearing the strong conviction of Millicent's words rekindled her faltering spirit. She stood up from the table, drew in a long deep breath, and announced she would be making plans for her immediate departure. Now, this was not at all the reaction that Millicent expected. They had grown close and bonded in their tragedy. They were each other's support system throughout this ordeal.

"Gracious, honey, what on earth do you mean you are leaving?"

Millicent's astonishment mirrored all over her face.

"It's time, Millicent." She hesitated momentarily and then continued, "I must get back to my writing. Besides, I've had a new book swirling about in my head for weeks. I dream it in the night and envision the words in the day. They are crying to be put down on paper and you, precious friend, just released my imprisonment here to go do it. Oh..." struggling to redeem herself. "Forgive me, I certainly didn't mean that the way it sounded. It has been so difficult for me," the words still awkwardly spilling out of the perfectly pastel lipstick mouth. "The waiting intertwined with all the beautiful memories of the moments Bruce and I shared are so painful. I truly need to go away from here and write my novel, 'Lost Love.' It will be therapeutic for me." The radiant blue of her eyes now misty from the moisture that clouded them. "Millicent, you saying Bernard told you in a dream for us to get on with our lives is like God speaking to us through your sweetheart. I completely trust your visions, your instincts, and most of all your intrepid faith. If you know our angels will return to us, then I know it, too!"

Melanie reached across the floral inlaid table and grasped her dear companion's soft slender hands. "Bernard is right. Look at it this way. God wants us to go on living. You are an innkeeper, and I am a writer. We must continue to act out our roles until that special day arrives. Besides, it will help to pass the time more quickly for the both of us. For the first time in months, I feel alive again. I feel filled with hope for the future. No more mooning around. And one more good thing has come from our discussion here this morning..."

Millicent quizzically looked at Melanie's new aura of sparkle. "Don't keep me in suspense, love. What, what?"

Melanie half giggling, "That Coast Guard dispatcher will be more than relieved not to be dodging my daily phone calls." Both ladies howled, knowing that their laughter was more of an enormous release of pent-up emotions. The two spent the rest of the day busily making the necessary arrangements to return to the lives they had led before the tragic interruption blew them off course. Millicent informed the Chamber of Commerce that she would be open for business the following weekend. Melanie called the local travel agency and booked herself on a flight the next day home to Colorado.

That evening she divulged her departure plans to a weary Millicent as they shared their traditional cup of nightly tea on the verandah.

"Millicent, you look terribly tired tonight. Are you not feeling well?"

"No, no, my dear. It is just that my mind is filled to the brim with so many thoughts of things to be done before I reopen the inn in a few days. Everything must be perfect, you know, for my guests.'

"Yes, I do know. That is why there is no other enchanted place in the world like this. I do so love it here. It breaks my heart to leave, but I must in order to write this particular book. I have to excommunicate myself from everything. It's the only way I can write... uninterrupted."

Sipping her tea in her own eloquent fashion, Millicent sighed. "I am going to miss you, lovey. You are like a daughter to me. I think of you as that, you know."

Sadly, Melanie rose to her feet, walked over to the stately woman's needlepoint cushioned chair and kissed her on the forehead. Spoken in barely a whisper, "I know. Good night, Millicent." She knew if she stayed a moment longer she would dissolve into tears, and she and her eyes were tired of crying. Besides she had wanted to call Babs, Claudia, Vivian, and Stephanie and tell them of her plans to return home. She talked to them weekly to bring them up-to-date on the "no news" of the missing men.

But, there were plenty of tears as both she and the gracious matron of the manor hugged good-bye the following day. It was one of the saddest days of Melanie's life. Millicent promised with her ivory hand on her Bible to impress the significance of her heartfelt words to Melanie, that she would call the instant she heard anything regarding Bernard and Bruce.

Once home, it took several days for Melanie to acclimate herself again amongst her familiar surroundings. Her life had changed so much since she had originally left for a ten day reunion with her dear old friends over two months earlier. Finally, ball-point in hand and a new legal pad, she was ready to pen her latest novel, "Lost Love."

The weeks turned into months, and the fall had mysteriously faded into winter. At first, she was calling Millicent constantly, but the calls began to taper off to less frequently. She knew Millicent would call with any news. Though, it was calming just to hear her lovely British accent. Recently, she detected a strain in their conversations. *The Enchantress* should have been recovered by now. The disturbing and eerie questions haunted them both as to whether the Bermuda Triangle had claimed their beloveds. Why hadn't there been any sightings of the boat? They each sensed the other's failing faith as to whether they would all be reunited again.

As the holidays approached, Melanie became despondent and slipped into a state of depression. She could no longer field the well meaning calls from her friends and family. Her sanity was becoming a source of concern to her. First, it meant leaving the beautiful but saddened Bermudian island, now she needed to get away again, though, this time to where no one could call and continuously remind her of how her life stopped the summer before. As hard as she tried, she could not bring herself to finish "Lost Love." How could she? The ending was still waiting to be finished. But now, there was the continual pressure from her agent. A publisher was demanding the final chapter before signing a lucrative book contract. A three novel deal...the dream of all writers. Finally, she had made it! Financial security, at least for awhile. A long while if she was not foolish and invested wisely. Melanie was unusually concerned about becoming a bag lady in her senior years. She had witnessed first hand from her own childhood how quickly her parents fell from the upper middle class bracket to bankruptcy within a year's time. She had to complete "Lost Love." The clock was ticking, and the publisher's impatience with her was escalating weekly as the deadline approached. Her agent phoned twice a day to see if his weary client had jotted down even one sentence on her dog eared legal pad.

Knowing what she must do, Melanie picked up the porcelain ivory French phone to call her travel agency and made a reservation on a flight the following day to Seattle, Washington. From there she had the agent reserve a rental car for the drive to her final destination... Orcas Island. A tiny secluded island in the chain of the San Juans only accessible by ferry. She was familiar with the island's circa 1906 hotel, a charming Victorian structure crisply painted in white with red trim. Surrounded by beautifully maintained old fashioned gardens with tall hollyhocks, hydrangeas displaying showy clusters of white, blue, and pink flowers, assorted colors of snapdragons, petunias, and breathtaking roses dripping from pristine white arched trellises leading into and out of the winding garden paths. The view was to die for! The inn nestled on a hill high above the picturesque harbor beckoned the ferry passengers in need of food and drink, as it was the first stop off the boat. The hotel also housed a jolly tavern frequented by guests and locals as well. There were only twelve guest rooms each appropriately appointed with an assortment of antiques. Not all expensive but decorative and tasteful.

At one time in its history, story has it, that the structure and its gardens had fallen into disrepair. For years it sat vacant, and then a woman investor fell in love with it, poured a million dollars into a redeeming facelift, and reopened it with a flair that proved successful.

As Melanie unpacked her bags, she knew she would be able to find her ending and complete her work enclaved in the warmth and charm of the stately hotel. It was off season, and no doubt there would only be a handful of guests celebrating the holiday season. And, they wouldn't stay beyond New Year's. The weather would be chilling to the bone accompanied by gray days. The manager, Mr. Haines, had politely informed his guest that after the first of the year, they would be doing the annual maintenance on the hotel. It was their slowest time of the year, and the only opportunity to get everything revamped and repaired for the next season. Of course, they would give her a reduced rate to offset any inconvenience she may endure during her extended stay.

The hour ferry ride had caused the seasick prone passenger to have a queasy stomach. The docking had been rougher too than any experienced in past visits due to the turbulent December seas. The hotel sat majestically high on the hill overlooking the dock. Melanie felt as though an old acquaintance was welcoming her home. She was so relieved that she responded that way. Since as of late, she could not count or predict her emotional state. Bruce, having touched and departed her life so abruptly, left an indelible scar. All that consumed her thoughts was what could have been. When she saw a family together, she envisioned Bruce and her with their two children. Or a couple admiring a diamond ring in a jewelry store, that could, no should have been them! Everything made her angry these days. She could not eat in a restaurant without seeing a romantic twosome staring dreamily into one another's eyes and feel the intensity of her loss. She swore to herself if there were any romantic couples staying at the hotel, she would have her meals in her room.

Christmas Eve arrived with all of the tradition that it rightly deserves. The inn was gloriously decorated with draping garlands garnished with red velvet bows and tiny white lights intricately woven throughout their fragrant branches. The owner had a magnificent collection of Victorian Santa Clauses, some quite exquisitely displayed throughout the parlor and entry hall. Even the many sconces in the elaborate velvet wallpapered dining room were decorated. The glow from the fireplaces in the living and dining rooms with their mantels heavily laden with evergreens and pine cones and candles exuded the warmth of the Christmas spirit. Oh, how she wanted to share this with Bruce.

The locals and guests all gathered for a festive evening of caroling. It was a scene from a Currier and Ives print, but somehow it was too painful for Melanie to endure any longer. Under different circumstances, she would have chimed right in and stayed until the last carol was sung. But, not this year. After struggling through the delectable ham dinner, dessert, coffee, and Christmas punch around the player piano in the parlor, the emotionally drained writer excused herself blaming a migraine headache as the culprit. Returning to her burgundy and ecru striped room, she threw herself upon the velveteen bedspread and cried for what seemed like hours.

Christmas morning was no better. Unable to face all the happy faces downstairs and the greetings of cheer, Melanie ordered her breakfast to be delivered to her room. She bathed, put on her make up, and did her hair into a chignon, like her mother had always done for special occasions when she was a child. Dressing in her traditional claret colored velvet robe with ivory lace collar and cuffs accented with tiny pearl buttons down the front, this part of her Christmas she refused to deny herself. She had worn that robe on Christmas morning for the past ten years. Afterwards, it would be carefully placed back in the tissue wrapping and put away until the following December 25th. She had seen the garment displayed on a mannequin in a posh New York department store while holiday shopping during a visit to her cousin's. Knowing instantly she had to have it, regardless of cost. The price was so ridiculous that in order to justify its expense, Melanie took an oath witnessed by her sister-like cousin, Susan, that she would wear it every Christmas until it fell apart. Not wanting that to happen, she only wore it the one morning a year.

The dreary weather did not seem to dampen the spirits that wafted up through the old worn hardwood floors from downstairs. Everyone was thoroughly enjoying the holiday morning. By afternoon though, a quietness bestowed itself upon the inn. Perhaps, some were still at church services, while others napped or took a walk. But, the guest in room twelve hardly noticed, for she had been busily writing since her breakfast tray was removed by the nice bellhop. The words had started flowing, and she could not write fast enough. The hours passed, and she wrote furiously. It was midnight that Christmas evening when the clock struck its final bong, and she dropped her pen upon the small antique writing desk where she had been seated for all those hours.

It was finished! How apropos, she thought, looking at the time. What a Christmas present this will be to her agent and publisher, not to mention to herself. After all, she realized it was her only Christmas gift. Keenly aware that it was divine intervention that took over her spirit those preceding hours. When she first started writing years before, she struck an agreement with the Holy Spirit to co-author all her writings. Sometimes she felt more moved than others. This was one of those times. Walking over to the lavish mahogany four poster bed piled high with assorted satin pillows, she knelt beside it to offer a prayer of thanksgiving, for not only supplying the final chapter's words but also for keeping her company throughout this special day when loneliness could have weighed heavily on her aching heart.

A pang of hunger nagged at her insides, but too tired to appease it, Melanie prepared herself for bed. Gently, she hung her beautiful robe on the satin and lace trimmed hanger, that she had brought especially for it. Never before had she worn it for so many hours. It always made her a little sad to put it away for another year, for she loved the elegant way it made her feel. The luxurious velvet caressed her skin. She loved the look of the old lace and the hue of the pearl buttons. But, Melanie was adamant about sticking to her self imposed rule not to wear it other than on the morning of December 25th. She secretly hoped it would last her her lifetime, if that would not be asking too much from it. If she continued to meticulously care for it, it could possible outlast her! "Oh, what a thought," she muttered. Hearing her voice made her realize she had barely spoken all day, with the exception of a *"thank you and Merry Christmas"* to the bellman who had removed her tray earlier that morning. Continuing to talk out loud, "I must will this robe to someone very special who would appreciate and carry on my tradition." Too weary to decide whom she should bequest her treasure to, the tired young woman tucked herself under the layers of sheeting, blankets, and comforter. She muttered softly, "Perhaps, my niece Jenelle." It was a matter that could wait but notifying her agent could not. She was most anxious to call him with the good news. If it had not been so late, she would have right then. "First thing in the morning." With that very last thought, she drifted off into the deepest and most comforting sleep she had experienced since her first nights at The Enchanted Isle Cottage, so long ago.

Her agent was more than delighted with Melanie's news. He was ecstatic...gleeful. When she gave him a brief synopsis of the final chapter and read him the last three pages, he became more demonstrative than she knew him to be capable of being. He kept reassuring her over and over she had a bestseller.

It seemed that his instincts were right on target, for the publisher shared his sentiments. He was moving up the press date for it to go into printing. He wanted it out ASAP. Also, his Hollywood director pal was interested in it for a screenplay and wanted Melanie to fly in to meet him to discuss a movie deal. Hanging up the phone, Melanie could not believe all that had transpired in the week since she had sent the manuscript to her agent. He was definitely earning his commission, she thought with a wide smile on her face. She had not felt this good in so long, deciding to stay on at the small hotel and recuperate from her months of anguish. The rate was dirt cheap, and she was the only guest since New Year's. It gave her the sacred opportunity to get back in touch with herself. She needed to reevaluate her life and get on with it. Her mourning over the loss of Bruce almost ruined her. But, somehow writing "Lost Love" had been like being in therapy for her. Now she was enjoying her incognito life. No phone calls, no talking to friends about the past, no ties to the past. She had even stopped calling Millicent. She had to let go of everything and everyone that reminded her of it. At least, for awhile. Perhaps a year...or more. Until she felt she could discuss it again without all the pain. Time had a way of healing, and she knew it would take a lot of it to heal her broken heart.

So, the next months were to be the busiest and most productive of Melanie's life. Her publisher's sense of urgency paid off handsomely. When "Lost Love" hit the marketplace, sales took off. Steve, her agent, had arranged for her to go on a ten city book tour to promote the hot novel to the public. They loved it and her! Hollywood had climbed on the "Lost Love" bandwagon, too. Zeroing in on the fact that the director friend of the publisher seemed to have taken more of an interest in her than just her literary talent, she seized the opportunity to advance her own desires by finagling him to let her work on the writing of the screenplay with the hired gun they already had on the job. At first, he wasn't pleased with trying to co-author *his* screenplay with a rookie, until he was introduced to the stunning author. In the span of sixty seconds, he did a complete turn-around. All the negativity he had spewed to the director only hours earlier, somehow dissipated when he locked into Melanie's metallic blue eyes where he lost himself. Her blonde hair casually fell off her tan shoulders, highlighting her bronze skin... thanks to the tanning salon she now frequented. Thinking to himself, "God, what a knockout. Not like any of the authors I've had to deal with over the years." Remembering them to be usually heavy with masculine features, an unattractive scent, and bossy as hell. His policy was to have as little to do with them as possible, letting their agents do the negotiations with him. But, every so often, someone like Melanie came along who insisted upon having hands on her own project...her baby, so to speak. Just like Amy Tan, when her Joy Luck Club was made into a movie.

Temporarily setting up residence in California and working round the clock with Ray on the screenplay took up every moment of Melanie's existence. She had completely dropped everyone from her life except the director Bill, her agent, publisher, and Ray. The launching of "Lost Love" consumed her entire being. When she wasn't flying off to do book signings, she was racing to the studio to supervise the production, as she was now a consultant. Neither Bill nor Ray wanted to let her escape from their lives. They had become a trio over the months of working together. Since Melanie knew no one in the Hollywood circuit and Bill and Ray were both bachelors, they were more than delighted to escort her about town. In the beginning, there was a definite rivalry between them for Melanie's affections, until the three of them got totally wasted one night at The Hard Rock Cafe.

"Look, guys, I need to clue you in on something. I am not, I repeat *not* looking for love. Only friendship at this point in my life."

It was only then under the influence of alcohol, that she revealed that "Lost Love" was a true story based on her life. That Bruce was truly her "Lost Love", that her heart ached for him. She envisioned his return to her life and would remain faithful to that dream. From that point on, Bill and Ray assumed new roles...as protectors. Anyone trying to put the moves on *their* Melanie would have to answer to them.

Things seemed to never slow down for her anymore. From time to time in a fleeting moment, reality confronted her as swiftly as a crashing wave slamming onto the awaiting grains of sand. Bruce was not a figment of her imagination, as she had to remind herself from time to time. She had not invented him as a fictional character in one of her manuscripts. He had been a real live person. Though, somehow through the severing of her past, he no longer existed for her as a memory but rather as a fantasy. A psychologist would certainly refer to this irrational behavior as a something-or-other syndrome. The conscious mind protecting itself from the painful reality that he was dead. His presence in her life was ever so brief but all consuming. Thoughts of togetherness for eternity had penetrated her total being, knowing she had at long last found her soul mate. But as briskly as he swept into her world, he was taken from it. The pain was so deep within her, she knew it would be a constant companion for the rest of her days. When asked, as she often was, if the hero of "Lost Love" was based on a real man, she would just pleasantly smile with a twinkle in her eye but never utter a verbal remark. She knew if a discussion commenced, she would totally fall apart and regress back into her pain. It was easier and healthier to pretend.

Finale

The weather had slightly improved since landing at the small airport in Burlington, Vermont. It was almost Christmas, and within the week, the weary author would be reunited with her family. As this was to be the final stop for the book signing tour, she was more than ready to put down the pen and start celebrating with her loved ones. The Thatcher Inn had dispatched a van to pick up the arriving guest. Melanie made herself comfortable while she enjoyed viewing the snow covered landscape and the hilly terrain dotted with the quaint farmhouses decorated for Christmas. It all looked so festive and flooded the chilled passenger with anticipation for the holidays. This picturesque spot held a special memory for Melanie, since she had spent several wonderful Christmases there as a child with her aunt and uncle and favorite cousin. Susan, now a mother of four, her husband, Bob, and their entourage were planning on joining Melanie Christmas Eve and staying until New Year's day, enjoying an old fashioned reunion together. Living in Pennsylvania, they planned to drive, taking in the pictorial scenes of winter along the way to the infamous maple syrup state. Melanie's sister, Laura, and her family were flying from Colorado. Her son, an Air Force pilot living overseas, made arrangements to take leave and join the family gathering. Her feelings of guilt for ignoring everyone in her personal life for so long resurfaced. On New Year's day, she would call Babs, Claudia, Stephanie, Vivian, and Millicent to wish them a happy new year and share with them all that had transpired in her life since they last communicated over a year ago. Now, at last, she was ready. She could face them and not disintegrate into a fragile sea of tears. Writing the book helped in the healing process, and time played a hand in her rehabilitation. Now, anxious to reveal her publishing success and her pen name, who knew, perhaps one of her cohorts may have read "Lost Love."

The crowds of shoppers were impressive as they waited somewhat patiently for a personally signed copy of Melanie's novel. Commenting to a well dressed older woman, "I'm afraid my hand is about to fall off." Receiving no sympathy from the awaiting consumer, as the lady made sure she shuffled her copy of "Lost Love" under Melanie's nose. It was obvious she wasn't about to leave without the autograph she had waited nearly an hour in line to receive. Her throbbing middle finger had an indentation as deep as the Grand Canyon, or so it felt from the pen she held too tightly. A bad habit she must break, she mused to herself. In a half hour, it would be over.

Finishing up on the 22nd allowed her some time to shop for gifts and rest before her relatives were to arrive at the inn. Feeling the holiday spirit, she decided to go downstairs and join the lively group in the knotty pine lounge with its massive rock fireplace glowing from the logs and the heavy scent of pine cones burning. Dressed in a forest green velour jumpsuit and a matching headband, she sauntered up to the cozy bar and seated herself next to a jolly living replica of Santa Claus.

"Excuse me, I'll have what St. Nick here is having," she addressed the bartender, who was busily restocking some beer bottles. The white haired patron next to her laughed a hearty chuckle and then offered some of his Christmas cheer.

"A specialty of the house, madam. A fine eggnog, but in need of a bit more rum and another dash of nutmeg."

The bartender still arranging the bottles in the bar refrigerator retorted, "Gus, you've been saying that for the last two hours. If I put anymore rum in that eggnog, you'll be D.U.I. driving that sleigh, and you know how Rudolph and the others feel about that. Besides, you've got a big night coming up."

Everyone roared with laughter. And, the funny thing was, it almost deemed believable. He certainly seemed the part.

Catching her own breather, Melanie had to ask, "I bet you are a department store Santa. Am I correct?"

"Ah, yep, missy. And, I am proud of it, too! Been Terwilliger's Department store Santa Claus for 32 years now. Look forward to it every year. My Mrs. was Mrs. Claus until she passed on five years ago, bless her soul."

Melanie noticed his rotund belly shook when he laughed, and his misty blue-gray eyes definitely twinkled when he looked straight at you. If his scrawny white beard had been fuller, she would have bet all she had, he was the real mccoy.

Apologizing for not waiting on her sooner, the barkeep turned around to face his patron, and his mouth dropped wide open. "Melanie! My God, is it really you?"

Stunned momentarily, she responded, "Buzz!" She stood on the rung of the stool to try to hug him over the copper inlaid bar. He raced around the end of the structure and grabbed her intently. They hadn't seen each other since their ten-year class reunion.

"God, lady, you look gorgeous as ever," as he stood back admiringly.

"Well, sir, you look terrific yourself," though she noticed he had less hair on top than when she last saw him, but that was years ago. For the next 45 minutes or so they reminisced , and all who were in the lounge seemed intensely interested in what they had to say to each other. Melanie was beginning to feel the fatigue of her day and the effects of the eggnog. She finally excused herself promising to return the next evening to keep Buzz company as he tended bar. Little did she know the impact the following night would have on her life.

At 7 o'clock sharp, feeling refreshed from a relaxing day of self pampering and a fun shopping spree, the sophisticated look Melanie selected included a winter white angora sweater with pearl droplets, matching tailored slacks, exquisite leather boots, pearl earrings, and her long blonde locks pulled back in a stunning barrette. She strolled into the festively decorated room for her pre-arranged rendezvous with Buzz. He was not there, but the inn's manager explained Buzz was down in the wine cellar retrieving several specially requested selections for diners in the adjacent dining room. He politely offered a glass of wine "on the house," which she cordially accepted. While awaiting the return of her friend, she glanced around the premises admiring the lovely decorations. A darling stuffed elf sat upon the antique cash register. Obviously handmade from the fine detail of his face. Vermonters were expert craft makers, and for many it was their livelihood. Just to the right of the register was a 5x7 framed photo. A sprig of evergreen from the garland hanging above had fallen over the corner of it, but not enough to cover the words, *Bernard's...Boat Builders of Bermuda.* Melanie's eyes froze upon the images that stood under the sprawling sign. Buzz standing in the middle had his arms around two men's shoulders. Blinking once, then again Melanie, as if in a trance, rose from the barstool and slowly walked around until she stood directly in front of the picture, never taking her eyes off it. There, before her was a picture of Bruce, Buzz, and Bernard. She could *not* believe her eyes!

"Pardon me, Miss, but only employees are allowed behind the bar." Startled by the voice, Melanie jumped and speechless she stared at Buzz.

"Hey, I didn't mean to frighten you," he softened his tone realizing that that was exactly what he had managed to do. Continuing to speak to the motionless beauty so smartly attired, "Melanie, you look as though you've seen a ghost."

Trying desperately to engage her tongue, it seemed to be an eternity before any words came out of her parched mouth. Stammering at first and not terribly coherent, Buzz became concerned as he tried to understand his old school chum. Garbled but audible, Melanie kept repeating the word "when" over and over.

"Do you mean when was that picture taken?" Appearing relieved to make communication, she shook her head positively.

"Last month..."

"Last month!!! But, that's impossible!!" Melanie's shriek startled everyone in the room. Buzz could see that something was terribly wrong. He swiftly walked around the bar and put his hands on his friend's shaking shoulders. Staring into her confused eyes, he started again softly.

"Last month while I was on vacation in Bermuda, I met the younger guy at a pub one night. I happened to overhear his conversation with another fella, that they were looking for another crew member to sail his catamaran to the Newport Boat Show in Annapolis, Maryland. It was his own design, and you should have heard him. Like a kid at Christmas."

Melanie still in shock, "Yes, *I* should have heard him! Better yet, been with him! I can't understand..."

"Excuse me, sir, but is it possible to get some service? I've been waiting for some time now, and my date and I are craving two of your house specialties...'The Thatcher Thog.'" Not missing a beat, Buzz jumped into action concocting the coffee and liqueurs topped off with nutmeg, whipped cream, and a cinnamon stick. Meanwhile, Melanie refused to bend for a moment and badgered him with so many questions that he finally yelled, "*STOP!* I can't possibly answer all your questions in ten seconds. Besides, you're not listening. You are too busy yakking. What is it about the guy in the picture anyway?"

"Barely taking the time to catch a breathe, she rattled on trying to fill Buzz in on the last fourteen months of her life.

In between filling drink orders, he listened attentively to her. Then, he relayed every moment he had spent with her beloved Bruce. Apparently, Bruce had given him a blow by blow reenactment of his harrowing experience with Bernard. Noticing Melanie appeared to be in a trance, he tried to pull her back into the conversation. Once she had digested all that her high school friend had just shared with her, she pole-vaulted off the stool to the nearest phone. Her fingers fumbled as her brain stumbled with the recall of Millicent's phone number. It had been such a long time.

Waiting for the connection to go through seemed like an eternity to her. Finally hearing the ringing of the phone until a voice interrupted, "Good evening The Enchanted Isle Cottage."

Breathlessly Melanie squealed, "Millicent! Millicent, is that you??" Though, she knew it was from her voice.

"Yes, yes this is Millicent. To whom am..."

"It's me, Melanie. Oh Millicent is it true? Are they alive??"

In a very shaken response, "Oh, my Lord! Melanie, my dear, where are you? Where have you been? We've called everyone who ever knew you, well, those who we could reach. We have been looking for you for months! Yes, Yes, my dear, Bernie and Bruce are alive and very well now. Oh my, Bruce will be exuberant to learn you are alive...and well, I take it?" she asked with a note of concern.

"Oh yes, I'm fine." Clearing her throat from all the welled up emotion, "It's a long story, but I've been incognito for the past year. I couldn't stand the pain of losing Bruce, and I had to finish my novel, and...oh, who cares!? I just want to know about Bruce and Bernard!"

"Well, luvey, they're both here, or I should say at the boat yard. Melanie, they have truly become like father and son, especially after their harrowing experience. I believe they bonded, as it is referred to these days. There is so much to tell you, dear. Will you be coming straight away? I'll prepare your room for you."

"That would be perfect. I'll catch the next available...." A dead silence fell over the phone lines. A long moment later, Melanie muttered, "I can't come right now." Realizing her family were enroute to spend the holidays with her and they, too, had not seen her for a year and a half. She just couldn't leave without having spent at least a few days with them. That much she felt compelled to do.

"Dear, are you all right?"

Melanie explained her predicament to her sweet friend, and of course, she understood.

"Shall I tell Bruce you'll be arriving after the new year?"

"No, Millicent, don't tell him anything. I want to surprise him on New Year's Eve. What a perfect way to begin the new year. Don't you agree?"

"Well, luv, I don't know how I'll be able to keep this news from him. I just hope I won't slip and give it away that we've spoken. Oh, mercy. This will truly be one of the most difficult tasks I have ever consented to. Lord help me."

"Millicent, please you must do this for me. I don't want Bruce to *hear* about me...I want him to *see* me. It means everything to me to do it this way.

Feeling overwhelmed with the immense responsibility of agreeing to keep a secret of such magnitude, the older woman sighed heavily into the phone receiver. Sounding weak, she responded in a meek voice, "I'll do my very best, dear, to honor your wishes. But, you had better say a little prayer, for I will need all the help I can get."

"For sure. You can count on an angel to be sitting on your shoulder to remind you to shhh. As a matter of fact, be on the lookout in your mail for one to arrive shortly." Melanie had seen a darling angel pin in a tiny shop the day before. First thing in the morning, she'd purchase it and send it to the hostess of The Enchanted Isle Cottage special delivery. She immediately dismissed the thought that it may have been sold. Assuring Millicent that she would call her from the airport on the 31st to apprise her of her arrival time, she bid her good-bye along with her love and best holiday wishes.

The next few days were joyful for Melanie being reunited with her loved ones, and yet a part of her was absent...at least emotionally. She wanted desperately to go to Bruce but knew she must wait. It was only a matter of days before she would be in his arms again. Finding the patience was the difficult part. She knew if she were to divulge Bruce's existence now to her family, they would insist she leave them and go join him. As much as that thought delighted her, it was deceitfully cloaked in guilt. Knowing herself too well, she said aloud, "I'd feel so guilty I'd be miserable. They came to see me, and I will not cop out and disappoint them."

As it was, Melanie was going to have to cut their visit short by departing New Year's Eve but didn't plan to mention that until the day before, knowing they would understand and wholly support her decision. At the same time, she was aware that her relatives would scold her for not going to Bruce's side immediately upon learning of his return. But, this was her choice, and the one she could most easily live with. Family was a number one priority and should not be shunned. With the deaths of her parents and brother, she placed a supreme value on her surviving kin. Besides, Bruce did not know that she was cognizant of his being amongst the living.

December 31st arrived. The blonde beauty had hardly slept a wink. Her anticipation and anxiety took over her entire body. Sleep seemed futile. Deciding to pack helped to whittle away the long sleepless night so as to be ready for her early morning departure.

While enjoying a long warm bath, she reminisced over the previous days with her loved ones: the fireside chats, singing carols around the old player piano in the parlor, and popping in and out of each other's rooms in their p.j.'s, and of course, the beautifully inspiring service at the small country church Christmas Eve. The joy of Christmas morning together followed by a delightful mid afternoon dinner were memories she would not have traded for anything or anyone, to say nothing of the fun filled days of skiing and comical rides down the hillside on the inn's old toboggan, looking forward to the awaiting hot chocolate back at the homestead. "Yes, I made the right decision to stay. These recollections I will cherish forever."

Looking at the wall clock through the reflections of the misty mirror, the time had come to dress, gather her bags, and say her farewells. She hated to leave them all, and yet, could not wait for her feet to touch the soil of her precious island out in the middle of the Atlantic. A new life awaited with her Prince Charming.

Naturally, the flight seemed to take forever. Though, she realized it was just her anticipation mounting with every passing moment. Melanie continually envisioned Bruce's face. The look of surprise when he would see her. She couldn't wait any longer. "Dear God, please may the time pass quickly until I am rejoined with my love."

The door of the airplane opened, and she was the first off and down the steps. Hurriedly, the former resident and guest made her way to the wall of pay phones. Just as she promised, she called Millicent, hoping Bernard or worse yet, that Bruce would not answer the phone. If that happened, she would simply hang up, wait, and re-dial.

"Happy New Year's Eve from the...."

"Millicent! It's me. I'm here! I am finally here," Melanie slowing her speech down so her friend could understand her.

"Oh! Dear, I am so pleased. Every time the phone has rung today, I've hoped it was you. Listen, luv, I have Arthur on alert to pick you up and bring you here. I'll give him a call, and he should be there shortly, if he isn't already."

Once outside the terminal, Melanie saw the familiar face wiping his brow and waving to her. He was third in a row of taxis awaiting to drive the incoming tourists to their destinations. Pulling up in front of her, Arthur briskly rounded the English cab and hugged his fare.

"Oh, miss, welcome home! And, Missy Lombard and I are hoping you will be making our island your permanent home."

"Oh, Arthur! I am so glad to see you." She hugged him back as tears rolled down her cheeks. The ride along the exquisite bougainvillea lined coastline with its shimmering aqua waters was the best New Year's gift she could have imagined. Just being back on the precious tiny mid Atlantic island under such glorious circumstances was a dream come true. Within the past week, her life had completely turned around. Now that she was here, the anticipation of seeing *him* was mounting with each passing minute. She could hardly stand the wait. Realizing she was lost in her thoughts and had barely spoken a word to her driver, she said, "Arthur, I don't mean to be rude. How have you and your family been during my absence from your beautiful isle?"

Clearing his deep throat, "Nice of you to inquire, Miss Melanie. Thankfully, they are all well. And, you look the picture of fine health. I take it that you've been very well, too?" Suddenly, as if choked by his last words, he promptly tried to backtrack his conversation. Awkwardly stumbling and obviously embarrassed, he desperately tried to correct his verbiage. "I mean to say, I know from Mrs. Lombard you were so upset that you went away for a year."

Not sure if he was asking a question or merely making a statement, his companion took over the conversation. Melanie explained in an abbreviated version, the course that her life had taken since their last encounter.

"Oh, Arthur, this is certainly a happier occasion, thank God, than when I last saw you. That was truly the unhappiest day of my life. I never thought I would be returning. Life surely has many surprises in store for us, doesn't it?"

As Arthur responded, "Yes, miss, more than we can ever know." The familiar sound of scrunching pebbles indicated that the taxi had started the descent down The Enchanted Isle's driveway.

"Oh, Arthur, I am so excited I can hardly breathe."

"Well, don't stop or we'll have another crisis on our hands, and we are all still recovering from the last one. Now, my orders are to take you around the back to the kitchen entrance. Mr. Bruce is not suppose to be here, but just in case he stopped by, Mrs. L. said we should take all necessary precautions to protect your surprise."

"You're a dear, Arthur. Thank you for being such a caring friend. You are one of my favorite people, in case I never told you."

"No, Miss M., you never did, but I feel honored. Thank you."

With those last words spoken, he helped her inside with her luggage. Offering to carry the floral tapestry suitcases upstairs, Arthur returned to the kitchen. There, he found Millicent and Melanie in a touching, heartfelt embrace, tears streaming down both their cheeks. The silence hung heavily. They held hands at arm's length and searched each other's eyes for lingering signs of the pain that had been so evident the last time they looked into each other's windows to their souls. None there! The pain all gone was replaced with a radiance that sparkled with luminescence. God had healed their grief by answering their prayers, and they were both keenly aware of the fact...and so grateful.

Feeling a bit odd and in the way, Arthur unnecessarily cleared his throat to let them know of his presence in the room. An involuntary reflex when he felt nervous or uncomfortable.

"You two ladies look mighty pleased to see each other."

Answering in unison and with a slight giggle, "That we are, Arthur." Breaking their embrace, Millicent offered the Bermudian gentleman a cup of tea.

Accepting her invitation, the stout man seated himself at the ceramic inlaid table. As the tea brewed, she set a dainty floral covered dish once belonging to her grandmother, before him. His eyes grew wide when he saw the homemade scones and shortbread.

"Oh, mum, these look delicious. My Mrs. will scold me for ruining my appetite for dinner, but I can't refuse such an offering."

Joining him at the table, Melanie sat stoically taking in the familiar surroundings. "I cannot believe I'm here. It's like a dream. Incidentally, Millicent, where is Bruce? I would like to bathe and glamorize myself before I see him. I wouldn't want him to walk in on us."

The steam spiraling its escape from the silver pot as she poured her guests their tea, "Not a chance of that, dear. My Bernie is under strict orders not to let Bruce out of his sight. He is to keep his protégé away from here, until he has checked in with me."

As if on cue, the rhythmic ringing of the phone called to their attention. "There he is now. I swear the man is psychic. Hello, Luv."

Melanie noted that the mistress of the manor did not answer the phone with the normal Enchanted Isle greeting. She arrived at the conclusion that it was not only Bernard who was clairvoyant.

After a brief conversation, she replaced the phone's receiver into its cradle. Turning directly to her fair haired guest, "Well, it seems our Prince Charming has quite a New Year's Eve planned. He had a chat this afternoon with my hubby. Apparently, he has decided to start off the new year with a bang. According to Bernard's interpretation, Bruce is ready to celebrate his coming out of the past. He's all riled up about commencing on a new life." The older woman paused a moment and staring intensely into her daughter-like friend's eyes, she softly spoke. "Bernard said Bruce is going to ask Sandra to marry him tonight on the stroke of midnight as a symbolic gesture of proof to himself that he is shedding the scars of the past fourteen months of heartache. I knew he had been seeing her on business matters. Since she couldn't entice him with her grand scheme, she settled to work for him as a sales rep for his new catamaran." The fury rose into her eyes.

Millicent's words had hit Melanie with a hurricane force of their own. Proposing to Sandra! Sandra working for him! The words came from Millicent's mouth clearly. Her conscious state heard them, absorbed them into her brain, and now they were swirling around so fast in her head, that she felt almost faint from dizziness. The healthy glow had drained from her face and was replaced by a stark look of white with greenish overtones.

Arthur immediately rose from the table, as if on alert to make a fast run to the hospital. Melanie appeared to be deathly ill. Millicent regrouping her own stunned composure, did what any staunch British soldier would do in battle...and that was how she viewed the situation on hand, she squarely grasped Melanie's trembling shoulders.

"Listen, dear, the battle is not over yet. We have until midnight. I know if Bruce knew you were here, he could never go through with his disastrous plan. He has seemed very lonely these last months. He won't date anyone, and I think that is why Sandra would be a logical choice. She has made herself totally available to him. She worships the ground he walks on." Shaking her head, "It is almost distasteful to see her sacheting all around him. I told Bernie she suffocates the poor fella. Bruce is an impressionable man. He has often expressed how he respects Bernard's and my marriage and how much he wants the same for his life." Fumbling in her apron pocket for her handkerchief to catch a falling tear, "I can't believe he is throwing in the towel and settling for someone he is obviously not," and she emphasized the *not,* "in love with."

Well, we aren't going to let this happen. Bernie mentioned that Bruce is taking Sandra to the New Year's Eve gala at The Sonesta Beach Hotel across from Henry VIII's. I know they are probably sold out, since it is their biggest function of the year, and they go all out, but we've known the manager for years. I'll call him now. There are going to be three more added to their guest list! Now, dear, you go upstairs and take a long hot bath. Be sure to use the aromatic oils in the small basket by the tub."

Nearly backing into the other guest standing behind her, "Oh, Arthur! I had forgotten you were still here. Well, it seems life is never dull, since these two young people have invaded our island. Will you and your lovely Louise be out and about celebrating?"

No longer resting against the counter and standing erect as the tiny woman addressed him, "Oh no, madame. The Mrs. and I always enjoy a quiet evening at home. We have for years."

"Nonsense, Arthur! Go home and surprise her with flowers and an invitation to really bring in the new year. Please join us at The Sonesta. I'll make our reservation for five. After all, you've certainly been a part of all this since the day you and your overloaded taxi delivered those five American beauties on our doorstep."

Obviously honored, the appreciative gentleman accepted the invite with pleasure and agreed to meet at the hotel about eight o'clock.

Alone in her kitchen, the realization of what she had just done had a profound impact. What if she could not finagle five tickets to the ball.

She had gone out on a limb...a place where such a conservative person did not normally venture. As frightening as it felt, it was also exciting, challenging. Without another moment of hesitation, the stately woman leafed through her address book for the private number of the hotel's manager. Relieved when she heard his voice, she minced no words, told him what she needed, and the circumstances behind her grand request. Before he could respond, she brilliantly decided to offer a bribe to enhance the chance of an affirmative answer by extending a complimentary night at the inn for him and his wife. She was ready to pull out all the stops for this evening.

"Millicent Lombard, this must be very special to you. In all the years I've known you, you've never asked a favor. And knowing you as I do, this occasion must be of the utmost importance. I'll be honest. I've turned down several of our well known residents and some hand-some bribes, but I cannot say no to you. But, you must give me your solemn oath, you won't ever divulge how you managed to twist my arm. I don't want to make enemies."

Feeling riddled with guilt for what she had done, Millicent assured her colleague that not even a whisper would ever leak from her sealed lips. She would be in his debt forever, and then she threw in two nights at her inn instead of the one initially offered.

"Accepted with pleasure. My wife and I have always wanted to stay at your lovely home. We'll make it a much needed mini-getaway. The tickets will be held at the concierge's desk under your name. Have a wonderful evening, Millicent. I'll drop by your table to wish you and Bernard a *Happy New Year.* And, one last favor for a friend who I know did not dare ask for another. I will make sure that you are seated near Mr. Hinds' table."

Exuberant, Millicent thanked him so many times that he finally had to excuse himself. He was needed to fulfill many tasks before the posh event.

Adrenaline rushing, the Grande Dame raced up the elegant oak staircase to notify Melanie that all was set. She was ecstatic. Now, what to wear was her next dilemma. Scouring her closet for something festive was to no avail. She and Bernard did not usually attend dressy affairs. Feeling like Cinderella without a dress for the ball, she began to panic...slightly. Glancing at her watch it was 4:30. On a shopping jaunt one day last week to purchase a linen tablecloth, she had noticed a beautiful dress adorning a boutique window in a nearby parish. Swiftly turning pages in the phone book, she found the shop's number. Yes, they would be opened until 5:00. After checking, yes, they happened to have her size in a petite. Hurriedly, she grabbed her purse, forgetting to take off her poppy print apron until she started the engine of the car. Once driving, her practical nature informed her that she could wear the dress she had worn to her niece's wedding the year before. "Oh, I had completely forgotten about it," she said aloud. It hung in a garment bag in the attic. She mused to herself that it would make a fine back-up dress if the outfit in the window did not work out. She had never owned a dress with sequins before. This was going to be the night of nights. And that called for sequins!

Arriving home thirty-five minutes later with a gaily colored dress box under her arm, Millicent flew through the kitchen door. Bernard was enjoying a mug of ale seated in the alcove's rocking chair.

"My dearest, where have you been?" Spotting the box, his response with surprise, "Shopping on New Year's Eve?"

She quickly explained the reason for the purchase, and the coup she pulled off with the manager of the Sonesta. "Yes, luv, we will be helping destiny bring the right couple together. You know as well as I do that Bruce doesn't love Sandra. He's become fond of her over these months, and I know he's grateful to her for helping him get through the disappearance of Melanie, but he is not in love with her. I know in my heart that once he sees Melanie he will be asking her to marry him!"

"I see how your mind is working. Let's hope things work out the way your heart is telling you, Mrs. Cupid. If nothing else, it should prove to be a most interesting New Year's Eve. Even I'm looking forward to celebrating and welcoming in the new year. We just lived through quite a year." With those words, he walked over to his petite wife and hugged her dearly. "I love you, Millicent Lombard."

Peering up into his soft gray eyes, "I know you do, and I love you, Bernard Lombard. So much so, that I'll make you a snack to tide you over until the big shindig. We'll be meeting Arthur and Louise around eight in The Sonesta's lobby."

The bath was so relaxing that had it not been for the bomb about Bruce and Sandra, Melanie knew she would have drifted off to sleep in the warm scented tub waters. This came as such a shock, but like Millicent said, "The battle wasn't over yet." She was right, too! If she had to fight for this man, she would with every fiber of her being. She had waited too long, cried too many tears, and had come too far to slink off into the horizon unannounced. Bruce was going to see her tonight! The next two hours were allotted for primping and preparing for the most important encounter of her life. It was strategically imperative that she look her absolute best, nothing short of that would do. Now, facing her greatest challenge, she was determined to be victorious. A sense of peace fell over her, and she knew...she just knew.

At 7:30, the confident blonde descended the grand staircase, feeling beautiful on the inside and hoping it was reflected on her outside appearance. If Bernard's reaction was any indication that she was successful in her beauty prepping, then she had achieved her goal...at least the first one of the evening. Both Bernard and Millicent showered her with endless compliments to the point that she became quite embarrassed. Melanie insisted it was her spectacular dress, a Bob Mackie creation which she bought while in Los Angeles. At the time, there was no occasion in mind, but it was so gorgeous, she knew she must have it. One day, she would be in need of such a dress! Remembering to thank her guardian angel, whom she was sure was responsible for nagging her into making such an extravagant purchase.

On the living room coffee table was a silver bucket with champagne and three crystal flutes. "Come and toast with us." The couple radiated. Bernard looked more handsome than Melanie had ever seen him. Decked out in a smashing black double breasted blazer, charcoal gray pin striped slacks, a pale blue shirt, complimented with a paisley satin ascot, and matching handkerchief in his breast pocket.

Millicent beamed with pride as she glanced over him, "He spruces up pretty well, don't you think, ducky?"

"Yes, he looks incredible, and so do you! Millicent, you look so beautiful."

"Well, as someone recently said, 'It's the dress.'" They all chuckled as they toasted to an evening of magic and perfect outcomes.

Finishing their glasses of bubbly, Melanie asked if they could hold hands, and she said a short prayer, "Father, please be with us this evening, and may your will be done." Then hugging each of them, she shouted, "We're off to the magic isle!" The Sonesta sat majestically on its own massive rock surrounded by water.

Arthur and Louise met them as they entered the doorway of the lobby. Compliments were circulating around the small entourage on how well they all looked. Bernard retrieved the promised tickets from the concierge and ushered them to the grand ballroom. The Glen Miller Orchestra was playing Millicent's favorite song, "String of Pearls." People were still arriving, while others were already on the dance floor. Once seated at their table, Melanie strained her neck to see if she could spot her beloved, noticing that the small table set for two to their left was not occupied. The napkins and party hats appeared not to have been disturbed, concluding that Bruce and Sandra hadn't arrived as yet.

Barely able to participate in the conversation at the table, Melanie was obsessed with scanning the room continuously for a sighting of Bruce. Becoming nervous at the possibility he may have changed his plans, she whispered her concern in Millicent's right ear.

"Nonsense!" Trying to reassure her friend, "One does not commit to the expense of these tickets and then not use them."

The cost of the tickets had totally escaped her. Melanie now felt an overwhelming pang of guilt. They would have not spent the money to be out, if it had not been for her. She insisted to no avail that she pay for all five tickets. As they all became so engrossed in the argument, no one noticed that Bruce and Sandra had just taken their seats. Before he actually pulled his chair up to the table, the voluptuous brunette had whisked him off to the dance floor. The music was spellbinding.

Now having caught a brief glimpse of *him*, Melanie could barely sit still. She just wanted to run to his arms, but they were filled with Sandra. The vixen was in her glory, too. Perhaps, Bruce had already proposed, and that was why they were late arriving. Sandra did not appear to need music. She was making her own. Overexaggerating her dance steps and swooning all over her date, it was obvious that she had an early start bringing in the new year. At first, Bruce did not seem to mind and was enjoying himself. He twirled her around and around, grabbing her and pulling her into him. Melanie couldn't stand to watch anymore. She was beginning to feel physically sick to her stomach. Just as Millicent leaned over to pat her knee, there was a loud commotion on the dance floor. It seemed that Sandra did one too many twirls and collided into one of the musicians...the drummer. She knocked over the cymbals, which made a hellacious bang. Bruce, obviously very embarrassed, swiftly escorted his date off the floor and back to their table. She loudly insisted they make a toast, and to appease her, he raised his glass of champagne. It was at that moment, when he glanced around to see if the occupants at the nearby tables were staring at them, that he saw *her.* His fingers immediately released the glass, and he froze. The sound of the crashing glass caused more of a commotion. Two waiters flew over to the table and attempted to clean up the broken crystal. Instantly, a new flute of champagne was placed on the small table. Bruce still had not moved. Sandra trying again to make a toast was becoming increasingly annoyed when she could not get a response from her escort. Finally following his line of vision, she, too, dropped her glass. Though, hers only spilled and did not break.

"Oh my God! Oh my God!! Where did she come from?" The shrill of Sandra's voice was enough to bring Bruce back to reality. He jumped up from the table, which now sent the toppled glass to shatter on the floor. The same two waiters once again flew over to make the necessary repairs and replacement. Each giving the other a look of disgust.

Melanie rose to her feet the moment she saw Bruce approaching her table. Speechless, he engulfed her in his arms. Long moments passed and still not a word uttered or a movement made. People were staring and commenting, "This looks like a scene from a movie, Harold. I wish you'd react that way when I come home after a week visiting my sister."

"Well, hon, I'm sure those two have been parted for more than a week!"

Arthur stood up and asked Louise to dance so a chair would be free for Bruce to sit down. Catching the gesture from the corner of his eye, he broke the embrace and motioned them to be seated. His eyes filled with tears, he looked at Bernard and Millicent. Bernard feeling the need to say something, "How's this for a New Year's surprise?"

Bruce still welled up with emotion, couldn't utter a word. So Millicent piped up with the explanation of how and when she and Melanie had first communicated the week before. How Melanie did not wish to talk over the phone to him. She had to see him in person. She had waited so long. As Millicent unraveled the yarn, they never stopped staring into each other's eyes. The spell was broken when a loud and obnoxious Sandra bumped into their table while seating herself in the unoccupied chair.

"Well, Melanie, I see you, too, have returned from the missing. You two are sure a pair with your disappearing acts." Perhaps it was a Freudian slip, but she could have bit her tongue for referring to the two of them as a pair. It was obvious to the other four seated that they were meant to be a pair. Millicent tried valiantly to engage Sandra in a conversation in an attempt to reduce the mounting pressure that hung heavily over them. Not about to be coerced, Sandra barraged Melanie with a million questions. Realizing she had a right to know, Melanie told her tale in an abbreviated version. Meanwhile, Arthur and Louise needing a break from dancing, decided not to interrupt the table of five and took their places at the vacated table. The two waiters seemed relieved to have the new arrivals and quickly brought them fresh glasses of bubbly obviously under the assumption the former occupants had left.

As Melanie wound up her story, it was evident that Sandra was bored to tears. She had consumed everyone's glass of champagne, since the Lombards and Bruce were captivated by the twists and turns her life had taken.

Inebriated, Sandra raised her glass to make a toast. The others raised their empty glasses to their astonishment.

"To friends and lovers reunited. Just so there isn't any confusion, you're the friend, and I am the lover." She sneered at Melanie and downed its contents.

Everyone was shocked. Millicent said curtly, "With a toast like that, I am glad my glass is empty."

"Hear, hear!" was echoed around the table.

It had been a long time since Bruce had seen Sandra in such a condition. It became evident to him that she had been on her best behavior to win him over, and now was feeling confident that it was a fait accompli. Seeing her true colors come to life was such an awakening to what a life would be like married to such a chameleon. He would be miserable. Instantly, while glancing across the table at a woman who in a matter of two hours would have become his betrothed, he felt sick and relieved. With mascara smudged and her lipstick smeared, she repulsed him. All he could think of was getting as far away as possible from her and escaping with his Melanie, the true love of his life. He knew he had to remedy the situation, and he had to do it *now!*

Excusing himself, he leaned over to whisper in Melanie's ear, "May I please have this dance?" Without hesitation she glided onto the dance floor with her prince. To follow suit, Bernard and Millicent joined the couple as did Arthur and Louise. As the waltz ended Bruce knelt down on one knee looked into Melanie's adoring face and proceeded to propose. "Melanie, I don't want to wait one minute longer. Would you do me the honor of becoming my wife." A loud squeal and a thud were all that could be heard. Sandra, quite intoxicated toppled off her chair as she screamed with disgust. Bernard signaled the waiters to remove her from the floor. Still squealing, "You're supposed to be asking meee" as the dining room doors closed behind them. Feeling rather awkward by this time, Bruce began to rise. Melanie nearly knocked him over as she planted a huge combo kiss and "YES" on his lips. The applause was deafening. There were cheers and congratulations from all in the room.

He gently pulled up her chin and placed a lovely kiss on her soft lips. "I want you to be in my life forever."

Epilogue

The picturesque setting of Bermuda provides the backdrop for the infamous group for a gala Valentine's Day wedding...where it all started. Separated by diverse circumstances, they were once again reunited in paradise.

Among the guests attending were the other four of the Fabulous Five and their loves: Claudia and Derek, Stephanie and Sean, Vivian and John, and Barbara and Lance...also reunited. And of course, Bernard and Millicent and Arthur and Louise. Millicent and Bernard opened their inn for all the arriving guests. Since the wedding was not until mid-afternoon, Millicent prepared a delightful breakfast for all her honored guests including Arthur and Louise. At 10:00 o'clock Bruce, Derek, Lance, John and Sean arrived, as they were lodging at the nearby cottage where Bruce had stayed. Just as before the girls were dashing in and out of each others' room, Millicent glowed. "This brings back such fine memories," she remarked to Bernard. "I know, sweetie, I love seeing you this happy again."

The rafters of the magnificent house were filled with the scrumptious smells wafting up from the kitchen. Louise offered to help Millicent with the lavish preparations, "My there is a lot of commotion up there!"

Millicent smiled, "Yes, isn't it wonderful, my girls are back."

February is not noted for the best weather in Bermuda. As the clouds threatened to hamper the outside affair, Melanie suggested at the dining room table they clasp hands and say a prayer, "Thank you, dear Lord, for bringing us all together, for this fine day and please bless this marriage, oh, and a sunbreak over the ceremony would be sooo appreciated."

The setting for the wedding could not have been more perfect. Perched on the highest point in Bermuda at the Fairmont Southampton overlooking the pink sands of Horseshoe beach the small ensemble of friends gathered. Bernard and the guys that morning had set up numerous decanters of flowers all grown in Millicent's mini greenhouse.

When Melanie arrived dressed in ivory looking like a vision from heaven, she gasped when she saw the setting, "It looks like a scene from a storybook! This is truly a dream come true."

She then joined her betrothed, and as if by magic the sun broke out and drenched the hilltop with its warm rays. The ceremony was not only spiritual but magical, it touched every heart. Barb looked into Lance's eyes and he squeezed her hand. It seemed to have that affect on each couple gathered there. Millicent snuggled up against Bernard and warmly smiled, "It's complete now."

Arthur drove the getaway taxi draped in hearts and flowers.

The End

About the Author

M.J. Hinds has drawn upon her extensive traveling experiences, as well as having been a resident of Bermuda and Jeddah, Saudi Arabia. As a former innkeeper/owner of The Anniversary Inn, originator of Fashions for Fun Boutique, flight attendant, and airline supervisor, she's been on the ground floor of two start-up airlines, America West and Mc-Clain and spent time as a public speaker and model, she has gathered much ma-terial that has been transformed into a non-fiction book and a novel. Her published works include Dreaming of Innkeeping and Reunion In Paradise. Non-fiction works to be published are; Prince Charming, He Lives and, Enshalla . . . Saudi Arabia, Anyone?

She is a grandmother and resides with her husband Bruce and their Old English Sheepdog, Oliver in Port Orchard, Washington.